Some Like It Hot

EMMA FOXX

Copyright © 2024 by Emma Foxx

All rights reserved.

No part of this book may be reproduced in any form or by any electronic or mechanical means, including information storage and retrieval systems, without written permission from the author, except for the use of brief quotations in a book review.

About The Book

I've always been the feisty side-kick who's up for anything. I don't need to be the main attraction. I'm fine being the fun girl who always has a hot take on a good time.

For instance, the night I sneak into the Chicago Racketeers New Year's Eve Party, I find myself trapped in an elevator with a gorgeous grump of a hockey player, before we're rescued by a sexy fireman who catches Mr. Hockey's hand in my . . . shapewear.

Talk about hot.

But the temperature only rises from there.

Turns out, the grouchy goalie needs a fake fiancée to earn his inheritance. I'm not *real* girlfriend material (my ex was clear about that), but I agree to help him out with the temporary farce.

Then I run into my ex-boss—the one I shared a steamy kiss with just before I quit. I'd forgotten how devastatingly dirty and charming the British golden retriever billionaire can be. And that cinnamon roll firefighter? He wants me too.

Did I mention he and my billionaire are also into each other?

Each of them makes me feel desired and adored, but when it's all four of us together we're absolutely on fire.

Good thing this is only until the inheritance is finalized and my billionaire goes back to London. This could never last for long without someone getting burned.

CHAPTER 1
Blake

SLID RIGHT IN THERE. *Like me between Elise's thighs.*

I grip my tumbler tighter and concentrate on not crushing it as I remember the taunt hurled at me on the ice earlier tonight as the puck passed me into the net.

It would be just my luck to end up with a sliced-open hand and not able to grip my stick for the next game. Travers would fucking love that.

Plus, this glass probably costs a thousand dollars.

Instead of smashing the tumbler, I lift it to my lips and take a long pull of the expensive whiskey. Then I take a deep breath and look around the room. I'm in a party room on the top floor of a hotel with my entire team after a big win this afternoon over the Dallas Dragons. It's New Year's Eve. I should be happy, partying, getting ready to celebrate the start of a new year.

Instead, Justin Fucking Travers is on my mind. More specifically, the woman Justin Travers slept with—is possibly still sleeping with—and the fact that I hate that fucking guy.

Most of the Racketeers, my hockey team, the best in the league and the one that *is* going to win the championship this year, dammit, hate Justin Travers. For good reason. He's a cocky son of a bitch, who not only scored their only goal tonight (a fact I can't shake as the Racketeer's goalie) but he's mouthy as hell.

Still, none of them have as good a reason to hate him as I do.

Namely, Elise Starling.

I shouldn't care that Elise and Justin hooked up.

I *don't* care that the gorgeous, sassy brunette with the make-a-grown-man-beg lips and make-a-man-grown-man-weep curves clearly has terrible taste in men.

It's all about Justin Travers having anything that he thinks I want.

Have Elise and I flirted? Yes.

Have I had a few dirty dreams about her? Of course.

Would I have welcomed her into my bed for a hot night, or even a long steamy weekend? No question.

But I don't *want* her. Not to keep. Not for long-term. It's not like I'm in love with her.

So the fact that Justin keeps bringing up the fact that he's been with her like she's some kind of conquest, like he's won some contest between us, rankles. It's disrespectful as hell to her.

Plus, I just don't want Justin Travers to have anything nice or anything that makes him happy. Definitely not any*one* that I would love to see naked.

"I'm heading out," Crew McNeill tells us, draining his glass and setting it on the high round table that I'm standing at with him, Alexsei Ryan, and Jack Hayes. "Got a wife and a baby girl to start the new year with."

"Not to mention our boss and our team doctor," Alexsei says with a chuckle.

"Yeah, them too." Crew grins.

McNeill is married to a woman who is married to two other guys. One of them is our team owner, Nathan Armstrong. The other is Michael Hughes, our team physician. Their wife, Danielle, just had their first child, a baby girl, about a week ago. They all live together, of course, and Crew is head over heels for his wife and daughter.

Crew only showed up tonight at the party because he had to. It's one of the things we do. We're a team. A family. It's important we celebrate together, just like it's important that we come together after losses.

But the amount of time we spend at these celebrations and group pep talks varies. Like the way Armstrong came to the party, made a *very* short speech, and then left about five minutes later.

Of course, he's the boss and can do whatever he wants.

Crew at least hung out for the past hour.

"Trust me," Crew goes on. "We had to talk Dani out of coming tonight. You know she loves these parties with the team. Especially now that Luna comes to all of them too." He inclines his head toward where his sister is talking with a group of wives and girlfriends.

Alexsei's face softens and his smile grows as he looks toward Luna. "I love that I can have my people here."

Luna is Crew's sister, but she's Alexsei's girlfriend.

"Are you sure she's here with *you*?" Jack asks as our assistant coach, Owen Phillips, wraps his arms around Luna from behind and says something in her ear that makes her laugh.

Alexsei grins at us. "I didn't say I'd be the only one in that storage room having a quickie with her later."

Yes, Luna is with Owen *and* Alexsei. And they're all with Cameron, Alexsei's best friend and boyfriend.

The poly-relationships are becoming an epidemic around here.

Watching them all happen over the past year has been cool. They're all having fun, treating each other well, and clearly healthy and happy. I'm happy for them.

These guys are younger than me, but I'd consider them my best friends on the team. Crew and Alexsei are a lot more laid-back and fun than I am, but I can tolerate them for a lot longer and more often than some of the other players. They might seem like goofballs at times, but they're serious when it comes to hockey. They work their asses off and it always shows on the ice. When McNeill, Ryan, and Hayes are on the ice, we all feel better.

I respect them. That's what it comes down to. The guys can do whatever they want off the ice and outside the arena, but I haven't busted my ass for almost ten years, beat my body up to the point that my hip hurts every fucking day, and put off my retirement for another year to just mess around. We came within one game of winning the championship last year and by God, we're getting that trophy this year.

Then I'm retiring.

"Guess it's you and me kissing at midnight," Hayes tells me.

I chuckle and lift my drink again. "No thanks."

"You got a better offer?" he asks.

"Yes."

"Who?"

"Literally anyone else," I tell him with a smirk.

He laughs. "Fuck you."

"Not that either. But thanks for the offer."

He laughs harder. "You wish you'd get an offer this good."

Alexsei is also grinning. "Not the way you swing, Wilder? Not even once in a while?"

I know that Alexsei is *with* both Luna and Cameron. That's great for him. He seems completely in love with them both. I lift a shoulder. "Never have. But to each his own."

"Would you share someone?" Hayes asks. "Like McNeill and Ryan do?"

I think about that. I don't really like a lot of other people. That's always been true. I have a very small inner circle and the only social outings I partake in have to do with my hockey team. Since I was recruited by the Racketeers straight out of high school, they've been my social circle and my surrogate family all of my adult life. So I don't know, like, or spend time with many people.

But do I need to *like* the other guy I share a woman with? Probably not. That's not what it would be about, right?

It would be about the woman.

Immediately, Elise's face flashes into my mind. And her body.

I haven't seen her naked. Much to my disappointment. But

I've imagined it. I can't help it. She is exactly my type. Great breasts, round ass, thick thighs, hips I could really sink my fingers into. Those lush lips. Those huge brown eyes. That long dark hair just perfect for wrapping around my fist.

Would I share Elise? Witness her coming absolutely, completely undone at the hands of another man? Be a part of overwhelming her with pleasure and lust?

Yes.

I don't even have to think about it.

Elise is a strong, bold, independent woman who knows exactly who she is and what she wants. Watching her lose control and come apart would be the hottest fucking thing I can think of.

With anyone but Justin Prick of the Year Travers.

No way did Travers blow her mind, though.

No fucking way.

"Yeah," I finally answer nonchalantly. "Depends on the girl and the guy, or guys, I suppose, but I don't have a reason to say no across the board."

Hayes looks surprised. "No kidding."

"You don't believe me?"

"You're just not very social and that would be…pretty damned social."

I actually feel myself grin. "Would it though?"

"Let me guess," Ryan says. "You're not a big talker, even in bed."

"Not true," I tell him. "The things I can talk about in bed happen to be some of my favorite topics."

McNeill laughs. "So you're chatty and gregarious in bed? Good to know."

Gregarious is pushing it. "Let's put it this way. On my list of top ten favorite things, breasts and pussy make the top two. So yes, I tend to be enthusiastic. And when it comes to talking, I don't just use the letters STFUATTDLAGG."

Hayes frowns. "What's that stand for?"

McNeill and I share a grin. "Google it," I tell Jack.

"I have to know. What else is in your top ten?" Alexsei asks. "And please don't say your hair."

That makes me snort. "Beer, West Wing reruns, sharks, hockey, fishing, donuts, my grandmother, and hammocks. Not necessarily in that order."

They're all just looking at me now with varying degrees of surprise and amusement.

"And on that note," McNeill says. "I've gotta go."

He heads for the elevators and Alexsei beelines for Luna and Owen, leaving Jack and me at the table finishing our drinks.

"I guess my Top Ten was a party buzz kill," I tell Hayes.

"No shit. Where the hell do we go with sharks and hammocks?" He grins. "You stayin' til midnight, you sentimental bastard?"

I sigh. That's still an hour away. I don't want to. I'm fucking tired.

I'm only twenty-nine, but I don't recover after games the way I used to. My hip pain that used to only occur every once in a while has been getting more and more frequent and now it's after every game, in spite of top-notch medical care from the Racketeers physicians and physical therapists.

I really probably should have hung it up after last season, but God, we were *so* close. I *know* we're going to win the championship this year. I've got one more season in me.

"Nah," I say. "I think I'd rather ring in the new year in my hot tub, to be honest."

Hayes nods. "Then you won't mind if I ditch you to go talk to the waitress?"

I follow his gaze to the pretty blonde who has been circulating with trays of hors d'oeuvres all night. I had noticed that we had plenty to eat all night. Now I realize she had an ulterior motive.

"Absolutely not. Go for it," I tell him.

He grins. "Thanks. Happy new year."

"Happy new year, man."

I watch him approach the woman and witness her huge smile

when he says hi. Wonderful. Hayes will have someone to kiss at midnight after all. I'm going to kiss a bottle of Blanton's in my hot tub and toast to a championship victory in six months.

My gaze finds Alexsei, Owen, and Luna. Cameron is with them now. I knew he was here somewhere. They're all laughing together. Alexsei's hand is resting on Luna's lower back, and she's leaning against Owen's side, his hand on the back of her neck. They look so happy and in love.

Good for them.

I love seeing people happy like that.

It's not for me. I've been married to hockey since I was old enough to slap a puck with a stick.

My love for the game hit early and hit hard and I've never had time, energy, or interest in anything else since. My dedication to the game, my travel schedule, the publicity—which includes attention from lots of women—has proven to be too much for the couple of women I *have* tried dating. And that was a long time ago. They accused me of caring about hockey more than them, and they were right.

Plus, I love being alone. Like *love it*. The idea of having someone around, in my life, in my decisions, taking up my time, twenty-four seven makes me itchy. Then you add to that their friends and family, social obligations like family dinners, birthdays, vacations…nope. Not for me. I don't need anyone in my life like that.

My plan after hockey is done is to head to the woods of Minnesota to my family's secluded cabin and to finally become the hermit I've always dreamed of being.

I watch as Cameron leans in and kisses Luna. It's a little strange to see while she's standing with two other men touching her with clear possessiveness. But it also looks very natural. She reaches up and runs a hand down his face, her smile soft. Then she smiles up at Alexsei as Owen kisses the top of her head.

The four of them look right together. That's the only way to describe it.

I wonder what Elise is doing tonight. And with who.

I frown. Okay, so Luna is Elise's friend and boss at the bakery Luna owns and where Elise works part time. *That* is why I thought of her. Not for any other reason.

Not because of what Travers said to me tonight about sliding between her thighs.

Not because I can't shake how much I fucking hate that Justin has been with her.

Not because whenever Elise is around I can't keep my eyes, or thoughts, off of her.

Clearly, she doesn't even have to be around for me to be thinking of her.

Dammit.

I straighten, look around to see if there's anyone I need to say goodbye to, decide that no, I'll see them in a couple of days.

I start for the elevator. No one else is leaving yet, so I'm waiting alone. Which is perfect. The good mood the guys helped me capture is gone. I want to go home, where I can soak my annoyingly painful hip in my hot tub, sip my favorite whiskey, and watch the clock roll past midnight and into my official retirement year.

The doors to the elevator swish open and I start to step forward, only to stop when I realize a couple of late comers are getting off.

Then my brain registers who they are.

It's Wade, the guy who dresses up as Sammy the Malamute, the Racketeers mascot.

And Elise.

Because of course it is.

She's dressed in a curve-hugging black dress that leaves her shoulders bare, plunges low in the front, showing off her mouth-watering cleavage, and black heels. Her dark hair is in large curls that fall softly around her shoulders and those lips—the ones that haunt my dreams—are painted crimson.

She looks so fucking gorgeous.

And she's staring right back at me, those kissable lips parted in surprise.

Slid right in there. Just like me between Elise's thighs.

Justin Travers' voice echoes in my head and I growl, stepping forward. I take Elise's upper arm and step her back into the elevator.

"What the he—" she starts to protest.

"We need to talk," I tell her, punching the button for the lobby.

I have no idea where we're going or what exactly I'm going to say. I haven't spoken to her in months. I've never spoken to her one-on-one, but that ends tonight. I have to get her out of my head and, I suppose, this seems like a rational way to do it.

Maybe I just need to hear her say that Travers sucked in bed?

That she is absolutely not still seeing him?

That he treated her well?

Or do I want to know he was a dick to her? That would give me a very good reason to slam his sorry ass into the boards the next time I see him. On the ice or not.

"Uh…"

I glance back at Sammy. I mean Wade. "She's fine. Go have fun."

He lifts a brow at Elise and I appreciate the fact that he's asking *her* if she's fine. I look down at her, also awaiting her answer.

This is a little nuts. She doesn't really *know* me. If she doesn't want to be alone with me, I'd understand, I suppose.

She frowns up at me, but then nods. "Yeah, fine."

"Okay, see ya," Wade says, ambling off into the party.

The elevator doors slide closed and Elise Starling and I are suddenly alone.

Together.

For the first time.

In a small, enclosed space.

I turn to her. She turns to face me.

"I—" I start.

She just waits.

All I have to do is ask, 'Are you still dating Justin Travers?' Or 'Was Justin amazing in bed?' Or 'Did Travers break your heart?' Any of those would start the conversation that I think I want to have.

I want to know about her and Travers, right? That's what's been driving me crazy. That's what I've been wondering about. It's about my rivalry with that dickhead who is the only Dragon to score on me in the last eight games between the Racketeers and the Dragons.

But when I open my mouth and actually speak, I say, "You look absolutely incredible and you smell amazing."

Her eyes widen. Mine do too.

That's what I want to say first?

But...it's the truth. Suddenly it's all I can think about.

She's stunning. Truly. Her hair, her eyes, that damned *mouth*. My palms are tingly with the need to run over her curves, feel the silkiness of her skin, to see how quickly I can make her catch her breath.

It's only fair. I don't feel like I'm breathing too easily.

"Th–Thank you," she finally stammers softly. "I wasn't expecting that."

I step closer. "You didn't know that I think you're gorgeous?"

"I..." She wets her lips and shakes her head. "I don't know."

I like this. She looks a little ruffled and honestly, the times I've been around this woman and we've talked, even teased, she's seemed very confident. I like thinking I can maybe throw her off her game a bit.

I step closer again. Now I feel her body heat and if she takes a very deep breath, her breasts will brush my chest. "I do. I want you to know that. And I think you should also know that I've been dying to kiss you since the first time I ever saw you."

Her eyes widen.

"Are you surprised by that?" I ask.

She shakes her head. "No. I know that you've wanted to kiss me."

Now my eyes widen. "Oh, really?"

"Of course. I'm just surprised you're saying it. I figured you were going to keep fighting it." She takes the tiny step that separates us. "For whatever reason you were giving yourself."

I lift my hand, sliding it into her thick, silky hair. "You think I've been fighting it?"

I have. And in that moment, I have no idea why. I know it will come back to me, but with her spicy, citrusy scent drifting up around me, her eyes watching me with heat and a confidence that makes my dick harder than it's been in a very, very long time, and those lips that I'm going to *have* to taste before the year is over, I can't think of anything else.

"You have," she says softly, her warm breath dancing over my lips.

That's when I realize I've bent over, my mouth just centimeters from hers. I grip her hair and tip her head back.

"Well, I'm done with that," I tell her.

"You are going to be *so* pissed at yourself for putting this off," she says in a breathy promise.

I grin at her sass just before my mouth covers hers.

And just as the elevator jerks to a stop and we're plunged into darkness.

CHAPTER 2
Elise

MY MOTHER LIKES to say that the first time my father kissed her, it felt like the entire world stopped. Which is adorable and romantic. Considering they wound up divorced when I was a kid, it's not exactly the stuff of happily-ever-afters, but she meant it in a one-kiss-and-your-dad-and-I-knew-we-had-a-future kind of way.

This is *not* what she meant.

Not a literal stopping of a giant mechanical steel box that could plunge us to our death at any second.

Blake Wilder, the Racketeers notoriously superstitious and very grumpy goalie, has barely put his lips on mine when the elevator jolts to a grinding stop. I'm ripped from sexy to startled so quickly, I fall backwards and slam into the handrail under the mirrored wall.

"Oh!"

Pain radiates throughout my hip as I try not to lose my balance in my high heels. I'm teetering on the edge of disaster when big, strong hands land on my waist and steady me.

His breath is warm in my ear. "You okay? Are you hurt?"

Even though it's so dark I can't see him, I can *feel* him. His enormous body is everywhere, and it's both comforting and crowding. I feel like I can't breathe. That isn't romantic either, because I'm about two heartbeats away from a full-blown panic attack.

I hate elevators.

All small spaces, really, but elevators in particular. Not for any reason. I've never been trapped in one before—oh, God, I'm trapped in an elevator—but because they shudder and groan and break down constantly in dozens of movies and books and presumably in real life.

Half the reason I jumped at the chance to move into Luna McNeill's old apartment over the bakery is because it has one flight of steps and no death box.

But I refuse to let Blake know I'm internally freaking the fuck out.

Show no weakness.

"I'm fine," I say, even as my hip throbs incessantly and I'm mentally calculating how long we can survive without fresh oxygen. "Though I just had to wear the fuck-me cage heels, didn't I?" I add, lightly.

Blake chuckles, his deep voice rolling over me like warm honey. "*Huge* fan. And it's New Year's Eve. What else would you wear?"

"Precisely. Though I wouldn't have moved an inch if I was in sneakers. My balance is amazing." Normally it is even in heels. I live in them because I love the way they show off my calves and give me a height advantage. Doing the pinup model pageant circuit has made me stumble-proof for the most part.

But Blake had broken my concentration when he bent down to kiss me, something I've not-so-secretly been wishing he'd do for months. We've only met a few times, but there was a sizzle between us. We flirted a little, he fished for a compliment, I refused to give it to him.

That's all it's been. I had assumed he was the type of guy who would have pursued me if he was interested, but he hadn't and

I'm not a woman who chases men. That was that. A missed connection, nothing more, nothing less.

So yes, I was distracted by his sudden insistence we talk and his very direct compliments.

And no one can anticipate an elevator screeching to a halt without warning.

"Are you sure you're not hurt?"

His hands start to wander up my sides and over my arms, making me shiver in the dark. My eyes are adjusting to the lack of light, and I can see his long hair brushing his shoulders, his strong jaw and his thick beard, his firm lips, and the curve of his nose. I can't read his expression but I can read his body language. He's planning to pick right back up where we left off.

"I'm not hurt." Except for the bruise on my hip that's probably forming as we speak.

I press my back against the wall and grip his forearms for balance as much as to stop him. Because while I do want to make out with him and show him what he's been missing, he's not grasping the obvious.

"We're stuck in an elevator," I point out. "We should call someone."

"You don't think it will just start back up?"

I give a huff of impatience. "Why would it do that?"

I sense his shrug more than I see it. "I don't know."

"Exactly. Let's be proactive here. Isn't there an emergency call button?"

"I don't think this is an emergency."

The hell it isn't.

I lift my ridiculously tiny clutch purse and unclick it to retrieve my phone. I command it to turn on the flashlight.

"Ow, fuck," Blake complains as the light hits him directly in the eyes. His hand lifts to cover his dark brown eyes, and he hisses a little. "Damn, girl."

I'm unmoved.

I need to see the elevator panel to push the button and get the hell out of here.

I was diagnosed with ADHD and anxiety as a child and while I've learned to manage both, accepting that certain things like my inability to maintain a clutter-free apartment will never change, panic can still pop up at random times. It's why I quit my corporate job as an executive assistant's assistant over a year ago. Well, that and the British billionaire boss that I had a huge crush on and happened to kiss one night when we were working late alone. But the *main* reason I quit was because I learned I couldn't force myself to be organized when I'm not and that it's better to embrace being a creative, while minimizing stressful situations.

This is an obviously stressful situation.

"Move your big body," I tell Blake, pushing around him, flashlight bouncing erratically as I search for the panel.

There it is. The red button. I push it triumphantly, half-expecting the elevator to light up and start descending immediately. Maybe some confetti to drop. A bass beat to start thumping in celebration.

Nothing happens except Blake moves in right behind me on the pretense of squinting at the panel. His thighs brush my ass.

"I don't think that was necessary," he says.

I try to glance back at him, but all I can see is his dark suit covering his massive shoulder. "Are you aware we're trapped and no one knows it?"

I'm already late to this party. No one is going to send out a search party for me. In fact, I wasn't even on the invitation list. Dani Larkin Armstrong Hughes McNeill, or whatever her actual name is now that she's married to *three* men, just had a baby a few days ago, so she clearly forgot to add me to the attending guests list after she invited me. Which is totally understandable and wouldn't have been an issue, aside from a sour-faced security guard who did the whole *you're-not-on-the-list* thing.

There was no way in hell I was going to text Dani given the hour and the fact that she literally just gave birth, but I wasn't about to give up either. Not after spending an hour and a half doing my hair and makeup and looking this damn hot. I was going to text Luna and every Racketeers player whose number is in my phone until someone came down and vouched I'm not a spy or a stalker seeking entrance to their private party.

Fortunately none of that was necessary because Wade, who wears the team mascot costume at the hockey games and is obsessed with my boobs, strolled into the lobby stoned right then and told the security guard I'm his girlfriend. For a guy who looks like he's spinning out on the astral plane half of the time, he has his sharp moments.

Unlike Blake right now, who seems to be deliberately misunderstanding me.

"What's the rush? We've got all night." His eyes narrow. "Unless you have plans?"

"Yes, they involve the free food and booze at the party I was about to walk into when you accosted me and forced me to stay in the elevator with you." That's a gross exaggeration, but now he's just annoying me.

"I did not *accost* you."

"What would you call it?" I demand. "We need to talk," I say slowly, in a poor attempt at Blake's demanding and rough voice.

He actually starts laughing.

Not the reaction I was expecting.

Grumpy Blake is sexy.

Laughing Blake is deadly.

As in the murder of all my inhibitions and hopefully my pussy. He may be annoying and we may die of suffocation or dehydration in this elevator, but after we're safe, I wouldn't mind having sex with him. I haven't hooked up with anyone since that prick hockey player Justin Travers, who had a tiny dick and somehow blamed that genetic shortcoming on me. It left a bad taste in my mouth, literally, and I feel confident Blake has more than a Vienna sausage in his pants.

"What's so damn funny?" I ask.

"Is that really what I sound like?"

I turn my flashlight on him. He's smiling and rubbing his jaw. His eyes narrow at the light, but he holds my gaze. "I think I sound more like this—we need to talk."

He says it the same way he did earlier. Demanding. Confident. *Growly.*

I'm momentarily and blissfully distracted.

"What do we need to talk about anyway?" The only thing I want to discuss is our escape plan.

He doesn't address that. "Are you scared that we're stuck in an elevator?" he asks. "Don't lie."

"I'm *not* scared," I lie.

He clearly doesn't believe me. He cocks his head and studies me for a second before nodding. "It's going to be fine, Elise. Here, I'll call the front desk. I'm sure there are maintenance personnel on site."

I sigh in relief. "Thank you. That's a great idea."

"Come here." Blake pulls me up against his chest with one hand and rubs my back comfortingly as he pulls his phone out of his pocket with the other. "I'll call the front desk."

Dropping my hand holding my purse, I press the other one against him so that the flashlight on my phone is facing his chest, dimming its brightness.

Blake is talking to someone. "Yes, this is Blake Wilder, with the Racketeers' private party in your lounge. My guest and I are on the elevator and it's stopped moving."

Relieved that he sounds confident and calm, I lean forward, just a little bit, wanting to feel the strength of his muscles and how good it feels to have his arm wrapped around me. He's built like a lumberjack and instead of lifting logs, he could be lifting me up against the wall later tonight. The thought makes me shiver in anticipation, heat swirling down low between my thighs. I love big, strong men.

His hand is drifting down from the small of my back onto the curve of my ass. His fingers flex and I give a soft moan of approval. Blake glances down at me, his eyes darkening with desire. "Yes, thank you, we appreciate it. Happy New Year."

He ends the call and gives my ass just the smallest of squeezes before he lets it fall away. "The hotel already knew we're stuck in here. The fire department should be here in ten minutes."

Now I'm fully reassured. Firefighters always save the day. "It was me pushing the button, wasn't it?" I ask. "That's how they know."

Blake gives a grunt. "Maybe."

So he's that guy. Can't admit when he's wrong. Or maybe when someone else is right.

Either way, it's not great.

Good thing I'm not in the market for a boyfriend.

Just hot hookup New Year's Eve sex.

"So." I take a step back, wincing at the soreness in my hip. I massage it through my dress.

Oddly, I suddenly realize he's limping a little as he shifts to the left.

"What's wrong with your hip?" I ask.

"What happened to your hip?" he asks at the exact same time.

"You first," I say. I'm instantly sympathetic. Goalies do a lot of squatting, sliding, hip rocking… *so* much body movement.

What started out as sympathy suddenly has me visualizing Blake Wilder hip thrusting naked. I clear my throat and try to steady my phone in my hand.

"Just a hazard of the job." He shrugs. "You?"

"Just bumped it when the elevator stopped." I stare at him, my flashlight trained at him. "What did you want to talk about? Anything other than that you obviously saw me in this dress and had to kiss me?"

"Can you take the spotlight off of me?" He crosses his arms over the barrel of his chest.

"Can you answer the question?"

Blake lets out the world's biggest sigh. "What the hell happened with you and Justin Travers?"

Whatever I thought he was going to say, it wasn't that. I stare back. Why on earth would he care about that now, after all these months? "That's none of your business."

"He's an asshole."

"I'm well aware of that."

There is momentary satisfaction in his expression before his nostrils flare and his eyes narrow. "Did he hurt you?" he demands. "I'll fucking kill him. Tell me the truth, Elise."

I'm fascinated by the display of what… jealousy? I'm not sure if it's about hockey or me or both, but I can admit that there is something sexy as hell about his reaction. What woman doesn't want a touch-her-and-die moment from a protective guy?

"He didn't hurt me. He was just a jerk."

Blake is silent, watching me. He seems to decide I'm telling the truth. "Did he suck in bed?"

"Okay, just stop right there." I hold my hand up. "That is really none of your business." Then because I don't owe Justin Travers anything and I'm still nauseated and possibly in need of therapy by the fact that he decided to clean himself off post-condom on my childhood teddy bear, I give Blake what he clearly wants to hear. "But yes, he was terrible in bed." I hold my pinky finger up as a visual display.

Blake's eyes widen. "For real?"

I nod.

"Well, damn. Holy shit." He chuckles. "Justin Pinky Dick Travers. I fucking love the sound of that."

Clearly, whatever perceived threat there was before has instantly been minimized. "I didn't love it."

"I'm sorry." He doesn't look sorry. He looks thrilled.

"I shouldn't have said anything." It wasn't about the fact that Justin wasn't well-endowed. I can work with small. I can't work with bad manners and a selfish, accusatory attitude. "Don't go spreading that around. It's not his fault."

"He's a total asshole," Blake says. "And now I know why. He's overcompensating."

I make a noncommittal sound.

"He didn't overcompensate?"

Not even close. He accused me of being too wet, and that's why he kept falling out during sex. For the record, I wasn't even damp by that point because he was so rude about the whole thing. But I didn't even tell Luna and Dani the truth about what happened. Luna would have been outraged and Dani would have been sad and it wasn't that important in the end. I just chalked it up to a night that could have been better spent and moved on. After throwing my teddy bear in the washing machine.

"Why does it matter?" I ask.

"Because you deserve to be worshiped in bed." He takes a step forward and cups my cheek, gaze drifting over my lips.

Well, yes, please..

I turn my flashlight feature off and shove my phone back in my purse so my hands are free. "I one hundred percent agree with you," I murmur, grateful for my heels as I slip my arms around his neck. "Know anyone who is up for the job?"

Blake responds by kissing me.

It's not a questing, tender kiss.

It's dominating and demanding and rough.

It's him laying possession to my mouth, tongue sweeping between my lips to tangle hotly with my own.

Immediately, I'm lost.

His hands are cupping my cheeks as we grapple with each other in a sexy tussle for control. I lose, instantly. He has me backed against the wall, hands above my head before I can even blink. I gasp, already out of breath, already wet and aching, already desperately wishing I wasn't wearing fucking shapewear under my dress.

"Your mouth is so fucking perfect," he says, pressing another hard kiss on me.

Then he nips at my bottom lip like he can't stop himself, like he wants to consume me. The roughness of his beard is only heightening my awareness of how close he is to me. I can feel his hardness pressing against my middle as he palms first one breast, then the other, teasing his thumb over my nipples beneath my dress. He tries to take the neckline down for better access as he runs his lips over the swell of my breast, but it doesn't budge. I'm poured into this skintight son of a bitch, and there is no wiggle room.

"God, your fucking body," he growls. "I want to rip this dress off you and taste and touch every single inch of you."

I want that too.

He smells like the woods. I don't know how that's possible, but he does. He smells like he just chopped a week's worth of firewood before bathing in a spring river. It feels like I've fallen into a fantasy where the rough lumberjack stumbles upon the naked virgin washing her clothes in the river and she is torn between running away and letting him have his way with her.

Only I'm no virgin and I know exactly what I want. And it's not running away.

I moan softly. "Fuck me," I beg breathlessly. "Now."

I'm never shy about telling men what I want and need, but it's crazy how fast he's shot me from zero to ninety.

"No condom," he says, shaking his head.

"No, God, no," I say in disappointment, letting my head fall back against the wall, hard. I hit it again for good measure. "I don't have one either."

"I've got you," he says, simply.

I take it to mean he's going to get me off, which I definitely approve of.

I'm going to enjoy returning the favor.

He yanks my leg up onto his thigh and shoves my dress up to my waist. His hand roams up my thigh. Right over my shapewear. He roams and roams, teasing me without meaning to. He is just trying to figure out how to get them off. Considering it took me ten minutes to get into it, he has his work cut out for him.

"Where the fuck does this thing end?" he asks, clearly bewildered, pulling back to glance down. "What are we working with here?"

I laugh softly. "Shapewear." Or as I like to call it, my rolls wrangler. At least it stops under my boobs. I had actually intended to wear the bodysuit version, but I couldn't find it in my bedroom, closet, or dresser, which isn't uncommon. I frequently lose track of clothing—and everything else—in my chaotic apartment. I've learned to pivot without much distress.

Blake lifts his head to stare at me. "Why the *hell* would you do this to yourself? Your body is fucking gorgeous. I've been fantasizing about it for months." He grips my thighs. "I want all of this."

"Thank you. I appreciate the enthusiasm." I'm not going to bother to explain to him about thigh chafing in dresses. "Just yank it down. It's right above my waist."

He doesn't need to be told twice. He has my dress right up under my strapless bra and slips his fingers between my flesh and the stretchy fabric. He peels it down with a hard yank, frowning. He's clearly very offended by shapewear, which I find kind of adorable.

I hold on to him as he lifts first one of my feet, then the other, removing the shapewear. He holds it up and shakes it.

"I'm going to burn this stupid thing." Then he drops it and runs his rough hands over my bare thighs, hips, my stomach, giving a sigh of pleasure. "So much fucking better. So soft, so damn sexy."

"If you were angling for a blowjob, you've totally earned one," I tell him, digging my nails into his biceps.

Then he has one, then two fingers buried deep inside me without warning, and I lose the ability to speak or think.

"Oh, fuck yes, Elise. This pussy is perfection."

"Blake," I breathe. I don't know what I want to say other than that. His fingers are huge. Massive. Skilled. Rhythmic.

He buries his lips near my ear, murmuring in encouragement.

"Yeah? You like that? Does that feel good to have my fingers fucking you?"

"So. Good."

"You want another finger?"

I nod eagerly, panting too hard to answer with words.

He slips his thumb over my clit, massaging it as he adds his ring finger to the first two.

"Oh!" He's stretching me with each stroke. Then he flicks his tongue over my earlobe as he works my pussy.

"You're going to come for me, you sexy little vixen. Now."

The words are commanding and rough.

I'm not always fabulous at following orders, but this one is easy.

I shatter all over him, giving sharp cries of pleasure into his shoulder, rocking my hips to get the most out of his fingers.

"That's it."

I'm still shaking and holding onto him, trying to catch my breath, when a metal grinding sound has me lifting my head in panic. "Oh, shit."

Blake yanks my dress back down to cover my naked lower half. He steps in front of me right as the elevator door pries open and a light washes over us.

"Chicago Fire Department. Everyone okay in there?"

Blake clears his throat. "We're fine."

Or devastated from an orgasm. He can speak for himself. My hands are shaking as I smooth down my dress and glance around his shoulder to see if our rescuers caught a glimpse of anything. Like my bare ass.

A handsome face is peering down at us. This man has the brightest, bluest eyes I've seen in my entire life. He has a crooked and warm smile.

Damn. Chicago's finest.

Happy New Year, girl.

CHAPTER 3
Aidan

"THIS ONE IS GOING to be easy," I tell Matt, my co-worker on the CFD, as we stroll into an upscale hotel. "Stalled elevator with entrapment is the easiest type of call to get on New Year's Eve."

Matt is a veteran in the department and he gives me a cynical look and shakes his head. "Still so wide-eyed with enthusiasm. You make me feel fucking old, you cheerful little shit."

I give him a grin as I carry the step-ladder easily with one hand. "I am not wide-eyed. I just happen to like my job. Oh, and you're actually *ancient*, you crusty old fuck."

Matt just snorts. This is our way of showing camaraderie with each other. Too much kindness makes him visibly uncomfortable. I'm used to it and I'm cool with our dynamic. He reminds me of my grandfather, who retired from the department ten years ago. He shows love with insults.

"I'm assigned to power," Matt says. "The elevator inspection on file says it's a traction elevator and the maintenance man is meeting me upstairs to let me in. I'll radio you from the penthouse. Keep 'em calm."

"Will do." The penthouse isn't the top apartment with sweeping views of the skyline. In elevator terms, it's the room above the elevator shaft with the motor and shiv and other mechanics. Matt needs to kill the power to all the elevators in the hoistway before we open the door. Not ideal for a night with lots of guests in the hotel, but it's necessary for everyone's safety. We'll just have to do the recovery as quickly as possible.

I head over to the elevator bank with our third, Wyatt, who is smart and efficient as hell. Wyatt loves to take the lead on the actual mechanics and leave the people part to me. He's a social guy outside of calls, but on site, he focuses on logistics, whereas I love helping people. I get along with everyone, from kids to the elderly, and everyone in between. I've been told I have a reassuring face. I'm better at victim rescue than he is.

"This is a hoistway door. Just a drop-key hole," he says. "They're between one and two. Easy."

I knock on the elevator door and call out in a booming voice, "Chicago Fire Department. Just stay calm. We're going to get the door open and get you out in just a minute."

There isn't a response. Hopefully, they just can't hear me and aren't injured. Sometimes the car jumps when it stops. Or more typically, someone panics from the enclosed space. The emergency light and fan should be running, but it's still unnerving to a lot of people to be trapped even briefly.

"Sucks they almost made it to the first floor," Wyatt says as we head for the stairs to climb to the second floor. "And it's thirty minutes to midnight." He gives me a grin. "Hope they're feeling friendly in there."

"We'd better hustle. No one wants to ring in the new year stuck in an elevator. Especially with strangers."

My younger sister had commented yesterday that it sucked that I am ringing in the new year at work, but I don't mind. I'd prefer it's me on duty—single guy, no kids—than the crew with spouses and families. They deserve to be at home with their loved ones.

Though I'd also prefer not to be single. I like being in a relationship, but the past year has been a bit of a dry spell for me. I had a girlfriend for four years in my early twenties, but it ended when she moved to Los Angeles. I loved her, but I love Chicago, my family and my job too. I couldn't sacrifice all of this to be sitting in traffic on the expressway all day. Or at least that's my vision of L.A. Then about nine months ago I briefly dated a guy who looked good on paper—until he stole a thousand bucks out of my nightstand. I can be a little too trusting, I admit it.

But I'd rather give people the benefit of the doubt than assume the worst from jump. If that costs me a grand, so be it.

It has me a little hesitant, though. I've been sticking primarily to hookups the last few months, which means a kiss at midnight with a special someone wasn't going to happen tonight anyway. I'm happy to be at work.

Our radios crackle. It's Matt. "Power's out. Go ahead."

"We're up." I set the ladder down and open the hoistway door in the shaft. "Gate restrictor."

I step back to let Wyatt check out the safety door. They all open slightly differently and he loves to figure them out in ten seconds or less. He considers it a fun personal challenge. I consider it boring.

I call out again. "Fire department. Step away from the door please and we'll have you out in just a minute. Happy New Year, folks!"

Wyatt rolls his eyes at me. He already has the gate restrictor open, but it usually stops at around three inches for another safety mechanism. He pushes down a handle and then the gate is open.

Because the elevator is between two floors, several feet of the car is now accessible. I pop my flashlight and my head in and announce myself again.

What I see are two people making the most of the time trapped. I'm looking down on them, but I see a large man in a suit with his hand up a woman's dress. A very sexy woman's dress. I see lots of smooth fair skin, cleavage, and wavy brown hair.

Lucky guy.

They leap apart from each other and blink up at me.

The face of the woman matches the body. She's gorgeous. Pouty red lips, long lashes, an elegant nose. I bet she has dimples. Damn, I love some fucking dimples. On a woman's face and on her ass. I love to kiss them. I smile at her. I'd say it's in reassurance, but it might also just be in appreciation for how beautiful she is.

"Chicago Fire Department. Everyone okay in there?"

"We're fine," the man says.

I fight the urge to grin. He doesn't sound fine. He sounds like he just got cock-blocked and is none too happy about it. Can't say I blame the guy. The woman is smoothing down her dress and if I'm not mistaken, her purse and panties are lying on the floor of the car.

"Oh, thank God!" the woman says breathlessly. "I'm so glad you're here! That took forever."

Her male companion frowns at her. I wouldn't call him conventionally good-looking. More like rough and tumble, which can be sexy, but the scowl on his face ruins it.

"What's the distance?" Wyatt asks me.

"Within protocol." If the car was more than thirty-six inches from the floor, we'd need to call in a safety crew and our battalion chief to assist. "Ladder."

The woman has rushed to the front of the elevator and is raising her arms up like I'm just supposed to haul her out of the elevator by her armpits. Which I could, but it's much safer to use a ladder.

"Ma'am, I need you to step back so I can put a ladder down for you."

"Ma'am? For fuck's safe, I'm twenty-eight! Don't ma'am me until I'm at least forty."

Sexy *and* sassy. I find that hot as hell. Too bad she has a boyfriend.

"Sorry. Miss. Can you step back for me, please?"

"Just please get me out of here." She does obey though, taking two steps backwards.

"Elise, give him room." The guy gently takes her elbow and tries to tug her further away.

She gives a huff of impatience.

I let the ladder down. Already anticipating she's going to just leap onto it, I caution her. "Let me secure it. I'll give you the go-ahead when it's safe."

"Thank you," she says. "You're a lifesaver. Literally." She smiles up at me.

Yep, dimples. Very nice.

Damn, if I don't feel like puffing my chest out just a little at that. As I check to make sure the ladder is stable, I comment, "Looks like the emergency lights and the fan didn't go on. Hope it wasn't too hot in there."

She shoots a bemused look at her boyfriend. "It was actually *very* hot."

"I can imagine," I say, casually.

But something about my tone gives me away. The guy gives me a sharp glare.

I ignore it. "Okay, miss, you can climb up. Just slow and steady, no running."

She grips the ladder and puts her heels on the first rung. She teeters a little, and I have a hell of a view of her bouncing breasts before she recovers. I wasn't trying to look, but my angle and those breasts? It was unavoidable.

"Don't forget your purse."

"Oh, crap, Blake, my purse. Can you grab it?" she pleads, glancing back over her shoulder. The movement makes her lose her balance. "Ah!" she squeaks.

I'm in a squat and I reach out with both hands and press them firmly on her forearms to secure her against the ladder and prevent backward motion.

Her boyfriend has his palms square on her ass and they remain there the entire time she ascends the ladder. I would say he is concerned for her safety, but I also get the sense he's staking his claim.

I get the message loud and clear. I don't hit on other guy's girlfriends. That's not my style. Plenty of people in the single pool to play with.

She's eye level with me now and I release her arms and shift back to give her room. I use a professional tone. "You're doing great. Just a few more steps." I make a point *not* to look at her chest, even though her dress seems to have stayed down around the fourth step while she kept climbing.

"Damn it." She lets go with one hand to tug her dress up.

I reach back out in alarm.

She's doing a one-armed flapping thing while saying, "Oh, shit, oh, shit, oh shit!"

But her boyfriend pushes her forward again.

One of her breasts has popped out of her dress. Not all of it. But like eighty percent of it. I definitely see areola. Clearing my throat, I decide to keep my eyes on hers and get her on the hotel floor before I tell her or she'll just let go of the ladder again.

In fact, I think I'll let her discover it on her own so I don't get a fist in the face from her boyfriend, who is fucking huge. Not that I couldn't hold my own with him, but I can't fight back when I'm on duty.

But once I take her hand and help her up onto the floor, the dress is covering more. She immediately tugs it up further, which is good because I don't want Wyatt to get a view of a nip slip. From what I understand from talk around the station, he gets to see plenty of bare breasts very regularly. He doesn't need to see this woman's too.

"You good?" I ask her.

She nods, blowing her bangs out of her eyes and tossing dark curls over her shoulder. "Holy shit. That was a workout." She swivels her hips like they're stiff and she needs to loosen them up.

I'm almost fucking speechless. Is she a burlesque dancer? Because that would not surprise me at all.

She turns. "Blake, do you need help?"

His answer is a grunt.

He clears the floor, her purse in his hand.

"Thank you." She retrieves it from him before he's climbed out of the car. "Where's my phone?"

"In your purse."

"And my... never mind." She makes a "whoopsie" face and grins.

He doesn't grin back. "In my pocket."

Once he's out, I gesture for them to move away from the door. "You sure you're okay?"

"We're fine."

I retrieve the ladder and then step back to let Wyatt secure the gate restrictor again.

The sexy woman named Elise goes to the panel on the wall and hits the up button.

"The power is out for all the elevators," I tell her. "Give us five more minutes and they'll be back up and running."

"Where the hell are you going?" the guy named Blake asks her.

"To the party. It's almost midnight. I desperately need a cocktail." She says this like it's obvious.

Clearly it is to her and not to him.

"I'm going home," he says, wincing a little as he takes a step toward the lobby.

"Seriously?"

"Seriously." He stares at her.

She stares at him.

Trying not to inadvertently be involved in their personal business, I busy myself with radioing Matt now that Wyatt has the hoistway door closed again. "All clear. Power can be restored."

Blake leans over and tucks Elise's hair behind her ear. "Goodnight, Elise. Happy New Year."

"Happy New Year, Blake." She doesn't sound angry, she just sounds a little mystified.

I'm mystified too. I wouldn't care if she wanted to party all damn night before going home with me. I'd wait out last call and enjoy showing her off on my arm in the process. And what fucking guy leaves his woman to get herself home? On New Year's Eve, of all nights, when car services and cabs are impossible to get and the train is chock full of drunks?

An asshole, that's who.

He heads toward the lobby and she untucks the piece of hair he put behind her ear. She adjusts her dress again and gives me a smile. "Champagne for one, then."

"Big party up there?"

She nods.

"Then enjoy your night. Your boyfriend is missing out on having a gorgeous woman on his arm."

"He's not my boyfriend."

That's the best damn thing I've heard all night. "No?"

"Not at all."

"The power is back on," I tell her.

She pushes the elevator button again. "What about you? Do you have a significant other who is home alone tonight? That must be hard."

"I'm single."

Wyatt clears his throat from behind me. I adjust my ball cap. We're not in full gear, just black pants and T-shirts. If we had needed a full safety crew, they would have come in gear. I know what Wyatt is thinking.

That I should get her number.

He's right. I should.

"Oh." She smiles at the news of my single status. "Too bad you're working. You could be my plus one."

I pull my phone out of my pocket and swipe it. "Give me your number and maybe we can make that happen another night." I hold it out to her.

She takes it readily and puts her number in. "What's your name?"

Right. I'm an opportunist but clearly off my game. "Aidan. It's a pleasure to meet you, Elise."

"You, too, Aidan." She hands my phone back. "Happy New Year."

The elevator door to her left dings and opens. She eyes it. "When you fall off a horse, get right back on, right?"

Her bravery impresses me, though she does take a deep, bracing breath.

A lanky kid in his early twenties steps off the elevator. "Oh, damn, Elise. There you are. The Racketeers party is lit. Where's Wilder?"

"He went home."

That's when it clicks. Racketeers. Blake Wilder. He's the pro hockey goalie. I'm not a huge hockey fan, but I know the name from when games are on at the station.

I guess he's taken one too many hits to the head with a puck to leave this gorgeous woman standing here alone. His loss, my gain.

"Does this mean I get a kiss at midnight?" the young guy asks, hopefully.

She sighs. "Wade, you're like my little brother. Knock it off."

I hide a grin. This woman is something else.

"Can't blame a guy for trying." He shrugs. He gives me a wave. "Yo, firefighter dude, what's up?"

"Just saving damsels in elevators."

"What?" He looks thoroughly confused.

Elise steps onto the elevator, nudging Wade out of the way since he's blocking the door from closing. She blows me a kiss right as the door glides closed.

I immediately text her.

> Let me know when you make it upstairs. This is Aidan.

Then I realize that might freak her out.

I text her again.

> Not that I'm concerned the elevator will stop again. It won't.

I can't guarantee that, but I don't want to scare her. She texts back.

> I'm not afraid of that. I'm only afraid of bad hair days and I almost never have those.

I grin.

> Good to know. Enjoy your night.

Do I care that she was doing whatever she was doing in the elevator with a professional hockey goalie?

Not in the least.

I'm not afraid of anything either.

CHAPTER 4
Simon

"I DON'T UNDERSTAND KISS CAMS," I say as I look down on the Racketeers arena from the owner's private box.

My cousin has owned the hockey team for years, but I've only seen them play a handful of times. I follow their record and standings, but I don't really watch hockey and the only player's name I know is Crew McNeill, and that's only because he's also married to Nathan's wife.

Rugby is more my game, and Nathan humors me once in a while when he's in London by accompanying me to a match so I come watch his beloved Racketeers play once a year or so when I'm in Chicago.

"What's to understand?" Nathan asks as the camera zooms in on a couple who grin, wave, and then lean in to share a kiss. "It's an annoying activity in between periods that entertains the crowd, for some reason."

"That's exactly my point," I say, fighting a grin. "Why do people like watching other people kiss?"

I don't really care, but Nathan's adorable wife Danielle told me the story of how she met two of her husbands because of the kiss cam in this very arena when I stopped at their townhouse to see their new baby girl last night.

Her two husbands who are not Nathan.

From what I can gather, were it not for the kiss cam, Nathan might have gotten Dani to himself—at least for a while—so the whole thing annoys him. Which means I need to bring it up however I can.

"Because people are strange and love to watch other people act like fools."

I laugh. "And what if someone is sitting next to someone they don't want to kiss?" I ask. I find people watching entertaining, unlike my stuffed shirt of a cousin.

I know that Dani was actually on a blind date with a guy she did not want to kiss when the kiss cam found her in the crowd on that first fateful night.

"They certainly don't *have* to kiss them," Nathan says with a scowl.

I chuckle. It is so easy, and fun, to tease my cousin. While he has certainly relaxed since meeting Danielle, he is still one thousand times more uptight than I am.

He's always been serious, and as he got older and took over more responsibilities for the North American arm of the Armstrong family business, he became grumpier and grumpier.

That makes no sense to me. How can you have billions of dollars and be anything but absolutely chuffed?

Sure, there's responsibility, but we also have the ability to give thousands of people jobs, turn out products and services that can make the world better, and at the same time live lives that are pretty fucking easy and comfortable.

Money can't buy happiness, so they say, but it sure can buy a lot of things that make it easier to enjoy yourself.

I chuckle as the camera actually finds a couple that doesn't want to kiss. The guy holds up a sign that says SHE'S MY SISTER. They were obviously prepared.

Then the camera pans to where the mascot, a huge silver and white dog, dressed in a vest and fedora, is standing on the steps.

He's pulling a laughing woman to her feet, then dipping her back and kissing her.

I straighten as he pulls the woman upright again, and the camera zooms in on her face.

I swear my heart stops.

"Holy hell," I mutter.

"You okay, Simon?" Nathan asks.

I can't tear my eyes away from the woman, but I nod. Am I *okay*? I'm fucking fantastic.

I just found Elise.

"How do I get down there?" I ask Nathan, not taking my eyes off of her.

She's just as drop dead gorgeous as I remember. Tonight, she's dressed casually, instead of the business attire I'm used to seeing her in. She's wearing tight, dark jeans, and a Racketeers hockey jersey. But because the mascot pulled her out onto the steps with him, I can see her from head to toe. She's wearing high heeled black boots, her dark hair hanging in large curls around her face and down her back. And the lips that I have been thinking about for fourteen bloody months are painted a cock-teasing crimson.

But more than anything, more than the curves, more than her hair, more than that mouth, it's the way her face lights up when she smiles.

I would know her anywhere.

That is the woman who walked into my office one day almost two years ago, grabbed me by the balls—metaphorically, not literally—and made me wish for the first time in my life that my last name was not Armstrong and that I didn't have millions of dollars to my name. That I was just a regular guy who she would agree to go out to dinner with. And then just a little over a year ago, the woman who finally let me kiss her. And then disappeared from my life.

"Down where?" Nathan asks.

The camera has moved off of Elise and I've lost track of her.

I turn to my cousin. "I need to find the woman the mascot was just kissing."

Nathan looks at me for several beats. He narrows his eyes. "Are you fucking kidding me?"

I shake my head with a frown. "No. Why would I be kidding?"

"Did Danielle put you up to this? Or was it Crew?"

Okay, if anyone was going to put me up to something to mess with Nathan, Crew is a pretty good guess. But I'm dead serious. "No. Nathan, I know that woman and I need to talk to her. Right now."

I can't believe she's here. I looked for her after she quit. We kissed and then the next day she just didn't come back to work. Accessing her employee files to find her address was probably not completely ethical, but I didn't care. I needed to know that she hadn't quit because of me because then I would have to apologize and talk her into returning to her job.

But she'd already moved. I resigned myself to the fact that she didn't want to be found. She could've walked back into my office at any point. Hell, she had my number. I'm still convinced to this day that she knows I would've welcomed any contact.

Which means she didn't want to have contact.

I chalked it up to just one of those things. It could have been something, and then it wasn't. But if she is within the same building as I am at the same time, I am going to find her and talk to her.

If for no other reason, than to assure myself that she is fine and I didn't somehow fuck up her life.

Nathan studies my face and apparently decides that I am completely serious. He nods. "Fine." He pulls his phone from his pocket and presses a couple of buttons. He puts the phone to his ear. "Wade, I need you to go get the woman you just kissed." He pauses, then frowns. "Elise?" His eyes find mine.

I give him a single nod, telling him that yes, that's the name of the woman I am talking about as well.

"Yes. Go get Elise and bring her up to my box."

Perfect. We can have a private place to talk.

"Yes, right now." Nathan pauses, then rolls his eyes. "You can do that afterward," he says heavily.

I can't help it, I smirk.

Finally, Nathan hangs up. "I don't know why I keep that kid on staff."

"He's going to get her?" I ask.

"As long as he doesn't forget or get lost between where he is and where she's sitting," Nathan says dryly.

"Thanks."

"You want to tell me what this is about? How do you know Elise?"

I narrow my eyes. "How do *you* know Elise?"

"Elise is a friend of Danielle's. She works part time for Crew's sister, Luna."

That makes me frown. "What does Luna do?"

"She owns a bakery."

She quit working for me at a very high paying, comfortable executive assistant job with fantastic benefits, to go work for a bakery?

"So how do you know her?" Nathan asks again.

"She used to work for me. She was my assistant's assistant."

"And why do you need to talk to her?"

I take a breath and blow it out. I study my cousin. He's a very good guy. He's also madly in love, managing a complicated but clearly real and fulfilling relationship with three other adult humans, and he just became a father. Maybe he'll understand this.

"I wanted to ask her out when she quit and walked out of my life, disappearing without a trace," I tell him. "After I kissed her."

Nathan just blinks at me for about five seconds. "I see," he finally says.

"I haven't seen or talked to her in fourteen months. I just want to know that she didn't quit her job because I crossed a line."

There is a knock at the door to the suite and Nathan looks

toward the door, then back to me. "Well, looks like here's your chance."

My heart thumps hard with anticipation. We had undeniable chemistry, me and Elise.

"Come in," Nathan calls.

The door swings open and a guy in a big furry dog suit, minus the head, leans in. The man in the suit is not at all what I expected. He's young, early to mid-twenties, with blond, shaggy hair, a scraggly beard, and a somewhat goofy grin that somehow manages to look nervous at the same time.

"Mr. Armstrong? Elise is here."

Nathan nods. "Come on in Elise."

The mascot steps back, and she moves into the room.

She's looking at the mascot and reaches up to pat his cheek. "Thanks, Wade. And seriously, that's the last time for the kiss cam. That's three games in a row that you've come for me."

The grin the kid gives her is definitely not nervous. It's big and full of affection. "You're such a good sport. And the social media account is now all about us going out, you know."

I frown as she laughs. "I know. We have to stop encouraging them."

"There's no negative for me here," Wade tells her.

"Sweetie, you're a big talker," Elise tells him. "But I keep telling you, I don't think you have what it takes to keep up with me."

"And what is that, exactly?" I ask, interrupting their exchange, even though it's clearly not serious.

I'm ready to have Elise's full attention on *me*.

And I get it when she swings toward my voice, sees me, registers who I am, straightens, and her eyes widen as her mouth drops open.

Nathan steps toward the door. He nudges Wade out as he steps into the hallway. "I'm going to go check on a few things," he says. "Take your time."

Then he's gone, pulling the door shut behind him.

"Hello, Elise," I say, tucking my hands into the pockets of my dress pants. I want to reach for her. I want to stomp across the room, back her up against the wall, and kiss the hell out of her.

I haven't forgotten her taste. I haven't forgotten the feel of her lips. I haven't forgotten how it feels to press my body to hers. I haven't forgotten how her sweet little moan of desire sounds.

It was a damn good kiss.

And now she's right here in front of me and it's taking everything in me to hold back.

"What the hell are you doing here?" she asks, her voice breathless.

"Watching hockey," I say, going with the simplest answer.

She looks around, as if confused. "How are you here? How do you know Nathan?" Then she laughs softly. "Or do all you hot rich guys have some private club or something?"

There are of course private clubs for very wealthy people but I give her the real answer. "Nathan and I are cousins."

She stares at me. "You've got to be kidding." She frowns and shakes her head. "Armstrong. Why did it never occur to me that you have the same last name?"

I open my mouth to respond but she goes on, "Maybe because you're British? You live in London. Nathan's from here. There have to be a million Armstrongs in the world."

I wait just a moment to see if she's finished, then I say, "Our grandfathers were brothers. My grandfather moved to London to run the family business office there. He met my grandmother, who is British. My father grew up in London, as did I. We've always overseen the European branch of the business while Nathan has been in charge of the North American branch."

She lifts her hand and rubs her forehead. "How is it possible that I became friends with the woman connected to your cousin?"

I lift a shoulder. "Fate. Obviously. "

She scoffs. "Yeah. Sure."

But I'm serious. Is it fanciful to believe in things like fate and soulmates? Maybe. Would people be surprised that a billionaire businessman is whimsical? Maybe. But who better to believe in things like luck and fate than someone who is living a life like the one I live? Most everything good in my life had come to me through luck, good timing, and charm.

"I was disappointed you disappeared without a trace," I tell her, cutting to the chase. It doesn't really matter how we ended up in this moment, only what we do now that we're here.

Her eyes widen. "Oh."

I take a step forward. "I tried to find you...Not just because of the job, but because of me. I wanted to see you, date you, after that kiss, and I hate to think you didn't know that."

She presses her lips together and crosses her arms. "I had to leave. We couldn't do that."

"Why not? We did it very well."

I'm still pissed I hadn't kissed her before I did. I'd wanted to for months. She'd only worked for my company for about six months. I'd thought I had time. I was enjoying getting to know her. Enjoying our flirtation. Enjoying letting her know me and building on our chemistry to the point of I-can't-take-it-anymore.

She laughs. "I was terrible at my job. And I just kept getting worse, it seemed. And then I was throwing myself at the boss. I had to get out."

"That's not how I remember it," I say, taking another step forward. "And even if you did, your boss was very happy to catch you."

Her brows pull together slightly in an adorably confused look. "It was inappropriate."

"It wasn't. We don't have a policy against employees dating. They—we—just have to disclose it. We were two grown, consenting adults."

"It was inappropriate to *me*. I was bad at my job. Thinking about staying there just because of my feelings for you felt wrong." She bites her bottom lip, watching me. Then she says, "After we kissed and I realized that my feelings were even stronger than I thought and realized you might feel some things too, I knew I *had* to leave right then...or I maybe never would. And I would have felt terrible about myself keeping a job I didn't deserve, or like, just so I could be close to you." She pauses. "I'd already done that for about three months."

Fuck yes. I love that. I probably shouldn't. It obviously bothers her. But she had feelings for me. That's all I can concentrate on.

"We could have worked it out," I tell her. "But here we are now, not working together. Let me take you to dinner."

She shakes her head and backs up toward the door. "I would drive you crazy, Simon."

I step toward her. "Yes, you would. You *did*. In every good way."

"No," she protests, stepping back again. "I'm not talking about *that*. I'm unorganized, messy, late all the time. Not just at work at a job I don't understand or like. I'm like that *all the time*. In everything. Even the stuff I love."

I frown. I'm not following. "Elise, why would I care about that?"

"You would," she insists. "I worked for you for six months. I know that you value organization and competence and professionalism and...I'm not those things."

"I have an assistant for those things. I don't need those things from you. Not when you're not on the payroll, and I'm discussing getting to know each other on a personal level."

Her eyes widen yet she steps back, right into the door. She fumbles for the knob, her gaze glued on mine. "We're not a good fit."

"We could be an *excellent* fit," I say, making sure she understands the full innuendo.

She sucks in a breath.

"Simon...go back to London and forget me. I'm fine. I'm *good*. You don't have to think about me anymore."

"I'm here, in Chicago, until the end of March," I tell her. "And there's no way in hell I'm going to forget you. I was gutted when you disappeared, thinking I was responsible for you quitting your job."

She twists the knob and steps forward to pull the door open. "You're not responsible for that. I absolve you of all guilt. The job was a terrible fit for me. So you can go forth and live your life and not feel bad about it."

"I'd feel better about my life if you were having dinner with me."

She stares at me. "You could have *any* woman."

"Good to know. I want *you*."

She hesitates in the doorway. Then she shakes her head. "I have to go."

Don't push her. You don't have to push right now. I tell myself that even though everything in me is screaming to take her into my arms and kiss her again.

"Okay," I say, begrudgingly. "I'll see you soon."

"That sounds ominous."

I smile. I don't believe her. I can tell her heart is pounding and her adrenaline is pulsing. Her cheeks are flushed and she keeps wetting her lips. "Does it, love? Or does it sound tempting?"

She swallows hard. Then she says, "Bye, Simon," and turns and literally *flees*.

But I just smile.

Now I know she has feelings for me. Now I know why she left. Now I know where she is. Now I can find her.

And I fully intend to.

CHAPTER 5
Blake

"TWO LEMON DROP MARTINIS."

The server nods. "Very good, ma'am."

I raise my eyebrows at my gran as he walks away. "Rough day?"

She snorts. "They're not both for me. We're celebrating."

"You're the only woman—or man, for that matter—I'll drink a lemon drop martini with. What exactly are we celebrating?"

I love these lunch meetings with Gran. We try to get together twice a month. It gets her out of the house and me out of my head. It's especially welcome today because I need a distraction after I left Elise standing in front of the elevator banks the other night. I left because I wanted to take her straight home and rip that sexy dress off of her and taste every single solitary inch of her glorious body. That she wanted to go to the party instead threw me off my game and I just decided it was better to leave than to spend two hours trailing around behind her at the Racketeers party after I already told everyone there I was leaving.

It would have revealed way too much about how this woman owns my thoughts.

"Speaking of women, how's your love life?"

So much for being distracted.

I sit back in my chair and eye my grandmother. She looks smug, which is worrisome. Gran is both scheming and competitive. I definitely get my competitiveness from her, and subsequently my dad, but I'm way more of a straight-shooter than she is.

"Who was talking about women?" I ask, suspicious that she has a friend with a granddaughter who "would be perfect for you."

"Not you. That's the problem. You know I've told you this before, but if you're gay, you can tell me. It won't change anything. I'll love you exactly the same."

Oh, Christ. I rub my beard. "If I was gay, I would tell you. I promise. Hell, I would proclaim it loudly. But I'm not. Thank you, though, I appreciate your support."

Gran is seventy-eight and still full of spunk. She raised five boys on a farm in Minnesota and then sold it with zero hesitation when my grandfather passed away. Since all of her sons scattered across the United States, she moved to the Chicago suburbs so that she can hop on a plane at O'Hare and visit any of them on a moment's notice. One of my uncles also lives here, and she's only fifteen minutes away from him and his wife, so it's been a good move for her.

She is addicted to games on her phone, cheap online shopping, and coordinating her shoes to her purses to her sunglasses. Today she is sporting light purple hair to match her enormous purse, which rivals my equipment bag in size.

She just might be my favorite person on the planet.

"Are you seeing anyone?"

She is also obsessed with ensuring all of her grandchildren are married by the age of thirty. But mostly me. I don't think she harasses my cousins as much, frankly, but she likes to tell me with a wink it's because I'm her favorite.

The server saves me from the question. He deposits two martini glasses in front of us, lemon peels floating, sugar on the rim.

"What are we celebrating?" I ask, eyeing the drink. I'm not big on sweets. Or alcohol. Or sweets in my alcohol.

The question is a natural deflection, but I am curious.

Her answer could be anything from she bought a shower caddy on Amazon to one of my cousins expecting a baby to she booked a trip to Napa.

She takes a sip of her drink and murmurs in approval. She sets it down and levels me with a look. "I'm selling the lake house."

My glass is halfway to my mouth and I immediately set it back down again. "What? Already? I thought you wanted a few more years. It's good timing though, since this is my last season. I can be up there by July."

I love the lake house. It's way up north in Minnesota and is my retirement plan. I can't wait to retreat to the woods and fish all day and sleep on the screened-in porch at night, away from social media and traffic and press conferences. I had hoped to spend a few weeks there this summer, but hell, this is even better. I can sell my condo and move right in.

I lift the martini glass to my lips and take a sip. She's right. This is a celebration.

"Oh, not to you," she says.

I choke on the drink, spraying some out onto the glass. Coughing, I thump my chest and set the glass down. Hard. *"What?"* I demand in a tight voice. "You said the lake house would be mine."

Only a few of my cousins have expressed any interest in it, and none of them have the money to pay Gran market value. Lake property has skyrocketed. I had assured her I would take excellent care of it and allow family to visit in the summer on a rotating schedule.

"I said it would be yours when you have a wife and a family."

I just stare at her, shocked. "What the hell does that mean?"

"I'm putting it on the market because it's too big for you. It's not a single man's house. It's five bedrooms. It's meant for a family."

She can't be serious. She looks serious. But she can't be.

"So, what, you're punishing me because I've been too busy with my career to reproduce?"

"Plenty of men play hockey and get married and have babies. You just don't want to. And no, I'm not punishing you. But that property would be a waste with just one lone bachelor hermit rattling around in it."

Even though I frequently refer to myself as a hermit, I'm offended she said it.

"I'll just outbid everyone," I tell her. "You know I have the money."

Checkmate, Gran.

"I won't accept your offer."

Not checkmate. Damn it. The wheels start turning in my head. I know better than to argue with her. She's too stubborn. I can form a company and buy it in a trust…

"Don't even think about trying something shady, like buying it as an LLC. I'm going to require video interviews with all parties making an offer."

I stare at her. "You're serious," I say flatly.

"I'm serious."

"You would take away what you promised me?"

"I always said when you're married and have a family."

"You did not."

"Didn't I? Well, I thought it."

"Gran," I say with a frustrated groan.

She sips her martini again and opens her menu. "I think I'm going to order the crab salad."

This is not cool. I want that house. I've spent nearly a decade envisioning myself living there after I leave hockey for good. I want to plunge into an icy cold lake and shake off the joint inflammation I have from playing goalie for twenty years. I want to see a bald eagle in the trees, damn it. I want a fucking fire pit filled with wood I chop myself.

"I have a girlfriend," I tell her, impulsively.

Maybe if she thinks I'm dating someone, I can still get the house.

"Oh? That's lovely. What's her name?"

"Elise."

Now why the actual fuck did I say that?

Maybe because she's the only woman in my head and has been for months.

Gran seems interested. "What does she do?"

"She works in a bakery," I say, triumphantly, because I know this answer. If Gran digs any deeper, I'm going to run out of details. I can't exactly tell her the extent of my knowledge about Elise is her job and the fact that she makes the sexiest little sound when she comes. "Called Books and Buns."

"That's a cute name. Isn't that Luna McNeill's bakery?"

"Yes. That's how I met Elise. I was with Crew and Luna and Elise were out having a drink."

That much is true.

"I've always wanted to go there. You should take me to pick up some desserts."

Uh... "Sure. Any time."

She smiles at me. "Is it serious?"

"The bakery?"

She gives a sound of impatience. "Your relationship with Elise."

Oh, God. I'm lying to my grandmother. But I'm in too deep already. "Yes. Yes. So serious. Like, really serious." I'm using my hands to talk, which is a tell that I'm lying. I drop them onto my lap and swallow hard. I'm already in it, now I have to win it.

That house is *mine*.

"I'd love to meet her. If you're thinking about marrying her."

Who the fuck mentioned marriage?

I'm sweating in my flannel shirt. "I'm sure she would love to meet you."

If she knew my grandmother existed.

"Wonderful. After I get back from Florida. I'll be back at the end of the month."

"Sure." And after I beg Elise to play along and pretend she's my girlfriend.

"So she likes the lakes region? She's happy to move up north with you?"

I highly doubt it. Elise seems like a nightlife and grabbing an Uber kind of girl.

I also can't tell if my grandmother actually believes me or not, but she seems willing to play along.

So I nod. "Absolutely."

"Then this is wonderful, Blakey!" She raises her glass in a toast. "I'm so happy for you. We really are celebrating!"

Celebrating the death of my retirement dreams unless I can convince one very self-assured woman, who's probably pissed at me right now, that she has any reason whatsoever to help me.

Charm isn't my strong suit.

I lift my glass up and clink Gran's.

"Ninety days," she adds, casually. "I want to meet her and see you're in love within ninety days or the house goes on the market."

I drink the lemon drop martini all in one giant swallow.

CHAPTER 6
Elise

> We need to talk.

> Who is this?

> Blake

HE CAN'T BE SERIOUS. Is he actually serious? He left me standing by the elevator with no panties and no explanation as to what happened between us and then he sends me a text with the exact same words he spoke to me when he pulled me on the elevator? Maybe he is trying to be funny, and he just has a dry sense of humor. He obviously got my number from someone so he put effort into reaching me, which is even stranger given he left me standing outside the elevator after basically destroying me with his fingers.

He could have asked for my number then.

I don't respond.

Because, one, I'm busy creating social media posts for my online pinup dress business I'm trying to expand, and when I have more than one thing going on, I get flustered and lose focus.

Two, what the hell am I supposed to say to that?

And three, I already have one very cute firefighter texting me *and* my former boss's boss popping up out of the blue.

Both of them seem very clear in their interest, unlike a certain grumpy goalie.

Who was an amazingly fantastic kisser.

With very large hands and talented fingers.

I haven't had fireman or billionaire fingers making me happy…yet…so Blake does have a couple points up on Aidan and Simon, I'll admit.

Damn it. I don't want to think about Blake when it's much more fun to think about Aidan, who has been texting me and chatting in a very normal getting-to-know-you kind of way.

Simon is a little scary to think about, but in a good way. I could really fall for him, given half a chance. Hell, I already have. I had months and months of random encounters with him where I saw he was charming and funny and very flirty. Running into him was a shock that I'm still feeling butterflies over.

My phone dings again.

> Can we? Talk?

I huff in impatience.

> I don't know, Blake, can we?

I slap my phone down on my nightstand and survey my next outfit option I've flung across my bed. It's a hunter green tulip skirt that I'm pairing with a mustard halter top and a mustard cardigan that has tiny white and brown foxes on it. I get dressed quickly, belting it with a chunky black and gold waist-cincher-style belt. I study myself in the mirror, fixing my cleavage and smoothing out my hair. I'm skipping the shapewear because this halter wouldn't work with a full body-suit and Blake left the elevator with my bottoms in his suit pocket. He's probably tossed them out, which is annoying because they cost sixty bucks and I'm constantly on a tight budget.

Designing my classic pinup clothing and making it myself is time consuming. It sells really well at my vendor table at competitive shows, but I'm still working to gain traction on social media. It takes time to gain a devoted following, but I'm optimistic about the growth. As it is, I'm always pressed for time because of my shifts at the bakery and sewing everything myself. My pieces are one and done. Nothing mass produced. Some are custom ordered to size. But generally, I do plus size and model it myself.

Last month, I did a special line of petite pinups and I forced Luna to model them for me. She was initially reluctant, but then her boyfriends all got so hot for the idea, it was an easier sell than I expected. After this current rotation goes up, I've promised Lydia, who is a senior in high school and also works at the bakery, that I'll do a Retro Teen line with shorter skirts.

My bedroom looks like Black Friday at Walmart. There are clothes and shoes thrown everywhere and the bed isn't made. I have a sweet tea problem and there are half-filled tumblers on both nightstands and my dressers. Last night's dinner—pizza in bed while watching Netflix and texting with Aidan—is on the floor. My vanity is strewn with brushes and lashes and balled up tissues. I've always been like this, and it doesn't bother me. If anything, there is something comforting to me about knowing where all my stuff is. If everything is neatly tucked away in drawers, I forget I have it and don't use it.

Every few days, I do a garbage sweep and dust and vacuum, so nothing is dirty. It's just colorful chaos. But I know it bothers other people. That's been drummed into me my whole life.

My father tried to punish me into tidiness as a child but it didn't work and he still takes it as some kind of personal failure. I missed many a Friday family movie night because I couldn't join in until my room was clean. I never understood what was the big deal, and we had lots of fights about it. He and my mother used to fight about it too, because my mother wanted me to go on ADHD medication and my father didn't. She would argue how could he expect me to focus if he wouldn't allow me the prescription that could help? She wasn't wrong and to this day, he and I don't have the greatest relationship. They're also divorced.

My mom is awesome and supportive of me wanting to pursue a creative career.

I touch up my lipstick and head downstairs in my heels. Navigating stairs in platforms is good practice for appearing glamorous and confident both in dealing with clients and participating in pinup competitions. I started doing them just as a confidence boost and to meet other women who share my love of vintage clothing, then I realized they spark my creativity. Trying to create fashion to match a contest's theme like "spring" is a fun challenge. For that particular contest, I did spring cleaning, with a yellow swing skirt, a blouse and floral apron, and yellow rubber gloves. I pinned my hair up with a dusting rag and wore pearls. It was meant to be a take on the so-called ideal of the fifties housewife and I took first place.

Lydia jumps up when I enter Books and Buns, ready to take over my phone. I hand it to her. Shooting vintage style clothing in the bakery is a match made in pink heaven normally, but the mustard sweater is going to clash, so I tell her, "Let's go to the bookshelves." I've grabbed a pair of fashion cat eye glasses.

"Oooh, sexy librarian," she says. "I love it. This is what I want to look like next year in college."

Lydia is literally the physical opposite of me in every way. She's thin, has straight hair, no hips or boobs, and olive skin. But pinup is a state of mind. It's about embracing the feminine and she loves to wear dresses, so I give her an encouraging smile. "You're going to kill it at Ohio State."

"I'm actually terrified," she says cheerfully, opening my camera on my phone. "You have a text, by the way."

"From Aidan?" I ask as I test a few leans and poses in front of the bookshelves.

Aidan's texts have been cute facts about himself and random

questions for me, like do I like chocolate chip versus peanut butter cookies and am I a beer or wine girl? I now know he was raised by a single mom and hates sushi, among other things.

"No. Blake."

I groan. Of course it's Blake. He's not a man you get rid of by ignoring.

She swipes the text away.

"What did it say?" I ask, in spite of myself.

"I didn't read it. That would be rude."

"But you saw his name. You must have seen the message, too."

"Partially." Lydia blinks at me. "Are you ready?"

She's going to fucking make me ask outright or grab the phone from her. "What did it partially say?" I ask, striving for nonchalance.

I don't even know why I care. He clearly only kissed me—among other things—in some effort to prove he was better than Justin Travers. He just wanted to win, because competitiveness is in his blood. Hell, it was probably some sort of weird superstition. Part of a new year ritual. He certainly seems to have all kinds of quirks on the ice from tapping his stick three times before the puck drops to lifting up his shirt and adjusting his pads every time a puck gets past him. Not that I've studied him or anything. He's just obviously very set in his ways.

"It said, "Just talk. I won't touch you," she says, wrinkling her nose.

"Oh goodie, that sounds so enticing. Just text him back and tell him to come to the bakery tomorrow morning. I'm not doing this stupid texting back and forth thing."

"You want me to text him back for you?" Lydia looks horrified.

"Yes, as me. Just what I said. Come to the bakery tomorrow morning. Nothing else."

"Okay." Her fingers fly over my phone. "Do I say you're not doing the stupid texting thing?"

"No, just to come to the bakery."

"I feel like I'm cheating on Brady," she grumbles. "This is weird."

Luna, who was removing pastries from the case for the night since it's closing, instantly yells out, *"You're cheating on Brady?"*

Lydia's face goes pale. "No! Of course not!"

As much as Luna likes Lydia, Brady is her boyfriend's kid. Fortunately, I can stop her head from exploding. "I told her to text Blake back as me and she's feeling weird about it. No one is cheating, no one wants to cheat. Calm down."

"Oh." Luna winces. "Sorry, Lydia." Then she seems to register what I said. "Wait, Blake Wilder is texting you? That's exciting."

"Is it?"

I told Luna about our great elevator escape and what happened in the dark prior to the fire department's arrival, and she was almost as disappointed as I was that he didn't go back up to the party with me.

"Isn't it?" she asks, eyebrows raising.

I give a noncommittal shrug and direct Lydia to start taking pictures. I run through a series of poses while she grabs the shots.

"How do those look?"

Lydia shows me my phone. As I'm swiping through the images, Luna appears behind us and checks them out.

"Elise, you are seriously so photogenic, oh my God. You look amazing."

"Thank you." They're not bad. I'm actually pretty pleased with the way the skirt is falling and the lighting.

A text pops up from Blake.

> I'll be there at 7.

"Seven?" I exclaim. "What is he, my grandfather? Who the hell is up at seven when they work at night?"

"The Racketeers don't play tomorrow," Luna tells me. "They have practice at noon. It doesn't matter, anyway. You'll be working by seven."

She's right, but I'm determined to be annoyed with Blake for any and every possible reason I can be. I swipe the text away. "Let me go change."

It takes me ten minutes to change into a red wiggle dress that hugs every ample curve I have. I strap on black Mary Jane style platforms and attach a black fascinator to my curls. It's tempting to put on a statement necklace, but I don't want to distract from the dress, which can make any woman in existence feel like a certified bombshell.

I head back downstairs.

CHAPTER 7
Simon

THE FACT that the sweet woman who I want to absolutely eat up works in a bakery is perfect. I step through the door of Books and Buns, and am met with the sound of a tinkling bell overhead and the mouthwatering aroma of butter, vanilla, cinnamon, and chocolate, and I'm instantly delighted.

There are a couple of women sitting at a small table near the window, and an older gentleman with his newspaper, a coffee cup and an empty plate at a high table closer to the counter, but it is relatively quiet. I'd chosen to come after noon, assuming the bakery was busier in the morning.

Finding out where Elise works was easy. Nathan had returned to his box at the Racketeers arena after Elise had departed and had taken one look at my grin and asked if I was going to see her again. When I said, 'yes, as soon as you tell me where to find her', he'd given me the name and address of the bakery. I chalk it up to him being madly in love and now a dad. I'm not sure the old Nathan would have given the information up as easily, but the new Nathan is head over heels and understands the need I'm feeling. I *have to* see her.

I'd given Elise a couple of days and yes, I'd hoped that

perhaps she would reach out to me, but I wasn't surprised that she hadn't. Not only had she been flustered the other night, but she clearly has a stubborn streak. Whatever it is that makes her think that nothing can happen between us is rooted deep.

I look forward to convincing her she's wrong.

Starting today.

The tiny woman behind the counter has blonde hair that's almost white with pink streaks through it, is wearing a bright pink apron, and greets me with a friendly smile.

"Welcome! Can I help you?"

"You must be Luna," I say, giving her the smile I use when seeing my grandmother, asking my assistant to do a particularly annoying task for me, or buying from the lovely ladies who run the fresh produce market down the street from my building. It's my charming-but-I'm-not-flirting smile.

"I am. Have we met?" Luna asks.

"No. I'm Nathan Armstrong's cousin. He told me all about your bakery and that you and Danielle used to be in business together."

Her eyes widen. "You're Simon?"

Ah, ha. Someone has mentioned my name. I hope it wasn't Danielle. Or that it wasn't only Danielle, anyway.

I tuck my hands into my pants pockets and work on acting nonchalant. "That's right. It's nice to meet you."

"Nice to meet you, too." Her smile changes from friendly to sly. "Are you here to try my macarons?"

"Of course. And eclairs." Everything in the bakery case looks amazing.

She laughs lightly, the sound making me smile. "I don't think we should start our friendship off with a lie Simon."

"Are we going to be friends?" I ask.

"As long as you treat Elise well, we will be," she says. "I care about that girl and she deserves a great guy."

Excellent. Elise has mentioned me. By name.

"That is completely my intention. Is she here?" I ask, deciding there's no reason to tease or joke about why I'm here.

"Actually, she's—"

"*Simon?*"

I turn to find Elise standing just inside the wide, arched doorway that separates the bakery from the attached bookshop. She's wearing a curve-hugging red dress that makes my mouth go dry. Her hair is gathered to one side, and she has a black hat with netting falling partially over her right eye. She's also wearing chunky black heels and sheer black stockings.

I feel my entire body straining toward her, but I make myself stay in place and give her my charming-I'm-definitely-flirting-now smile.

"Hello, Elise."

"Oh my God, what are you doing here?"

"You really don't know?" I ask her.

She presses her lips together.

"I'm here to see you. To charm your pants off." I let my gaze track over her slowly. "Though I'm very pleased to see you're not wearing any." Now I walk toward her. "Fuck me, Elise, you're stunning."

She wets her lips but pulls herself straighter and says, "So you have graduated to stalking now?"

My smile widens. "Yes. I had to see you."

She crosses her arms over her midsection. "I don't think that's a good idea."

"I know that's what you *think*. But I'm more interested in how you *feel*." I stop in front of her. "You've been thinking about me."

"I see your ego is intact."

"You told Luna about me." I grin. "But did you only tell her about the other night at the hockey game, or did you tell her about making out with me in my office before thoroughly ghosting me?"

"I—"

"Both," Luna fills in as I lift a hand and run my thumb over Elise's silky cheek.

Elise shoots her a look. "Okay, enough of you two talking." Elise takes my hand and pulls me toward the steps. "You don't believe that I'm too much of a mess? Come on. I'll show you."

I wrap my hand around hers, loving the feel of her delicate bones and soft, warm skin. I'll follow her anywhere. I glance back at Luna. She's just smiling as she watches us go.

"Thought she's into the firefighter," the man at the tall table says.

"She is," Luna says brightly. "Isn't it great?"

Firefighter? Who is the—

But any questions fly out of my mind when I step off the top step into the little hallway on the second floor and follow Elise through the door and into what is clearly her apartment.

"You work here and live here?" I ask.

She drops my hand and stops in the middle of the main room. She faces me and crosses her arms. "Yep."

"That's convenient. Did you move here after you quit working for me?"

"Yes."

"That explains why I couldn't find you."

She tips her head to the side, studying me. "You really tried to find me?"

"Of course."

She sighs. "You make it sound like that should be so obvious. But we didn't have a relationship, Simon. You never declared any feelings for me. I kissed you *one* time."

"It was a hell of a kiss," I tell her. "There was unfinished business."

She gives a little laugh, but shakes her head in disbelief. She reaches up and pulls the hat from her head, tossing it onto the coffee table. "Simon, you're a rich, good looking, charming, intelligent, amazing guy. You could have anyone. There is no way that one kiss with me was that life altering." She bends and unstraps her shoes, kicking them off to the side as she asks, "What is really going on? Is it that you just want something you think you can't have? Or you just want to have a fling while you're here in Chicago?"

I step toward her, my toe kicking a box that rattles, but I don't even look down. "It's chemistry, love. I'm not trying to explain it. I don't need to. It's one of life's fun mysteries. I just want to enjoy it. I'll admit after you left, I was worried, and curious, about what caused your quick exit. But yes, I was intrigued by you. I wanted you. The chance to get to know you better, to finally have you if I can, won't leave me alone now that I've found you again."

She narrows her eyes. "I think maybe you're a little crazy."

"I've been called worse."

She spreads her arms and looks around the room. "Okay, well, this is it. This is the real me. If you're not crazy now, I'll drive you there soon enough."

I look around her apartment. Before this, she was the only thing in the room that mattered. Now I take in details.

It's cluttered. Her coffee table is piled high with catalogs and papers, a plastic container of bright beads, another with multi-colored gemstones. There are dresses spread out on nearly every piece of furniture, and there are shoes lying all over the floor. Scarves and necklaces dangle from lamps. More scarves and belts and gloves are draped over the back of chairs. There's nowhere to sit on her couch save one empty cushion. The others have pillows piled high with dresses, stockings, and shawls draped over them.

Behind the sofa, the room opens into what would typically be a dining area. There is a table there, but it holds three different sewing machines, various tools, including scissors, tape measures, and the like.

There are more reams of fabric stacked at the end. Bolts of fabric are propped in one corner and more dresses on hangers are suspended from the chandelier over the table. Every single chair has what looks to be catalogs or more fabric on them.

The walls are covered with sketches and photos, pinned and taped up.

To the left is an island that separates the dining area from the kitchen. It, too, is covered with books, catalogs, material, shoes, bags, and other accessories.

I look down and see that the box I kicked is full of what looks to be jewelry. Pieces of varying sizes and colors fill the plastic tub.

Finally, my eyes meet Elise's again. "What are you trying to tell me?"

"My apartment always looks like this."

"What is all of this?"

"I design dresses. I make them. I also model them. I compete in pinup model contests."

I had no idea. That's so interesting. So unique. "That's amazing."

"You think so?"

"Of course. Love, you're a knockout and obviously passionate and talented. Show me your designs."

"What?" She laughs. "No."

"Yes. Elise, I insist."

"Well, you can't insist. You're not my boss anymore."

I give her a grin. "Hmm... you might like my bossy side."

I see her eyes widen. "Oh?"

I chuckle. "You have no idea how many times I thought about summoning you to my office, ordering you to bend over my desk, and fucking you until you screamed my name so loud the entire upper floor could hear you."

Her breath catches. "Geez, Simon." She puts her hand on her chest. "You can't just be sweet and charming one minute and then dirty and hot the next without any warning."

I grin at her. "Oh, but I can. You'll have to get used to it, I guess."

She bites her lower lip, then says, "We'll see if you stick around."

I look around her apartment. "Does all of this bother you? Do you want me to hire you a cleaning service or get you an assistant?"

She looks surprised for a moment. Then she shakes her head. "No. I'm fine. It bothers other people."

"What other people?"

She laughs. "Everyone, Simon. Everyone. My parents. My ex-boyfriend. Luna, though she won't say it. Definitely you."

I step toward her again. "This is at least the third time you've mentioned me. Where is that coming from?"

"I worked for you. I saw your desk, your calendar, your office. Sonia made sure that I knew we had to keep everything neat and organized. You like things a certain way. Even your coffee order."

I relax. Now I understand. I step close to her again. "Doesn't everyone have a particular coffee order?"

She nods. "Sure. But Sonia made it sound as if it was the end of the world if we messed it up."

I lift my hand and brush the back of my knuckles over her cheek again. I cannot wait till I can fully touch this woman. She's soft and warm on the inside and out.

"Everything you said, about the way that Sonia approached my daily schedule and my office and my desk, came from Sonia."

Elise frowns. "What do you mean?"

"I am...untidy, Elise," I confess. "I am unorganized. I hate calendars. I hate having my schedule dictated down to the minute. My desk was a disaster when Sonia came to work for me. I drove her nuts. It helped her do her job as my assistant to keep my desk neat and tidy, my calendar perfectly organized, and my office meticulously clean. She was a minimalist. And hiring her was the best idea I ever had. Because she did help me function better. Because I'm not like that at all."

Elise seems to take a moment to process that.

"I want you, Elise. Messy, late, unorganized. I don't care."

"You don't even know me," she protests, though her voice is soft.

"You always bought an extra coffee for one of the other assistants, Marci," I say, ready to put my heart right in her hands. "She was a single mom and was always rushed in the morning and didn't have time to get her own. You always had an extra sweater at work because one of the girls, Holly, was always cold and never brought her own. You wore different earrings every single day for a month before starting to repeat them." I look down at the box at my feet. I realize what I'm *really* looking at. "You collect jewelry?"

She nods, looking like she's so stunned she doesn't remember to argue with me or push back. "I love to shop in vintage shops. I also make some of it."

I smile. "You had three different perfumes. One that smelled like lilacs, one that smelled like lemons and vanilla, and a spicy one that was musky, maybe amber or something?"

She nods again, slowly, as if she can't believe what I'm saying.

"I would call you into my office sometimes for no real reason, just because I wanted to have the scent of you linger for a little while."

"Simon," she says softly.

"I like you, Elise. From all the little things I noticed, to the big things like how funny and sarcastic you are. I think you're special and I want to get to know you better. Where's the harm in that?"

She takes a deep breath, then says, "I have ADHD. I spent my life in a house with two parents who I drove crazy. My mom was a lot more loving and understanding about it, but my father was a perfectionist, and he hated how messy and scatter-brained I was. It took a while to get a diagnosis, but even when we did, he didn't believe in medication for it. He said I just needed to pay more attention and try harder. So I've had to cope and adapt as best I can. I'm medicated now, which helps a lot, but there are just things that are a part of who I am."

I frown. The ADHD makes sense. I can't imagine a parent understanding something like that about their child, but refusing to pursue every avenue for help. But if that's what she grew up with and dealt with, then her inability to believe other people can want to be close to her adds up.

She swallows hard and continues, "I will be late for things. I will forget dates and anniversaries. I will forget to text back. And none of that means that I don't care, I just forget. And then feel terrible and beat myself up. I've lost a lot of friendships. I've lost a couple of serious boyfriends. I don't even have a great relationship with my parents honestly. All because of that. People don't like coming over. I don't like having people over. My place is a mess, but it makes me happy. I know where things are. I not only need to have all my stuff out, I like having my stuff around me. And I can't do jobs like being your assistant. I quit because I was terrible at it and I didn't want you to find out because I didn't want you to have any negative thoughts about me. I stayed longer than I should have because I liked being around you. I was afraid of getting in too deep."

I give her a few seconds to be sure she's finished. Then I say, "Thank you for telling me all of that."

"I used to try to hide it, but that never worked in the end. I can't compensate for long enough to really make relationships work, so I decided to be upfront with people from the start."

She's telling this to turn me off. To convince me we can't work before we've even started. But she's also showing me a very vulnerable side. She's opening up and letting me in and it makes me want to take care of her and prove that everyone who didn't stick around, who made her feel like there was something wrong with her, and that she messed everything up, was not worthy of her.

"I hope this means that you are going to give me a chance. Because we absolutely were, and are, going to get in too deep," I tell her, my voice husky.

She wets her lips, then takes a tiny step closer to me. "I'm sorry in advance for missing your birthday."

I huff out a small laugh. "Do you really think that a guy like me, with an ego like mine, won't remind you a million times?"

I see her shoulders relax, and she smiles, which makes the tightness in my chest loosen slightly.

"The thing is, I don't think you have that big of an ego after all."

"Is that a good thing or a bad thing?"

"It must be a good thing," she says, her voice softer now. "Because I like you. I really like you, Simon."

Thank God. "Let me take you out."

She arches a brow. "Out?"

"Yes. Out. On a date. A fancy dinner. Dancing. A show. Turks and Caicos. Wherever you want to go."

Her laugh is louder and freer now. "Dinner or Turks and Caicos? That's quite a spectrum."

I shrug. "Dinner *in* Turks and Caicos." I cup her cheek. "Let me spoil you. Let me show you how much I want you. Just the way you are."

She hesitates, then takes the final step that presses our bodies against one another. She slides her hand up my chest to the back of my neck. "I have a very good idea about how you can show me how much you want me."

My body heats and my heart starts pumping but I say, "This doesn't have to be about sex tonight. I want more than that."

"I believe you. I want more than that too," she tells me.

Her fingers continue up into my hair and I shiver at how good it feels to feel her nails drag over my scalp.

"But I really want this," she says. "I've wanted this for a long time. I've had so many daydreams about you."

I groan softly and my hands move down her back to her waist. "Please tell me they involve my desk and you in some of those fuck-me heels you used to wear to the office."

"Please tell me all about *your* daydreams," she says huskily.

I slide my hands to her ass and squeeze. "You have no idea how fucking dirty we made my very neat and tidy desk."

She breathes out as if in relief. "Oh God. You have no idea how much I wanted to mess up your desk."

"We are very much on the same page. We can always do Turks and Caicos later."

She laughs. "I need to put on heels if we're going to do this right."

"Yes, you do." I look around and spot a pair of cherry red heels near the armchair. I point. "Those."

CHAPTER 8
Simon

SHE GRINS and slips out of my arms to retrieve the shoes.

She balances on one foot as she slips the first shoe on and I say, "See? There are all kinds of perks to not putting your shoes away. They'll always be available when I need to bend you over the couch."

She sucks in a little breath, then gives a little moan. "Thank God you're a dirty talker."

I move in behind her as she puts on the other shoe, skimming my palms down her sides to her hips. I bring her back against me when her foot is back on the ground.

I press my already aching cock against her ass. "You like dirty talk?"

"So much. And I'll tell you a secret—most women do. But it has to be good."

"I don't want to talk about other women. I just want to know what *you* like. What you love even." I press my mouth to the bare skin beneath one ear.

She shivers in my arms. "I like your hands and mouth on me very much."

"That's a very good thing. They're both going to be all over you, repeatedly."

"Also, I think I'm going to like being fucked in my heels. But that's never happened before, so I'm not sure."

"Fuck yes," I growl against her neck. "Love, the more firsts you give me, the happier I'm going to be." I run my hands from her hips, down her ass and down her thighs. God, this woman's curves make me crazy. "Make me the happiest man in Chicago and tell me that you don't have to be anywhere until late tomorrow morning."

She leans back against me and says, "Early morning. I have to open the bakery."

"But I can have you all night?"

She nods. "Yes."

That's all I need to hear.

I spin her and pull her in close. I wrap her hair around my hand and tip her head back. The heels put her at the perfect height that I barely have to bend to seal my mouth over hers. She makes a sweet little moaning noise as our mouths connect. I lick over her bottom lip, demanding entrance. I need to fully taste her. Now.

Sweetly, obediently, she parts her lips, her tongue meeting mine as I take her mouth fully. We kiss, just drinking each other in for long, hot moments. I've thought about our first kiss so often that it feels surreal to be kissing her now. But even as I realize this is truly only our third kiss and should be more or less an introduction and discovery between us, it feels like I've been kissing this woman forever. And I know that I might never want to stop.

I don't feel that it's egotistical to say that I've had a lot of women in my life. Men too. I love meeting people, love flirtation and romance, and I fucking love sex. I've definitely enjoyed many relationships over the past two decades since I first lost my virginity.

But it's not hyperbole to say that Elise is a stand out.

For one, I've never had to wait this long to have someone I wanted. But it is not just wanting what I can't have, or the thrill of the chase. It's truly that I've had time to reflect upon how much I want her. And in all the months since I met her, I have been unable to come up with a single reason to not give pursuing her my all if we ever crossed paths again.

Yes, it's mostly instinct, chemistry, a gut feeling, but none of that has ever steered me wrong in business or in life. I'm certainly not going to ignore it now.

I turn her and walk her back toward the couch. There are so many things I want to do with and to this woman. But we might as well start with the primary fantasy for both of us.

I lift my head when her ass hits the back of the couch. "You know if you had ever given me the green light when you worked for me, I would've taken you the first time at my desk."

She takes a deep breath. "It would've happened sometime when we were alone in the office. Probably late. I would have come into your office to see if you needed anything before I left for the night and you would have said that what you needed was me. And I wouldn't have been able to say no."

I run my thumb over her lower lip. It's wet and pink from my mouth. "I would've made you say yes. Clearly and loudly. You would've known exactly what I wanted and what you were agreeing to."

She nods.

"But we wouldn't have been able to wait to get to one of our apartments or a hotel. And the number of times that I wanted to squeeze your ass, or smack it, when you were in my office, leaning over to give me my coffee or a file, that's how I would've taken you. Leaning over my desk, the skirt of one of these pinup dresses hiked up around your waist, your panties around your ankles, tits spilling out of the top of the dress, your hands gripping the edge of that desk, where I would have been taking calls and meetings and signing papers, but thinking of how it felt to sink into your sweet pussy over and over."

Her cheeks are pink and she's breathing hard now. Her gorgeous breasts are heaving against the front of her dress. This one is so much like the ones she wore to the office, that I am aching with the need to peel it off of her.

"That's exactly what I always pictured," she finally says. "You have no idea how many times I used my vibrator picturing that very thing."

I groan. "Bloody hell, love, you might kill me tonight."

She laughs. "I hope not. I'm just getting used to the idea of having you."

If she hadn't stolen my heart before, that response comes damn close. I know she still thinks that this isn't going to work, that somehow she's going to turn me off or frustrate me to the point that I walk away. It sounds like that's happened to her repeatedly in the past. That actually makes my gut clench with the need to not only prove that wrong, but yell at and possibly punch every person who's made her feel that way in the past.

But then her fingers are at the first button on my shirt and she starts unbuttoning it and all my thoughts scatter.

"Next time you come over, wear a suit and tie, okay?" she asks. "I mean, you look amazing right now, but the daydream did include your suits."

I suddenly can think of nothing else, but bringing this woman intense pleasure and making her understand that she has me wrapped around her little finger. "I can have someone bring a suit to me in the next twenty minutes."

She laughs and keeps unbuttoning. "My God, you don't even realize how ridiculous that sounds?"

"My God," I mimic back to her. "You don't even realize what I'm willing to do to make you happy."

Her gaze bounces from my chest up to my eyes. She just stares at me for a moment. Then she says, "Never mind. I don't need a jacket or tie. I'm so fucking turned on right now I can barely breathe."

"Excellent," I tell her. My hands go to her waist, and I begin gathering the fabric of her dress up. "You don't mind if I don't take this fully off do you?"

"We can't fully undress," she says, finishing with the buttons and running her hands over my bare skin, from the waistband of my pants up to my chest.

Having her hands finally on me makes me hot and hard all over. I shudder with the lust that's coursing through me.

"We're in your office," she says. "Even if it's after hours, it would be too risky to undress entirely."

"Good point, Miss Starling," I say, calling her by her last name as I did when she worked for me.

The only time I used her first name was the night that we did finally kiss for the first time. That was at my desk, though. And even just kissing her ruined my concentration at my desk for days afterward. Every time I sat there on a call, or in a meeting with someone across the expanse of mahogany, I thought of her and could conjure her taste.

She starts unbuckling my belt as I get the material gathered at her waist. I look down and freeze.

I'd known she was wearing the sheer black stockings. But I had no idea they would be thigh high with lace tops.

"Holy hell," I grit out.

She just watches me taking in every inch of her, her bottom lip caught between her teeth.

"These need to go," I keep my eyes on hers as I hook my thumbs in the tops of the silk and lace black panties. I slide them over her hips and then strip them down her thighs, letting them fall to her ankles.

She kicks them to the side.

I can see the pulse pounding at the base of her throat and I lean in and press a kiss there.

I don't look down yet at what I've uncovered. I won't be able to help myself once I do. I reach behind and pull down the zipper of her dress. Then peel down the front, freeing her gorgeous breasts. They are cupped in a matching black bra, which I also unhook. I let it drop to the floor and take in the sight of her full breasts with the dusky pink nipples spilling out over the bodice of the dress.

"You are the most gorgeous thing I have ever seen," I tell her, my voice rough with lust and emotion.

This woman is a treasure. Every inch of her is gorgeous and unique and I feel so lucky to be here with her in this moment.

"Touch me. Please," she says, taking one of my hands and lifting it to her breast.

I gladly mold my hand around her, squeezing, kneading, then plucking at her nipple.

I lean in to kiss her, absorbing her moans and gasps.

I play with her breasts until I cannot take it anymore and I have to take a nipple in my mouth. I lick and suck until she's pressing against me, her fingers tangled in my hair, and my name on her lips.

I lean back and look at her gorgeous face, her cheeks pink, her eyes wide and dreamy looking. "Are you the one needing some assistance right now, Miss Starling?" I ask, running my hand down her belly, over her hip and between her thighs. I barely skim over her mound and she cries out.

"Yes, please Simon."

"What do you need?" I ask, staring into her eyes.

"Fuck me. Simon, please. Bend me over and just fuck me."

Need stabs me in the gut. My cock is hard and begging to be freed. "Do you want my fingers?" I slide them through her wetness, my middle finger rubbing over her clit. Then I slide two fingers into her slick heat. My cock pulses at the sweet tightness I discover. "Do you want me to make you come like this, love?"

She gasps and grinds against my hand, but shakes her head. "No. More."

I reach up with my other hand, grasping the back of her neck. I pump my fingers deep, circling her clit with my thumb. "Tell me what you want, Miss Starling. You came to my office. Told me you were here to help me in whatever capacity I might need. Now you're begging *me* for help."

She nods quickly. "Yes. I'm sorry, sir. But I need your cock."

A wave of lust hits me hard. "Christ Elise," I mutter.

She gives me a cheeky grin and for that, I lean in and kiss her hard. Then I lift my head and spin her to face the back of the couch. "Brilliant girl, you've come up with a way we can help each other. Let me fill up this sweet cunt with my cock."

She shivers. "Yes, sir."

She bends over the back of the couch and for a second, I simply stand and marvel at the magnificent sight. Her heavy breasts hang free from the top of her dress, and I reach around and cup them, plucking at the nipples and making her moan. Then I run my hand over the curve of her ass. I squeeze both globes, relishing the softness and how I'm going to be able to grip her tightly as I pound into her.

"I've been thinking about this nonstop since the hockey game," I tell her, squeezing and kneading the flesh. "I hope you can actually take what I want to give you."

She looks back at me over her shoulder, her expression open and happy. "I can take whatever you want to give me, Mr. Armstrong."

I rip open the front of my pants, shoving my boxers down, and taking my cock in hand, giving it three long angry strokes. Her gaze zeros in on my cock and she licks her lips.

"Oh, I can't wait to feel those perfect red lips around my cock. But first I need your pussy."

She nods quickly. "Yes, please."

I grab my wallet and fish out a condom before shoving my pants to the floor. I roll it on, then grip her hips.

"Do you have any idea how fucking gorgeous you are right now?"

"I hope gorgeous enough that all you can think about is fucking me hard and deep."

She's fucking perfect. "It will be my pleasure."

Without another word, I line my cock up and thrust. I don't take it easy. I don't have the impression that Elise needs it tender and slow. And if the way she arches and pushes back into me and her loud, "Yes!" is any indication, I am completely right.

I set up a quick, hard pace, and she's with me every step.

She gasps and moans, giving me lots of "oh God!", and "Mr. Armstrong!", and of course, my favorite, "Simon!"

She's everything I thought she would be and more. She's hot and soft and tight and enthusiastic. And I know even before I come that I will never get tired of fucking this woman. I want her in every position, every situation I can dream up. Anything and everything that will bring this woman pleasure—whether it is a chai latte or a trip around the world or mind-blowing orgasms—I want to give it all to her.

Soon my orgasm is barreling straight at me.

"Elise, I need you to come, love," I say through gritted teeth.

"I'm so close. I'm so close, Simon," she pants.

I reach around and find her clit, rubbing over it, then pinching. "Come on me, sweetheart."

She shatters, her pussy gripping me as she cries out my name.

I let go. I pound into her until my balls draw up, and I feel everything in me explode into her.

"Elise! Fuck!"

I pump one last time, then slump forward over her back, kissing her shoulder, then pulling out, I tug her to stand, then turn her so that I can enfold her in my arms.

She wraps her arms around my neck, her forehead against my chest, as we both breathe hard, trying to catch our breath.

Finally, I pull back and look into her face.

She gives me a happy, slightly goofy smile.

I drop a kiss on her forehead, then pull the top of her dress up and the bottom of her dress down.

"Bathroom?" I ask.

She points and I head in that direction to deal with the condom.

When I return, she is leaning on the back of the couch, still breathing a little hard.

She gives me another smile. "That was fun, Mr. Armstrong."

"As expected." I pull her up and give her a long, sweet kiss. Then I lift my head. "So? Dinner in Chicago or Turks and Caicos?"

CHAPTER 9
Elise

WE STAY in Chicago for dinner.

And for the next four rounds of sex.

Simon is... a god.

His mouth, his hands, his cock.

Whether he's on top, behind me, or under me, the orgasms are guaranteed and the best I've ever had.

I knew he would be. And this is definitely part of the reason I didn't want to sleep with him before. Simon is the kind of guy you don't get over. The kind of guy you think about thirty years later with affection and an ache in your chest for what could've been, and probably some tingles, even three decades later, remembering the things he did to you.

I didn't want that.

I still don't, but clearly resistance is futile.

He's the first guy I've let into this apartment.

He's actually only the third *person* to be in this apartment. Luna and Dani have been here. I mean, it's above Luna's bakery and she's my landlord. She owns the building and used to live in this apartment before she moved in with her boyfriends. I couldn't really keep her out. But she visited as a friend.

It's been a long time since I even let a girlfriend close. I've just learned the hard way over the years that people find my messiness a turn off. Or strange. Or gross.

I mean I get it. There's I-didn't-have-a-chance-to-pick-up-before-you-got-here and then there's...what I've got. But I've accepted this. Does it mean I keep people from getting close? Yes. But I spent my childhood and teenage years trying to keep my parents happy and beating myself up about the messy condition of my bedroom, my locker at school, my inability to keep track of assignments, the fact that I was late to almost everything. I'm done with that. The ADHD is not my fault. This is just who I am. And with the medication and some coping mechanisms I've learned from therapy and online, I manage to adult adequately ninety percent of the time.

Okay, maybe eighty percent of the time.

But I also know that I have to know someone really well and trust them implicitly before they get inside my inner sanctum.

Or I have to be trying to push them away like I was with Simon.

But he's still here. Despite the mess in my apartment, he managed to fuck me on three different surfaces. Sure one of them was my bed. But the couch and my sewing table saw action.

And he seemed to truly think having my dresses and shoes spread out was a good thing. When I kept refusing to show him every single dress I'd ever made, he decided to pull out the I'm Your Boss fantasy again and made me dress up in four different outfits.

He also seemed actually interested in what I do and impressed by the fact that I made the outfits that he found completely hot and stripping me right back out of.

I study him as he sleeps. He's so beautiful. And charming, and funny, and stupidly fun and laid-back for a billionaire.

He's too good to be true. Which has a partial wall still up around my heart. But he managed to smash half of that thing down in only a few hours.

I glance at the clock and groan.

It's five-thirty in the morning. I have to get up.

I have a deal with Luna that comes with living in this apartment. I agree to be the one that gets up and gets everything started in the bakery first thing in the morning. It's a perk to be able to walk downstairs in whatever I want to throw on and get the ovens going. It also knocks some money off my already ridiculously low rent.

But five-thirty in the morning is really fucking early, especially if you didn't get a lot of sleep the night before.

Still, I grin as I sit up and swing my legs over the side of the mattress. I don't mind being kept up the way Simon kept me up.

I also know I'm going to be a little sore today. The way he worked out, bent me over, and stretched me out hasn't been done in a very long time.

I feel a big hand slide over my hip and an arm wrap around my waist tugging me back. "Where are you going?" a husky voice with a British accent asks.

God, he's sexy. "I have to go get things started downstairs in the bakery. But I'll bring you breakfast when I come back up if you want to hang around."

I really want him to hang around.

That thought hits me and my heart trips.

Yeah, I'm in trouble here.

And yes, I know it's because Simon knows about my greatest weakness and is still here, being sweet, sexy, and charming.

"I definitely want to hang around. And it's not just because of breakfast." He lifts my hand to his lips and presses a kiss. "Or I should say, what I'm interested in eating isn't down in that kitchen. Hurry back."

I shiver with desire. "I will." Then, because I can't help it, I lean over and kiss him. "I'm glad you're staying."

Then I quickly slip out of bed. I dress in loose, light blue lounge pants, and a gray tank top with no bra since no one's going to see me.

An hour later, I've got all the morning basics finished and cooling, and I head back upstairs with cranberry-orange muffins for Simon and to shower and get dressed for the day.

Simon is sitting on my sofa, in the one clear spot where I sit to read and work. He is scrolling on his phone, dressed in only his boxers, but seemingly completely happy and content.

Out of habit, my body tenses, and I look around, bracing to see that he's tried to tidy up, or organize things in some way.

Every single person, except for Dani and Luna, has done that to me. My parents always did it, though my mother did it more to keep my father's blood pressure down. My boyfriend did it. Another boyfriend actually hired a professional home organizer for me. I *wept* after she left because I had no idea where anything was. All I saw were plastic bins everywhere. I even had girlfriends who did it under the guise of trying to help. They simply thought that I didn't know how to organize things. They didn't understand that if I put things away, I wouldn't remember where they were, and wouldn't be able to find them again when I needed them.

They also didn't understand that all of their "help" embarrassed me and made me feel infantilized and like they thought I couldn't take care of myself.

I can admit that my system isn't perfect, but the more I've read and connected with other people who have ADHD, I realize that I'm not weird, or wrong. Our brains are just wired differently and we need to live however we need to live.

But nothing seems to be different. Just that I know I have a hot Brit sitting on my couch in his underwear.

Simon looks up at me and smiles that I-think-you're-amazing smile that he seems to always give me. "Morning, love."

God, his voice, the way he calls me 'love', just everything about him makes me melt.

A flash of guilt goes through my mind. I'm kind of texting with Aidan with the intention that we're going to see each other. But I barely know the firefighter. He seems nice, he's definitely hot, and he does seem interested, but we just met. I know nothing about him other than what he does for a living. And that he's pretty cocky. He asked for my number after finding me making out with another man.

I almost groan. Yeah, then there's that other man. But nothing is going on with me and Blake. Blake Wilder has very nice big hands and fingers that definitely know what they're doing when they're up underneath a woman's skirt. But that's it. He walked off instead of spending the rest of the night with me. He didn't even want to stick around for a New Year's Eve kiss.

But he texted you. He wants to see you.

Yes, I'm being flooded by texts from two different directions.

But Blake's grumpy and not at all sweet, romantic, or even really charming like Simon and Aidan are.

Still, Simon and I *just* started this whatever-it-is. I didn't know he was going to show up yesterday. I haven't done anything wrong.

You should tell Simon about Blake and Aidan.

What should I tell him? There's nothing to tell. You aren't dating either of them.

Yet.

Shut up.

Great. Now the voices in my head are arguing with one another.

"Morning," I say, giving Simon a genuine smile. "How do you feel about cranberry orange muffins?"

"Can I eat them with you sitting naked in my lap?"

I laugh as I hand him the plate with two muffins. "I have to get ready for work. So no."

"Can I eat them while watching you shower?"

I laugh again. "They might get a little soggy."

He laughs. "Fine. I'll stay outside the shower curtain. We can just chat while you get ready. How long do you work today?"

"Just through the morning rush actually," I tell him.

"Then what?"

"I was going to sew for a little bit, but I could be talked into something else." I gave him a grin. "Except Turks and Caicos. I don't quite have that much time."

"We can do anything. Think of something."

"What do you want to do?"

"Spend the day with you."

My heart flips.

Okay. I might need to stop texting Aidan and Blake.

Suddenly, a loud squealing pierces the air.

I jump and frown, trying to place the sound. I turn toward the door, realizing the sound is coming from the bakery.

Simon is on his feet. "That sounds like—"

"The fire alarm," I fill in. I feel the blood drain from my face. "Oh…shit."

Immediately I run for the door. "Oh shit, oh shit, oh *shit*!"

"Love, hold on," Simon says.

I rip the door open and start for the stairs.

"Elise!" Simon's loud, firm voice stops me two steps down.

I look up at him.

"Slow down," he tells me. "You need to be careful. You don't know what's going on down there."

"I know, but it's the bakery. It's obviously something I did. I was just down there!"

He comes down the steps. He stops on the step I'm standing on. "Maybe. But you still need to proceed with caution. You are more important than anything in that bakery."

My eyes immediately fill with tears. "It's Luna's bakery. I can't…"

Simon takes my hand and squeezes it. "It's going to be okay. Come on. *Slowly*."

He proceeds down the steps in front of me, pausing at the bottom to survey what's going on.

My heart is in my throat. Luna has been one of the best friends I've ever had. If I damaged her bakery, set her kitchen on fire, did something to make her hate me…

"There's no smoke out here, there's no flames I can see," Simon reports.

I take a deep breath as we both step down into the bookstore. "Okay." I'm only partially taking in what he's telling me. But it sounds good. His tone is reassuring, and I love that he's holding my hand.

We head for the bakery side of the building.

"There's smoke coming from the kitchen," he says, pausing in the doorway between the two businesses. He turns to look at me. "Stay here."

I grasp his hand tighter. "No. You can't go in there alone."

"I'm fine. I'm going to check it out. Stay here."

A little part of my brain recognizes that he's protecting me, and I love that.

The bigger part of my brain realizes that this man, who I really care about, is heading into a fire that I probably started. In one of my best friend's kitchen.

I obviously cannot let him do that. "Simon, don't—"

Just then, there's a loud pounding on the front door.

I jump and swing toward the door.

"Fire department! Open the door!"

There are firefighters gathered in front of the glass door and window.

Well, perfect.

I look at Simon. "Do not go into that kitchen."

He sighs. "Fine. But I'm answering the door."

I frown. "No, I—"

"Don't have a bra on." Simon fills in just as he starts for the door to let the Chicago Fire Department in.

CHAPTER 10
Aidan

"SEE YOU ALL LATER," I say, giving a wave to my crew as I head for my locker. My twenty-four-hour shift is done and the new crew is on duty.

I'm looking forward to catching a little more sleep and then taking my little brother, who is still on winter break from college, curling. I've always thought it was a bit of a puzzling sport, but according to my brother everyone is doing it and I'm as competitive as the next guy. I embrace every opportunity to show my siblings who is the biggest and the strongest. In a friendly, we-love-each-other-way, of course. My family means everything to me.

I'm just grabbing my coat when I hear the call.

"Smoke detected from home security system. Books and Buns bakery," the dispatcher says.

That gives me instant pause. That's the bakery where Elise works. She's talked about it in our text exchanges. There can't be another bakery with that same name.

Dispatch gives the street address, but I barely hear it. I'm following the crew to the truck.

"What the hell are you doing, Burke?" Shelly asks. "You're off-duty."

We don't work together often, but Shelly is around thirty-five and looks very sweet but is an absolute beast in the gym. She's American Ninja Warrior level athletic. But she isn't going to stop me from riding along on this call.

"I know a woman who works there. I need to make sure she's okay." I shoot Shelly a look that brooks no argument.

She doesn't want to waste time debating it. "Fine. But you know you can't go in."

"Got it." I can't battle any blaze, but that doesn't mean I can't get eyes on Elise to see for myself that she's unharmed.

Two minutes later, we're roaring down the street. I text Elise.

> Saw the call. Are you okay?

She doesn't respond. I call her, worried she is still in the building. Which is irrational. If the business has a security system that goes directly to 911, surely it alerts employees, and has both an alarm and sprinklers. She doesn't pick up, hopefully because she's busy exiting the building or isn't even at work, but is blissfully unaware of what is happening from the cozy comfort of her own apartment.

There is no visible smoke coming from the building when we arrive, indicating either a small blaze or one that's already been contained.

I hang back to let the crew do their job, but I can see immediately through the large glass windows that Elise is standing in front of the door. She looks fine.

Then the door is opened by a man wearing nothing but boxer shorts.

Immediately, my colleagues usher the man and Elise out of the shop and make entrance.

I call for her when she comes out, tears in her eyes.

"Elise! Thank God you're okay."

She's dressed in flip-flops and lounge pants and a tank top. I've heard of casual Friday at work, but this is next level. It's also

January, and fucking freezing outside, so I peel my coat off as I make my way to her.

"Aidan!" She swipes at her eyes. "I don't know what's happening. I started the croissants this morning and the muffins and I was tempering some chocolate for Luna, and then I went upstairs and the alarm went off. We didn't go into the kitchen, so I don't know what's happening and I'm freaking out that there might be real damage."

She pauses for breath and looks up at me. Her lip is trembling, and she's shivering from the cold. Her nipples are tight pebbles beneath her cotton tank top.

All I can think is how damn happy I am to see her. Not one single hair on her head appears to have been harmed. Sighing in relief, I put my coat around her shoulders and pull her up against me.

"I'm glad you're okay," I tell her gruffly. "And I don't see any smoke, so I'm sure whatever happened, it's not that bad."

Then I glance over her shoulder and see the man who unlocked the front door. He's dressed—or mostly undressed—in only boxer shorts. He's running a hand through his hair when we make eye contact.

I almost suck in a breath at the sudden and unexpected instant attraction I have to him. His eyes widen and the corner of his mouth turns up, slowly. His gaze sweeps over me, taking in the way I'm comforting Elise, but more than that, he's checking me out.

The feeling is mutual. I'm intrigued by that strong jaw, the straight nose, and a lean, but muscular chest. Under the circumstances, his stance is fairly casual. He seems confident that all will be well, in spite of a fire crew having just pushed past him, and the fact that he's standing in nothing but his underwear in January. He has a muffin in his hand. A muffin, for fuck's sake. It's thirty degrees outside and he looks like he's stepped outside to start his day in his private garden.

I find that confidence sexy as hell.

"I take it you two know each other?" he asks.

He's British.

Until right fucking now, I never knew I had a thing for British guys.

But I know now.

At least this one.

He's older than me by about a decade, also not my usual type, but I never argue with the power of attraction.

"We met on New Year's Eve." I reach my hand out around Elise's side. "I'm Aidan."

"Simon." He grips my hand.

It's a firm shake. And it lingers too long.

His fingers are long and cool, and he gives just the slightest small stroke across my palm before he releases my hand.

My cock reacts, hardening. Elise's thigh is pressed against me and the way I've turned to reach Simon's hand, my coat has slipped off her right shoulder and her nipple is brushing against my chest.

He's shifted closer, right behind Elise. We're all in a tight cocoon.

I glance down at Elise. Her lips have parted. She can feel my erection against her, has even leaned into it a little. Confusion clouds her expression.

"Wait—" Elise pauses and looks back and forth between me and Simon. "Oh." Understanding dawns on her. "*Ooohh*." Then she grins. "Well. This just all got a lot more fun."

"It certainly did," Simon says.

His voice is husky, but amused.

And while my body reacts positively to that, and to Elise snuggled up against me, my brain is struggling to catch up.

"I'm confused." Not by the obvious—she and Simon clearly just rolled out of bed. But the logistics are baffling to me. "How... why are you here in pajamas?"

"I live above the bakery. I guess I didn't tell you that since we just met."

Now it all makes sense. "Got it. So you put some baked goods in the oven and then went back upstairs?"

She nods. "Exactly."

"She brought me a sample to taste." Simon waves the muffin in his hand. "Then the alarm went off."

"Aren't you cold?" I ask him. He's not even wearing shoes.

"Freezing my bloody balls off," he agrees cheerfully.

"Here, take Aidan's coat." Elise tries to give him my coat, but he waves her off.

"You keep it, love. Can't have every man on the street staring at your chest."

"I agree." There is a crowd gathering now. A woman walking her bulldog, an older man with a newspaper tucked under his arm, a couple of guys in their twenties in chef's pants.

"I'll get you a blanket," I tell Simon, stepping back and heading to the truck.

It doesn't bother me that Elise spent the night with Simon. If anything, I find the idea hot as hell. Especially since they both seemed happy to acknowledge we all share an attraction. But I'm not sure what any of that means.

I grab a blanket as Shelly is coming out the front door. "No one inside," she tells me. "Just a small stovetop fire. Kitchen towel. It had already gone out on its own."

"Good. So no real damage?"

She shakes her head. "No. Just a saucepan as a casualty and some minor smoke."

"Elise said something about chocolate."

Shelly nods. "Glad your friend is okay."

"Me too." I return to Elise and Simon and shake the blanket loose so I can drape it over his shoulders.

I could have handed him the blanket to wrap around him himself, but I want the opportunity to invade his personal space. To cement for him my intention.

It's a miscalculation though, because once I have my arms wrapped around him and we're staring into each other's eyes, I want to kiss him. I want to walk him back up against the brick wall and claim his mouth with mine.

His eyes darken before drifting down to my lips.

"Thanks," he says, huskily. "I'm impressed with the fire department's prompt and *thorough* efforts."

I release his shoulders. "I'm not even on duty. Just got off for the day."

He grins. I realize the way my words sounded.

I clear my throat and Elise reaches out and squeezes my hand.

"I didn't know you have a boyfriend." I want to ask point-blank if it's an open relationship, given she was kissing the hockey player in the elevator the other night and texting with me, but I wait for her response first.

"This just happened. Simon used to be my boss. Now he's more," she says simply.

"Much more," Simon adds.

She looks at Simon, who gives her a go-ahead nod. She turns back to me. "But I still want to get to know you, Aidan. If all three of us are okay with that?"

Simon gives me a charming smile. "I'd love to get to know Aidan, too. What do you think, Aidan?"

I've never had a threesome just fall into my lap like this, because that's clearly what they're both suggesting.

It's fucking amazing.

I'm very attracted to both Elise and Simon, and I feel like I've drunk six cups of coffee. Excitement is buzzing in my veins. "I'm free tonight."

They glance at each other. Elise smiles at Simon and nods.

He turns to me and claps my shoulder. "I love a chap who doesn't waste time."

"It seems like we all know what we want."

I'm fixated on both Elise's tank top hugging her gorgeous breasts and the feel of Simon's hand on my shoulder.

Damn. I can't wait to be naked with these two.

"If I hadn't almost burned down the bakery, this would be a perfect morning," Elise says.

That makes me laugh. "Let me see what's going on in there before Simon gets hypothermia. Wouldn't want him to lose any important body parts."

"God forbid," Elise agrees.

Simon makes a face. "Christ."

"I'll be right back and then I'll give you instructions on how to slowly warm up after your body temperature has dropped."

"Cute and practical," he says. "A winning combination."

That makes me grin. "I'm the full package, what can I say?"

I squeeze Elise's hip before walking away, feeling both their gazes pinned firmly on me.

CHAPTER 11
Blake

"ELISE, you are an amazing woman, I would love to get to know you better, I think we could have a lot of fun, I'd love to spend a bunch of time with you in the next few weeks."

I frown as I stalk up the sidewalk toward Books and Buns.

That sounds stupid.

"Elise, you are the sexiest woman I've ever…" I groan. "Don't mention the elevator. Come on, man." I take a breath. "Elise, I need some help, and you're the first person I thought of."

First thought of? Hell, her name practically fell out of my mouth.

But this request needs to be perfect. Straight to the point. But… nice. I need her. I need a favor. A *huge* favor. That I've already gotten her into.

Fuck. I'm not even sure Elise *likes* me.

Oh, she liked my hands and mouth the other night. But me? In a boyfriend sense? Not so sure about that. Or a *fiancé* sense? Nope, probably not.

I might just have to use my hands and mouth to convince her…

My heart rate picks up and my cock stirs.

Damn. I'm going to confront—no, that's a bad word. I'm going to *sweet talk*—Elise, and I need to do it *without* a hard-on.

I shove a hand through my hair and keep walking.

It's fucking early to be preparing for a big, important conversation.

I'm used to being up to work out or for early morning skates. Waking up early isn't a problem. Being friendly, even charming, is.

Kind-of any time of day.

I like being straight to the point. And I make most of my points with a hockey stick. Or my hands.

Again, I think about where my hands were on New Year's Eve and how much both Elise and I enjoyed that.

I turn the corner and take two steps before coming to a sudden halt.

Books and Buns, the bakery where Elise works and where she told me to meet her this morning, is in the middle of this block.

I decided to come right when they open, because I can't wait to see her.

Because of my grandma and this whole house thing. *Only* because of that.

That's what I'm telling myself.

But coming first thing this morning looks like it's a bad idea.

There's a huge crowd outside.

But then I really take in what's going on.

It's still five minutes before the bakery is supposed to open, but there are a ton of people gathered in front of the store.

Including a fire truck.

What the fuck?

The lights aren't flashing, and no one's running around or shouting. There's no big hose spraying water anywhere, so I assume things are fine but...

Firefighters show up for medical problems too.

My heart begins pounding, and I start jogging toward the bakery.

Elise lives in the apartment over the bakery. Where is she? What happened? Is she okay?

"Excuse me," I say, shouldering my way through a few people standing at the fringe. "Let me through." My size definitely helps in situations like that.

I nearly plow Luna McNeill over.

"Hey!"

"Luna," I say, as my hands shoot out to keep her from landing on her ass.

"Blake?" Her frown smooths out. "Oh, hi."

"Elise? Is she okay?"

Luna smiles. "Yes. She's fine. It was just a small kitchen fire. Easily contained. Everyone's okay."

I blow out a breath. I didn't even realize how tense I was until I heard that. "Is she around?"

"Yes. Somewhere. She's kind of…busy."

"I need to find her."

Luna smiles again. "That way." She points. "Good luck."

I don't know what that means. I start moving through the crowd again, people parting for me easily now.

Until I get to the firefighters.

"I need to get through," I tell the one in front of me. He's shorter than me, not as wide, but he's solid, that's for sure. Still, he's between me and Elise, so he needs to move.

He turns. "I don't think so. You need to stay back."

I realize I know this guy. It's clear the next second that he recognizes me, too.

"Oh, elevator guy."

"Firefighter guy," I respond.

"You can just call me a firefighter," he says with a half grin. "Or Lieutenant. Or Lieutenant Burke. Or Aidan."

"That's… a lot of choices," I say, for some reason feeling confused.

"Aidan is probably easiest."

"Okay."

"And you're Blake."

"How do you know my name?" Unless he recognized me from the Racketeers. Maybe he's a hockey fan.

"Elise called you Blake."

"Oh. Why does it matter if we know each other's first names?" I finally ask.

"Because I think maybe we're going to see each other around. A lot."

I frown. "What do you—"

"Blake! Oh my God, I forgot you were coming over!"

I look up to see Elise hurrying toward me. With some guy behind her. He's got a blanket around his shoulders, but he's in only black boxers otherwise.

What the hell?

"Hey," I say. "What's going on? Are you okay? What happened?" I step forward, *past* Lieutenant Aidan Burke, and grasp her upper arms. I look her over.

She seems completely fine. She doesn't even have a smudge of soot on her face. It looks like she was awakened by the fire, though. She's got a large man's coat on, but she's in lounge pants and a tank top.

And that's it.

When the coat gapes, it's clear she's not wearing a bra.

I swallow and pull her in closer, instinctively trying to keep anyone else from noticing. Even though I'm the late-comer and everyone else here has already seen everything she's got on display.

I feel a stupid, but sharp, stab of jealousy.

Which makes no sense.

"I'm fine," she says. "It was just a mess up." She gives a light laugh. "Of course. I got distracted and left a towel on a burner. No major damage. Thank god."

I'm watching her face as she explains. Despite her laugh, she doesn't look amused. She looks embarrassed.

"I'm glad you're okay," I tell her. Then I feel like I need to add more. I squeeze her arms. "Everybody does stuff like that. No big deal." I look at the firefighter. Aidan. I roll my eyes. "Right? *Lieutenant*? It's no big deal." I give him a look that says he better agree.

Aidan nods. "Right. Easiest call we've had in weeks. No risk. No problem."

Elise blows out a breath. Then she gives me a wobbly smile. "Thanks."

"Of course." I rub my hands up and down her arms. I want to run my hands all over her. Without any layers of clothes between us.

"I'm so sorry I forgot you were coming over," she says. "I got distracted. I didn't even realize what time it was."

I look around. "You've had a lot going on." Then my eyes land on the guy in the boxers. He's right there. Still. And…he's in *boxers*. I narrow my eyes.

"Oh, hey, Blake," Aidan says. "This is Simon."

I look from one man to the other. "Okay."

"Simon, this is Blake."

"Hey, mate."

Jesus, he's British.

She's got a half-dressed Brit and a cocky firefighter here. No wonder she was distracted.

"Hey."

"You should know his name too," Aidan says. "Probably going to see him around a bit."

"A bit?" Simon asks.

"A lot?" Aidan asks.

Simon nods. "Definitely."

I frown. What the hell? I look down at Elise. She looks a little sheepish.

Uh, huh. Okay. Well… fuck.

It seems I have some competition.

Which is a stupid thing to think. Elise and I do not have a relationship. We kissed for the first time on New Year's Eve.

But I need her.

I need her to agree to this crazy, stupid plan I spontaneously hatched with my grandmother, who I do not want to lie to but who is strong-arming me. I need her to *not* be into another guy, or a *couple* of other guys, who could mess up the idea of us being a convincing madly in love couple for the next ninety days.

I need her to…

Fuck. I need her to want me. The way I want her.

Yes, I want her. Even without the house thing.

Dammit.

Well, 'competition' is one of my favorite words.

"I need to talk to you," I tell her, ignoring the other men.

"Yeah, so you said in your text," she says. "Can it wait?"

"No." That's probably an asshole answer considering what's going on here, but they just said it was no big deal, and I have a ticking time clock here.

She frowns, studying my face. "Is everything okay?"

"I need your help with something," I tell her honestly.

She looks confused, but nods. "Okay. We can go upstairs and talk." She frowns. "I think?" She looks at Aidan. "Is it okay if we go inside now?"

Aidan looks from her to me, then back. "I don't know."

I give a little growl. "Is it *safe* to go inside, *Lieutenant*?"

He looks pleased that he's pissed me off.

"Yes. But I should escort you, just to be sure."

"My clothes are in there," the Brit pipes up. "I need to go inside, too."

Well, I guess that answers any lingering questions about why he's here and not fully dressed.

I sigh. "Great. Let's all go inside."

Aidan talks to the firefighters who are still lingering around. Elise talks with Luna. And ten minutes later, we—the *three* guys—are following her upstairs to her apartment.

She pushes the door open and then stops in the doorway and turns to us.

We're single file on the steps, not able to all fit any other way.

I'm first, with Simon right behind me, and Aidan bringing up the rear.

"So, before we go inside," Elise says. "You need to know that I almost never have people over."

I frown. She clearly had Simon over.

"The apartment looks like a disaster but..." Her gaze finds someone over my shoulder and she smiles, then nods.

I look over my shoulder. I don't know which guy is giving her a silent pep talk, but when I see Simon's face, I assume it's him. He's looking at her with clear affection.

Great.

It wasn't just a one-night stand. They're not just fucking.

My ask of her is going to sound really stupid if she's got a *boyfriend*.

I mean, I'd love to ask him where the hell he was on New Year's Eve if he's so smitten with her. I'd love to ask her just what the hell our kiss in the elevator was if the Brit is so amazing. But I just grit my teeth instead.

I don't really have another choice here but to go ahead and ask my favor. Unless I can talk some other girl I know into pretending to be my fiancée *and* pretending her name is Elise.

"But?" Aidan asks.

"But this is how I like it," she says, lifting her chin. "It's *my* mess and if you don't like it, you can leave. I don't want any comments, I don't want any help cleaning it up, and yes, it's always like this."

We all wait after she stops.

"That's it," she says.

"Well done, love," Simon tells her. "Now I could really use a pair of socks."

Love?

She laughs and steps back. "Of course. Come on in."

We all file past her into the apartment.

The *small* apartment.

That is, in fact, a bit of a disaster.

I look around. All I can see are dresses. And shoes. But mostly dresses.

The sexy-as-hell dresses she always wears that remind me of Marilyn Monroe.

I love these fucking dresses.

The only time I've seen her out of them is when she wears jeans to hockey games. And *fuck* her hips and ass look amazing in fitted denim.

But yeah, I've had some really dirty thoughts about these dresses.

"Be right back," Simon tells us as he ducks into what I assume is Elise's bedroom.

I clench my jaw.

He spent the night. I'm just going to have to deal with that.

Hope Simon is cool with me pretending to be madly in love with his girlfriend for the next three months.

CHAPTER 12
Blake

"ELISE," I say, turning to face her, prepared to just spit it out.

But she's still in the damned coat and her pajamas. I'm sure the coat is Aidan's. She looks small in the coat. And she still looks a little dazed and definitely vulnerable and suddenly I can't just pile this craziness on top of what just happened to her this morning.

"Why don't you take a hot shower and change, too?" I ask.

She looks surprised. Probably because I'm typically not that nice.

"Good idea," Aidan says, stepping forward. "I'll make coffee. Do you want something to eat?"

She turns wide eyes from me to him. "I, uh…"

"Coffee's always a good idea," I say when she trails off. "I can go downstairs and get something from Luna."

"Or I can make eggs or something," Aidan offers.

"I can make eggs too," I say. Stupidly.

Aidan shoots me a smirk. "That's amazing. We can make eggs together."

I frown at him.

"Yeah," Elise finally says. "I…a shower sounds good. And coffee. Definitely."

She shrugs out of that coat, the move pressing her breasts against the front of her tank. She hands the coat to Aidan. I give him a sideways glance and notice that his eyes are definitely on her breasts.

Of course they are. Her breasts are amazing.

As Elise steps around us and heads into the bedroom, Aidan starts for the kitchen. I don't know if he's been here before or not, but it's easy enough to find the kitchen. Elise's apartment is small and I can see the kitchen from where we're standing.

He walks around the clutter without comment and I decide, while I want to follow Elise, I need to give her a little space. Simon's in there anyway, so I follow Aidan.

He rummages in the refrigerator and pulls out a carton of eggs, some cheese, and butter. Then he plucks some leafy greens and a tomato from the door of the refrigerator.

I frown. I've never seen anyone store produce in the door.

He turns with everything in his arms, and asks, "Do you really want to help or was that just a competitive reflex?"

I should say that I want to help, and while I can make eggs, I don't actually want to.

"You go ahead," I tell him as I lean back against the island opposite of the stove.

He doesn't say anything, but he moves to the counter next to the stove and begins prepping what I assume is an omelet.

"You want one?" he asks as he breaks eggs into a bowl that he retrieved from a cupboard.

"I'm good." I watch him for another moment. "So you've been here before." I say it as a statement rather than a question.

He shakes his head without looking at me. "Nope."

"Then how do you know where everything is?"

"She has things organized in a pretty obvious way. I definitely know my way around the kitchen. Do a lot of cooking at the firehouse."

Right.

"So are you fucking her?" I ask. I wince slightly at how blunt that comes out, but that's kind of how I roll.

He spares me a glance at that. "No."

"Oh." I'll admit I'm surprised. "So you were here just for the fire."

"Yup. This morning anyway."

"So there's nothing going on between you and Elise?" I ask.

"We've been talking ever since New Year's Eve. We're going out tonight." He pours the egg mixture into a heated pan that I didn't even notice he'd gotten out.

"Really?" I ask, not loving this new revelation. "And Simon is cool with that?"

"Well, he's coming tonight too."

"You're all three going out? Together?"

I hadn't considered that for even a second.

"Yep." Aidan leaves the eggs cooking and moves to the coffee pot. It's a single pod unit, so he pulls a mug from the cabinet above and inserts a pod in the machine, pressing a button to get one cup going.

"And how's that work?" I ask. I'm not asking about a threesome. I definitely know how those work. I'm specifically asking about *these* three. Who is with who, how this started, and so on. Maybe Aidan and Simon are together, and that's how Simon ended up here with Elise.

Aidan gives me a grin. "I imagine it's going to work very well."

"You guys haven't done this before?"

"Well, not the three of us. I've done this before. I get the impression Simon's done this before. But this will be a first for the three of us."

And that answers a lot of questions right there.

"What about Elise?"

Aidan picks up the cup from the little platform on the machine and holds it out to me.

I take it. I think I'm going to need the caffeine. At least.

"We haven't discussed specifics, but she was interested when we suggested it."

"And what was suggested? Exactly?"

Now I'm very interested. And it's not just because I'd like to know what's going on with these three. I feel my body stirring. I've shared women in the past and always enjoyed it. And if Elise is into more than one guy at a time, it could make this upcoming favor I need to ask easier. If she can still see Aidan and Simon, maybe she'd be more apt to say yes to helping me out. And there will be less pressure on the two of us and our fake relationship.

"Right now, it's just a date tonight. But I think we're all on the same page with how we'd like the night to end," Aidan says, starting another cup brewing, then moving to the stove to check on the eggs.

He's obviously very comfortable in the kitchen and can easily multitask.

I guess that's a good thing if he's going to be dating two people.

"What are you going to do tonight?" I shake my head and add quickly, "On the date part I mean." I don't need to know what they're going to do when they get back to the apartment.

Even though I kind of want to.

Suddenly, I'm picturing Elise with Simon and Aidan, and I definitely feel my body heat.

Elise is a gorgeous, feisty, passionate woman. It is not hard for me to imagine her with two men. Hell, maybe even three.

I shouldn't be surprised by that thought. I love sex. I really fucking love sex. And I've already had a taste of Elise. The image of her spread out, being pleasured from head to toe, is so easy to conjure. There's something about both Aidan and Simon that makes me think that could be a hell of a good time.

Aidan shrugs. "I assume a nice dinner or something. Simon strikes me as the type of guy who would like to spoil her a little. And I'm all for that."

"You're not into spoiling?"

"Oh, definitely," Aidan says, lifting his cup of coffee. "But I don't need a lot of money or fancy cars and clothes for my kind of spoiling."

The guy has an air of confidence about him that is obvious without being in your face. My competitive streak is constantly on edge. It's incredibly easy to poke my desire to be top dog. But Aidan gives off a quiet competence. As if he is completely sure of what he has to offer without having to prove it.

"Wanna come?" Aidan asks, lifting his cup for another sip.

I'm surprised by the invitation. I'm also surprised that I'm seriously considering it. But why not?

"I—"

"Much better."

Elise cuts me off as she comes into the kitchen.

She looks completely different. She's now in jeans, with a pullover hoodie that's a bright, kick-ass red color. The front has sparkly letters that read *Fun Fact: I don't care*. Her long dark hair is wet and twisted up into a messy bun.

She might be dressed down, but she looks like her usual confident self now.

Without a word, Aidan moves to the coffee pot and starts brewing another cup. Then he grabs a plate out of the cupboard and dishes eggs onto it.

Simon comes into the room and gives Elise a kiss on the back of her head before taking a seat on the only empty stool at the kitchen island. Then he pulls her in between his knees so that she's leaning onto him, her butt resting on the front edge of the stool. Aidan sets the plate and fresh cup of coffee down in front of them.

Simon lifts the cup and takes a sip before handing it to Elise. She smiles at him, then takes a long draw.

Aidan presents her with a fork. "Do you need cream or sugar? Hot sauce for your eggs? More salt?"

But rather than hand her the fork, he lifts a bite to her mouth. I watch as she opens her mouth and lets him feed her.

"Mmmm," she moans.

All of us are watching her raptly.

She chews and swallows. "They're perfect. Thank you."

And suddenly I wish I'd helped make them.

I clear my throat.

She looks at me. "Right. Okay, what did you need to talk to me about so badly?"

I look at her leaning against Simon, who is now, thankfully, also dressed. Though the clothes he's wearing are obviously what he wore last night. I guess that means he's not staying here on a regular basis.

So far.

Then I look at Aidan. He's watching me with an amused look.

He basically just asked me out on a date with the other two.

The three of them are going out tonight.

Aidan is not fucking her. Yet. That 'yet' is very obvious. It could practically be a neon sign. And Simon clearly has.

Elise definitely has the happy afterglow going. So it was good. And she's going out with him again tonight, which means she wants a repeat.

My gaze locks on hers.

Drop it.

No, you can't drop it. Just say you need a favor.

Just say it's about your grandma. Lead with the grandma.

Drop it!

No, you can't! It's just a favor. It's fake. It's temporary. Lead. With. It's. Fake.

But when I open my mouth and actually speak, what comes out is, "Elise, I need you to marry me."

The kitchen is completely silent for five ticks on the clock above her sink.

Then Simon starts chuckling, Aidan says, "Didn't see that one coming," and Elise says, "What the hell are you talking about?"

I blow out a breath. "I want to buy a house. It's where I want to retire. It's been my dream. But my grandmother won't sell it to me unless I can convince her that I am in a serious relationship and won't move to the Minnesota woods all alone and become a hermit."

She studies me.

Aidan and Simon just go back to drinking coffee.

Specifically, Simon keeps drinking Elise's coffee. I don't know why that annoys me.

I step forward and hand her my cup. It's still two-thirds full and apparently, she drinks it black too.

She looks down at the cup and then back up at me.

"Do you *want* to move to the woods all alone and become a hermit?" she asks.

I nod. "Very much so."

"So you want to trick your grandmother into selling you the house?"

I hesitate for a second, but then nod again. "Yes."

"Is she a terrible person?" Elise asks.

I give a short laugh. "No. Not really."

"Would I like her?"

"Probably."

"But you want *me* to lie to her too."

I nod. "Yes."

She laughs softly. "I do appreciate your blunt honesty." She takes a breath. "Why would I do this to a nice old lady?"

"I said she's not terrible, not that she's nice," I point out. "She's trying to manipulate my life. It's none of her business. She can't *make* me get married. If I want to live alone in the woods, I should be able to."

Elise is quiet for several seconds, then she nods. "Okay, I agree with that."

Thank God. "If I try to go around this demand, she won't sell it to me. Her attorney has strict instructions. And I don't want her to manipulate me, but I do love her. I don't want to fight with her. So, I need a fiancée. Ninety days. Someone to pretend to be planning a future with me until I own the house.

Then we can break up and she won't be able to do anything about it."

Elise frowns. "And I'm your best option?"

"Your name was the one that popped out when she asked me about this fiancée of mine."

She's clearly surprised by that answer.

"It's a favor," I insist. "I know it's huge. But I'll make it up to you."

Interest sparks in her eyes. "How?"

"However you want."

She doesn't say anything for a long moment. She just sits there, watching me.

I noticed that Simon's hand is on her hip and he's stroking up and down.

I narrow my eyes. "You don't seem upset by this," I say to him. He's the only one in the room who's actually slept with her. How can he be so completely nonchalant about two other men clearly wanting her? Is it really that casual between them?

"Why would I be upset? This is completely up to Elise. And you just said it would be fake," Simon says.

"Still, I'm famous here in Chicago. If she's dating me, it will make it into the media. Other people will think the girl you're sleeping with is going to marry *me*."

Simon gives me a cocky grin. "Seems like *you* should be the one who's worried. Your fiancée is fucking me on the side."

Suddenly, I kind of want to punch him.

Elise rolls her eyes. "Everyone needs to calm down." She looks at Aidan, then looks over her shoulder at Simon, then back to me.

"I want to keep seeing Simon and Aidan," she tells me. "Would that be a problem?"

I think about it. "I guess not."

"What if the media finds out? What would your grandmother think?"

I actually consider her question. The media and Racketeers fans will be no problem. Other members of the Racketeers family are already in poly relationships and people are supportive for the most part. Then I think about my grandmother. Then I actually chuckle.

Elise looks startled.

"As a matter of fact, my grandmother would probably think it was great. She was just telling me how the house is way too big for one guy. Her greatest fear is me dying alone. If I brought home a girlfriend and two boyfriends, she'd probably be thrilled."

"You're going to fake date all of us?" Elise asks, a smile tugging at her lips.

"I'll introduce *you* as my fiancée. But if people find out that the four of us are seeing each other, or whatever, I guess that's okay." I really don't give a shit what people think about me. And this would not be a cause for my grandmother to take the house away from me. So *c'est la vie*.

Elise looks at Aidan and then Simon. "What do you guys think?"

Simon shakes his head. "I'm fine. I've never dated a famous hockey player before. Could be fun."

Aidan nods. "Same. I'll be the envy of the entire firehouse."

"I'm cool with the four of us being linked together. I have no problem sharing," I say, my eyes resting on Elise. I'm gratified to see her cheeks get pink with my comment. "But," I say, meeting first Aidan's gaze, then Simon's. "I'm straight."

They both shrug.

"Fine," Simon says. "Though a tad disappointing."

Just a tad? I give a grunt of acknowledgement.

"Understood," Aidan agrees.

I look at Elise again then. "Okay then, what do you say? Will you marry me?"

A smile curves her beautiful lips. "No. But I will be engaged to you until your grandmother sells you the house."

A weight seems to lift off my shoulders and give her a genuine smile. "Thank you."

"Am I right to think the two of you have not been out on a date?" Simon asks.

"Yes, you're right," Elise says.

"Then I think you should go out tonight. Get to know each other. Make a public appearance just the two of you before we spring a foursome on Chicago." His eyes find Aidan. "Let me take you to dinner."

And damn if Aidan doesn't blush just a little. He nods. "That sounds nice."

I look at Elise. "Can I peel you away from this charming British billionaire?"

She laughs. "I suppose."

Simon squeezes her hips. "Temporarily," he says. But then he nudges her toward me.

She stops right in front of me, looking up, breathing a little faster.

"You could've asked any woman in Chicago," she says softly.

I lift my hand and cup her cheek, remembering the silky feel of her skin from New Year's Eve. "Not a single other woman even came to mind."

She blows out a breath. "Dammit Wilder, that was a pretty good line."

I smile as I bend to kiss her, my lips hovering just above hers as I say, "I have all kinds of good things in store for you."

And when I do kiss her, with a cocky Brit, and a smug firefighter looking on, the only thing I can think is *damn, this was a really good idea.*

CHAPTER 13
Simon

I MIGHT BE LAYING *it on a bit too thick*, I think as I look around the restaurant I've bought out for my date with Aidan.

My thirteen-year-old niece Portia likes to call me a "try hard," meaning I put a lot of effort into getting people to like me. Granted, the cheeky little minx never objects when it involves me showering her with spa days and trips to St. Tropez. But as I eye the servers standing at the ready and the piano player tickling the ivories in the corner, she's not wrong.

I might be trying too hard.

But when I locked eyes with Aidan Burke as he competently and yet gently placed a blanket around my freezing fucking shoulders this morning, I damn near drowned in his blue eyes.

I'm a bit of a romantic.

Am I physically attracted to him?

Fuck yes.

He is big and muscular and I'm guessing hard in all the right places.

But it's more than that. There's also something utterly charming about him. He seems protective and caring. His voice is deep and filled with self-assurance.

He has a crooked smile, for fuck's sake.

I can't be expected to stand strong against that.

Which is why I'm standing in the middle of this hushed and dim restaurant in a suit, impatiently waiting for him.

All while realizing this is probably a bit over-the-top for a working class firefighter from Chicago. As the third generation of a wealthy family, I take money for granted and don't always realize how spending it so freely might come across to those who weren't born with my privileges.

Too late to worry about that now.

In spite of what Portia claims, it's not to buy affection. I just want people I like to enjoy themselves. In turn, that makes me happy.

Aidan strolls through the door, in khakis and a button-up shirt, and immediately draws up short. He runs his hand through his short, dark hair, an Apple watch on his wrist.

I walk over to him and pause three feet in front of him and give him a smile.

"Where is everyone?" he asks.

"Private dining event tonight."

"There's thirty tables in here." He looks a little baffled, and his voice has dropped to a hushed tone.

"And they'll be empty all night. I thought it might be easier to get to know each other if we can actually hear what the other is saying."

"I think I'm underdressed."

"I think you're *overdressed*, but we can get to that later." I give him a grin.

Aidan chuckles softly. "You didn't have to do this," he says, as he jams his fists into his pockets.

"I don't have to do anything. I do things because I want to."

The moment doesn't feel right to kiss him, even though I'm aching to. With his hands in his pockets, I can't even embrace him in greeting, and I can sense he's a little uncomfortable.

So instead, I gesture to the table that is designated for us, right by the windows. The lake is an inky blue-black expanse beyond the glass. Snow and ice cling to the edges of the shore and it's stark and beautiful.

"Have a seat. Drink? They can make you anything you want."

Aidan takes a seat and looks out at the view. "Wow. This is all incredible. Thanks, Simon. But you didn't really have to do this."

"Aren't you worth it?" I ask, as I sit, genuinely curious. He's rubbing his jaw now.

My question makes him drop his hand. It picks at his ego, which I assumed it would.

"Oh, I'm worth it." He gives me a cocky smile. "I just don't want you to think this is…transactional."

That surprises me. I raise a brow. "Of course not. Financial disparity doesn't make this transactional. I take it you're not used to being treated?"

"Uh, no. I was raised in a traditional family with working-class values. When I date women, I pay for everything."

"And when you're with a man?" I flick my napkin open.

"I still pay if it's a relationship. But I've only had one boyfriend. Mostly, I date men casually and we split the tab."

"If it makes you feel better, you can split the bill with me."

His face blanches.

I laugh. "I'm kidding. Just sit back, please, relax, and enjoy yourself. That's all I want. Order whatever you want and let the man who has money he doesn't deserve to have treat the man who, I'm certain, deserves everything he has. Unless you want to go somewhere else, which would be perfectly fine with me. I just want to spend time with you."

It matters to me that he feels comfortable.

Yet I'm also turned on by the fact that he doesn't care about money. That's rare in my world. I've got plenty of people around me, both currently and in the past, who only want what I can give them. Whether it's material items, exposure to my social circle, or clout in the company, a lot of people want something from me. Those are all transactional in one form or another.

But no one acknowledges or admits that.

That Aidan clearly needs nothing from me is very appealing.

Aidan hesitates, then he shakes his head. "No. This is perfect, thank you. I just want to get to know you, too."

I gesture for the server to come over. "I'll have a whiskey, neat."

"Can I get a beer?" Aidan asks the server, who nods and lists what he has available.

Aidan orders a domestic beer, and I fully relax. Aidan is obviously confident in being himself.

"Are you from Chicago originally?" I ask him.

He nods. "Born and raised. Third generation firefighter. My grandfather, his two brothers, my uncle. All firefighters."

"That's incredible. What a legacy. Siblings?"

"I have a little brother and sister. Raised by a kick-ass single mom," he says proudly. "Dad went to the store for milk when I was five and never came home."

I wince. "Ouch."

Aidan shrugs. "Fuck him. His loss. My mom is a nurse, and she did an amazing job raising us."

"So taking care of others is a family trait."

"I guess so."

"And you have been the man of the house since you were five." That explains a lot.

"I guess that is also true. My mom never remarried or anything. She never even really dated. Too busy, she said."

The server sets down Aidan's beer and my whiskey. I raise the rocks glass and take a sip. "Well, my parents are still married, but they despise each other, so that's not a great thing, either."

"Why don't they get divorced?"

That makes me smile. I'm too old for the relationship to be anything but an irritation now. I mostly see them separately unless it's for large family gatherings. "Ah, that would require compromise and they are both terrible at that. My childhood home was a battleground. I was thrilled to go away to school."

"For college?"

"Year three. When I was eight."

Aidan chokes on his beer. "*Eight*? Jesus."

"Trust me, it was preferable to rattling around in a drafty old manor house in the middle of nowhere with nothing but a suit of armor to play with. My sister is eight years younger than me. So I was happy to escape and gain the companionship of my schoolmates."

"When you put it that way, that is an improvement. So how did you end up in Chicago?"

"My family has an American branch of the company. My cousin runs it. He also owns the Racketeers. Nathan Armstrong."

"No kidding? Is that how you met Elise?"

"Elise used to work for me. She was my assistant's assistant, and according to her, she was rubbish at it. She quit over a year ago. I ran into her two nights ago at the Racketeers game, and well, here we are."

He nods. Then he pauses with his beer to his lips, lifting his eyebrows. "Was she rubbish at it?"

I pretend to glance around the empty restaurant and put my finger to my lips. "She wasn't the best at it. But that's our little secret."

Aidan laughs warmly, and it washes over me. "I won't tell a soul. I'm a steel fucking trap."

"I bet you are."

"I'm going to ask a stupid question," he says.

"Anything."

"What the hell is neat whiskey? I've always wondered that but not enough to look it up."

It's such an innocuous question I laugh. I thought he was going to ask me something difficult to answer. "It just means it's served room temperature, with no ice, no mixers. Just straight whiskey from bottle to glass. It makes the flavor bolder. Hotter."

"You like it hotter?"

Now he's flirting.

A warm feeling settles into my stomach, and it's not the whiskey.

"I do. I take it you know all about heat."

"I know how to put out fires, that is true. Do you want to order now?"

"Are you hungry?"

"Starving."

He grins. But then he looks at the table. "I don't see a menu."

"You can order anything you want and they'll make it for you."

His jaw drops. "Oh, come on, that is just too much pressure. I need options at least."

"No. Because then you'll order the least expensive thing on the menu, won't you?"

His face turns an adorable shade of red.

I chuckle. "Are you a vegan, vegetarian, pescatarian?"

"No."

"Then how about a filet?"

"That sounds great."

I turn, and the server instantly appears. I order for both of us.

When I turn back, Aidan is eyeing me. "How do you do that?"

"Do what?"

"Make the server understand you need something when you don't do anything? You just looked at him."

"That's his job. It would be insulting to him if I waved my arm around like a madman."

He drains his beer. "I think you're doing it to me right now."

"Doing what?" My heart is suddenly drumming a hard beat in my chest.

"Letting me know what you want by looking at me."

"What do you think I want?"

"Me."

"Then it's working."

. . .

After we eat dinner and continue to casually chat and get to know each other as we stroll down the sidewalk outside of the building, Aidan tells me, "Our next date, I'm taking you into my world. I want to see you squirm a little."

Second date. I love the sound of that.

I eye him. "You're going to enjoy watching me squirm?"

"Kind of."

"What will we be doing? Do I need special shoes?"

Aidan laughs. "Maybe. I'm debating between darts and bowling. Both take place in sticky dive bars."

Dear God.

"Please don't use the word sticky. I'm begging you." I'm laughing with him. "But I'm willing to try anything once and I'm sure it will be highly entertaining to the locals to see the aging Brit attempting to bowl."

The January air is like glass shards slicing through my face, but I steel myself against it, not wanting the night to end early. We're just walking without a plan. The two whiskeys I drank have warmed and loosened me up.

"How old are you, if I can ask?"

"I'm thirty-eight. You?" Aidan definitely looks younger than me, but I don't worry about age differences. I just like to feel a connection with someone, and I do with him.

"Twenty-seven."

"And your life is where you want it to be?"

Aidan seems like a man who is very content with himself and his place in the world.

"Yep. I'm just missing a special someone."

That both sends a thrill through me and a wave of regret. "Aidan, I don't live in Chicago full time, just so you know. I'm here for ninety days this time, then back to London."

He glances over at me. "That's the same timeframe Blake has for this whole fake engagement, isn't it?"

I nod. "I think so."

"So let's just have fun while we can. You and me, Blake and Elise, the four of us."

I nod again, throat tight. I want to say more, but I don't want to make promises I can't keep. "Brilliant."

"Hey." Aidan stops walking.

"Yes?" I stop walking.

Aidan invades my space. He puts his hands on my shoulders and walks me back against the wall. His gaze drops to my mouth.

Then he kisses me.

He's good at this.

That's all I can think as his lips take mine, firmly, confidently, fully in control.

He smells like aftershave and something else I can't put my finger on.

As his tongue teases my lips apart, lust licks at me.

But before I can wrap my arms around him and return a proper favor, he pulls away and gives me a smirk.

"I just wanted to say that."

"That was worth saying." I clear my throat, a little fucking rattled by this man, if I'm being honest.

"And thank you for dinner."

"You're welcome. Want to go to the bar at the hotel I'm living in?"

"I'd love that."

"We can have a drink and text Elise."

We start walking.

"How do you think that's going?" he asks.

"Elise probably has him on his knees."

He chuckles. "I think we're all going to take turns being on our knees."

We make eye contact, and lust has me in a chokehold. I picture me the night before, down between Elise's soft thighs, lapping at her sweet pussy. Then I visualize being on my knees, drawing Aidan's cock between my lips. Then him doing the same to me, taking me deep, his dark hair bobbing over my swollen erection.

"I certainly fucking hope so."

Aidan groans. "How long of a walk is it to your hotel?"

I flick my arm out. A cab immediately pulls over to the curb. "I don't walk unless I'm hiking in the woods. Which, come to think of it, I never do either. I was only walking now to be polite."

He shakes his head. "You're something else."

"Something you like though." It's not a question.

"Definitely something I like. Definitely *someone* I like."

I give the driver the name of the hotel and then I spread my legs out so my knee bumps Aidan's.

"Text Elise," I command my phone.

"What do you want to say to Elise?" my phone intones back to me.

"Make sure Blake buys you a ring." I raise my eyebrows up and down at Aidan. "He can afford at least three carats."

He laughs.

I tuck my phone in my pocket and place my hand on Aidan's knee.

CHAPTER 14
Elise

SO I'M ENGAGED to Blake Wilder.

How the *fuck* did that happen?

I mean, I was there. I remember it. I even remember it making sense at the time. But now we're out, dressed up, holding hands as we walk toward a restaurant, and someone has already spotted us and yelled, "Wilder! Who's your girlfriend?" And he answered, "Her name's Elise, and she's a lot more than just my girlfriend."

So…this is real. And weird.

Blake has a reservation, so once we arrive, we're immediately led to a table across the restaurant. It's an upscale Italian place and he tells me it's one of his favorites. It seems most of the staff knows him and he greets several people as we pass their tables. He never lets go of my hand, and when we get to the semi-circular booth along one wall, he steps back to let me ease in first. His hand grazes over my lower back and hip as I move past him. He slides onto the bench beside me, not stopping until his thigh is pressed right up against mine.

The waiter comes over immediately, pouring us ice water, and asking if we'd like to see the wine menu.

"Are you a wine drinker?" Blake asks me.

"Sometimes. I like a lot of things."

His gaze drops to my lips and I press them together. I didn't mean that the way it sounded. I can't seem to help flirting. What is going on? I'm going to call it the Simon effect. It really might be, because that man has made me feel pretty fucking good about…everything. Especially sex. "Do you want wine?" I ask Blake.

"Not a wine guy, really," he admits. "But please have whatever you want."

I really kind of want a couple of tequila shots but that is not the vibe for tonight. Probably. At the moment, anyway. But if I'm lucky, then later…

I clear my throat, tamp down my inner floozie, and tell the waiter, "I'll have a vodka martini."

"Bring me whatever ale you have on draft," Blake tells him.

"Of course. I'll give you a few minutes with the menu."

"I hope you like Italian," Blake says. "I realize just now I should've asked. They do have great steak and salmon here too."

I open the menu. "I love Italian. This is great."

He seems relieved, and I wonder if Blake brings women here often. "Do you date a lot?" I ask.

"Define 'date'." He looks amused.

Yeah, that's what I thought. "You seem like you have plenty of attention. Of all kinds, including female. But I'm wondering if perhaps you don't need to date them."

"So I seem more the type to take them home, fuck them, and not call them the next day?"

He's a straight shooter so I decide I can be too. I pick up my water glass. "Yes."

He chuckles. "Well, I guess that's not *entirely* wrong. But I usually call them a few times. And I've at least talked to them at the bar or an event or two before I take them home."

I know 'the bar' is the regular hang-out where the Racketeers like to gather. I've been there a few times, and it makes sense that he could meet women there and get to know them at least a bit.

"But you aren't friends with any of them after you…stop calling them?"

He narrows his eyes. "Why do you assume that?"

"Because you asked *me* to be your fake fiancée. We barely know each other. We made out once. Seems if you had someone you'd taken out even a couple of times, she would be a better candidate."

He sips from his water glass, watching me. He sets it down and says, "You're right. I don't stay friends with women I fuck. And I don't date. I have avoided anything serious on purpose. I don't intend to stay in Chicago, so it's always seemed silly to fall in love with a hometown girl. And the fake fiancée thing seemed complicated to go into with anyone else."

"But it's not with me somehow?"

"You seem like a no bullshit kind of person. I really like that about you." One corner of his mouth curls. "And…" He shakes his head. "Your name just popped out when I was talking to my grandmother. You were obviously on my mind. I guess it seemed like a good way to spend more time with you."

I'm not sure what to make of that. I like that he's been thinking about me. Probably too much.

I don't need this. For one, he's grumpy and blunt and literally just said he has no intention of staying in Chicago. Letting myself develop feelings for him would be stupid. So, I can tell myself not to do that but…what if I can't? Clearly we're going to be pretending to be close. We're going to go on dates, hold hands, probably kiss.

For another, I just had my world rocked last night by Simon, and now Aidan showed up and seems to want to make it a threesome.

A shiver of desire goes through me at that thought. Wow. Simon and Aidan are clearly into each other as well as being into me and that is so hot…

I blow out a breath.

I don't need Blake Wilder.

Why did I agree to help him out in the first place?

You had no hope of saying no when he asked you a question. Any question. But especially one that involved getting to see him more.

My inner voice is very annoying, but she's right. And I don't know what to do with that realization.

The waiter returns before I need to comment. And goes over the evening specials. We both place our orders—lasagna for Blake and lemon garlic linguine for me—and he moves off again, leaving us alone. Blake leans back, his beer cradled in his hand.

"So tell me about this cabin that's so important you'll fake having a fiancée to get it," I say.

"It's gorgeous. Five bedrooms, four baths, huge balcony that looks out over the lake and a screened-in porch. We have our own dock. It's surrounded by trees. The closest neighbor is a mile away. Woodburning fireplaces, amazing hiking, quiet, you can see so many fucking stars."

I smile at how easily he launches into the description, and the softness in his voice. He's relaxed talking about it and it's clear that it means a lot to him.

"A lot of memories there?"

"The best. We went up every summer, often in the fall too. The leaves are amazing. It was one of the few times that my family was all together, no crazy schedules."

"Are you close to your family?"

He nods. "Definitely. When I started playing hockey, things got a little crazy. There was lots of traveling, the schedule was nuts. But they were totally supportive. It was actually tough making the decision to come to Chicago."

"Really? Even to play professional hockey? Wasn't that your dream?"

"My dream was to play for Minnesota." He chuckles. "I was actually disappointed to be drafted by Chicago at first. I'm happy to be here now. But it's far from home. I'm ready to go back."

I sip from my martini glass and study him. I'm surprised for some reason to see this softer love-of-family-and-home side of him. This cabin matters to him because he has roots there. I like that about him.

"Does your grandmother know how you feel?"

"She does."

The waiter delivers our salads, and our conversation pauses again. But when he leaves and we start eating, Blake picks the conversation back up.

"It's my sense of family and home that's hurting me with her, actually," he says, scooting the cucumbers and onions to the side and mixing dressing over the rest of his salad. "She knows that home and family are important and she's worried I'm letting my chance pass me by. She's afraid I'm going to end up just being the fun uncle."

I snort. "Fun? Does she have you mixed up with someone else in the family? Are there a lot of cousins or something? Is she easily confused?"

He just grins. I like that I can poke at him and he takes it in stride.

I take another drink, then ask, "Why won't she just let you have the cabin because you love it? She doesn't think a woman would ever go up there with you?"

"I wasn't exaggerating when I said that I want to go up there and live alone. Away from the world. Unplugged. My least favorite part of being a professional athlete is all of the PR that goes with it. I hate social media. I don't love fan meet and greets. Really hate talking to the media after games. I just wanna play hockey. And when I'm done playing hockey, I just want to hike and fish and enjoy nature."

"But really *all* by yourself?"

"I'm really good at being alone."

"You don't think you'll get lonely?"

He gives me a little smile. "If I want human connection, I know how to get into the cities. And I expect I'll be back in Chicago to visit from time to time."

I feel my stomach flip and tell myself that's stupid. He's teasing. Yes, he's insinuating that when he misses sex, he knows how to find it. But the comment about visiting Chicago isn't necessarily about me.

And I remind myself again that I have two other guys who also seem to want to spend time with me.

Of course, one of them, the one who, after only one night, I am already feeling some pretty strong feelings for, is going back to London at the end of March. Blake and I aren't the only ones who have a deadline.

My stomach dips at that reminder, but not in a good way.

"So you and Simon? And Aidan?" Blake asked, as if reading my mind.

I pick up my martini and take a sip. Then shrug. "Yeah."

"But this is new. The three of you haven't been together before. Or yet."

"I see you and Aidan were chatty in the kitchen."

Blake grins. "I was curious, I'll admit."

"I guess if I showed up at your apartment first thing in the morning and two other women were there, I might be a little curious."

He laughs. "Would you be ready to talk about making it into a foursome right away?"

I laugh. "No. That doesn't sound nearly as much fun as what we talked about."

I feel his hand on my thigh, heavy and hot. He strokes his thumb up and down my inner thigh just above my knee.

"Why did you say yes to this? To helping me, I mean?" he asks.

Dammit. I can ignore answering that question for myself, but how can I avoid answering him?

"Seemed like it could be fun," I tell him. That's not a lie. There is something that sparks in the air between Blake and me that does always make me enjoy myself. "And I guess I didn't have a good reason to say no."

"I'm glad. I do think it could be fun. Maybe we should go over some rules. Talk about what we're gonna tell people."

He seems to have abandoned his salad, his hand still on my leg.

I set my fork down too and pick up my drink, taking a gulp. "That's probably a good idea."

"Okay, I've been thinking about this," he tells me. "I think we should go on a public date, like tonight, once a week."

"That seems fair."

"You'll need to meet my grandmother, of course."

I'm already nervous about it, but I nod. "Sure. Whenever."

"You also need to come to my games. I really feel like a fiancée would be at all of my home games. Wearing my jersey."

I smile. "That's kind of a thing isn't it? Guys like to have their girls in their jerseys."

He frowns. "Well, yes. Obviously."

"Why?"

"Shows you're proud of me." He leans in. "Shows everyone you're mine."

A hot shiver dances down my spine. "I don't have a jersey with your number and name."

"I will take care of that."

Inadvertently, my gaze drops to his mouth.

"And you need to spend the night at my place five times a week when I'm not traveling."

My gaze bounces back up to his. "What? No. Come on."

His voice drops lower. "Elise, if you were my girl for real, you would be in my bed every night. If we were actually engaged, I'd have you moved in. You need to be at my place a lot."

"But I'm not *actually* your girl," I say, my voice breathier than I would like. "So we need to negotiate that."

"Because of Simon and Aidan?"

"Yes. In part."

"I see."

I decide to say something that's been on my mind but that I hadn't decided on for sure. Until now. "Maybe we should—"

He squeezes my thigh. I have to clear my throat.

"Maybe we shouldn't...I mean, you and I...shouldn't do the spend the night thing. Or the sex thing..."

His hand slides up higher.

I take a breath and keep going. "That might just make this unnecessarily complicated. There's Aidan and Simon."

"I don't mind that you're with Aidan and Simon," he says. His hand is squeezing and running up and down my thigh, pushing the skirt of my dress higher.

"I know," I say, my voice a little husky now. "And that's...nice. But this thing with us is fake, and it's not with them. I might have a real...thing..."

His thumb brushes over the elastic that crosses between my pussy and my thigh. I suck in a breath. *Focus!* "...with them. And there's a timeline with us. And..."

"Elise."

I finally look up from my salad to meet his eyes.

"Take your panties off."

I feel my eyes widen and heat pool in my core. "What?"

"Take your panties off. I need to touch you."

"But...why?"

"Because I'm going to remind you that even ninety days between us is worth something and this—" He strokes his thumb over the silk over my clit. "—is real no matter what else we're saying or calling things."

"But...dinner," I manage.

"Yes. We're going to eat dinner. And I'm going to finger fuck you while we do it. And get this pussy nice and wet and ready for the *three* men who want you."

Holy...crap. What am I supposed to say to that?

Besides, *yes, please*.

"I really am surprised that you're cool with sharing with Simon and Aidan," I say instead.

"You don't think I'd be okay with sharing?" His thumb brushes over my clit again.

I grip the edge of the table and squeeze. I shake my head. "Honestly? No."

"Well, you have no idea what a fucking turn on it is to watch a woman that you're into being pleasured by another guy who is really into her. One of my favorite things is making a woman come. I don't mind having help. Whether it's toys, role-playing, fantasies, or another guy. I'll admit I've never had *two* others, but if that's what you want, my ego is *huge*, and I can handle it." He leans in and presses his thumb firmly against my clit. "I look forward to watching you lose your mind and hearing you scream all night."

That is maybe one of the hottest things I've ever heard. I blow out a breath. "I wasn't actually worried about your ego. But glad to hear it."

"But, with *four* of us, I'm also cool with going over to one of their places some of the time."

I stare at him for three seconds. Then I scoot away from him, glance around the restaurant, reach up under my skirt and tug my panties down.

I lay them in his lap.

His big hand clenches around them.

I smile and lean in and put my mouth against his ear. "This is why I said yes to you."

He catches me as I try to lean back. He cups my face, keeping my mouth close to his. "You need three cocks to keep you satisfied?"

I nod against his lips.

He growls and seals his mouth over mine, kissing me deeply.

We're interrupted when the waiter returns with our entrées.

I sit back, taking a deep breath. Ninety days. That's all I have with him. That's all I have with Simon, too.

But damn, it seems like these might be the hottest, best three months of my life.

My phone buzzes in my purse as a text comes in. I should ignore it. It might be Luna or Dani wanting more details. Or reporting something else that landed on the Racketeers' Instagram page. It could also be an online order though, and I like to respond to those quickly with a follow up message, letting the person know I received the order.

"Sorry," I murmur to Blake as I reach for my purse.

"No worries," he assures me as he tucks my panties into his pocket.

Whew. I'm so revved up. I'm not sure I can even eat.

I pull my phone out and swipe across the screen. The text is from Simon.

I laugh.

"Everything okay?" Blake asks.

"Simon says you need to buy me a real engagement ring. You can afford it."

He frowns. "Well, of course. It'll be huge too. My girl isn't going to have some dinky little piece of ice on her finger."

I grin and type.

> He says of course. He's offended you would think otherwise.

> Good. Now tell him to bring you to my hotel. We're in the bar waiting. We both want to see you.

My chest feels warm even as the rest of my body heats.

I start to type, but another text comes in from Aidan before I finish.

> Both of you.

Oh…yes.

I look up at Blake. "Simon and Aidan are inviting us over after dinner. To Simon's hotel."

Blake's mouth stretches into a wicked grin. "Who knew proposing to a girl with two boyfriends could be so much fun?"

CHAPTER 15
Blake

ENGAGEMENT RING SHOPPING.

It's all in my head now, taking Elise to a jewelry store, letting her pick out whatever diamond—or other stone—she wants. Then putting it on her finger. Having it flash every time she lifts her hand to smooth her hair, or touch up her lipstick.

Having it sitting like a rock on her hand when she's gripping my cock with her fist, her cherry red lips descending down the length of my shaft...

I shouldn't care about the ring.

It shouldn't even be in my head.

The only ring I should care about is the one I'm getting when the Racketeers win the championship this year and I can retire.

That's what I should be focusing on.

This relationship with Elise is fake. It's all fucking fake.

She's doing me a favor.

Yet, I can't get it out of my head. Dating her, hanging out with her, putting a ring on her finger.

Or the fact that she has two guys who want to fuck her tonight with me.

That she even tried to suggest she and I wouldn't get naked with each other is fucking laughable.

"Did you really think you were going to sleep over at my condo and we were *not* going to have sex?" I ask, amused, after I've paid our dinner check and we're heading out of the restaurant.

Elise huffs a little. "I was trying to keep this all straightforward. Simple. Uncomplicated."

I run my palm over the small of her back as I guide her out the front door. Then drop it lower, to the curve of her generous ass and give a squeeze. "It's already complicated. I've *touched* you, remember? Me sleeping on the couch isn't going to change that or make this any less complicated. I wouldn't sleep a damn wink knowing you're curled up on my pillow, bare skin on my sheets."

Just the thought has me clearing my throat.

"How do you know I sleep naked?" she asks, but she sounds a little breathless. I don't think it's from the blast of cold air we encounter when we step outside.

Her ass is pressing back against my hand even as she pulls a knit cap onto her head and down over her ears.

This woman.

God. I'm really fucking playing with fire.

But I love to win.

And I have to taste Elise from head to toe. I need to bury myself in her heat.

"You are one fucking hundred percent a sleep naked girl. Don't even try to deny it. You're comfortable in your skin and that is so damn sexy."

She makes a noncommittal sound, but I know I'm right.

"Do you sleep naked?" she asks.

"You'll have to find out." I gesture to the right. "My truck is down here."

"Of course you drive a truck," she mutters. "You're huge."

I lift my fob to start the engine and get the seats heated. "I'm not small. Besides, I can't drive a sports car in the woods."

"So many trees in the woods," she remarks, shaking her head

and smiling. "Lovely to look at, but definitely not my dream. I bet you can't even get food delivery service."

"Nope."

Is that a pang of disappointment I feel?

I frown to myself.

It's not like Elise strikes me as a woman who wants to hike and fish. Nor do I need companionship.

"I'm not cut out for subsistence living," she adds.

"Uh, not being able to order food day or night is not exactly subsistence living."

"It is to me."

I tell myself I'm disappointed by her reaction because of my grandmother. Elise needs to be convincing. "Make sure you tell my grandmother you love the woods."

I open the passenger door and she climbs in. She pauses, boots on the runner, and pins me with a gaze over her shoulder. "I know the assignment."

Grunting, I just nod, and she settles into the seat. I push the door closed and go around to the driver's side.

"These seats are heaven," she said, wiggling her ass back and forth. "Toasted buns. I love it."

All that wiggling isn't helping me focus. Lust is continually clouding my thoughts, which are already muddled enough. "Where is this hotel?"

She rattles off the address, and I put it in my phone.

It's close by, which is good. I need her naked. Now.

Watching her break as three men take her is going to be hot as hell.

I'm about to say that out loud when she fiddles with her earring and says, "By the way, I have a pinup competition in a few weeks and I think you should be there. If I'm spending half my free time at hockey games, you should support me too. That's what a fiancé would do."

"Pinup competition?" I have a sudden vision of her strutting across a stage in heels and a bikini in front of drooling judges. "What is that, exactly?"

"It's a pageant for women who love the retro pinup look. Lots of dresses and heels and vintage hairstyles. The theme for this one is winter wonderland."

I have no idea what that means, but I nod firmly. "I'll be there if I can. Do you do those frequently?"

"Three or four a year. They're fun for me and good advertising as I try to launch my clothing line, Sugar Starling. That's my pinup name. Miss Sugar."

Now I do groan. "Are you fucking trying to kill me? *Miss Sugar*?"

As I almost run a red light, she snorts. "It's going to take more than that to kill you."

"Do you wear a bikini?" God, I hope she does.

"No. It's *dresses*. I need my shapewear back, as a side note."

"What shapewear?" I know exactly what she's talking about. That vise-like contraption that doubled as underwear. After I went home I admittedly raised it to my nose and then gripped my cock and got myself off, remembering the whole time the way she pumped her hips against my fingers and her soft cries of pleasure.

Then I threw the stretchy underwear thing away.

I don't think she needs to squeeze herself into anything.

"Blake."

"What?" I glance over at her.

Her look is full of censure. "Those were expensive."

"You don't need them."

"I didn't ask your opinion."

She's right, of course. It's none of my business. "I'm sorry. I'll replace them. But only if you agree to also get one of those bras that has a hole for your nipples. And panties with the slit for my tongue."

Her jaw drops. Then she laughs. "That's very specific."

"I have very specific tastes. You and your incredible body."

"Well, how can I say no to that?"

"You can't," I agree.

I find a parking spot. "We're here." I'm edgy with anticipation, just like I am before every game. "They're in the bar?"

"Yes." Elise presses her hand to her belly. "I have butterflies, I'm not going to lie."

"You've never done this before?"

She shakes her head. "Not three guys, no. You don't think they changed their mind, do you? Or that I'm reading their invitation wrong? Maybe they really just want us all to have a drink together and nothing more."

That's laughable. "Uh. No. I don't. This isn't a casual meet up."

When we walk into the bar, we immediately spot Aidan and Simon, sitting at a four top table. The bar only has one other lone patron at the actual bar. The guys have chosen a cozy corner, where the lighting is low and far enough away from the bartender that our conversation probably won't be overheard.

Perfect.

They hear Elise's arrival because both swivel to look back at the entrance to the bar. There are no doors, just a wide entrance off the lobby. But the floors are marble and her shoes have little heels that make a clicking sound.

It's Elise's siren call.

It certainly drives me crazy, so I understand how they're equally drawn to her.

Simon gives her a charming smile and raises his glass up in salute.

Aidan shifts in his chair, his smile slow and filled with desire.

Then they both flick their gazes to me.

I nod in greeting. I glance down at Elise. She's taking a deep breath. She feels my gaze and looks up at me.

She seems nervous, but if I'm reading her right, it seems more like excitement, not doubt. "You don't have to do this," she says. "I'll still pretend to be your fiancée publicly."

I grip her cheeks with both of my hands and stare into her

beautiful eyes. Then I kiss her, taking her mouth in a demanding, hungry kiss. I pour myself into tasting her, crowding her space, sweeping my tongue into her mouth.

She moans softly when I pull away.

"I never do anything I don't want to do," I tell her. "Except for Racketeers press conferences."

She laughs softly. "Good to know."

"Now let's go join these guys so you can tell them exactly what you want."

I take her hand. I don't know why. I'm not really a holding hands kind of guy.

Who the fuck am I kidding?

I may be willing to share Elise and our engagement may be fake, but I still want to establish I'm an equal player.

"Hello, love," Simon says to her as we approach. He stands up and kisses her cheek. He holds his hand out to me. "Good to see you again, Blake."

He says it as if I haven't seen him in his underwear.

I shake his hand. "Hey, what's up?"

Social situations are a breeze for this guy and part of me envies that, the way I have in the past with friends like Crew McNeill and Alexsei Ryan. They always know what to say.

Aidan is the same way. He may not be as charming as Simon, but he always seems comfortable and friendly. He gives Elise a smile as he pulls himself to his feet.

"Hi." He gives her a hug and shakes my hand as well.

Simon gestures for us to sit down and he casually leans back in his chair, resting his calf over the opposite knee. "How was dinner?"

"Delicious," Elise says. "How about you two?"

"My filet was perfectly prepared," he says, lifting his fingers in an "o." "The chef is amazing."

"There was no one else in the restaurant," Aidan tells her. "Simon arranged for private dining."

"Oooh, that sounds very fancy. You're on your A game, Simon, I love it." Elise sits down next to Aidan.

Simon launches into a detailed description of their dinner dishes.

I drag out the chair beside Simon and listen to them make small talk for another five minutes before I can't stand it.

I fucking hate small talk.

"Is anyone having sex or are we just going to talk about the braised whatever-the-fuck all night?" I demand.

Elise cuts off mid-sentence and gapes at me.

Aidan snorts.

Simon chuckles.

"What?" I ask Elise. "That's what you want, right?"

"There's nothing wrong with a little conversation," she says. She lifts Aidan's beer to her lips and takes a long swallow.

"My suite is just an elevator ride away," Simon says. "But Elise sets the pace, Wilder. We do it her way."

Aidan's arm has come around her shoulder, and he's giving it a reassuring squeeze. "Exactly."

I reach over the table and take her hand, sliding my thumb down her palm. "Would you like to go upstairs right now and get fucked by three men, sugar?"

CHAPTER 16
Aidan

"SO ALL FOUR of us together? Right now? Tonight?" Elise asks. Her eyes are wide and filled with hope and desire as her gaze flicks from Blake to Simon to me.

I look at the other two men but then focus on her as I laugh roughly. "Oh yes, sweetheart. I'm in."

I was content to hang out at the bar and talk for a while, but I'm eager to get her and Simon upstairs and naked. Any doubt I might have had about her wanting Wilder to join us is eradicated by the look on her face.

"I think it's a brilliant idea, love," Simon tells her.

She meets Blake's gaze. He gives her a nod. "Fuck, yeah, you know I'm in."

She takes a deep breath, then grins. "Wow. Yes. This is what I want. But I don't even know what to say or do now."

Blake shoves his chair back to stand, his expression serious. "You just let us take care of you. Let us worship you all night. All you have to do is say yes, no, more, harder. Anything you don't like, you tell us to stop. Anything you do like, you ask for more." He lifts a hand and runs his thumb over her bottom lip. "Or maybe you can *beg* for more."

She swallows hard, then nods. "Okay. Where do we start?"

I exchange a look with Simon.

I love that she's eager for this. This is going to be amazing. It's obvious that Blake is going to be more dominating than either Simon or me. Which is fine. I don't need to compete with the goalie. Then again, I think Wilder gets off on a little competition. I can push him when he needs it, too.

"We pay the tab and go upstairs." I stand up too and offer her my hand, which she accepts.

Simon is on his feet. "The bartender already knows to put the bill on my room. Does anyone need a drink sent upstairs?"

I shake my head no. I want a clear head for this.

Elise smiles at me and squeezes my hand before releasing it when she stands. "No, thanks."

Blake doesn't say anything, just strides to the bank of elevators and punches the up button.

The door slides open immediately, and he gestures for us to go in first. Elise brushes past him and he watches her with hungry eyes. It surprises me he's willing to share her. I have a sneaking suspicion he's in deeper emotionally than he even realizes.

Simon follows, and he gives her a kiss. Elise reaches out her hand for me. I take it and lean against the elevator wall.

"If this gets stuck, I'll get us out."

She laughs softly.

"Hit the PH button for me, Wilder," Simon says.

Of course his room is the penthouse. I'm a little in awe of Simon's casual wealth.

Once we're in the luxurious suite, Elise clears her throat and rips the knit hat off of her head. "Now what?"

"Well, I'm going to pick your sweet ass up and carry you into the bedroom, lay you down, and we're going to absolutely feast on you," Blake tells her. He bends, clearly intending to literally lift her up.

She laughs and steps back. "Well, that's not necessary."

He frowns at her. "It is absolutely necessary."

"You don't have to pick me up. I'm not even sure you can. No offense. But I can walk in the bedroom myself."

Blake narrows his eyes. "Fucking dare me."

Her eyes widen. "What?"

"I *am* going to pick you up. I *am* going to carry you into the bedroom. And if you say something like that again, I'm gonna put you over my knee and spank your ass."

She stares at him, her mouth open.

He lifts a brow. "I throw big ass fully grown hockey players around. You're nothing."

She shakes her head. "No. I was thinking about the spanking thing."

I grin. Simon actually gives a little groan.

Blake doesn't say anything. He simply steps forward, grips her ass, and lifts her up against him.

She wraps her arms and legs around him, laughing. "But if I let you carry me, you're not going to spank me."

"Who said that?" he asks, giving her ass a little swat. "There's lots of reasons to spank you. One of them can be just that you want it." He starts down the hall. "You're going to quickly catch on that you can have whatever you want from us."

I shake my head and look at Simon. "This is going to be a lot of fun."

Simon is watching them go. "Yes. Yes, it is."

Then he turns and kisses me so briefly it makes me moan.

We start after them. Blake already has Elise on the bed. He's stripping. He pulls his shirt over his head and Elise is watching, fascinated. I can see why. The guy is ripped. Of course he is. He's a hockey goalie. But he's huge. Bigger than I imagined. And I am not embarrassed to admit that I definitely imagined it.

After seeing how hot they were together in the elevator, it was very difficult *not* to imagine it.

I watch Elise taking in every detail of his cut chest and abs, the ink on his shoulders and arms, and the way he lifts his hands to his hair, gathering it back into a low ponytail. Clearly, he's going to be busy doing things that he needs his hair out of the way for.

I think I could just watch these two together for the next few hours and be very happy. My own personal, live action porn.

"It occurs to me that you haven't even kissed her yet," Simon says, looking at me.

I look at Elise. She licks her lips. "That's true."

Blake looks over. "So?"

"Good point, Simon. I'm thinking maybe I should go first," I say, poking the bear just the right amount.

Elise deserves to have him growly and jealous over her. It's great that he's so open to sharing her, and we are going to make sure this is the best night of her life, and hopefully there will be other nights, but Elise needs to know that Blake really wants her. Hell, I want to be sure *Blake* realizes that.

"You not kissing her seems like bad judgment on your part," Wilder tells me, kneeling on the bed and bracing himself over Elise. He lowers his head and gives her a long, deep kiss.

"Why do you get to go first?" I ask, taking my time to strip my shirt off as well. "I mean, she's kissed both you and Simon. It's kind of my turn."

Blake doesn't move from where he's braced over Elise, except to turn his head to look at me. "Yeah, but there's only one person in this room for me to kiss. You've got another option. Why don't you kiss him if you're needing a kiss so bad?"

Elise peeks around his shoulder to look at Simon. I grin at Simon, too. "Well, it's not a bad point."

"In fact, it's a very good point," Simon agrees. He reaches out, cups me by the back of the neck and hauls me in, crushing his lips to mine.

I kissed him first on the sidewalk, but he definitely takes control this time. His mouth moves over mine possessively, hotly. I'm hard and I grip his shirt, keeping his body against mine.

I hear rustling, but I don't know who is taking whose clothes off. And it doesn't really matter right now. I am very happy as

Simon's hands travel from my waist up my ribs and back down as our tongues stroke and thrust.

"Jesus, you're gorgeous," I hear Blake mutter.

Now I have to pull back to look at Elise. From what I understand, this is Blake's first time seeing her naked, but it's also mine, and I don't want to miss a thing.

He's gotten her out of her dress and she's lying on the sheets in only a black satin bra. No panties.

"Oh, you beautiful, naughty thing," Simon says.

"It's Blake's fault," she says, blushing. "He took them at the restaurant."

"Well done," Simon tells Blake.

I agree, but I can't look away from Elise. Or form words.

She looks like a fantasy come to life with all that creamy skin, those soft, gorgeous curves, pink lips, dark hair against the white sheets.

"Go on," Simon says softly, nudging me toward the bed. "Trust me, you want to get in there."

I glance from Elise back to him. I've had great, even adventurous sex before, but I'm not sure I've ever had a situation as open as this. Simon clearly wants Elise, but he definitely wants me as well. And he wants me and Elise together. This feels very unique, and I'm going to relish every second.

I move toward the bed. Elise's smile is sweet, sexy, and welcoming. She stretches out a hand toward me. "I am definitely ready for my first kiss from you," she tells me.

"Is your fiancée okay with that?" I give Blake a smirk.

"Depends where you want to kiss her," he tells me.

He leans in, scooping under Elise's ass and pulling her to the end of the bed where he kneels, spreads her thighs, and gives her pussy a low, slow lick.

Elise moans. "Oh *god*."

Blake lifts his head to say, "This is mine right now. I'm not moving until she's crying out my name."

Jesus. That is so fucking hot.

"You can kiss her anywhere else though," he tells me.

He doesn't look at me. Or Simon. His eyes don't leave Elise, his gaze hot and possessive.

Damn, this guy already has it bad. I wonder if he realizes it.

"Well, that leaves me lots of delicious choices," I say, moving in closer to the bed.

But Elise can't make any requests, because she's busy gasping and crying out as Blake eats her. There are lots of, "oh my God" and "Blake!" coming from her gorgeous mouth.

I feel a slight jab of jealousy, simply because this man is clearly making her feel so good. But I was right. I could just watch these two together and be perfectly happy. And very horny.

Simon seems to sense how much I'm enjoying myself, because he moves around the bed and reaches underneath her to unhook her bra.

"You gorgeous thing," he murmurs as he peels her bra from her body, revealing the most gorgeous breasts I have ever seen.

He cups them, then rolls the dark pink nipples between his thumb and first finger as he bends and presses a kiss to her mouth, swallowing down the cries telling Blake she's getting close.

Blake shifts and slides two thick fingers into her pussy and I have to reach down and adjust my cock.

I knew this would be hot. I'm with three people who are clearly open and comfortable about sex and what they like and need. But how quickly we went from zero to sixty is amazing.

As Elise wrenches her mouth away from Simon to cry out as she comes apart around Blake's fingers, lust hits me hard and hot. I'm not sure I have ever been this turned on. She's amazing. Her body is soft and curvy and an entire buffet of delights, and the fact that there are three men here with her, determined to enjoy her all night, make her come over and over again, seems completely right.

She deserves this kind of sex, this kind of appreciation and pleasure.

She was made for it.

She's taking deep shuddering breaths as Blake rises up between her legs, licking his fingers, his eyes glued on her. Simon strokes her hair back, away from her face.

"You're so fucking perfect, love," he praises.

"That's only the warm-up. *Now* she's ready to go," Blake says.

I finally move. I kneel on the bed beside her, opposite Simon, and lean across, sinking my fingers into Simon's hair and pulling him in for a kiss. He comes willingly. We kiss deeply, and I know that he is still playing with one of her breasts. My other hand strokes through her hair, the silky strands sliding between my fingers and over my palm. I feel another surge of lust. I want to wrap her hair around my hand to hold her head as I fuck her mouth. She'll take it. She'll love it. This is going to be the best night.

I pull back from Simon and look down at her. She's watching us, breathing hard. Blake is still standing between her legs, letting her drift back down to earth, letting Simon and I figure out what's next.

"Kiss me, Aidan," Elise says finally, her voice soft, the pleading grabbing me by the balls.

I growl and lean over, tugging on her hair just slightly, sealing my mouth over hers. It's our first kiss, but I don't ease in. I take her mouth hungrily, my tongue stroking along hers firmly.

I feel Simon's hand running along my shoulder and upper back. The mattress dips and I hear Simon say, "Seriously, Wilder?"

Blake gives a chuckle. "Feel free to shove me out of the way and take my place. But this girl needs to be filled up."

She whimpers into my mouth.

I don't stop kissing her to look, but I assume Blake is getting ready to fuck her if no one else is.

I move my hand down her body, over her breast to her belly and down between her legs. She arches up into my touch.

It's the first time I'm kissing her, and she's completely naked, spread out on the bed, having come on another man's tongue, and

I'm stroking over her clit, then sliding my fingers into her hot, wet pussy, and it feels completely natural.

I lift my head and stare down at her. "What do you need?"

Her head rolls back-and-forth on the sheets. "I don't know. Everything. All of you."

"Have you ever taken two cocks at once?" Simon asks, his hand stroking back and forth over her stomach.

Something about the way he asks the very dirty question with his accent makes me chuckle.

He quirks an eyebrow at me, but we are both pulled back to Elise when she says, "No. But I want to. So much."

Again three masculine groans fill the room.

"You're a fucking dream, aren't you?" I ask, pressing another kiss to her lips before I straighten.

"How about a cock and some fingers tonight?" Simon asks, his hand stroking down now over her inner thigh.

She's breathing fast but nods. "God, yes. I want all of you to do the dirtiest things you can think of to me."

I suck in a quick breath, but the three of us look at each other.

Elise is a firecracker, but the look we exchange says that we all agree she's probably not quite ready for *that*.

Between the three of us, I'm thinking I might be the most innocent. I am also looking forward to the things these men might want to get up to.

"Good thing we have ninety days," Blake says. "This is definitely not a one night list."

Simon nods his agreement.

Elise giggles and we all focus on her again. We're all smiling as she looks from Simon to Blake, then to me. "I realize that you're all more experienced at this group thing, but I'm pretty sure whatever we're going to do requires you to all get rid of your pants."

We laugh and get off the bed to start working on our buttons and flies.

I'm already certain I've never had this much fun during sex.

I've definitely liked the people I fucked. I've had some good relationships. But, strange as it seems this early in, and particularly in this exact situation, I feel a sort of camaraderie here that's never been present before. Maybe I've been missing out not having two other guys and a girl all at once.

But the next moment, I realize it's not the number or the gender of the people I'm with—it's *these* people. There's a chemistry here, a mix of personalities, a connection, that will be impossible to replicate.

I look at the woman on the bed as I strip out of my clothes. It's clear Elise isn't sure where to look first. She has three men that she's attracted to and planning to sleep with all undressing at once.

I grin. Poor thing. What a terrible problem to have.

She sees my grin and matches it. Yeah, she knows just how fucking lucky she is right now.

I climb back on the bed, naked, and start kissing her again.

Damn, I like her.

And that's a very good thing. Because she and I are going to be the ones left behind when Blake and Simon no longer need our hot little arrangement.

At least there's one of them I won't have to say goodbye to.

CHAPTER 17
Elise

MY ENTIRE BODY is on fire.

These men, these three incredible men, are all here for me. Because of me. I have never been this turned on in my life.

Oh, I know Simon and Aidan have something between them. It's so obvious. And I love it. I can't explain the lack of jealousy. I love the way they look at each other, the way they laugh and talk, the heat that simmers between them.

I care about them both and I like the idea that there's someone else to show them how incredible they are, too.

I completely understand what Blake said at the restaurant about how exciting it is to watch someone you care about be pleasured by someone else that cares about them. I love watching Simon and Aidan flirt and talk and touch. Where typically I'd expect insecurity, there's only appreciation for them both and a deeper heat that makes me want them both even more.

As for Blake...well, I know he has a timer set on our time together.

But *this* moment? Right now in this bedroom? All eyes are on me.

I feel like I do when I'm up on stage modeling and everyone is watching me, taking in the details of my design, my look, my attitude, and they're smiling and nodding and murmuring their approval.

Except this is that times a million.

I'm turning on three sexy, experienced men who could have whoever they want in bed. They've chosen to be here with me and they've put *me* center stage.

Because I don't know what happened exactly, but something flipped a switch in Aidan.

He's suddenly stretched out next to me on the bed and when he starts kissing me again, it's not just his mouth that's hot and hungry.

His hands roam, plucking at my nipples, then he replaces his fingers with his mouth as his hand continues down, again sliding over my clit, where he circles.

My hips come off the mattress, pressing closer.

Despite my recent orgasm and the sensitivity from Blake's mouth, I want more. I *need* more.

Aidan's fingers sink into my pussy and I moan in appreciation and frustration. Blake was right. I do need to be filled up. But I need more than fingers.

"Aidan," I moan.

"I know, sweet thing. I know. We'll give you everything you need," he says huskily against my breast.

He pumps his fingers deep, in and out, and keeps moving down my body, kissing, licking, giving me little nips. I'm wiggling under him, trying to press harder against his hand.

Then his hand is gone and I feel him move off the bed. I look toward him. "No," I protest.

Blake grips my hips. "Fuck, I love you greedy." His voice is rough and I feel tingles skitter over my skin.

"Easy sweetness," Simon says near my ear. He's now stretched out on my other side. His fingers stroke up and down my side to my thigh. He's watching my face. "We've got you."

I lift my hand to his cheek. "I know." I pull him down for a kiss.

His lips are hot and greedy on mine, and I'm lost for a moment.

Then Aidan is back at the side of the bed. He puts one knee on the mattress, leaning over to pinch a nipple, then takes it in his mouth, sucking hard. "You've got the best tits," he mutters.

I hear the sound of a condom wrapper opening, and prepare to feel Blake's cock at my entrance.

"You ready for me, sugar?" Blake asks, rubbing his covered head through the wetness he created with my orgasm.

I nod. "So ready."

"Hang on tight, beautiful," Blake says gruffly, gripping my hips.

I look up at Aidan. He's staring at me with so much heat in his gaze, I feel singed.

Blake shifts his hips and thrusts, sliding deep and we both groan.

"Fuck, Elise, you're…" He trails off as he pauses, then pulls back and thrusts again. "You're so fucking tight. You feel so damned good."

He's holding my thighs as he withdraws and then sinks deep again.

"Oh my God, yes," is all I'm able to manage.

Now Simon is kissing my neck, Aidan is sucking on my nipple, and Blake is stretching me so good.

Simon just fucked me last night, but I feel so tight around Blake and so full. I grip Simon's arm. With the way Simon is lying against me, I can't get my arm up to touch Blake.

I try to move my arm that's next to Aidan. I need to grab onto Blake's shoulder or something. I wiggle it out from between our bodies, but Aidan catches my fingers.

"You're good. You're all ours," he says gruffly. He draws my arm up over my head and pins my wrist to the mattress. "Simon and I are hanging on to you tight."

Simon presses more firmly against my side, and I feel him

wrap a hand around my closest thigh. "Damn right," he agrees. He pulls my thigh wider and higher.

Blake groans as he sinks even deeper. "*Fuck.*"

"Just let yourself go, love," Simon whispers against my ear.

I feel untethered. Like I have nothing keeping me grounded, no leverage.

But then I let out a breath and relax, sink into it, focus on the guys and…it's incredible.

Aidan and Simon hold me tightly between them, Blake fucks into me deep and hard, and I feel every inch of all their bodies, every touch, every kiss, every dark whisper, every dirty word, every bit of praise.

"You're amazing."

"Jesus, Elise, this is everything."

"We've got you."

I feel the coil of another orgasm start to tighten and I press my head back into the mattress, closing my eyes, letting it wash over me.

But…

The men who I was just considering gods and princes, move me.

Just as I'm on the brink.

"Hey!" I protest.

Blake jerks out of me and I'm rolled to my stomach. I feel a big, hot hand on my ass, while two other hands pull me onto my hands and knees.

They're talking but it's only in short words and they mostly seem to just all know and agree with what's happening.

"I liked what we were doing," I tell them. I might sound a little whiny if I'm honest.

Simon chuckles and I suddenly feel a hand land on my ass with a sharp sting. My head whips around to glare at Blake. "Hey!"

"Don't be too sassy," he warns. "Or we won't keep going."

My eyes drop to his huge, hard erection. "You sure you want to make that threat?" I ask.

He leans over, his nose nearly touching mine. "I'll jerk off and come all over your magnificent ass and not let you have another orgasm for twenty-four hours." He presses his thumb to my lips. "How about we use this pretty mouth for nicer things than being a naughty brat and doubting that your men know exactly what we're doing?"

Oh...damn. I'm in so much trouble. Because if Blake Wilder keeps talking to me like that, I will do anything.

And that goes against every independent and, yes, sassy, bone in my body.

He's watching me with a cocky smirk. "Say, yes, Blake, I'll be a good girl."

I shake my head. I'm not saying that.

He lifts a brow, then looks at Simon. "I guess she's *not* going to get ass play while sucking on the fireman after all."

Ass play? Wait...I didn't know *that* was on the table.

"Yes, Blake I'll be a good girl."

Blake chuckles darkly. "I thought so." He kisses me. "I really like when you obey me."

"Don't get used to it," I mutter.

He gives my ass another little slap.

But I don't hate it.

"I think you can trust Blake to make being a good girl worth it," Simon tells me.

I look at Blake, biting my bottom lip. I feel his hand smooth over my ass and I say, "Prove it."

He squeezes me, but gives me a little smile. "Promise." Then he says, "Come on, Lieutenant, let's go."

Blake moves around Aidan to slide onto the bed in front of me. "Miss your pussy already," he tells me gruffly. He slides down the bed till he's on his back. "Come on up here, beautiful."

I crawl up, my knees on either side of his hips.

He grips my ass and guides me back down onto his cock without another word.

I moan as he slides deep.

"Addicted to you," he tells me, squeezing my hips and moving me up and down his length.

Aidan moves closer to the bed, stroking his cock.

He just stands watching us for a moment, then he says, "Let's keep that sassy mouth busy." He steps close and reaches out, tangling his fingers in my hair and urging me toward him.

I catch on quickly. I lean over and lick the head of his cock, relishing his groan. Then I take him in my mouth, sucking hard.

We quickly find a rhythm between Aidan, my mouth, and Blake underneath me.

Then I feel cool gel hit my ass and I feel Simon's big warm hand spreading it over my backside.

I shiver. I try to pull back to say something, but Aidan tightens his hold on my hair.

Okay, I get it. I'm not supposed to talk. I'm just supposed to take whatever they give me.

And I fall right in line as Simon's thumb rubs over the tight ring of muscles, and I feel the sensations shoot through my body, causing my pussy to tighten around Blake.

God, yes. They can do whatever they want.

As Blake fucks me and Aidan rewards me with groans and "your fucking mouth," and "fuck yes, Elise," Simon continues to massage my ass, slowly working his thumb inside.

The sensation of having something there at the same time I'm being filled in my pussy is incredible.

I'm not going to last long.

And since my mouth is full, I can't tell them.

Two minutes later, my entire body tightens and I come apart. My pussy clamps down on Blake. I pull my head back away from Aidan to suck in a deep breath, and I scream out my orgasm.

"Jesus, you are stunning," Simon grits out. I turned to look at him over my shoulder and find him stroking his cock quickly. The look on his face tells me he's close as well.

"Come on me, Simon," I gasp.

He groans and tips his head back, pumping his cock faster. I turn back to Aidan, who has replaced my mouth with his hand. I knock it away and lean in, taking him deep.

"*Fuck*," he swears, but his hands return to my hair and he pumps into my mouth.

Blake grips my hips and thrusts up into me hard and fast.

"Gotta come," he pants.

He comes only seconds before Aidan grips my hair and says, "Swallow me."

His firm, dirty command sends another wave of desire through me, and I greedily swallow as he empties into my throat.

"Elise!" Simon roars as he comes, the sticky ropes hitting my ass.

I take a deep, shuddering breath.

Holy. Shit.

Aidan gently pulls my head back, leaning down to kiss me. Then I sag against Blake. His big hands stroke up and down my back as he kisses my forehead.

My eyes drift shut and don't open even when I feel someone—Simon, I'm guessing—washing me with a warm washcloth.

Someone then pulls a blanket up over me and Blake.

Oh, that's nice.

Wow, that was incredible. I feel amazing. I really, really like these three guys. I hope we can do all of that again. Soon.

But first I really need a little nap.

They've absolutely destroyed me in the best way.

CHAPTER 18
Elise

I WAKE up the next morning, a little sore, very happy, and alone. Though not entirely alone. Just alone in the bed. I can hear low masculine voices from the outer room.

I smile and stretch in the incredibly comfortable king bed in Simon Armstrong's opulent hotel penthouse.

Wow. Was last night even real?

But the fact that I am naked in luxurious Egyptian cotton sheets tells me that yes, it was very real.

Blake is not out there. He left shortly after midnight.

But there are two voices, which means that Aidan is still here, and that makes warm butterflies kick up in my stomach.

After I woke from dozing, Simon took me into his holy-shit-amazing shower and soaped me from head to toe. It wasn't sexual. It was sweet. Tender. He was taking care of me. I'd asked if he was okay that he and I hadn't actually really had sex and he smiled and kissed me and assured me that he was more than fine.

After we toweled off, we'd gone out into the living room to find that Aidan had ordered room service.

It was a simple charcuterie board and lots of sparkling water, but the guys had insisted I eat and hydrate.

I am not one to typically love being fussed over, and certainly not one to put up with being bossed around, but the way these men do it, it's very hot.

It was also interestingly, a team effort it seemed. None of them really took the lead. They all took turns handing me bits of cheese and bread and fruit, making sure my water glass didn't get empty, and holding my hand, brushing kisses over my cheeks, or in Blake's case, pulling my feet into his lap and massaging them.

I have not been the recipient of aftercare before, but it's clear these guys know what they're doing.

We snacked, chatted, and laughed almost as if the four of us have been doing it for months instead of only hours.

Then, when I started yawning, Blake had said I needed to go back to bed. I was happy to oblige. But Blake had stood, pulled me into his arms, given me a sweet kiss and told me he was heading home.

I was disappointed, but not surprised. He doesn't seem like the sleepover type. Especially with two other guys. Particularly on one of those other guys' turfs.

But he had promised to call me today and said that we would see each other soon.

I mean, of course we will. We still have to convince his grandmother we're engaged.

I'm eager to see him.

Blake Wilder. The grumpy goalie who wants to be a hermit in the woods.

Crap. I'm falling for him. Even though I know it will never be anything serious or long term. He didn't even stay the night but I'm still heart-eyed and eager to see if he texted me yet.

With that thought, I notice someone set my phone and a glass of water on the nightstand.

I reach for my phone.

And my dumb heart somersaults when I see three texts from Blake.

> You were amazing. Thank you for last night.

I blush and smile.

> I'm on the road for the next two days but I'll call you.

Oh, damn. I don't know his schedule at all. I should probably look that up.

> I can't stop thinking about you.

Whoa. Okay. I like that. And that's nothing to do with being fake engaged.

I take a deep breath and text back.

> Good luck with the games. I think about what else to add. I've never been a hockey WAG before. Should I offer a blow job for every save or something?

I giggle as I hit send. It's silly, but it feels girlfriend-ish.
I get a text back within seconds.

> You have no idea how many saves I typically have in a game do you?

> No. Sorry. <laughing emoji> <angel emoji>

> Well not to be cocky...

> Let's just say your jaw can't handle that, sugar. But I appreciate the offer.

Damn. I watch Racketeers hockey and I can't help but watch Blake more than any of the other players. I've always been attracted to him. But... okay...

> I appreciate you looking out for my jaw.

> How about a good luck selfie? You in my jersey.

> I don't have one yet.

> It will be at your place around noon.

> Okay. I can do that. Let me guess... just the jersey? Maybe in some... interesting pose?

It takes a few extra seconds for him to respond to that message.

> <sweating emoji> I was actually just thinking of you in the jersey. With pants on even. Standing up and smiling your sweet smile. But now that you've offered...

I laugh, but my stomach also feels like I just went over the top of a rollercoaster.

He really did just want a regular photo of me in his jersey? That's... sweet. Ugh. He's not just the grumpy hermit goalie. That's my whole problem.

> I can send a variety. <kissy face emoji>

> Can't wait.

I take a deep breath and look around.

Blake's out of town but the perk to this new situation I find myself in is that there are still two guys here in Chicago I want to see.

Unlike Blake, Aidan had stayed over. Simon and Aidan and I had gone back to bed, but we hadn't had sex again. They told me that we were just going to cuddle. And then they were true to their word.

We kissed, hands had roamed, but they had tucked me

between them, and I'd quickly fallen into a very contented deep sleep.

I head into the bathroom. I pull a brush through my hair, splash water on my face, and then am delighted, though not surprised somehow, to find a new unopened toothbrush lying on the counter.

If it's not for me, I'll have to buy Simon a new one. But there is an open one propped inside a glass to the side of the sink that I assume is his.

I brush my teeth and then head back out into the bedroom.

What am I going to wear?

I don't think about that for long. I pad to Simon's closet and help myself to one of his shirts.

When I step out into the main part of the apartment, I find Simon and Aidan sitting at the little table next to the windows, sharing coffee and what looks like an assortment of pastries and fruit.

They don't notice me at first and I take a moment just to observe them together.

They're both stunningly good looking in completely different ways. Simon is distinguished, clean cut, sophisticated, and put together even when he's relaxing. He's in dress pants, a button-down shirt, with a tie hanging loose around his neck.

Aidan is more rugged. His idea of kicking back includes a lot more denim and cotton than Simon's does, I'm sure. Right now, he's dressed in what he was wearing last night. Clearly, he didn't expect to spend the night.

They look great together. They're both smiling, their voices low, with occasional laughter. My heart turns over in my chest and I feel myself grinning.

They clearly really like each other. It's more than just chemistry. The way they're looking at one another, anyone would think they were already a couple.

I like that. They're both really good men and if they've found something special with each other? That's amazing.

I think I'm happy that I set my kitchen towel on fire.

I push off the doorway and walk into the room.

Simon sees me first. His gaze tracks over me, taking in his shirt and my bare legs.

"Good morning, love," he greets me with a warm rumble in his voice and a smile. "How are you feeling?"

"Like I just woke up after the best night of my life," I tell him sincerely.

He holds out a hand, and I take it, letting him tug me into his lap. He kisses my neck as I smile at Aidan.

"You look beautiful," he tells me.

"Thank you," I say with a small laugh. "This isn't my usual morning attire."

"It should be," Aidan says, blatantly checking me out.

Simon squeezes my hip and says, "Cool it, you two. I have to be at a meeting in twenty minutes. I don't have time to be getting all wound up."

Aidan smirks at him. "I have the day off. I have all the time in the world to get all wound up."

Simon shakes his head. "Not fair. If you're going to ravish our girl, you can at least have the decency to do it after I leave. I can't walk into this meeting with an erection."

My stomach flips and I don't know if it's the promise of ravishing, their playful back and forth, or the easy use of 'our girl'.

Or all of the above.

Aidan chuckles. "Fair enough." His eyes find mine. "What do you have planned for the day? I was hoping maybe we could spend it together."

My chest warms. I've now spent one-on-one time with Simon and with Blake, but I haven't with Aidan yet. I nod. "I have a few errands to run but after—"

Aidan cuts me off. "I'll go with you. We can make a day of it. I'll take you to lunch after your errands."

My eyes widen. "You want to run errands with me? I have to shop for some fabric."

"Of course. It's about spending time with you. Not specifically what we do."

That is so... nice. None of my boyfriends in the past ever took the slightest interest in my dress designs and none ever shopped with me. I don't talk about it that much with anyone else really, except for the other designers and models I meet at shows. To have someone in my personal life willing to spend time on it with me is new and...wonderful. I find myself having to swallow before I say, "I'd really like that."

"That's perfect," Simon says. "Then you can come back over here and I'll take you both to dinner. I should be finished around six."

Aidan smiles at us as if *we've* given *him* some kind of award or trophy. "Fantastic. I go on shift tomorrow for twenty-four-hours. So this sounds like the perfect way to spend my day. And night," he adds before lifting his cup for a sip.

Simon runs his hand over my hip and gives me another kiss on the neck. "I agree."

I agree too. I think I might still be sleeping and dreaming.

CHAPTER 19
Aidan

"HOW DID you get into pinup modeling?" I ask Elise as I watch her sort through the racks of scarves and hats in the vintage clothing shop she pulled me into.

She looks up with a smile. "It kind of started with things like hats, actually."

"Tell me."

I love just watching her and listening to her. I haven't been able to pick up on a favorite color or specific style she gravitates to yet. She likes an eclectic assortment of things. Kind of a 'when she sees it, she knows' vibe.

And it makes me smile. It's like her taste in men. The three she was with last night are pretty different from one another, but she clearly likes us all. And maybe that's why. We all bring something different to the table.

Blake is intense and bossy, and when he's attentive or sweet it probably feels extra special.

Simon is over the top in romancing her and making her feel like a queen. But he's great at sharing. He wants everyone to be happy.

Then there's me. I fall in between, I suppose. I'm definitely open to sharing thoughts and feelings and want her to feel worshiped in the bedroom, but I'm practical. I'm happy eating sandwiches and shopping for things she likes. I don't need to buy out a restaurant. As for sharing, I'm good with it as long as Elise is. But if that changes for her, it changes for me.

"My mom," she says, moving to another table and running her fingers over the beads of the necklaces displayed. "My dad was... particular. I didn't realize it until later because I was focused on myself and how I was never good enough for him, but after they divorced I started thinking about my mom too and I realized that he was always picking at her too. In different ways, but one of the ways she escaped was to do community theater."

I follow her around the table, watching her pick up earrings and examine them before putting them back. We shopped for a couple of hours before stopping for lunch at one of my favorite sub shops. I do know now that she doesn't like mayo and does like pickles, and I've filed even that little bit of information away.

She's already bought fabric. And two new pairs of shoes. She told me two bolts of fabric were for a special order that had come in the past week for someone else, but that two of them were for dresses for herself. She seems sheepish about buying things for herself, and I want nothing more than to take everything out of her arms, lay it down on the counter, and buy it all for her. I want her to go crazy. I want her to have everything she wants.

Okay, so maybe I'm not *totally* practical when it comes to her. I *would* be more over-the-top maybe if I had a black diamond credit card like Simon does. But I grin. Between Simon and me, we could spoil this girl exactly the way she deserves.

He'd want to buy her real diamonds while I know she prefers costume jewelry, but he'd be able to buy out the entire thrift shop for her.

My mind goes to the third man who was a part of spoiling her in bed last night.

Yeah, okay, all three of us could spoil her right. I think Blake Wilder has more feelings for Elise than he even realizes.

Fortunately, I only have to deal with one man who isn't good at emotions. Simon is an open book. He's extremely easy to read, but is also very forthcoming with his thoughts and feelings. He was nearly giddy this morning having both Elise and me still in his bed, then being able to have coffee with me while she slept in.

It would be very easy to fall for that guy.

I have to keep reminding myself that he's leaving. Chicago is not his full-time home. It sounds like he comes back often, which could be fun. If Elise and I keep dating, maybe we can see Simon whenever he's in town.

Still, it's very important for both Elise and me to remember that there is an expiration date on this foursome.

"I loved being with her backstage for the plays she did," Elise goes on as she plops another hat on her head, looks in the mirror, then turns and gives me a smile.

She looks adorable in it. But I've thought everything she's tried on has looked great. And I'm very aware that it's about the woman and not the accessories.

"It was amazing how she could transform from my mom into a completely new person. I asked her how she did it and she said that the makeup and hair and clothes helped. That when she dressed differently, she felt different."

"That makes sense," I say. "When a call comes in and we all get into our gear, it's like a switch flips. We go from just guys and girls to firefighters. Our gear is obviously functional, keeping us safe, but being in it also helps with focus and mindset."

Elise's eyes sparkle a little when she looks at me. "Exactly. When I was in high school, I discovered the pinup look because of a show my mom did. It just hit me. It was absolutely my style. It was the first thing I really felt good in. So I started trying to create the look myself at thrift stores and using what I had. Then I got into making pieces. And as I got further into design and making my own, I discovered the modeling circuit. I met amazing people, and I got a huge confidence boost." She smiles. "There's nothing like the feeling of being up on stage and showing off something you've created."

As she talks, her entire face lights up. She is passionate and animated and I wish I could take a picture and capture the moment.

"Here," I say, handing her a gorgeous red dress I noticed as soon as we walked into the shop. "Try this on. I want to buy it for you."

"I can make this for a fraction of the cost," she laughs, fingering the tag.

"I'm sure. But this way you can wear it to dinner tonight."

Her eyes widen. "Where are we going for dinner? This is a little overkill."

"I'll send a photo to Simon and tell him to match up the venue with how you look. I guarantee he's going to want you in the dress. Dinner will be a very secondary concern."

She blushes prettily, but I can tell that the compliments matter. I hope she knows every one of them is genuine.

"Try it on," I urge. I might not have a credit card with a limit like Armstrong's, but I can splurge on this girl.

She shakes her head. "You are not buying me this dress."

"I am."

"Aidan, you don't have to."

I step closer to her. "Would you let Simon buy it?"

"I would protest."

"But it would be easier to let him buy it."

She sighs. "Yes."

"Would you let Blake buy it?"

She pauses, then nods. "Probably. Mostly because he wouldn't ask, he'd just do it."

"Then you have to let me buy it. I am going to get just as turned on looking at you in it, imagining stripping you out of it," I tell her, lifting my hand and tucking a strand of hair behind her ear. "And if I buy it for you, that means I get to be the one to undress you. And take the first taste of everything that's underneath."

She takes a shaky breath. "That only seems fair, I guess."

"Please do this for *me*. Don't let those guys have an unfair advantage when it comes to dressing and undressing you."

She laughs softly, breathlessly. "Is that the rule?"

"If you let me buy this dress it is," I say. I love teasing her. I love making her blush. I love making sure she knows that she is the most gorgeous woman I have ever seen.

"Well, if it's a *favor* to you…."

"Exactly. And this dress is really hot, isn't it?"

She looks down at it. "It's fire engine red hot."

"It sure fucking is."

She presses it against her chest, then lifts up on tiptoe and presses a kiss against the corner of my mouth. Then she turns and heads for the dressing rooms.

I'm smiling as I wander through the store waiting for her. Until I find something that I absolutely must have. Yes, she'll be wearing it, but it will be for *me*. Okay, *us*. The guys. I'll share. But she has to have this too.

I grab it and head for the dressing room. I knock softly. "Elise, this too."

She cracks the door, peeking through. She sees what I'm holding and her eyebrows arch. "Oh, really?"

"I'm begging you," I tell her honestly.

She reaches through and plucks the black garter belt and sheer stockings from my fingers. "Begging. I like the sound of that."

She shuts the door again, and I lean back against the wall. "Let me know if you need help with a zipper or anything," I say.

"Oh, I'm fine," she tells me.

A couple of minutes later, she opens the door and comes back out. In what she was wearing before.

I straighten from the wall with a frown. "You're not getting it?"

She gives me a smile. "I'm definitely getting it. And the stockings."

"I don't get to see you try it on?"

She shakes her head. "You'll see it tonight. It'll be a surprise."

"You want to see me spontaneously combust the first time I see it?"

She grins. "Exactly."

I fall just a little bit more in love with her.

"Brat."

She laughs. "And I was wondering if you'll take me somewhere that I've always wanted to go but have never been."

"Over and over," I say huskily.

She gives me that half-surprised-half-delighted smile again. "I mean an actual place, but that was a really good answer."

"I'll take you anywhere, El," I tell her sincerely. If I need to sell my truck or start bartending on my days off to afford a trip, I'll do it.

"So you'll give me a tour of the fire house?"

I stare at her. That's all? "You want to tour the firehouse?" I was definitely not expecting that.

"Of course. I'd love to see where you work. You spend so much time there and I know it's really important to you. Your job isn't just a job. It's really something you have to believe in. I'd love to know more about it." She looks around the shop. "You've taken an interest in my life." Then she looks up at me again. "I want to know about yours, too. And that way I can imagine where you are when you're not with us."

It's like she reached right into my chest and squeezed my heart like a sponge.

She thinks about me when we're not together and she wants to see the place where I spend so much of my life.

And she used the word 'us' so easily.

"And," she adds, giving me a flirtatious little grin. "Firefighters are extremely sexy in case you didn't know."

I move in closer, sliding one of my hands to her ass and giving it a little smack. "You have to behave if I do. I'm the only firefighter you have eyes for."

"Well, I can't promise that," she says. "But I promise to only misbehave with you."

I grin. "Good answer."

I wonder if Simon and Blake are feeling as tightly wound around her finger as I already am.

"Of course I'll take you to the firehouse," I tell her. "I would love to show my gorgeous new girlfriend off to my crew."

She gives me a surprised, but very pleased, smile at my use of the term girlfriend. Is it fast? Maybe. But what the hell else would I call her? I love being with her. I intend to keep fucking her. I want to spend all my free time with her, I can't wait to introduce her to my family, and I want to know everything about her.

If that's not a girlfriend, I don't know what is.

CHAPTER 20
Aidan

TWENTY MINUTES LATER, we're walking through the doors to Fire Station Seventeen.

"Burke!" one of the guys, Wyatt, calls when he notices me. "What the hell are you doing here? You do understand how days off work, right?" But his eyes are on Elise.

And the grin that stretches his stupid face is all for her.

"Yeah, well, when a gorgeous woman says she assumes firefighters are humble, hard-working guys, you have to take the opportunity to prove her right," I shoot back.

He laughs. "Humble? I don't think I know that word. Can you use it in a sentence?"

I really like Wyatt. He's definitely hard working and I trust him in any and every situation we would ever find ourselves in. But humble? No. I'm pretty sure he does not know that word. "Sure," I say. "Those of us who are hardworking, *and humble,* get to bring gorgeous women to the firehouse."

Wyatt laughs. "I gotta get me some of that humble then." He extends his hand to Elise. "I'm Wyatt. Very nice to meet you. Though I feel like we've met before…"

"She was in the elevator on New Year's Eve. You caught a glimpse of her when you weren't geeking out over key locks."

Wyatt shoots me a glare before giving Elise a nod of understanding. "That's right. The damsel in a hot dress."

"I'm Elise," she says, giving him a smile that makes me slide my hand to her ass and squeeze. She looks up at me with a sassy grin.

Wyatt gives me a look. "Didn't know you acted on that."

Yeah, yeah, there can be a lot of down time between calls around here and we all get to know each other pretty well. Serious relationships do come up and no, I haven't mentioned I texted Elise. But now I want to tell everyone everything about her.

"You must have been worried about bringing her around and having her realize she has far better hot, charming firefighter options," Wyatt says, giving Elise a wink.

She laughs.

I roll my eyes at him. "That's why I brought her during *your* shift. Nothing to worry about at all."

"Right." He grins at Elise again. "Well, if you ever need *anything* this guy can't give you, let me know."

Elise leans against me and I wrap an arm around her. "That's sweet but I've got all the hoses and poles I could possibly need, thanks."

Wyatt snorts. "Good to hear." He claps me on the shoulder as he steps past me. "See ya Burke. Don't let sweet Elise here keep you up all night."

I look down at her. "A little tired on the shift will be worth it."

I take her hand and we move further into the station. We say hi to a few more of the crew. I show her the bays where the trucks are parked and don't even try to contain my smile when she exclaims about them and runs her hand over the shiny red sides. She's disappointed to find out that we don't have a dog, but I show her the calendar we shot this year and that I (okay, and others) were holding dogs from the shelter. She's placated when I inform her that they all got adopted after the calendar came out. She also takes one of the extra calendars from the stack and tucks it under her arm.

I take her into the common area, the kitchen, and then we stop by the office of our chief.

"Hey Chief, I wanted to introduce you to someone."

Luke looks up from his desk, then his eyes settle on Elise and his eyebrows arch.

She seems to have that effect on pretty much all men, as far as I can tell. I can't wait to tell Simon and Blake how enamored all of the firefighters are with our girl.

"Hey Burke. Spending your day off with us?"

"Elise wanted to see where I work."

He focuses on her. "Elise, it's nice to meet you."

"Hi."

I look down at her again. Is her voice a little breathless?

I am definitely telling Blake and Simon about *that*.

Luke leans back in his chair. "Burke here is one of our finest. You have good taste."

"I agree." She gives me a smile. "Though after meeting your whole crew, I definitely feel that Chicago is in very good hands in general."

Luke just nods. Then he looks at me. "Well, a firefighter does need to be good with his hands and has to be able to handle the heat."

Jesus. I roll my eyes. Luke comes off as gruff and demanding, but I know a few things about him that not *every* member of the crew is privy to. Luke is single and does date and he likes things pretty spicy. He's not actually flirting with Elise, though another guy might take it that way. But he's definitely not talking about the job right now.

Subtle, he is *not*.

"*Anyway*," I say. "I'm going to show Elise around a little more. Don't want to interrupt your very important work, Chief."

"Appreciate you looking out for me," he says, nodding. "Really appreciate you brightening my day by bringing Elise by."

I put my hand on her lower back and turn her toward the door, shaking my head at my Chief. "Knock it off."

He smirks. "Bye Elise. Hope to see you again. "

"Bye," she says with a finger waggle.

I nudge her out into the hallway and pull his door closed behind us. Then I look down at her. "You were flirting with my boss."

She widens her eyes. "I was not. I was being friendly to your boss."

"Yeah, with your pretty brown eyes, and your luscious mouth, and your flirty little smiles, and your gorgeous curves."

She giggles and I love the sound.

"I can't help any of that," she protests.

I look up and down the hallway, then grab her hand and tug her toward the third door on the left. My sleeping quarters. I push her inside and shut the door behind us.

"Oh wow, you actually have a little bedroom?" she asks, taking in the built-in bed with the stacked storage drawers underneath, the hooks on the wall, and the fold down desk and chair inside the small room.

"Every station is a little different. We were lucky to have a remodel not that long ago. When I started out, we had an open room with a bunch of bunk beds, but they've done studies showing that firefighters are often sleep deprived and to improve on that, remodeling and providing private rooms or at least partitioned spaces, helps." I shake my head. "They could have asked any firefighter and he or she could have told them that without needing a *study*."

She smiles and looks around. "Is this the one you use all the time?"

I nod. "I share it with another guy. We work opposite shifts."

She turns in the small space, then goes to the bed and sits on the edge, bouncing up and down. "It's pretty comfortable."

I nod. "Not quite like at home, definitely not as nice as what's at Simon's," I say with a grin. "But I don't sleep too bad here."

I move in close to her, our knees bumping. I gaze down into her beautiful, upturned face. "You know, it occurs to me that when you were talking about having plenty of hoses and poles to keep you satisfied, that I haven't been a part of that yet."

Her eyes widen. "Of course you have. I remember you definitely being there last night and I was absolutely turned on and having a *fantastic* time because of *all* of you."

I can't believe that I only kissed this woman for the first time last night. I feel like we have been seeing each other much longer than we have.

"Have you ever been fucked in a firehouse, Elise?" I ask, cupping her cheek.

Her eyes immediately widen with interest, and she shakes her head as she wets her lips. "No."

"Would you like to be?"

"Very much." She pauses.

I take a hand and tug her to stand, then trade places with her. "It'll have to be quick, and you'll have to be quiet. These walls aren't super thick."

She shivers and I know it's with excitement.

"Yes sir, Lieutenant."

Oh, fuck, I like that.

I reach for her, sliding my hand underneath the hem of her long shirt. "Drop your jacket," I command softly as my thumbs hook into the top waistband of her leggings.

I start tugging as she slips out of the jacket and tosses it to the side. Her fingers go to the buttons on her shirt, but I shake my head. "Can't undress you fully, but need this sweet pussy." When I get her leggings and panties to her ankles, she steps out of them.

I run my hand back up her inner thigh, then cup her pussy. She's already wet. "Are you wet for me? Or all the firefighters here?"

She smiles. "You. Definitely you."

I don't know if I believe her completely, but that's a good enough answer. I slide my middle finger into her.

Her hands go to grip my shoulders and she moans. "*Aidan.*"

"Oh, I fucking love hearing my name on your lips," I tell her.

She's breathing faster already as I circle my thumb.

"Climb up and straddle me."

She does as I command without hesitation. My lap is now full of sweet, wet, willing woman, and I have never been happier inside this fire house.

"Kiss me."

She leans in and presses her mouth to mine. My hand that is not finger fucking her, cups the back of her head and I deepen the kiss. Our tongues tangle as I add a second finger and feel her shudder.

I pull back. "Condom. Left pocket."

What can I say? I'm an optimist. Especially after Simon essentially gave me the green light to have fun with her by myself today. The three of us guys haven't really discussed any rules about what happens when the four of us are not together, but she's been on dates with both of them and I know she and Simon have slept together. If Blake hasn't taken advantage of one-on-one time with her, that's on him.

"Put it on me," I say against her mouth, pumping my fingers in and out.

She reaches between us, fumbling with my fly and zipper, but manages to open my pants and when I lift my hips, she pushes my pants and boxers out of the way. She gives me two long, firm strokes and I groan. "Jesus woman."

"I love that you're so hard already," she breathes.

"I've been hard since I woke up next to you this morning," I tell her. "Every single thing about you, about this day, just being with you, turns me on."

She rewards me for that answer with another deep kiss. Then she rips open the condom and rolls it down my length.

Regretfully, I remove my hand from her hot cunt, my only consolation that my cock will soon be deep in this gorgeous, amazing woman that has already become so important to me.

"Come here," I mutter as I grip her ass and bring her forward and then down on my cock.

I sink into her and we both moan into one another's mouth.

She feels so fucking good. We're not doing anything kinky, nothing unusual, nothing neither of us hasn't done before, but it feels new.

I start moving her, but she happily joins in, sliding up and down, dragging her tight, hot walls along my length. Our rhythm is steady but fast, and deep.

I would love to have her fully naked, but just being inside her, filling her up like this is enough for now. This is our first time, but I already know it's the first of many.

"You fucking feel like heaven," I tell her. "Jesus Elise, you're so damned good."

Her pussy clenches around me and she half moans, half laughs. "How is this *this* good?" she asks. "We're not even naked. And I want you naked so much."

"We've got time," I promise, squeezing her ass. "Just need you right now. Just need to make you come apart."

"I'm close," she tells me.

I reach down between us, circling over her clit. She moans and starts riding me even faster.

God, I wish I could see her tits bouncing. I want to suck on her nipples. I want to make her scream. What was I thinking pulling her in here where none of that can happen?

I press my mouth against her neck and nip gently.

She gasps, and then her pussy is clenching as she comes, my name on her lips.

"Oh my God, Aid—"

I clamp my hand over her mouth to muffle her cry, loving that she *can't* stay quiet.

I don't know if there's anyone in any of the other rooms, but there could easily be someone walking past the hallway.

Her pussy milks me, and I feel my climax slam into me.

I bury my face in her neck, gritting my teeth as I come hard.

Last night, with her gorgeous lips wrapped around me was amazing, but it's nothing like being buried deep inside her.

I resist the urge to shout, but I thrust and thrust and thrust until I'm completely empty.

I hug her against me, breathing hard, stroking my hand up and down her back.

We stay like that for a few minutes, but we can't stay as long as I would like.

Eventually I squeeze her. "Okay, so welcome to Station Seventeen."

She laughs softly and kisses me, then pushes off my lap.

I grin at her as I stand.

I open one of the drawers where there's a box of tissues. We clean up a bit, but once we're dressed again, I lead her down the hall to the women's locker room.

"I'll meet you right back out here."

After we both clean up more fully in the locker rooms, I walk her out, our fingers linked.

Wyatt sees us and calls out, "Great to meet you, Elise!"

She waves back to him. "I can't wait to *come* back."

I swat her ass even as I laugh. "You are so much trouble."

She nods. "I know. That's why I'm hooking up with *three* guys who seem to like trouble."

I lean in and say huskily, "Actually, I think we love it."

Her surprised, happy smile convinces me that I'm definitely falling for this woman. Fast and hard.

CHAPTER 21
Simon

"SHE'S UPSTAIRS WITH BLAKE," Luna McNeill says as Aidan and I approach the counter at Books and Buns bakery. "She just got off."

I raise my eyebrows. Aidan snorts. We exchange a grin.

Luna laughs. "She got off of *work*, you dirty boys. Her shift ended."

"So she's getting off then," I say cheerfully, eyeing the row of pastries in the case. "I doubt Wilder could resist the urge to get his hands on her first."

"I agree." Aidan glances toward the stairs. "Should we just go up or text her first?"

"If you think I'm going to waste an opportunity to barge in on Wilder unannounced then you really don't know me at all."

Aidan just clears his throat, but doesn't respond.

I glance over at him. His expression is reserved.

We've just got back from having lunch together in my suite, something I had hoped would be more sex than salads, but he didn't make any moves, so I didn't either.

He and I haven't had sex yet, even though it's been over a week, and I want him desperately.

I sat through three courses with a raging hard cock waiting for him to indicate in some way he wanted to move the feast to the bedroom, but he didn't.

He's clearly holding back, and I know why.

Aidan attaches to people.

He's already attaching to Elise. His blue eyes go soft whenever he looks at her, and he can't resist the urge to touch her whenever he's around her. Not just sexually, but casually. A hand on her back. A sweeping of her hair off of her cheek. Brushing his thigh against hers in the car. He constantly peppers her with little kisses and she laughs easily when he's around, soaking up his attention.

In sharp contrast, he's pulled back from me. He actually showed very little enthusiasm about having lunch together in my suite, suggesting a hot dog stand instead.

A fucking hot dog stand.

Nothing kills romance like questionable pork in a stale preservative-filled bun.

But he's distancing himself from me because I'm heading back to London.

He knows this is temporary, and he's protecting himself. Protecting his *heart*.

Because when he doesn't know I'm looking, I see the way he looks at me too—with growing affection.

And I love it.

It feels incredible to have a man who is as solid and caring as Aidan look at me like I'm someone worthy of his love.

Not because I buy him things.

Not because I can introduce him to influential people or take him on a luxurious vacation.

But because he likes *me*.

It's pushing me to the edge of falling head over ass for him.

How to handle it isn't entirely clear to me yet, but I do know that I don't want to initiate sex. I feel confident if I did, he would tumble into bed naked with me, and I don't want him to have regrets. It has to be his idea.

Patience isn't my biggest virtue, but my mum always said the harder you work for something, the sweeter it tastes.

Ironic coming from a woman who never worked for a damn thing in her life, but a valid sentiment.

Speaking of sweets, I point to the row of pain au chocolat. "I'll take four of those. One for each of us."

"I don't need one," Aidan says. "I'll just take a coffee. Black. Thanks, Luna."

Aside from his fondness for domestic beer and steak, Aidan is a healthy eater. He has no sweet tooth. He's also stubborn. He's already pulling his wallet out to pay for his coffee and I don't say anything. I just let him pay for it.

I can't remember what kind of coffee Elise drinks, which makes me feel terrible. But in all fairness, the morning after I stayed at her place, I was deliciously distracted. "A latte for Elise?" I guess. "And two more black coffees."

I suspect Wilder drinks his black just to punish himself. He's that kind of guy.

Luna packages up my sweets and puts the coffee cups into a travel case. I give her a generous tip. "Thank you. Much appreciated."

"Don't keep Elise up all night," she warns us. "She's opening again tomorrow and I don't think my blood pressure can take another kitchen fire."

Even though she's smiling and clearly teasing, I still wince. "I feel responsible for that. She was utterly desperate to get back to me."

Luna laughs. "Oh, I bet."

Aidan shakes his head, but he's smiling. "Ready? I feel like this is going to take more than ten minutes."

The plan is not to have sex tonight, though I won't object to it.

We're supposed to be creating a mutual history for Blake and Elise so that when they meet his grandmother, they have a solid lock on knowing each other and their relationship timeline.

I'm looking forward to it because I want to know every little snippet about Elise that I can.

Also, I can't wait to torment Blake.

He's fun to poke.

And I don't mean that literally.

"I feel like this could take *hours*," I agree. "He's as stubborn as you are."

"I'm not stubborn," Aidan protests in surprise as we head toward the stairs.

I eye the coffee in his hand pointedly.

He makes a face. "Much."

"We'll just have to get the basics down. Family background, how long they've been dating, that sort of thing."

We climb the stairs.

"Do you think they can pull off lovey-dovey?"

"I don't see why not. They've seen each other naked."

"That is true."

Jostling the coffee carrier and the bag, I knock on the door. "We're here." I start to turn the knob.

"Should you just go in?" Aidan asks.

"It never occurred to me not to."

"But that seems…"

"She's expecting us." I knock again to appease his sense of politeness.

I don't get a response.

But I can clearly hear Elise moaning inside.

That has me turning the knob and shoving the unlocked door open.

What greets us is a thing of beauty.

Elise is naked, her ass moving up and down as she enthusiastically rides Blake on the one uncluttered spot that exists on her couch. Her hair is cascading down her pale back as his big hands grip her waist. I can see his pants are still partially on, and he's still wearing a shirt.

"Simon! Aidan!" she calls out, clearly startled.

For some odd and utterly adorable reason, she covers her bare breasts when she half-turns to us.

"I would say they're pretty convincing," I tell Aidan, glancing back at him over my shoulder. "That screams lovey-dovey to me."

Aidan is intently staring. "That is straight up hot."

"Oh, God, should I stop?" Elise asks breathlessly, even as she continues to bob up and down on Wilder's cock.

"No," Blake growls. "Don't you dare."

"Don't stop on my behalf. I'm enjoying the view." Watching Elise take her pleasure is gorgeous. I adjust myself in my pants.

"Absolutely not," Aidan says. "I want to see you come, El. You're going to come so hard, aren't you?"

His voice has lowered, and his attention is rapt on her.

"Yes, yes, I am!"

"Then do it," he tells her. "Soak Wilder with that sweet pussy."

"Fuck yeah," Blake says.

She releases her breasts and puts her hands on his shoulders. Then she grinds her clit against him while he uses his strength to lift her up and down.

Her head snaps back and she breaks.

"Jesus fuck," I murmur. "You're so beautiful, love."

Wilder is coming with gritted teeth and a rough groan.

Then Aidan is behind her, shifting her hair off her dewy shoulder and pressing a kiss there. "That was incredible."

"Oh my God," she laughs softly. "That was an accident."

I set the items I'm carrying on her coffee table. "Your clothes fell off by accident? Or the orgasm. In either case, I understand. Happens to the best of us. I brought you a latte."

"I was in the shower and Blake got here and... well, anyway, thank you. I'd love a latte. I usually try not to add sugar, but that sounds amazing right now."

Her cheeks are pink from exertion as I hold my hand out to her to help her climb off of Wilder's lap.

Legs shaking, she brushes her lips over mine. "Hi."

"Hi." I wrap my arms around her and kiss her more deeply,

running my palms over her spine. Her bare skin is warm, and she smells incredible—like sex and cinnamon.

My very own sweet treat.

"I should put some clothes on." She steps back and stumbles a little over Blake's enormous feet.

He catches her, but she does tumble back down into his lap. He tugs her hair and tilts her face to him, giving her a tender kiss that makes me smile in amusement. There's a soft side there beneath all that facial hair and grumbling.

She lifts her hand again and Aidan takes it this time and it's his turn to claim a kiss.

I love that this is so easy, the four of us.

It feels natural.

Right.

Which makes my chest tighten.

Elise slips past Aidan and pulls a silky piece of floral fabric off of a pile of clothes on her dining table. A second later she has it on and belted.

"Of course you have a silky robe," I groan. "You are truly the perfect woman."

She giggles. "Being at home isn't an excuse to not look cute. Fashion is a full-time job."

"You get no argument from me." I shove a pile of papers off of a chair and take a seat. "So. How do we ensure Grandma believes yours is a love story for the ages?"

Elise bites her bottom lip and glances at Blake. He's pulled his pants back up and zipped them. He stands up with a wince, condom in hand and disappears into the bathroom without a word.

"Did we interrupt something?" I ask, half-joking, mostly serious.

She shakes her head. "Nothing more than what you saw."

I study her. She looks a little bewildered herself.

But she adds, "I didn't mean to exclude the two of you…"

Aidan takes her the latte and cups her chin. "Hey. This is about *you.* You call the shots here. We all agreed to that, I'm pretty sure. You're allowed to do whatever you want with us, separately or together." He glances over at me. "Right?"

"Absolutely." I open the bakery bag. "I'm content with my pastry. We need to focus on Operation Cabin Procurement. Would you like a pain au chocolat?"

"I would love one." She takes the pastry from me and bites into it immediately, giving a moan of pleasure. "So good."

I love that Elise enjoys food and isn't on a permanent diet, like some women I've dated in the past. She doesn't deny herself life's little pleasures and I find that, and her, incredibly sexy.

Aidan's eyes have darkened, watching her flick her tongue across her lip to catch an errant crumb, but he sticks to the plan and just lifts his coffee to his mouth.

Blake returns and I realize he's limping a little, though he's trying to hide it. "You okay?" I ask in concern.

He nods, but it's clear he's in pain.

I follow him into the kitchen, where he's grabbing a glass and filling it with water. I'm opening a cabinet for a plate I don't actually need when I see him lift his closed fist to his mouth and shake pills in. He quickly swallows.

"New injury or old?" I ask, striving for casual.

He glances over at me. For a second, I don't think he's going to answer.

But then he says, "More like permanent. Hip flexor tendonitis. Inflammation of the iliopsoas muscle and tendons from overuse. It will probably get better after retirement though."

I'm no expert on hockey, but even I know the goaltender goes up and down repeatedly during a game. Overuse seems like an understatement.

"I see. I'm sure you're getting excellent medical treatment, but I know a great massage therapist if you need one."

He nods. "Thanks." He hesitates, then adds, "I appreciate it."

"Sure." I shoot him a grin. "And I'm happy to take over the task of fucking Elise from behind while you lay on the bed."

He rolls his eyes. "Very fucking generous, Armstrong. You're a real pal."

But we're both chuckling though as we return to the living room. Aidan and Elise are squeezed onto her couch together and he's blowing on her coffee to make sure it isn't too hot.

This guy. Always the protector. The caregiver.

I love that we all bring something different to the table.

Blake chooses to lean against the wall and now I understand him better. Sometimes what appears to be aloofness is just him being in pain and not wanting to show it. He's resting his hip right now, not excluding himself from our group around the coffee table.

"We need the story of how you met," I announce. "Elise, go."

"We met at a bar."

"We met through Crew and Luna," Blake immediately protests.

"At a bar."

He makes a face.

"What, that isn't romantic enough for you?" I ask.

"Not really. That's so basic."

"But it's the truth." Elise sips her latte. "It's always better to stick to the truth when possible. Lies can trip you up."

Blake just grunts.

"What about your first date?" Aidan asks.

"I took her to dinner, then afterward we had a foursome with two other guys."

That makes me laugh. "I suggest you skip the foursome part unless you want to give grandma a stroke."

"Tell me about your family." Elise takes another bite of her pastry. "I know you have a sister, but I don't even know where you grew up."

"Minnesota. How about you?"

"South Bend. I moved here for the fashion and the food. What's your sister's name?"

"Brooke. You're an only child?"

She nods.

"Are you a cat or dog person?" Aidan asks.

"Dog."

"Cat," Elise says.

"What kind of toothpaste does Elise use?"

"This isn't immigration, for fuck's sake. It's my grandma."

"But do you know? You were just in her bathroom."

Elise eyes him curiously. "If you know the answer to this I'm going to be amazed. There's a lot going on in my bathroom."

"It's Crest gel. Cinnamon flavor."

Aidan and I look at Elise.

Her jaw drops. "He's right. Was that just a lucky guess?"

"No one uses cinnamon toothpaste, El," Aidan says. "That is not a lucky guess."

It does explain why she smells like cinnamon all the time. I just thought she magically absorbed the bakery scent into her skin.

"The only reason I know that is because it's the only item in your bathroom that is recognizable to me. All the rest of it is girl shit," Blake admits.

"Girl shit. Fair enough." Elise eyes him with clear affection. "That's so romantic."

"I can be romantic."

"I'm sure you can."

But then he shocks all of us by digging in his pocket and pulling out a ring box.

Elise gasps.

"Okay," Aidan says. "I like where this is going."

Blake moves over to Elise and he drops down onto a knee, giving zero indication that he's in any pain at all. He flips open the box. "Elise, will you fake marry me?"

For a second, her eyes light up when she sees the ring, which even from my seat several feet away, I can see is high quality. That's a clear-cut diamond.

Then Elise shutters her expression. "Of course I will fake marry you."

She lets him slip the ring on her finger.

But I realize that Elise, for a brief moment, wanted it to be real.

We're all in dangerous fucking territory.

But I have no intention of stopping what we're doing.

CHAPTER 22
Blake

MY FUCKING hip is killing me.

Thank God we're going into the third period.

This game seems to be taking forever. I know it's only in part because of my hip. I've been playing well, the other team hasn't scored on me yet, and our guys are playing with real fire tonight. But some games are like this. Some go by in a snap and others are grueling and I could swear they take days.

Part of it tonight is because I am having to truly force myself to concentrate.

Part of my mind is on my hip, part of it is on the text from my grandmother that came in as I was still in the locker room before the game. She's back in town from her Florida trip and ready to meet my fiancée.

Of course, she needs to meet Elise. How am I going to convince her that I am madly in love and that Elise will be living with me happily ever after in the cabin if the two women never meet?

I'm just not sure I'm ready.

That takes things to another level.

Things weren't supposed to get to 'levels' at all.

Elise is doing me a favor. She's an acquaintance who agreed to pose as my fake girlfriend for three months. That's it.

But… that's not it. It's already more than that.

I like her. Being with her is easy and fun. I look forward to her texts. I *love* fucking her. When I was out of town, I was actually eager to get back to Chicago so I could see her. And not just to get her naked.

That was not supposed to happen.

I haven't even seen her *that* much. Or fucked her that much. Definitely not enough.

But dammit, it has been enough.

Enough to complicate everything.

As the rest of the team warms up for the last period, I let my gaze do something I've been fighting all night.

I find Elise in the stands.

Warmth floods my chest and I have to actually fight a smile.

She's not just here. She's here wearing my jersey. I'm sure there are social media posts about it even now.

She's also not here alone. She's sitting behind Dani and Luna. But more importantly, she's sitting between Simon and Aidan.

More importantly? Where did that come from?

But I know very well. Because Simon and Aidan are here to watch me too. Sure, they are here to keep Elise company, but the three of them are at this game because of me.

It's unusual for me to have people in the stands.

Most of my family lives too far away for it to be a regular thing. All of the people I consider friends are on the team, so they're not in the stands watching, of course. My grandmother does make it to a game here and there, but she prefers to watch my games on television. She hates dealing with crowds. She says that she can follow the puck more easily with the help of the cameras, and I know the cold air makes her joints stiff.

It's nice having them here.

It's really fucking nice to have Elise in that jersey.

It's also very nice to be thinking about going home with them after the game.

Sometimes I have plans after a game. Sometimes they involve a woman.

But I don't think I've ever looked forward to after games as much as I have since the four of us have been hanging out and hooking up.

I'm feeling things that I didn't expect. And that I probably shouldn't be.

I'm *fake* dating her.

But are you? A little voice in my head asks. I mean, we might be faking how serious it is, and that we're engaged and going to be owning a cabin in Minnesota together, but we're kind of *actually* dating.

We do *actually* go out on dates. We talk. We flirt. We text. We fuck.

I mean…that's dating, isn't it?

Whistles split the air, indicating the period is about to start and I take a deep breath and re-focus. I've got more hockey to play. I can't be thinking about my love life.

I'm as superstitious as the next goalie, so I start my pre-period ritual.

I run my hand through my hair twice, tap my helmet against each of my shin guards before placing on my head, then tap my stick three times against the left side of the net, three times on the right, then three times on the top. That's me putting my "force-field" up. It started when I was a kid but, hey, it works. Then I'm ready to go.

Just a few more minutes until I can be with Elise.

"I didn't realize how much hotter it would be watching you play after we've had sex," Elise says in my ear as I hug her in the back hallway after the game. "Now I know how much power your hips have and how capable your hands are and what those shoulders look like bare naked." She shivers. "So. Hot."

When I walked out of the locker room and saw her standing

there with Luna and Dani and the other wives and girlfriends, my heart had done a little flip-flop.

Fuck. I really am getting into this thing between us, aren't I?

Then she says things like that and I'm *really* into it.

I lift my head and grin down at her. "You had no idea at all? You're honestly trying to convince me that you never thought about fucking me while watching me play before? I don't believe that for a second."

She lifts one shoulder. "Of course I did. And I always thought you were hot when you played. I guess I didn't realize it could get even hotter."

I lean in and put my mouth against her ear. "I'll have you know that partway through the second period I was rethinking the whole blow jobs for every save thing. I was killing it out there and I am becoming *very* fond of your hot little mouth."

She laughs and her warm breath brushes over my neck as an equally warm feeling rushes through my chest. "No longer worried about my jaw getting tired?" she asks.

"Well, I figured they don't have to all be at once. Not all in one night, you know? We can save them up. There are my days off, after all. And a long off-season."

She's still smiling but her eyes are studying me now. "You're retiring after this year."

Right. Shit. "Yeah, I mean I'll need a few things to get me through those first few months, right?"

Which is also insinuating that she'll still be around then. That we'll still be doing things that involve my dick in her mouth.

But this is all *temporary*. As well as being fake-ish.

Fuck. Why is that all so easy to forget?

I start to pull back a little, but her arms tighten around my waist. "I am very happy to keep tally marks of how many saves you make and reward you for every single one."

I look at her. Is she offering to make this go past the ninety-day mark?

And do I want that?

"You don't even have to keep track," I say. "That's a stat that other people keep track of for us."

She gives me a grin. "Even better."

I keep an arm around her as she says goodbye to her friends and we head down the hallway toward the parking lot.

"My place?" I ask.

"Simon and Aidan asked about that. Simon said we're welcome at his place, but yours is fine too," she tells me.

I wait for a second to see if I feel a stab of jealousy or annoyance.

Neither come.

In truth, not only is it hot to be with Simon and Aidan with Elise, but they're making it easier to keep some distance between me and this girl.

Seeing her sitting in the stands, having her waiting for me in the back hallway, just having my number on her back, is making me feel more attached to her than I ever expected. I've been attracted to her, wanted to take her to bed, even thought that taking her to a few social functions would be fun, but I didn't expect to want things like waking up in the night and finding her head on my chest and wanting to lay and listen to her breathing. I didn't expect to love her little fashion shows where she tries on new dresses for us. The dresses are sexy, of course, but her excitement, creativity, and the way she approaches her passion with joy and a smart-as-a-whip business mind, is also a turn on. She's smart, sassy, and almost too self-deprecating.

I wish she could see how amazing she really is.

All of this combines to make me want to pull back a little. I haven't felt invested in a woman in longer than I can remember. I want to know how her day was, how her various dress projects are coming along, how many orders she got this week, what she had for lunch, for fuck's sake.

That is too much.

So it's a good thing that Aiden and Simon are part of this. I need to pull back.

"Simon's place is great," I say. The fewer memories we make in *my* apartment, the better. Then they won't haunt me when this is over.

"Great." She pulls her phone out and sends a quick message.

Her phone pings a couple seconds later.

She smiles at me. "They'll meet us there."

"Did they bring you to the arena?" I ask as I guide her to my truck in the players' parking lot.

She shakes her head. "I got an Uber. I figured since I'm seeing three guys, the chances of having a ride home after the game were pretty good."

I help her up into the passenger seat of my truck, then impulsively lean in to kiss her lips. "Thanks for coming tonight."

She looks surprised and I brace myself for her to remind me that it was part of our deal.

But, instead, she says, "I loved it."

"You look really fucking good in my jersey."

She grins. "Let me guess. That means I'm keeping it on in bed later?"

"It does," I confirm.

Two nights ago, Aidan brought her a Chicago Fire Department T-shirt, which he insisted she wear while we fucked her.

I've been dreaming of getting him back with this jersey.

Which I know he knows.

Which makes it even more fun.

Dammit, I like those guys too.

Great.

"By the way," I tell her. "When Aidan's fucking you, you have to be on hands and knees."

She looks very interested. She is always ready to go for all three of us and we can't get enough. "And why is that?" she asks.

"So he has to stare at my name and number the entire time."

I shut the door while she's still laughing. I'm also grinning as I get in. I barely even wince as my hip twinges.

Then I take us to my girlfriend's other boyfriend's apartment.

CHAPTER 23
Aidan

FOR TWO FUCKING weeks I've been dancing around what is happening between me and Simon.

Which emotionally, is a lot. I'm falling hard for him and trying not to.

Physically? We haven't even kissed again.

For two torturous weeks I've been waiting to see if he will try to get me naked, and he hasn't. I've bounced between disappointment and total gratitude.

I know if we share the intimacy of sex, I'm not going to be able to resist my deeper feelings for him. Then when he heads back to London, I'll be emotionally fucked. Devastated.

But I also know that Simon isn't holding back because he doesn't want me that way. He wants to have sex with me. He's holding back because I'm holding back.

For a guy who always has a smile and a charming comeback, who can navigate any social situation, he's very intuitive. It's what makes him so capable of talking to anyone and making them feel like a million bucks. He understands people.

He sees *me*.

And he's giving me space to sort out my head all on my own.

I think he grasps the reality of it—if he rips my shirt off and slips a hand down my pants, we're having sex.

But he wants me to be sure.

It makes me care about him even more.

Blake is out of town playing hockey.

Elise is working tonight, finishing up a custom order for a client.

Simon asked me to join him at this corporate fundraiser event for cancer research and so here I am, dressed in a suit that makes me feel ridiculous, gripping a beer bottle like it's a life raft, and watching him work the crowd.

He makes every person he speaks to feel special. He remembers names, spouse's names, whose family member had cancer, and asks pointed questions about how they're doing. His assistant is hovering, trying to give him facts and stats to use as talking points, but he waves her off repeatedly.

"I may be shit at keeping my desk clean, but I've got this," he tells her.

He makes me feel special too.

My suit is off-the-rack and yet twice he's told me how good I look and how much he appreciates me being here.

He also leaned in and murmured, "Though I *really* appreciate you wearing nothing at all when we're fucking our gorgeous girl."

He introduces me as his date, "a firefighter who saved me from going up in veritable flames."

I don't know how he can say shit like "veritable flames" with a straight face, but that's Simon Armstrong.

His voice, with that sexy-as-hell accent, has started popping up in my dreams nightly.

I'm getting better and more plentiful sex than I have in my entire life with Elise, yet I'm waking up every morning with a throbbing erection because of the British billionaire's voice.

It's driving me up the damn wall.

When Simon shakes a man's hand and tells him, "I knew you

had this beat, William, never doubted it for a minute," and the guy in his thirties holding hands with a crying woman, I know there is no use denying what I'm feeling.

I'm falling in love with Simon.

If we never touch each other ever again, I'm going to be heartbroken when he returns to London. There's no denying it. That's the outcome, because it's already too late.

We both clearly want to have sex, and I figure there's no reason to deny either of us that pleasure.

I'm going to be devastated either way when he leaves. So I can be heartbroken without ever having had the chance to share all of myself with him, or I can be heartbroken and have no regrets.

I choose no regrets every damn time.

No holding back, no more stilted dates, no fighting it.

Just wonderful fucking memories.

An hour later, after I've done my best to support him, chatting with various people and encouraging them to donate what they see fit to, I'm resolved to make the most of the time I have left with Simon.

"You ready to head out?" he asks me.

"If you are, yes."

"I'm more than ready."

I look around for somewhere to set my empty beer bottle down.

Simon takes it out of my hand and does his magic trick, where all he does is lift and tilt the bottle and suddenly someone is taking it from him.

"My place for a drink?" he asks once we're downstairs. "Or are you calling it a night?"

"I was thinking you could come to my place," I tell him, loosening my tie. "If that's okay with you."

His eyebrows shoot up. "Your place? I'd love to. I can open your cupboards and poke in your drawers and learn all your secrets."

I laugh. "I don't have any secrets."

"I know. That's what I love about you."

He says it casually, but it punches me in the gut.

Damn it.

I've already fallen in love with him.

Twenty minutes later, I unlock my door and gesture for Simon to go in ahead of me.

"I don't know why I expected a dog to bound to the door and greet us," Simon says. "I guess you just seem like a dog lover."

"I do love dogs. It's just too hard with my schedule to have one right now. Maybe someday." When I have a live-in partner. That's who I need in my life in order to have a dog. That's what I want for myself.

"I love dogs too," he says. "Especially hounds. But I have the same issue. Not home enough."

He looks around at my compact living space. "This is nice, Aidan."

I have the upstairs unit of a brick duplex. I wouldn't call myself any sort of expert on home design, but I don't have secondhand furniture or a keg in my living room. I pride myself on living like a grown ass man, past my college curb-picked junk days.

"Thanks. It's still a little messy from my brother staying here over his Christmas break from school. He didn't want to stay with my mother because she still thinks he should come home at midnight. It offended her, but she's working through it." I toe off my shoes and offer to take Simon's coat that he's stripped off.

I hang up both our coats and note how he lines up his shoes under the bench, the shiny dress shoes sporting a damaging layer of Chicago snow slush. It makes me feel compelled to fix it.

"Do you want me to clean those off?" I ask.

"What?" He shoots me a look and unbuttons his suit jacket. "God, no. They're only my twelfth best pair." He gives me a wink.

I shake my head as I chuckle. "Half the time I can't even tell if you're serious or not."

"I never joke about Italian shoes."

He wanders into the living room and spends a few minutes cruising past my display of family photos and my grandfather's military awards, which he bestowed on me because my grandmother was tired of dusting them. I don't mind dusting, or any cleaning. It makes me feel productive.

"Is this you?" he asks, pointing to a picture of me and my little brother and sister dressed like ninja turtles for Halloween. "The green one."

"Yep."

"You were a cute kid."

I have my arm protectively around my sister, who was probably four at the time. "Thanks. I had a very good childhood."

"Lucky chap," he says lightly.

He has talked a little about his childhood with me, and the whole boarding-school-at-eight-thing still is hard to wrap my head around. "I'm sorry you didn't have that."

Simon waves me off. "Oh, my childhood was fine. Like I told you, I had great friends and lovely houseparents at school. I'm not crying over rich boy problems. But I can see how you grew into such a good man, Aidan. Seriously."

The compliment warms me inside out. "Can I get you a drink? I have cheap bourbon."

"My favorite."

That makes me laugh. "Liar."

"I'm adaptable."

He is. Blake and I basically crashed his relationship with Elise and he was totally willing to shift and give her what she needs—all three of us.

For now, anyway.

I still have no idea what will happen when Blake retreats to the woods and Simon is back in London. I hope it's me and Elise then.

But tonight is about *now*.

And right now it's me and Simon and I want all of him.

I pour Simon a drink and grab myself a beer. My heart is racing, my blood thick with desire. I hand it to him and say, "Come here. I want to show you something."

"If it's a pet reptile, no thank you."

"No. I don't have any reptiles." I strip my suit jacket off as I head down the hallway to my bedroom. I toss it over the chair I have in the corner and flick on a soft lamp. I set my beer on the dresser.

"The bedroom. What do you need to show me in here?" he asks, tone flirty but also a little hesitant.

I turn and close the gap between us, gripping the back of his head. "This."

Then I kiss him.

I almost sigh in relief. It feels amazing to have my lips on his again, to smell his expensive cologne up close and personal. To let go of my fears.

Simon immediately responds, putting his hands on my waist and tugging me closer as we move our mouths together in a hot, passionate kiss. Urgency explodes inside me and I flick my tongue across the seam of his lips.

He opens for me easily and the thrust of our tongues has me gripping his hair with taut fingers.

Simon pulls back, breathing heavily.

"I missed this," he admits.

"Me too," I say gruffly. Then I add, "More. I need more."

"Are you sure?" he asks.

"Yes." I nip his bottom lip. "Don't ask me again."

I shove his suit jacket down off of his shoulders so I can fist my fingers into the fabric of his shirt as I take his mouth over and over with mine, our tongues hotly tangled.

He pulls back again, making me groan in disappointment.

"I think I've figured out how our relationship dynamic can work," he says, as he runs his palms over my shoulders, lightly squeezing my biceps.

Hearing him say "relationship" sends a jolt through me. "How so?"

"You let me buy whatever I want for you and I let you boss me around in bed."

Oh, hell yeah.

Now I'm *really* turned on.

"It's the perfect power balance, don't you think?" He gives me a smile that rises slowly, confidently, deliciously.

"I can work with that," I say gruffly. "Now take your shirt off before I rip it off."

He obeys, but he's unbuttoning so slowly it's pure fucking torture.

"Not fast enough." I reach out and tear it apart, sending buttons flying.

Simon gives a low moan. "That's it. Take control, Aidan."

Then it dawns on me he was moving at a snail's pace on purpose. I tug his undershirt from his pants and slip my hand down inside them to give a hard squeeze on his dick. I begin to pump my hand up and down. "You are way more devious than I gave you credit for."

"I prefer clever." He is gritting his teeth now, grinding himself into my touch.

I stop stroking him.

"Fuck, why did you stop?"

"Now are you going to do what I say or not?"

"I'll do anything and everything you say," he pants. "God save the king."

I almost laugh, but I'm too turned on to do much more than give a strangled gasp as I slide my hand up and down his hard length one more time.

Then stepping back, I shove him onto the bed. "Everything off. Now."

I've seen Simon naked before, but I've never watched him strip for *me*.

He undoes his belt as he locks eyes with me and then shoves his pants and boxers down to his ankles.

Bending over, I yank them off his feet and toss them to the side. It gives me a perfect angle to brush my hand across his balls and stroke lightly up his dick.

"Fuck," he breathes. "Yes."

Just to torture him—and myself—I step back again, unbuttoning the top button of my shirt. When he reaches out to help me, I stop him.

"Nope. I'm in charge, remember?"

His eyes darken, but he nods.

Then I unbutton the rest of my shirt and yank it and my undershirt off in one fell swoop.

"God, you're so fucking hot," he says.

I'll take the ego stroke any day of the week. "It gets better," I say with a smirk.

"Oh, I know."

My pants hit the floor, along with my boxer briefs. I step between his legs. "Come here."

Simon doesn't hesitate. He drops his head down and eases his warm mouth over my cock. I hiss at the first contact.

"That's it. So good."

Good is a fucking understatement. Simon is working me from tip to shaft, slicking me up with his mouth, and I let my eyes drift shut briefly.

Then I open them again immediately, wanting to watch his shoulders, the top of his head, as he uses his hand to follow his mouth in a tight, hot slide. I don't want to miss a moment of this, knowing there's an expiration date on my time with Simon.

"Oh, yeah, suck it, baby," I encourage him.

He glances up at me and seeing his brown eyes soaked with desire while his mouth is full of my cock, almost undoes me.

I let him lick and suck, cradling my balls for another minute and then I can't take it anymore.

"Enough," I pant, pulling off. "I need you, Simon."

Digging in my nightstand I pull out lube and a condom, which I rip open with my teeth.

"Let me." He takes the condom from me and rolls it on my erection, squeezing the base of my shaft, while stroking himself simultaneously.

Bending down, I kiss him, hot and hard. Demanding. He tastes like bourbon and I feel almost drunk on the sensation of being here with him. I drop my knee to the mattress, ease him back onto the bed, crowding him.

As my tongue swirls over his, I tease between his thighs, testing his entrance by pressing the pad of my thumb inside. Simon moans into my mouth.

Breaking off the kiss, I lube up my fingers and start to work his hole with just the tip of my index finger, watching his face to gauge his reaction. "Good?"

"More," he breathes. "Give me more."

"Only when I say so," I tell him, my balls tight with anticipation. "Or you beg."

I continue to swirl a finger over him, teasing in and out, brushing over his thighs with the rest of my hand.

"*Aidan.* Damn it."

"That doesn't sound like begging to me."

My mouth is thick with desire, my cock resting heavy against his leg, and I'm driving myself as crazy as I am him. I'm used to Simon being a bit of a smartass, charming and quick with a comeback. He isn't saying much, just bucking his hips, trying to encourage me, his right fingers digging deep grooves into my forearm.

I tease and tease until I'm in a haze and he half-lifts off of the bed. He looks as desperate as I feel.

"Fuck me, Aidan. I'm begging you."

Lust and satisfaction punch me in the gut.

"That's what I wanted to hear." I reward him with first one finger, then two, easing deep inside him, stretching him.

He groans from the back of his throat, collapsing back onto the bed, grip falling off of me. "Jesus fuck."

I shove his knees up and apart and edge him above my fingers, stroking across his rim, before thrusting my cock in at the same time I ease my fingers out.

We both let out mutual cries of pleasure.

I pause, buried deep inside him, swallowing hard.

"You want me to fuck you?" I ask. "Say it again."

"I want you to fuck me."

I can't hold back anymore. I take him, pounding into him so hard I'm shifting him back on the bed. But I've waited weeks for this moment and now here I am, his body a tight fist wrapped around my dick, his moans everything I've ever wanted.

"You feel so fucking fantastic, baby."

As I slam into him over and over, I stare down at him, in awe that we got here. That I get to be with him, however brief.

"I'm close," I warn him through gritted teeth. "Holy fuck, you're just…"

His hands grip my ass and he squeezes, his gaze earnest. "Let me see you come. Drive it deep and just fucking let go."

I couldn't resist it if I tried.

My balls tense and I break hard, a moan tearing from my lips as he encourages me, raising his hips.

"You're so fucking beautiful," he murmurs. "Inside and out."

I've never been called beautiful before and it makes me feel… everything. My body is still spasming, buried to the hilt in his ass, and our gazes are locked, the connection intense, undeniable.

Finally, I ease up and pause, dropping my gaze to his dick while I drag in some much needed air. I feel fucking vulnerable all of a sudden, and I don't want to show him that.

I pull out and toss the condom on the nightstand while I collapse beside him.

He turns to kiss me, but I ignore the quest, and instead shift down a little so I can study his dick.

"You don't have to—

He starts to speak, then immediately cuts off when I cover him with my mouth.

"Forget what I just said. Yes, you have to," he says.

I chuckle, lips vibrating on his warm skin. That sounds more like Simon.

Working him with my mouth and hand, I cup his balls and ease a finger into his ass.

"Too much," he pants. "Got to come."

I don't stop. Instead, I take him deep and open my throat.

When he moans, his hot cum lands in the back of my mouth, and I swallow all his salty pleasure.

Easing off, I wipe my bottom lip and smile up at him over his dick, flicking my tongue over the last bit of moisture pooling on his head.

"That was embarrassingly fast," he says.

"My fault," I say with a grin.

He nods. "Yes. It absolutely fucking was your fault. Brutal tease. I loved it."

That makes me laugh. Happy and satisfied, I withdraw my finger and lay down beside him. This time when he tries to kiss me, I lean in, giving him a deep kiss.

"Do you need anything?" I ask him. "I can go get some water."

He shakes his head. "Don't you dare leave this bed. I don't need anything. Just you," he says simply.

"Works for me." I stretch and turn the lamp off.

Simon closes his eyes and lightly runs his fingers over my chest. "I'm wondering something."

"What are you wondering about?" I ask as I pull the comforter up and over our sweaty bodies.

"Dogs," he murmurs, half-asleep.

"Dogs?" That's the last thing I expected him to say.

"Yes. What breed we would get if the world wasn't a cold, heartless place conspiring to keep us apart and devoid of furry companions."

My heart just about stops beating in my chest.

That's about as close to a confession of love as I ever expected to get from him.

I run my hand over the back of his hair. "I like golden retrievers."

But he's already asleep.

I lay awake, just savoring the feel of him sprawled over my chest under the blankets, the snow gently falling down outside my bedroom window.

It takes me damn near two hours to fall asleep.

CHAPTER 24
Simon

"THIS ISN'T AN ISSUE," I say with false confidence as I glance around Elise's bedroom. "So where do we start to look? What is a likely place?"

Elise is running around the room in a full-blown panic, tossing pillows and dresses and jeans in all directions as she desperately searches for her driver's license, which she needs to show at the pinup competition this afternoon. I start on her makeup table, shifting items around, looking for the ID card.

"I don't know! I don't even drive so I don't keep it in my wallet. I just always grab it when I'm going to a bar or somewhere they might card me." Elise has her hair in rollers with a cap over it and she's in her bra and panties.

If she wasn't so distraught, I would enjoy the view, but I feel terrible that she's so stressed out.

"Why do I even have a driver's license if I don't drive?" she asks rhetorically. "I should just get a state ID. Maybe I'll do that next week. I have Thursday off. I wonder what Blake's schedule is like that day? If he's out of town, I'm definitely free all day because you'll be at work and Aidan always works Thursdays."

She's already lost focus.

I notice she does that when she's under pressure. Whatever is the main issue that is causing her stress gets mentally shoved to the side and replaced with something she has a solution for. While she's contemplating next week and a fictional trip to the DMV, she has stopped looking for her license and is rechecking her roller suitcase, which is stacked on top of her bed and filled with carefully folded and packed items for the competition.

The suitcase was packed last night. I lounged on the sofa and listened to a finance podcast while she worked on it. I didn't go into the bedroom because I knew talking would distract her, so I left her to it.

Everything clothing and makeup wise she has ready to go because those are important to her.

Details like the location of the competition and her license were left until right now, as we're supposed to be walking out the door to drive to Milwaukee.

That was her answer when I asked for the location of the competition. Milwaukee.

"Where specifically?" I asked her five minutes earlier.

That had sent her fruitlessly searching through her email for the vital information.

Which somehow had jogged her memory that she needed her license and now here we are.

"What is the name of the competition?" I ask her as I open the drawers on her vanity. More makeup.

"It's the Milwaukee Pin Up Contest. That's the actual name."

Easy enough. I text my assistant.

> Find me the venue and address for the Milwaukee Pin Up Contest happening today. Book hotel nearby and have light refreshments sent to the front desk of the venue under my name. Water, protein bars, etc. Check contest rules and send me highlights. High urgency.

Elise has already indicated we need to stop for snacks en route, but we're already thirty minutes behind schedule. The competition starts at six and it's already two. At least I put her prop box in the car last night. I have no idea what was in there, but she told me it was for the performance portion of the pageant.

"Do you think I can just tell them I lost my license?" she asks, remembering what she's supposed to be doing as she zips her suitcase shut.

I'll give them a thousand dollars if I have to. But I have one more quick thought. "Do you have a passport? I'm sure you can use that instead."

Her eyes light up. She's in full makeup already, just planning on dressing and touching up her hair at the venue.

"I do," she says. "My mom took me on a cruise to Mexico for my twenty-second birthday. Have you ever been to Mexico? It was really beautiful. I went through two entire tubes of sunscreen though because I burn so easily."

There it is again. The wander.

I redirect. "Do you know where the passport is?" I ignore her other comments.

This is the first time I'll have spent two nights in a row with Elise and I want her to enjoy herself, not be fretting about getting there on time.

"Yes! I think." She dashes over to her closet, which affords me a fantastic view of her breasts threatening to spill out of her bra from the movement.

Bloody hell. I can't allow myself to be distracted either.

"I have a box with important documents. It's in there because I haven't used it in years. I think. I mean, why would I move it?"

That is an excellent question, but I don't rule the possibility out.

Now her ass is sky high in her black panties as she bends over and rustles around in the closet. "It's in here! And oh. So is my driver's license. That was smart of me."

I grin before I quickly school my features.

God, this woman is delectable.

"Brilliant, love. Then we're all set."

My phone dings. It's a series of attachments from my assistant with all the necessary information.

"I have the address for the venue."

"I guess I should get dressed."

"As much as I love you out of clothes, yes, that's a great idea." I take her suitcase off of the bed and drop it on the floor, pulling the handle up.

It seems wise to remove it from her view or she'll unzip it and start going through her clothes again to ensure she hasn't forgotten anything. I know she hasn't because she was completely confident the night before. After a month of dating Elise, I feel like I know her really well.

She still wavers sometimes between apologizing for her disorganization and shrugging it off as who she is. I've never had an issue with it. None of us are perfect, or even someone else's perceived version of perfection. Relationships are about meeting the other person where they are, and I hope that I've done that for Elise. She has done that for me. She never presses me about the fact that I have to go back to London or what that means.

What it means in my mind is simply that there will be periods of time where I don't get to see her or Aidan in person but that I can hop on a plane and return to Chicago for work or just because I want to.

By then, Blake will be living in the woods in his cherished cabin.

Which is a shame, really. Hell, I know that's what he wants, but the four of us work well together in my not-so-humble opinion.

With varying schedules and busy careers, we don't get to spend as much time together as a foursome as I think Elise would like, but it also means that whenever she wants company, she has some, even if it can't be all of us.

I take the suitcase into the living room and set it by the front door. I rummage through her kitchen, grabbing a couple packets of the trail mix I know she likes, and filling her jumbo water bottle up with fresh water from the refrigerator. I snag her a bottled iced coffee as well and put them all into a grocery bag.

Then I pop my head back into the bedroom. Elise is dressed in tight stretchy jeans, high heel boots and an ice blue fuzzy sweater that shows off the shape of her breasts perfectly.

"You look gorgeous," I tell her truthfully.

She laughs. "I have a hair net on."

"So? It's not covering your face. I can't wait to see you up on stage."

"Thanks, Simon." She takes a deep breath and adds, "I wish Aidan and Blake could be here."

"I know, love. Next time they can coordinate schedules better." Blake is out of town playing hockey and Aidan is on a twenty-four-hour shift.

She purses her lips, but then she nods.

"Okay, exit check," I tell her. "Phone?"

She raises it up to show me. "Check."

"Put it in your purse." If she doesn't, she's liable to set it down on a table on the way out as she picks something else up.

"In the purse. Check." She obeys.

This is a routine I've started with her and realized it actually helps me a lot, too. I'm just as likely to forget my phone as Elise without my assistant Sonia around.

"Phone, Simon?"

I hold my own up and show her I'm inserting in the breast pocket of my overcoat. "In the coat."

"Keys?"

She grabs them off the kitchen counter. "Keys. Car keys?"

I lift them up and show her. "License?"

She digs in her jeans pocket and waves the little plastic card at me. "Wallet?"

I pat my pocket. "Wallet. I think we're good to go. I grabbed some water too." I hold her coat out for her and she slips into it.

She turns her head for a kiss and I happily oblige.

"Thank you for coming with me."

"I wouldn't miss it for the world. I'm excited to see you kick ass."

Elise laughs. "Graciousness is part of the judging. I love meeting the other contestants."

I grab the grocery bag and her suitcase handle and we head out.

Elise astonishes me. Not only is she hands down the most gorgeous woman in the competition, she's a natural on stage. She walks with confidence in her heels, white stockings with snowflakes on them and a vintage white winter swing coat. She has her hands tucked into the muff, but pulls one out to blow a kiss to the audience.

It's obviously meant for the judges, but she does lock eyes with me as she does it and my heart damn near stops.

Clearing my throat, I shift in my chair. My dick is getting hard.

I glance over at the man sitting next to me and he is eyeing Elise with naked interest.

"Damn," he says. "That is one hot woman."

"Mine," I say.

"Mine what?" the guy asks, looking at me briefly in confusion before returning his attention to Elise, who is descending the steps off the stage.

"My woman."

I don't think I've ever said that in such a possessive way in my entire life, but fuck all, Elise is mine. This man can find his own pinup model.

"Ah. Lucky you." He grins.

I nod, satisfied he's got the message.

This was just the brief introduction to all the candidates, but Miss Sugar Starling is a clear hit. She gets a loud round of applause.

The next round is a question-and-answer segment and Elise sounds charming and eloquent as she discusses her hobbies, which include fashion design, baking, and swing dancing, which I did not know. Now I instantly have a fantasy that involves taking her dancing.

Not that I can dance.

But I will learn if that's what she's interested in.

There's another round of competition that I assume is some kind of talent portion, but it's more like performance art. Elise does a routine to music that involves shedding layers, starting with her coat, revealing a peacock blue velvet swing dress as if she's going to a cocktail party. One of her props is a martini glass, which she mimics sipping from and then poses.

Then, to my utter shock and delight, she manages to drop the dress in one casual maneuver and is in a sexy silk ice blue nightgown and tying her hair up with a ribbon. It's not revealing, other than her glorious cleavage. It's just a promise of good things to come, for the man lucky enough to be her partner.

I heartily agree with the man next to me.

Lucky me.

The whole routine is meant to simulate a night out for a woman in winter in the fifties and not only is her body displayed to perfection, so are her fashions. Her expressions are adorable and sweetly sexy. I'm blown away by how creative she is and so clearly in her element. Her focus is spot on and she's clearly enjoying herself.

When she takes second place, I'm both proud of her and convinced the judges got it wrong. All the women gave it their all, but she is the clear winner.

Finally, after a round of photos of the contestants and the top prize winners, Elise is free to come down and meet me. I give her a big hug and tell her, "You were incredible. I'm astonished by your poise. I would have froze up there with all those eyes on me."

She laughs and gives me a look, throwing her arms around me. "Oh, bullshit. You can charm a snake, Simon."

Then she kisses me softly and tenderly wipes off the lipstick she's transferred to my mouth. "Thank you for the standing ovation."

"You deserved it."

"At least you didn't catcall me. That would have been embarrassing."

"That's more of a Wilder move," I say.

She gives a shrug. "I don't think that will ever happen. We're meeting with his grandmother soon and then that's that."

I can't tell how she feels about losing Blake in her life, but I'm British and we don't pry. If she wanted to tell me, she would.

"Care for a cocktail?"

"Yes, I just need to say goodbye to all the other girls."

I watch her dash off and give hugs and big smiles and hold out her phone to exchange numbers and probably her design business information. I'm content to just soak in her pure joy.

When she returns, I murmur to her, "I need to serve you a martini while you're wearing that nightgown. Just so I can see it drop to the floor."

"I think that can be arranged."

We can't get out of that venue and to the hotel fast enough.

CHAPTER 25
Elise

THIS IS GREAT. *This is great. This is great.*

I keep repeating the words over and over as I rip the stitches out of the dress in my lap. Again.

I'm overwhelmed. I'll admit it. But I don't know what to do about it.

My show was a huge success, and I got eight orders afterward. Which is amazing.

And terrible.

What was I thinking? How am I supposed to get *eight* custom orders done on time? There's no way.

This is great. This is great. Your business is growing. This is what you want.

I feel tears stinging the backs of my eyes and I take a deep breath.

This *is* what I want.

I just need to figure out how to manage these eight orders. Having three sketches of each of the eight, all eight started, and second guessing myself on every one of them is *not* it.

I'll just—

Suddenly I hear a pounding on my door and, "Elise! Baby! It's Simon!"

My heart jumps into my throat and I drop everything I was holding.

"Just kick it down!"

That's Aidan's voice.

What the *hell*?

I frown at the door. "Just open it!" I yell. I'm sure it's not locked. I just ran down to the bakery...

I frown.

I don't remember the last time I actually went out or came in the door, to be honest. I usually lock it before bed, of course, but I slept only a couple of hours last night and that's because I fell asleep on the floor, using one of the might-someday-be-a-dress piles of fabric as a pillow.

The door bursts open and Simon and Aidan storm inside.

"Elise!" Simon finds me amongst the explosion of fabric, sketch pad pages, and cardboard boxes my supplies have been delivered in. He comes straight for me, sinking to his knees and pulling me into his chest. "Jesus, are you alright?"

My nose is smashed against his shoulder and I'm suddenly wondering when I last brushed my teeth. "Yes. Mostly."

He leans back, studying me. I look up over his shoulder to find Aidan glowering at me.

Glowering. Sweet, amazing Aidan.

"What?" I ask him. "What happened?"

"We were waiting for you at the hockey game," Aidan says, his voice tight.

"What? Oh, my God!" My gaze flies to the wall clock. It's eight-thirty on... I have no idea what day it is.

Well, obviously it's Tuesday because I'm supposed to be at the hockey game. I know better than to think that these guys have the wrong day and somehow *I'm* right.

"Oh my God. I'm so sorry." Obviously, Aidan is angry. Which is fair. And I'm not surprised. This is what always happens. I'm *shocked* this hasn't happened before now, to be honest. We've all been seeing each other for a few weeks and that I just now screwed up a date is a miracle.

"I just totally lost track of time." I push Simon back and shove material, scissors, my sketch pad and pencils to the floor. "Why didn't you call me?"

"We did," Simon says. "Over and over."

Fuck. Of course they did. I look around. I haven't seen my phone in hours. Probably since yesterday. It's here somewhere. I'm pretty sure. God knows how many calls and texts I've missed.

Fuck, what if some of them are from customers?

The idea of *more* customers dumps unwanted adrenaline into my system. I want more customers, but I swear if there's one more order on my phone, I'm going to burst into tears. It's too much all at once. I want steady orders. Orders I can keep up with. I want to feel like a badass boss, staying on top of things, and doing amazing work.

This isn't it.

Maybe it will never be it.

It's not like organization and time management are skills I possess. I can design and sew, but I need more than that if I want to run the business I want.

Then I look up at Aidan and Simon again.

Aidan. And Simon. Are here. In my apartment. Because I was supposed to meet them at Blake's game.

I completely forgot. I had a date with my *three* boyfriends and I forgot.

I let them all down at once.

I stand quickly. "I'm so sorry. I can just…"

But I can't get ready for the game *now*. It's way past the start and they're *here*. And I'm a mess. I would need to shower and get dressed and do my hair.

I look down.

Oh, *God*. I'm wearing shorts—something I almost never do—and a baggy shirt that I pulled from a pile on the chair in my room. I'm not wearing a bra and I haven't showered since before the pinup show.

My hand flies to my hair.

I have no idea how it looks, but I'm pretty sure it's not good.

I know Simon told me that he is a mess too, but he has people who keep him on schedule and organized. And Aidan... he so effortlessly takes care of things.

I *hate* them seeing me like this. A messy apartment is one thing. Seeing *me* as the disaster I am is frustrating.

"You have to leave," I tell them.

My heart is hammering and I have literally no idea what my next step should be.

I feel like I should shower. But I should finish these dresses. I should find my phone and check my messages. I should maybe eat. When did I last eat? I should maybe go to bed. My head feels a little fuzzy and I don't know if it's low blood sugar, or lack of sleep, or just a mental breakdown. Or all three.

"Elise," Simon says softly, stepping forward. He steps on my scissors, but he doesn't even look down. "It's okay. We were just concerned."

I shake my head. "It's not okay. I blew you off. *All* of you. I wasn't there for Blake."

"Blake is fine," Simon tells me. "He's also at work. He knows how to do that no matter who is in the stands. Or who isn't. He understands that you have a job too, and that you had a great show the other day and he'll be happy to know that you've got a ton of orders to fill."

I shake my head harder. "But I *forgot*. If I needed to work I should have *told* you all that. But I didn't. I just forgot."

Simon steps forward, taking my upper arms in his hands and squeezing. "It's okay."

I stiffen in his hold. "Please don't hug me. I don't remember the last time I showered. Or brushed my teeth. Or my hair."

His gaze softens. "You look beautiful."

I frown and shake my head. "Don't say that. That is not true. That just makes this all worse."

Finally, Aidan speaks. "Elise."

I look around Simon to him.

"We are not angry. We were *worried*. We were afraid you had a car accident. Or you were sick. I'll admit my memory flashed back to the fire for a minute, too."

I wince. I can understand why they might have thought about all of those things. Shit. It's sweet that they were worried and one more reason I suck at having a boyfriend.

"And yes," he goes on. "It is a little frustrating that you misplace your phone, and we're going to have to come up with a way to compensate for that. But we're obviously able to just come over and check on you. Which is what we did." He takes a step closer. "You're getting used to having three men who care about where and how you are. We're getting used to having a girl that sometimes loses track of time and isn't easy to check on. We just need to come up with some ways of dealing with that. But we are not angry with you," he repeats.

He holds out a hand, palm up. Instinctively, I reach out and take it. He tugs me toward him, and I brace for the hug.

But he doesn't hug me. He turns me toward the bathroom. "Get in the shower. I'll make you something to eat. Then we'll talk through your plan for the dresses. I'm sure you're feeling overwhelmed. Maybe we can just help you put a list together or something. But sometimes it just helps to talk it through."

I open my mouth to protest, then close it. That all sounds really nice. And it's a *plan*.

I haven't had one of those in a couple of days.

I know I'll feel better after a shower. And I genuinely don't remember the last time I ate. Also, I do need to talk through my plan. It also occurs to me that tomorrow, I have a few errands I need to do. I need to run to pick up some more thread and silk. But if I call ahead to the fabric store, Gillian, who knows me well, could pull those items out and one of the guys would be happy to pick them up for me.

I take a deep breath. "Okay—"

My front door bursts open just then and I scream and turn toward it.

There's a huge, wild-eyed, hockey player standing there.

"Blake!"

"Jesus Christ, Elise." He stomps toward me and wraps his huge arms around me, picking me up off the floor before I have a chance to protest that I don't look or smell very good. "I was so worried."

I hug him back, hoping that will make him put me down. But he holds me for several long seconds.

"Blake," Simon finally says. "You need to let her go. She really wants to take a shower."

Blake pulls back to look into my face. "Are you okay?"

I nod, not opening my mouth for fear of breathing horrible breath on him.

"She got caught up in her new dress orders and lost track of time," Aidan fills in.

I feel Blake relax under me. "Thank God."

I blink. He's *glad*?

He puts me down. "Fuck, girl." He runs a hand over my head and then down my back. "I was so fucking scared. I looked up and you weren't in the stands. I thought you were just running late. But then later I looked up and these guys were gone. And then they were gone for way longer than a concession stand run and I started to freak out."

I swallow hard. "I'm sorry," I whisper.

He finally looks around, taking in Simon and Aidan, and then the apartment. "It's okay. You've got a lot going on. I was just worried."

"Wait, how are you here?" Aidan asks. "The game's not over, is it?"

"No. I…" He blows out a breath and gives me a sheepish look. "I left."

"You *left*?" Simon asks.

I stare up at Blake. Oh, my God. I made such a mess here.

"I was benched," Blake explains. "I was playing like shit. They scored on me twice, so they pulled me. I figured if I wasn't going to help the team anyway, I could leave." He cups my face. "I needed to get over here."

"Oh my God, Blake." I shake my head. "I'm *so* sorry. This is so bad. It's all my fault."

"It's okay." He shrugs. "They'll fine me but what are they gonna do? Fire me?" He gives me a half smile that actually makes my stomach swoop a little. "I needed to be sure you were okay. It's just a game."

"But… you should have cal…" Then I realize that he probably tried. *Fuck*. The fact that I can't keep track of my phone is a *huge* problem. I have to get my shit together!

But he turns a frown on Aidan and Simon. "I *would have* just called, but I don't have your numbers," he tells the guys. "We need to fix that."

They both nod. "We do. We all need each other's numbers."

I look from one man to the next to the next. They're going to exchange numbers. So they can keep in touch. About me. I mean, maybe other things too, but I'm the reason they're including Blake.

That makes me feel… good. Cared for.

"Shower," Aidan tells me, his voice firm but gentle. "We'll get food and talk."

Talk. Right. They'll help me make a plan. That's what I need.

I look at them all again. They're here. Because they were worried. Because they care.

Maybe I don't need a plan. Or a shower or food.

Maybe I just need them.

Blake turns me and nudges me toward the bathroom door. "Go. You need help washing your hair or anything?"

I look up at him, trying to gauge if he's being flirty. But I think he's actually really just asking. I shake my head. "No. I'm just a mess, not injured."

"I'll grab you some clean clothes and put them on the counter," he says, nudging me again.

So I decide to just do this—focus on one thing at a time. Let the guys tell me what the next step is. That alone is a relief, to be honest. To just not have to make big decisions. Just one step at a time.

I take my time in the shower. I just stand under the warm spray for several minutes doing nothing else. I try to quiet my mind.

When I get out, I pull on the sweatpants and hoodie Blake laid out for me. He even added underwear. But no bra. Which is so great. I hate wearing bras at home.

I pull my hair up on top of my head, not bothering to dry it.

I don't even put moisturizer on.

I do brush my teeth though.

Then I take a breath before heading out to the living room.

If they cleaned up, straightened the room up for me, I will be appreciative. I will not freak out. It's fine. I'll find everything again. They don't know that if *I* don't put something away or move something, it makes it ten times harder to find. They'll have done it to help. I have to remember that and not get frustrated.

But when I step into the living room, it seems nothing has been moved at all.

It's still a disaster. But I can see where all eight partial dresses are. I know where my sketch pad is. I know where my scissors are.

I breathe out.

Aidan is in the kitchen and I can smell the grilled cheese sandwiches he's making. My stomach growls and I feel the tension leave my body.

Blake is sitting on the floor, propped up against one section of the wall. Simon is perched on the arm of the couch. Even the cushion that's usually clear is covered at the moment.

They stop talking when they see me.

Simon comes to his feet. "Better, love?"

I nod and go to him. "Much."

He pulls me into his arms and hugs me. "Good."

Over the next hour, we all eat. Blake places an order to have more bread and cheese delivered, since he eats four sandwiches himself. He adds several other things to the order and says, "Don't be fucking ridiculous," when I offer to pay him back.

When the order arrives, I'm delighted to find he included ice cream.

They also help me organize my projects.

I'm amazed at how they do it.

They simply ask questions. And then play the part of human clothing racks.

Blake holds project one in his right hand, two in his left.

Aidan takes project three and four.

Simon five and six.

Seven and eight are spread out on the couch.

They even let me scotch tape my sketches to their shirts and slacks so I can match my ideas up with the material.

Blake ends up with a hat on his head and a scarf around his neck.

Aidan lets me try five different purses with one of the pieces of fabric he's holding.

Simon wears a fascinator hat and a belt, which should be ridiculous but actually only proves the man looks good in anything.

The ideas are so much clearer to me now. Seeing them all displayed like this allows me to visualize them, move things around, and get a better idea of what needs to happen first and what can wait.

They also ask me questions. They make me think through how

long things will take, what my customers' expectations are, ways I can be more efficient.

And Simon records it all on his phone so I can listen to it later and remember the plan.

When I've got it all worked out, they help me hang everything up in an organized fashion around my dining table.

I even end up letting Simon buy me a clothing rack to keep in that area of the apartment. It really will be so much easier to keep things organized.

And then...I move everything off my couch, making organized piles on my dining room chairs, and we all collapse together on my couch for the first time, the three guys side by side and me with my head in Simon's lap, my ass in Aidan's, and my feet in Blake's.

Blake starts rubbing my feet, Aidan's hand splays over my stomach, and Simon starts playing with my hair.

And I don't think I've ever been happier.

"So," I say, looking down the length of the couch at Blake. "How was the game?"

"Good," he says. "Until I got distracted."

I grimace. That was a silly question. "I am *really* sorry. Good thing this will be over after your grandmother gives you the cabin."

He squeezes my foot harder. "Good thing?"

"You can't have a real girlfriend who's going to be a distraction like that. What if the team had lost?" We'd pulled the final score up and the Racketeers had pulled out the win even without Blake. We hadn't listened in on the press conference to see what, if anything, was being said about his poor third period. "But for now, while you're stuck with me, I'm really sorry and I'll...work on keeping my phone nearby." But I frown as I say it. My intentions are always good. I don't *mean* to misplace things. I don't know if there's a better solution.

"What if you had a landline installed?" Aidan asks. "You'd only give the number out to certain people so it wouldn't ring all the time, but if it's mounted on the wall in here, you couldn't misplace it and you'd have a number anyone could call if they really needed you."

I look at him and smile. "That's a good idea. Do they still install landlines?"

"I'll get you one," Simon says immediately. "Tomorrow."

"Elise."

I look at Blake. "Yeah?"

His voice is husky when he says, "I don't feel *stuck* with you."

My heart squeezes and I smile.

"And now that I have Aidan and Simon's numbers, and we can all get a hold of each other—" Blake looks at the other men. "I mean the benefit of there being *three* of us is that someone can always get to you."

My independent, don't-need-anyone ass immediately thinks, "That's ridiculous." But the part of me that's falling for these men, my *heart*, really likes that.

And then my stupid brain reminds me that all of this is temporary.

Blake only needs all of this until he gets the cabin. Simon will be going back to London. So no, they won't be able to 'get to me'.

But, on the bright side, I also won't be driving them crazy by losing track of time and missing dates.

CHAPTER 26
Blake

I'M massaging Elise's feet and wondering what the hell it means that I abandoned a hockey game—even on the bench—for this incredible, sexy, talented woman when I realize something.

"Where's your ring?" I demand.

"What?" Elise glances up at me, her head in Simon's lap.

"Your engagement ring." Her hands are crossed over her stomach and she's not wearing the diamond that I definitely overpaid for given this relationship isn't even real.

"Oh!" She lifts her hands. "It's in my jewelry box. I'm not used to wearing it and it was throwing me off when I was working." She studies me. "Are you mad? I didn't lose it, I swear."

I shake my head, throat tight. I'm feeling territorial and intense and all kinds of fucked up in the head, but I am definitely not angry with her. "I'm not mad. Even if you did lose it, I wouldn't be mad."

She could lose ten rings and I'd just buy her another one.

Whoa.

Where the *fuck* did that thought come from?

I know exactly where it came from. My stupid ass heart.

Until tonight, until I thought something terrible had happened to Elise, I had myself convinced this was all fake. Just sex.

Amazing, knock-your-fucking-socks-off sex.

But just sex.

Somewhere along the way, it became a friendship too. Not just with Elise, but with Simon and Aidan. We share a camaraderie. A team sport, so to speak.

The guys have been my defenders, deflecting any emotional pucks getting flung my way.

I don't have to face my emotions when they're around and we're all laughing and talking and pleasuring Elise. Because of that, ignoring that maybe what I'm feeling for Elise isn't just friends with benefits didn't feel wrong.

Neither did lying our asses off to my poor, unsuspecting, incredibly manipulative, emotionally blackmailing grandmother.

Now it doesn't feel *right* either.

"Because this isn't not real," Elise says.

It's not a question. She poses it as fact.

I'm so turned inside out, I don't even know what's real anymore. Everything feels muddy and complicated. Before I can protest that isn't really what I meant, she speaks again.

"But the ring was expensive, I'm sure. I'm taking good care of it, I promise."

Simon is brushing Elise's hair off of her face, but Aidan is eyeing me. I can feel the cool stare on me, even though I'm not looking at him.

"I trust you," I say simply. I do.

But it feels like there is more to all of this than I realized and my stomach is too tight still from my earlier fear to be willing to address it right now.

Or maybe I just don't want to face it.

Whatever the excuse is I'm telling myself, I know one surefire way to avoid any uncomfortable feelings.

Sex.

"Are you relaxed now?" I ask her, my voice casual, but low. "We can get you even more relaxed."

"How so?" she asks flirtatiously, her eyebrows lifting, the corner of her mouth turning up in a smile.

"What do you say, boys, should we give Miss Sugar some sugar?"

"Count me in." Simon nods enthusiastically.

"Anything to help our girl relax," Aidan adds.

Elise turns her hand and finds Aidan's dick with unerring accuracy. "I'd much prefer cock."

Aidan sucks in his breath as she strokes him.

"I think that can be arranged." Running my fingers over the bottom of her foot, I'm amused when she suddenly recoils and almost kicks the shit out of me.

"Stop! I'm ticklish."

I hold her firmly so she doesn't nail me in the chin. "Whoa, slugger, you're going to take out my teeth, and I'm already missing two."

She goes still and squints up at me. "You're missing two teeth? Where?"

"Well, they've been replaced with implants. But I'd like to keep the rest." Even as I say it, I tickle her foot again, relieved to be back in familiar territory.

Teasing, flirting, fucking.

I need to stick to the script we've all established together.

Elise starts to buck, trying to escape my touch. Aidan gives a groan.

"Oh, shit, sorry," Elise says as she yanks her foot away from me and stops thrashing. "Did I hurt you, Aidan?"

He shakes his head. "No. But all that wiggling, El, you're killing me."

His hand slips under her sweatshirt, and he palms her breast.

Elise stops moving and gives a breathy sigh that has me instantly hard. Her head arches back and her lips part.

"You should not have admitted you're ticklish," Simon says. "Because now I need to test everywhere."

But he doesn't tickle her. Instead, while Aidan is under her sweatshirt, clearly massaging her breasts and nipples, Simon glides his fingers through her hair and down over her temples, digging the pads of his thumbs into her pressure points. He traces her eyebrows, her nose, her cheekbones, all while watching her with affection and rapt interest.

"Does this tickle?" he murmurs.

"No," she whispers. "That feels amazing."

Aidan brushes his free hand over the apex of her thighs. "How about here?"

She shakes her head. "No. That feels amazing."

All of my crowded thoughts quiet and I just focus on Elise. On how beautiful she looks, her face pink from giggling, free of makeup, her hair a raven blanket spread out over Simon's thighs. She's a knockout when she's dressed to go out, but I like this look on her too. She's relaxed, fully trusting the three of us with her vulnerabilities, with the real her.

Even if the relationship is fake, she's showing me the real Elise, and damn it, I have some very strong feelings for the real Elise.

I may not know what to do with them, but I do know what to do with her right now.

This couch is really fucking small for three grown men and all I have access to is her feet, so I lift one foot and gently kiss her arch, before sliding out from under her and standing up. With one hand, I rip my sweatshirt off over my head from the neck.

Then I perch my large body on the coffee table so I can watch as Simon slips his finger into Elise's mouth, encouraging her to suck on it, as Aidan slides a hand into her leggings and starts to work her clit. Her thighs relax and she opens for him with a pretty little moan, before sinking her teeth into Simon's finger.

"Let me see that eager little pussy." I lean over and yank her leggings down to her ankles.

Elise has on red lace panties that pop against her fair skin and Aidan's big hand has them pulled out taut as his finger saws in and out of her. I can't see her cunt, but it's enough to have me squeezing my dick and adjusting it in my sweatpants.

"You like this so much, don't you?" Aidan asks, his voice thick. "Having three men worship you."

With Simon's finger in her mouth, she can only nod. But she rolls her hips, then pulls back to beg, "More, Aidan."

"Of course, baby, whatever you need." He adds another finger.

Simon removes his finger from her mouth at the same time and Elise gasps, arching up to pump into Aidan's touch. Simon shifts her head, turning her toward him. He undoes his pants, and she eagerly opens her mouth so he can ease his cock between her lips.

My body is tense and I realize I'm tapping my foot up and down, impatiently waiting to enter the game.

But I don't, because there is something so damn sexy about watching her open herself to these two men. Plus, I kind of enjoy torturing myself. I am a goaltender, after all. A born masochist.

I do reach out again though and ease her panties down for a better view. Aidan gets the message and raises her knee up by hooking his free hand under it so that her legs spread. I can see the moisture his touch is creating, see her pretty little plump pussy lips open wide, his fingers buried deep inside her. When he pulls back entirely to swirl over her swollen clit, she's glistening with dewy arousal.

Elise gives a cry of disappointment at the loss, her mouth slipping off of Simon's cock.

He grips her hair. "Don't stop, love."

Elise obeys, turning her head again so he can guide her to move over him, his dick disappearing between her lips over and over.

I swallow hard and resist the urge to fill her pussy with my own finger. Instead, I just reach out and swipe through her heat and soak my finger. Then I put it in my mouth, sucking off her taste and essence.

"You taste so fucking good."

Elise drops her head back, and Simon gives his erection a couple of pumps with his hand.

"Can you…"

She gives a shuddering sigh when Aidan eases a finger back inside her slit.

"What do you need, Sugar?" I ask her gruffly. "And from who?"

"Can you…" She closes her eyes briefly and then looks at me directly. "Can you finger my ass while Aidan fingers my pussy?"

I don't hesitate. "Whatever you need, you get. It's going to get a little crowded but you like that, don't you, you dirty girl?"

She nods, biting her bottom lip as Aidan continues to work her.

"Don't come," he commands her. "If you come, you will be punished."

"I won't come. I promise," she says, even as she sounds like she's going to. Her voice has lifted, her hips rolling frantically.

Aidan immediately removes his fingers. "Get in there, Wilder. Slick your fingers up."

Elise's shoulders slump. "God, I was *so* close."

Simon runs his thumb over her bottom lip. "That's why he stopped, love. We're just getting started."

"You don't want to come before you're getting double fucked, do you?" I demand. "Because we're going to start with fingers first but then you're getting two cocks tonight. That's what you want, isn't it?"

Her eyes are already glassy but the lust that darkens them at my words nearly undoes me. She nods eagerly.

I go down on my knees so I can be closer to her.

But of course, right then, my hip chooses to be a bitch and a sharp pain rocks through my leg. I mask the wince, but I make the mistake of looking at Elise to see if she's noticed. She hasn't. But right behind her, Simon meets my gaze.

He's definitely noticed. He tilts his head in question. I give a small shake of my head.

As if I'd let a little fucking twinge ruin the fun.

At this point, I don't even know what it feels like to be pain free.

Before Simon can say anything, I bury two fingers in Elise's cunt and soak them before easing down and massaging the tight little entrance she wants filled. Once I'm teasing inside with first one finger, then a second, Elise is panting in pleasure.

"Get in there, Aidan. Give this dirty girl what she needs."

"Simon, you have a better angle," Aidan says. "I'll just enjoy the view."

He makes a good point. Simon can slide a hand down over her breasts and her belly and work her more easily. He is pressing in and out immediately, taking the time to also tease at her clit.

I stretch her even more, getting her ready. She's falling into the zone, eyes drifting closed, giving over to the sensations of having both her ass and her pussy finger fucked.

Aidan is watching her closely, and he taps my shoulder after just a minute or two. "Stop, Wilder. She's too close."

I instantly obey and Elise protests by lightly kicking my arm. "Keep going," she demands.

She's flushed and irritated with us, especially when Simon removes his own touch.

I chuckle lightly. "You're a brat. Did you know that?"

She's actually pouting as she gives a heated, "I am not!"

Yet even as she says that, she's trying to force Simon's fingers back inside her.

Aidan takes her wrist. "No, El. Be a good girl."

"I suck at being a good girl."

That makes me grin. "We've noticed."

"Wilder, take this woman to the bedroom," Aidan tells me.

But Simon shakes his head. "No, Aidan, carry her fireman style. I think Elise needs to be flung over your shoulder right now, so I can smack her hot little ass on the way down the hallway."

I glance over at him. I know what he's doing. Sparing me the task of carrying her. It's not necessary. I could carry Elise through ten feet of snow with one hand behind my back if it means I get to fuck her at the end, but I appreciate his concern.

I'm not going to be a dick and reject his gesture.

"How does that sound?" I ask her.

She moistens her lips. "Great idea."

"You want that little ass spanked, don't you?" I give her a little pat.

Her response is to moan in approval.

I stand up and shed my pants, shifting the coffee table out of the way. I take Elise's hands and pull her to an upright position. It puts her face right in my junk.

"Well, hello," she says.

Then she flicks her tongue over my head.

I hiss.

"Not so tough now, are you?" she asks, sounding smug as she cups my balls.

Then she takes me deep.

This definitely wasn't the plan, but I indulge in the sensation of her hot little mouth clasping around my dick three or four times before I step back. Taking her hands, I spin her forward and pull her to her feet.

Covering her lips with mine, I give her a deep, passionate kiss.

Then I crack her on the ass. Hard.

She jumps and gasps.

Aidan groans. "You have no idea what a fantastic view Simon and I have right now."

I do. Elise has a perfect ass. It's full, bouncy, and super soft when you grip it.

It's one of the many reasons I love fucking her from behind.

I have a feeling Aidan and I are going to be arm wrestling over who gets to be the one to take her ass. Simon is more into her breasts, which works well. He can spend an hour sucking her nipples, which are highly sensitive. But both Aidan and I have an ass addiction.

I tug her hand and pull her away from the couch so they can stand up.

Aidan bends down and lifts Elise up with one arm under her ass. She shrieks, but she loves it. She's smiling and laughing.

"That's high enough," she warns him.

"Nope. You're getting the full treatment." He uses his hips and knees to bounce her up and over his shoulder.

Her hair is dangling forward, her sweatshirt bunched up around her waist. "This is ridiculous," she says, but her voice is filled with pure delight.

As Aidan starts down the hallway, Simon reaches out and gives her backside a soft little smack. It's gentler than what I gave her, but she responds to it by wiggling her ass in open invitation for more.

She loves what we all have to give her in equal parts and damn, if that isn't fucking hot.

Simon glances back at me. "You get her pussy, Wilder."

"I know what you're doing," I murmur so Elise and Aidan can't hear. "I appreciate it, but it's not necessary."

"Don't be a twat," he tells me. "This way I can see Aidan's ass, which I much prefer to seeing yours. I'm a selfish son of a bitch."

Then he gives me a wink and turns back, kneading Elise's ass with his hand.

I shake my head. He's letting me off the hook.

I've also never been called a twat in my entire life.

I'm actually going to miss the wise-cracking and thoughtful Brit when he goes home and I'm in the woods.

Who would have thought?

But that just reminds me that I'm also going to miss Elise.

I immediately tamp that thought down and enter her bedroom.

CHAPTER 27
Elise

I LOVE THIS.

The thought pops into my head unbidden and once there, I can't shake it. Obviously, I love having sex with three guys at once.

But it's *these* three guys.

That's what makes it so sexy and fun at the same time.

Aidan effortlessly tosses me down on my bed and stalks up between my legs to give me a hard kiss.

God, it's so sexy that he can carry me without breaking a sweat. I've never been a girl who needs to feel small—let's face it, I'm *not* small and I never will be. I like my body and my curves. I feel intensely feminine all the time.

But hell, it's still hot to be carried.

"You don't need this," Aidan says, stripping off my hoodie and tossing it to Simon, who catches it readily.

The two of them share a smile.

I know they've gone out together a number of times, but I'm definitely sensing heightened sexual tension between the two of them, which I'm enjoying.

Do I like it all being about me?

Well, obviously.

But I find it sexy as hell that they are into each other as well.

Simon gives an appreciative stare in my direction.

"Stunning," he tells me. "I do love it when you pout though."

That makes me laugh. "I do not pout."

"Love." He strips his shirt off and bends over to kiss me. "You pout like the best of them."

Then he turns his head and kisses Aidan, too. They swirl their tongues together inches from me, and I feel Aidan's cock jump against my thigh. I'm prepared to lay back, hands above my head and take in the view for a while, but the mattress sinks when Blake lays down next to me. I roll slightly toward him.

"Hi," I murmur.

"Hi." He pulls me onto his chest.

"No fair, Wilder," Aidan complains. "I was going to eat our girl's pussy."

"Too late. You let Armstrong distract you."

"It doesn't work like that." Aidan pops the button on Simon's pants with one hand and cups my breast with the other, teasing at my nipple. "Ladies' choice when we're together, remember?"

I shift my gaze from Aidan to Blake to Simon.

Is there some kind of power struggle going on here?

Then I realize that Blake is just being impatient. He's already nudging at my slit, which is a distracting and delicious sensation. My hips start to rock against him before I even make a conscious choice.

"What do you want, Sugar?" he asks me. "Tell us what you need."

"Oh, now I get to decide?" I demand. "Where was ladies' choice when I wanted to come on the couch?" I use the mattress to lift myself off of Blake's chest and pin him with what I hope is a flirty, not pouty gaze.

He just grins up at me and gives my ass a hard slap.

It makes my whole body bounce on top of him, and damn it, it feels amazing. I get very, very wet, which he knows because he can feel it on his hip. The grin grows wider.

"You want to come?" Aidan asks. "Then on your back, woman."

But I shake my head. "No. I was promised two cocks at once and I want them. *Now*."

We always talk about doing this, but somehow it never happens. Usually because they spend so much time eating me out that I'm a limp noodle by the time they're fucking me.

I'm wet and ready and relaxed enough that I won't tense up.

I rub up and down on Blake and dangle my breasts in front of him.

"You heard the lady," Blake growls, before he raises his head and takes a nipple into his mouth.

I moan enthusiastically as sharp pleasure rips through me. "*More.*"

Blake lifts my hips and seats me on him. "Oh, yeah, that's one wet pussy, baby. You're ready, aren't you?"

"So. Ready." I gasp and clench my inner walls down onto Blake as he thrusts up into me.

It pops into my head that this may be the only time we do this, but I banish the thought.

We still have weeks. Almost two months.

But just in case, I'm not letting this opportunity slip away to experience having two men deep inside me at the same time.

Aidan shifts in behind me, his legs on either side of Blake's. He lifts my hair and kisses the back of my neck. "Lean forward, El. Tell me if it's too much, okay?"

"Of course."

When I lean forward, bracing myself on the mattress, Aidan runs his hand down my spine and over my ass, teasing between my cheeks. Even that much, having his touch on me while Blake pumps up into me has goose bumps rising. Then Simon shifts in beside me and pets my hair, running a knuckle down my cheek. I instinctively suck on them when he brushes over my lips.

There is rustling as Aidan undresses and presumably grabs

lube, but then he's swirling around my entrance with his finger. "Good?"

"Yes. So good." All these hands, all these bodies crowding me, it never fails to allow me to dump every chaotic thought from my brain and live in the moment.

It's nothing but pleasure. Hot, sharp, aching pleasure.

"Look at me, love," Simon commands.

I turn obediently, seeing him watching me with hooded eyes. I open my mouth, wanting him, a finger, his cock, anything.

He just slowly shakes his head. "God, you're incredible. Wait until Aidan is inside you. Then you can have my cock, too. Just be patient."

"I want you," I plead.

"Relax, El," Aidan says. "You're tensing up."

Reaching for Simon has stiffened my back and shoulders. I force myself to open myself up more, to trust that they'll know what I need and when.

They always do.

"That's it, dirty girl. I'm coming in."

Then I'm shocked to feel the press of Aidan inside me.

It's fantastic. I feel full and loved from all angles.

My nerve endings are on fire. My pussy spasms.

Blake grinds into me.

I moan, loudly. "Oh, God, I'm going to come already. Oh, God!"

"That's it. Take it."

That's Simon encouraging me.

Blake is staring intently at me.

Aidan is sawing in and out of my ass with pounding thrusts that should be uncomfortable, but it's nothing but pure fucking bliss.

I fly apart, all wild cries and trembling arms as the orgasm rips through me, pulsating on and on

It's the best orgasm I've ever had.

Hands fucking down.

I'm still riding the waves when Aidan eases out of me.

"I can't hold off," he roars.

He rips off the condom and then I feel hot thick ropes of his cum land on my ass.

"Yes!" I say in encouragement, the sensation sending aftershocks through my cunt.

Which in turn makes Blake groan.

"Sugar, you're killing me. Sit up so I can see your tits."

Aidan takes my shoulders from behind and eases me upright.

I shudder, lightheaded, throwing my hair over my shoulder.

Then I put my hands on Blake's chest, riding him with all the energy I have left in my trembling body. He reaches up and squeezes my breasts, playing with my nipples.

"Perfection," he grinds out through gritted teeth. "Your body is fucking perfect."

Simon takes Aidan's place and cracks the palm of his hand on the curve of my ass.

"Yes! Spank me hard."

"You are such a dirty girl," he says.

Then he smacks me again, finding a rhythm that works with me bobbing up and down on Blake.

Aidan is on the side of the bed now, fisting his dick slowly, looking both satisfied and ready to go again at a moment's notice.

The stinging spanking is making the sweet friction of Blake inside me even sweeter and the combination has me shattering faster than I could have ever thought possible.

The second I come, Blake gives a loud yell. "Sugar, *fuck*!"

I feel the hot burst of him deep in me and I squeeze my inner muscles to milk it for him.

Then I'm limp and sprawled over Blake's damp chest, reaching for Simon. I turn my head. "Give me."

He laughs softly. "Just give me?"

"Yes. I can't do any hard work but fuck my mouth, Simon. I want to swallow you."

"Only a fucking fool would say no to that."

I open my mouth and he doesn't hesitate to thrust his cock between my lips, pumping hard.

"This isn't going to take long," he mutters. "You are the sexiest fucking thing I've ever seen."

I suck in my cheeks and open the back of my throat.

He's right.

In less than a minute, salty heat hits the back of my throat as he groans.

"Jesus," Simon breathes.

When he eases out, I swallow in pure cat-like satisfaction. "Mmm. That was the exclamation point I needed."

Blake shifts me to the side and I fall onto the bed boneless, mentally floating somewhere in the clouds. My legs are still trembling and I shiver, still feeling the little electrical aftershocks of the powerful orgasms.

"I've never been this happy. Ever. I could take on the entire world," I tell them all. "Once I can move again."

Simon chuckles and brushes my hair off of my cheek. "Sleep, love."

Aidan bends down and kisses the top of my head. "You were incredible."

Blake runs his hand down my arm lazily, up and down, in a gesture so tender I sigh in pure contentment.

Then I drift off.

When I wake up after dozing off for what I thought was just a few minutes, but was clearly longer, there's a glass of water on the nightstand for me. I sit up and take a sip, instantly aware that the warm body snug against mine isn't Aidan or Simon, but Blake.

He's asleep.

For once, it looks like he plans to spend the night.

He never does that with Simon and Aidan here.

The bed is too crowded for the four of us. I can admit that. It doesn't bother me that he leaves. He's in his final season of hockey and he needs decent sleep.

He also thinks I don't realize it, but when I have stayed over at his condo twice, he's gone into the kitchen in the middle of the night and wrapped both of his knees with flexible ice packs.

Blake's body is beat to hell from hockey.

So he must be exhausted to have just fallen asleep here.

Even cuddled against me, he has sprawled his legs out and taken over the majority of the bed.

Overcome by the fact that he rushed over here to make sure I was okay tonight, I watch him sleep, his hair a tangled mess. He needs better conditioner. Or to stop raking it back and dumping water on it repeatedly during games.

Simon and Aidan must have moved to the couch to try to sleep.

Which has to be virtually impossible for two grown men to do, spooning or not.

Easing out of bed, I pull on a T-shirt that's laying on the floor. I realize it's Aidan's. I can smell his cologne and it goes nearly to my knees.

As I pad down the hallway, I hear low voices.

I realize they're having sex.

Hey, now.

I grin to myself in the dark, pausing to watch them.

Aidan is on Simon on the couch, moving rhythmically as they give mutual low moans of pleasure.

God, they're cute together.

I feel a little bit of matchmaker smugness. They would have never met if it wasn't for my careless placement of a kitchen towel and I knew the minute they laid eyes on each other, there were sparks flying between them.

It's sexy as hell to watch them having sex.

But I should let them know I'm here.

I don't think they'd mind an audience, but I should let them know they have one.

I open my mouth to ask, "Want a third?" but before I can get the words out, Aidan shocks me by gazing intently down at Simon.

"I love you, Simon," he says.

It's earnest, emphatic, clear as day.

"I love you too," Simon murmurs. "God, so much, Aidan."

I'm shocked, frozen in the hallway.

I'm scared to move, because I've just overheard what was clearly meant to be a personal moment between the two of them, and I feel terrible that I'm eavesdropping.

But I'm also shocked that they're *in love*.

I thought we were all having a great time.

But not an "in love" kind of time.

Am I thrilled for them?

Absolutely.

But I can't help but think that neither one of them has told me they're in love with *me*.

It drives home that I'm an extra in their relationship. They care about me, of course. The sex is amazing. They take care of me in so many different ways.

But I'm not *necessary* to their happiness.

They've found that with each other.

Carefully, I take a couple steps back and hit a hard plane.

"Oof!" I say, before spinning around to face Blake, huge and naked.

He puts a hand up to his lips and tugs me back into the safety of the bedroom.

"I don't think they saw us," he murmurs. "Come back to bed."

I can't tell if he heard their expressions of love or not because the room is dark and his tone sounds even, but I'm too confused to ask him.

I'm not sure how I feel or how I'm supposed to feel.

Blake sits down on the bed with a deep sigh. "Come here."

He holds his hand out to me and I step between his legs gratefully.

He raises Aidan's shirt and presses a kiss on my stomach, of all places.

Then he hugs me around the waist, peppering kisses over my breasts.

I sigh and lean into him.

When he pulls me onto the bed and opens my thighs, I'm grateful for the dark.

Because even though I'm happy for Simon and Aidan to have found each other, and Blake to be getting his dream retirement, I'm sad for me.

Where does all of this leave me?

Alone.

That's where.

I hold on to Blake with both hands, achingly aware this is all ending soon.

CHAPTER 28
Elise

WE'RE MEETING Blake's grandmother at the bakery.

I'm not sure if that's a good thing or a bad thing.

On the surface, it's good. I love the bakery and feel at home here. She'll love our desserts. I should feel more relaxed here. And it's a huge compliment that she has always wanted to try Books and Buns.

It's been about two weeks since we first came up with our how-we-met story and we've filled in more details since then. We're ready for this meeting. But I'm so jumpy that I feel like I've already had four cups of coffee.

I suppose I'd feel that way no matter where we were meeting.

Why am I nervous though? This isn't real. It doesn't matter in the long run if she likes me or not.

But I want this to go well for Blake. The cabin is important to him, and if his grandmother does not believe that we are heading down the aisle, she might not turn the place over to him.

I will admit that there's a little jab in my chest when I think about him moving to Minnesota. Not only do I not want him that far away because I'll miss him, but I'm a little concerned about him becoming a hermit as well. He's a quiet guy. Not a people person. But he has seemed happy with the time he's spent with me, Aidan, and Simon. I kind of hate the idea of him up there in the woods all alone.

I take a deep breath and push through the swinging door, stepping out from the kitchen and into the main bakery with the tray of macarons, pain au chocolat, and éclairs.

I've already served both Blake and Heidi coffee and cappuccino. They are sitting at one of our tables near the front window.

Blake looks almost ridiculous in the tiny white wrought-iron chair. His hulking frame makes everything in the bakery look even more dainty and feminine than usual.

I've seen hockey players in here before. Crew McNeill stops by, and Alexsei Ryan is, of course, a regular. But even next to them, Blake is humongous.

"Good luck," Luna says softly to me.

I had to confess the fake engagement to her and Dani. I couldn't have them believing that Blake and I were actually getting married.

"Thanks." The huge diamond on my left hand catches the sunlight as I pick up three glass dessert plates. "It's going to be fine, right?" I ask Luna.

"Convincing her that you have feelings for Blake?" Luna asks. She gives me a wink. "*Completely* fine."

I don't know if I like that answer. I do have feelings for him. I want his grandmother to believe that. But I don't know if I want to be broadcasting it to the entire world. I don't even know if I want Blake to know that. That will make things a lot more complicated when it comes time to end this. I don't want it to be awkward when he says "Hey, thanks for the help. Really excited for the cabin. You were a real trooper."

"For what it's worth," Luna says, moving behind me to refill the coffee cup for the woman at the counter. "He clearly has feelings for you, too. It will be a very easy sell to his grandmother."

I don't know if that helps. It's not like it matters. I do think that Blake *likes* me. I think we went from casual flirtation to much more pretty easily. But I'm not a part of his long-term plan. He wants to live in Minnesota. I am a Chicago girl. My business is just taking off here. I am not the outdoorsy, live–in–a–cabin type of girl. At. All.

I just give Luna a smile, at a loss for words. Then I head for the table. I set the desserts down and hand Blake the plates. He chooses one of each of the desserts, setting them on one of the plates and handing it to his grandmother. Then he does the same for me as I take the seat next to him, the diamond ring heavy on my finger.

"You're a model. And you design your own dresses," Heidi says. "Tell me all about that. That's amazing."

I relax slightly and give Blake a smile. He told his grandmother about my business and that makes this first topic of conversation easy. There doesn't need to be any lies here.

"This has been absolutely lovely," Heidi says.

We have been chatting and eating for forty-five minutes. She loves the desserts, loves the cappuccino, and seemingly loves me.

We've answered every question, we haven't stumbled over a single thing, and Blake has visibly relaxed. He's leaning back in the tiny chair, and has his arm draped over the back of my chair.

"What have you discussed with your parents as far as the wedding?" Heidi asks me.

I carefully swallow the sip of coffee without choking and set my cup down.

"Um…we haven't discussed details at all yet."

Heidi frowns and I feel a trickle of trepidation. Dammit. It's been going so well.

"Oh. I was hoping for some news on a wedding date."

Blake shifts on his chair, but I don't risk looking at him for fear of giving away the *what the hell* going through my mind.

"We haven't set a date yet," he says.

"Really?" Heidi leans in.

"Yes, really," Blake says. "Why do you look confused?"

"Because that's confusing. Elise is wonderful. You're obviously completely enamored. There's a huge ring on her finger. Your retirement is coming up. Seems that you would want to get married before making a big move to Minnesota, especially because Elise will be needing to move her business and figure out how to continue with her modeling." She looks at me. "Or are you going to quit? I mean you're just getting started. You seem so excited about it. But that will be difficult from Minnesota. Or maybe not. Everyone is on social media these days."

I swallow. "Well, I…"

"Obviously we'll be traveling back-and-forth from Minnesota to Chicago whenever Elise needs to," Blake says easily.

"I see," Heidi says. "That will make fittings with your clients much more difficult. Of course, you can gain clients in Minnesota. Still, living way out there in the woods is going to make it hard for people to come to you. Are you able to travel and do fittings with clients hours away?"

Shit, shit, shit. I shouldn't have given her so many details about my business. I just get carried away when I'm talking about it.

I nod. "Of course. I'll become a traveling show." I smile. "I'll be in Chicago once a month. People will come to their fittings when I'm in town. And I'll do adjustments then. And I would love to expand to a Minnesota clientele. I can easily go to them." I have no idea if that's true, but it sounds good. "A lot of my customers are strictly online anyway." *It doesn't matter. All of this is fake. Don't panic.*

Heidi shakes her head. "Well, not *easily*. We are pretty off the grid up there." She turns her attention to Blake. "Have you not told her? You really should take her to the cabin so she knows what she's getting into."

"Of course I'm going to take her to the cabin," Blake says. "But we're going to work all of this out. Being together is the most important thing."

Heidi focuses on me. "Elise doesn't seem like the type of

woman to give up her career. Especially when *you're* retiring. You should just stay in Chicago."

I look at Blake. He's gritting his teeth. I smile at his grandmother. "We'll work it out. I love my job. But I also love your grandson."

Saying the words that I love Blake out loud, in front of him, to his grandmother, feels a little too real to me. I feel a shiver of awareness trip down my spine and realize Blake is staring at me.

His grandmother is watching us closely, so I give her a big smile.

"Well, that's obvious, dear," Heidi tells me. She looks at Blake. "I can't believe that you haven't told your parents about Elise. Everyone was so surprised when I told them."

He stiffens. "Who all did you tell?"

"Well *everyone*. I'm so excited. Your mother is obviously very upset you haven't told her. Why haven't you?"

"We were going to wait to announce it."

"Wait for what?" Heidi asks.

"After my retirement. When we had some of these details worked out."

"Oh." She doesn't seem worried about ruining the secret. "Well now they're all very excited. And I've decided that the cabin will be my wedding present to you. No need to go through all that silly paperwork."

I look up at Blake. His eyes are narrowed. "What do you mean?"

"Well, you, of course, will have to take over the property taxes and all the maintenance and everything, but I'll just give it to the two of you. I'll bring all the official paperwork signed and delivered to the wedding." She smiles at me. "I'll put both of your names on it."

"That would mean that you would expect us to get married before we move," Blake says. "You want us to just throw a wedding together?"

"Oh, even better," his grandmother says. "Let's have the

wedding at the cabin! You're not a big crowd guy anyway. I imagine you'd want to have a small wedding. We'll just have family and close friends. I'm sure all of them would be happy to make the trip to Minnesota. Then you can just move right into the cabin."

Blake doesn't say anything for a long moment. Then he takes in a deep breath through his nose. "Of course. Getting married right away makes sense. After all, me moving to Minnesota and Elise staying here wouldn't work, would it?"

His grandmother beams. "Exactly. I'm sure you'll want her to move with you when you go. And if you're going to get married anyway, might as well do it sooner versus later."

I feel like I'm watching a ping-pong game as I look from one to the other. I have no idea what to say here, and decide my silence is more helpful than anything.

But how are we going to do this? We can't have all of our family and friends go all the way to Minnesota for a fake wedding. What are we going to do? Pay off the minister? Get a fake marriage license?

His grandmother reaches under the table and grabs her purse. "I'm going to be late for my nail appointment." She stands and turns to me. "But thank you so much for getting together. Everything was delicious and it was delightful to meet you in person. We're going to be seeing a lot of each other." She leans over and gives me a kiss on the cheek, then does the same to Blake. "We'll talk soon."

Then she's out the door, and getting into the town car that appears as if by magic at the curb.

I blow out of breath.

Then I hesitantly look up at my fake fiancé.

"Well...*fuck*," are the first words out of his mouth.

"Yeah.. That's kind of a curveball."

He sits forward in his chair and rests his head in his hands. "Kind of? Fuck. She doesn't believe us."

I frown. "Is that what that was?"

He looks at me. "Yes. She knows there is no way that you are moving to the woods of Minnesota with me. She doesn't believe our whole thing at all. That's her way of calling me out. Because the woman won't just say it. She has to make me sweat. And she told my parents. I can't believe they haven't called me. They must not believe it's real either. Fuck, fuck, and fuck."

I chew on my bottom lip, thinking.

He sighs and sits back. "I'm gonna have to come clean. I shouldn't have lied to her in the first place."

"But you really want the cabin," I say.

"Yeah," he says. "I really do."

"Well then, there's only one thing we can do."

He looks at me. "Buy some land and build my own cabin?"

Right, he's a millionaire hockey player. I nod. "Okay, there's two things we could do. You could do that, and give up the cabin that is part of your childhood, something that means a lot to you and that in my opinion should be yours. Your grandmother is trying to manipulate you, and that's not cool. No matter how nice and sweet she seems."

"Okay, what's the other option?" he asks.

"We get married for real."

He just stares at me. He says nothing. He doesn't make a single move.

I shrug. "Come on. Let's just do that. There's no stipulation that we have to *stay* married. We get married, we get an official marriage license, and she can't doubt us then. She has to sign the cabin over to you."

"You would actually invite your family and friends all the way to Minnesota to marry me for real at the cabin?"

I shake my head. "I think we should say that we were swept away by emotion. Once she put the idea in our heads, we couldn't wait. We go get married in Vegas. Or down at the courthouse. Whatever. We just get married on a whim, tell them it was the most romantic thing ever. We can say that we'll do a ceremony or a reception some other time for everyone. But as long as we have a real, legal marriage certificate, she loses her high ground."

He studies me for long moments. It's almost as if he's trying to memorize my face. "You're extraordinary, you know that?"

I laugh lightly. "That's a nice way of saying I am slightly crazy."

"But you're doing this for me. You're not really getting anything out of it."

I'm able to genuinely smile at that. "I get to help one of my favorite people out."

He looks stunned. "I'm one of your favorite people?"

I lean in. "You know things about me that very few people do. You have been there for me in ways no one else has. You make me *feel* extraordinary. You make me feel special and cared about and beautiful, and like I can actually make one of the grumpiest people I've ever met happy. You have given me things. And yes, you're one of my favorite people."

It's actually not crazy to help him out at all. It makes me feel warm inside and out, considering what he's given to me.

He reaches up and cups my face. "You make me so happy, Elise. And you're one of my favorite people, too."

And then one of the grumpiest people I know gives me one of the sweetest kisses I've ever had.

CHAPTER 29
Blake

I HAVE a pastry halfway to my mouth when Elise steps into the bakery.

"Oh, my God," Luna breathes, standing behind the counter. "She looks so pretty."

Pretty isn't even the fucking half of it.

Elise looks like…a *bride*.

A stunning, glowing, gorgeous bride, smiling at me as she strolls across the room in a white dress that flares out at the waist and turquoise blue heels. She has a little hat on her head and a coat and purse over her arm. Her hair is done in little rolls that match her pinup style.

She looks like she's about to marry her soldier before sending him off to the war in Europe.

Instead, she's marrying me.

For real estate.

I instantly regret agreeing to this when Elise suggested we just go ahead and get married.

This isn't what I want for her—a fake wedding with a fake ring.

She deserves a full-blown wedding someday with the man of her dreams tearing up at the end of the aisle when he sees her. She should have a celebration with everyone she cares about present and I feel guilty that this might take away from that.

That she'll have to explain to a future husband why she was married to a hockey goalie for a couple of months, assuring him it meant nothing.

"Ready?" she asks me with a smile, bending down to adjust her shoe.

Her breasts threaten to spill out of her dress.

I make a sound somewhere in the back of my throat, but I don't say anything.

"I think he's speechless," Luna says, clearly amused.

"I have that effect on men." Elise stands back up. "Are you going to eat that?" She points to the pastry in my hand. "Or can I have it?"

I shove it at her. "You can have it." Then I take a deep breath. "You look amazing. I appreciate the effort. I kind of thought you'd just wear whatever, not a white dress."

She swipes her finger through the icing and pops it between her lips and sucks. "Nothing screams fake marriage like getting married in jeans. I don't think any woman would ever agree to that for her actual wedding day unless she's drunk in Vegas."

Elise told Luna the truth about what we're doing because she didn't want to lie to her friend. Which I understand. But it's also complicated. Who do we bring in on our sham marriage? Guilt is starting to claw away at my insides.

"You sure you want to do this? You can still change your mind, Sugar."

Elise just nods. "Sure, I'm sure."

It occurs to me I've never asked Elise how she feels about marriage. Maybe she thinks it's an outdated institution. Maybe she's not interested in marriage for real and that's why this doesn't seem like a big deal to her.

I could press the issue and open that discussion now.

Or I could trust that she's an adult who offered me a solution totally without any pressure from me and I shouldn't worry about it.

Elise doesn't do what she doesn't want to do.

That I do know about her.

I adjust my tie and bend down to take a bite of the pastry still in her hand.

"Blake!" she protests, laughing as she turns to protect her food from further attack. "That was half the sticky bun!"

Relieved that this is going to be okay, I press a hard smack on her lips. "Let's go get married."

"Good luck, you crazy kids," Luna says.

Thirty minutes later, we're standing in the hallway at the courthouse, waiting for the judge to call us in. We went yesterday right after talking to my grandmother and got the license. Elise is fixing her lipstick with a little mirror, and I'm struggling with the urge to pace back and forth.

I kind of feel like a dick that we haven't told Simon and Aidan.

But Simon is on a plane to London and Aidan is at work.

Elise didn't want to bother them when they're working.

With something apparently as trivial as *getting married*.

But I also heard Simon and Aidan in Elise's living room the other night.

They confessed their love for each other.

It was so raw and real that I felt guilty having overheard it. The moment was intended to be private, between the two of them.

Elise didn't seem surprised.

I wasn't either. You can see when they look at each other that those feelings go way deeper than sexual chemistry and friendship.

Hell, I'm happy for them. I hope they can work out their relationship in spite of Simon's planned move back to London.

"Blake."

"Yeah?" I look at Elise. I realize I'm gnawing on my thumbnail. I drop my hand and shove it in my pocket.

"Do *you* still want to do this?" she asks, arching her eyebrows. "You look like you're going to pass out. It's not real, remember?"

I stare at her, taking in her classic beauty, her delicious body, her perfect poise.

Her soft smile and her rich brown eyes.

I feel like I was just struck by a bolt of lightning.

Because I suddenly realize I want it to be real.

Holy shit, I'm in love with Elise.

Genuinely, deeply, fucking madly in love with her.

That's why my stomach is in knots and I can't seem to keep my leg from bouncing up and down.

I am in love with this sassy, confident, joyful woman and I want to marry her.

Not for the lake house, but for me.

To have and to fucking hold until death do us part.

I open my mouth.

The clerk steps up to us right then. "Blake Wilder and Elise Starling? We're ready for you."

My stomach drops to the damn floor.

I almost confessed to Elise I love her.

Which would have made this whole thing very awkward and weird.

I don't want her to feel obligated to marry me if she knows I have deeper feelings for her than she does for me.

So I hold my hand out for her. "They're ready for us."

Elise gives me a grin. "I heard."

She lets me help her to her feet and then she adjusts the cleavage of her dress with her free hand. I keep clutching her other hand, wanting to feel her skin on mine. I brush a kiss over her temple.

"When did you become so sweet?" she asks me, fondly. "Who stole my grumpy goalie?"

She did.

She stole my heart when I wasn't looking.

"Don't worry, I can still be a sour-faced asshole when you least expect it." It's light, playful.

Just banter.

Keeping it casual.

That's what I need to do.

Even if I'm feeling anything but casual as I'm holding her hands and standing in front of a judge vowing to keep and protect her.

She's smiling up at me and I'm studying her, searching her expression for any indication she might feel the same way as me, but she just looks like Elise—happy, confident.

"Do you, Blake, take Elise to be your lawfully wedded wife?"

"I do."

Oh, fuck me, I do.

I said it. I meant it. I'm not faking a damn thing.

And now I'm in trouble.

This can only end in me being emotionally destroyed.

"Do you, Elise, take Blake to be your husband?"

"I do."

She did.

Fuck, fuck, fuck.

"Then by the power vested in me by the state of Illinois, I now pronounce you husband and wife. You may kiss the bride."

There is a buzzing in my ears.

My hands are trembling a little when I cup her cheeks and meet her gaze. Her lips part and her eyes go soft. She sighs when I invade her space.

Then my lips are on hers and I'm drowning.

My wife.

She is my wife.

And I've never been happier.

She grips the lapels of my suit jacket and gives herself over wholly into our kiss, our mouths melding, tongues lightly intertwining.

It's the best kiss we've ever shared.

And I know I can't tell her how I feel.

Because she'll see it as a bait and switch.

She's marrying me as a friend.

I end the kiss, nibbling lightly on her lower lip, and easing my hands down off of her soft skin.

Elise sways a little on her feet.

Her cheeks are pink.

"Wow," she says.

"Was that sweet enough for you, Sugar?" I force myself to grin and turn back to the judge to hear the rest of what he has to say.

If I look at Elise, I'll blurt out everything and freak her the fuck out.

The clerk says, "Congratulations," and Elise leans against my left side, her hand still in mine.

Then we leave the courtroom married.

CHAPTER 30
Elise

I'M MARRIED. To Blake Wilder.

Wow.

I look up at him as we descend the courthouse steps, our fingers intertwined.

That is...just wow.

I feel a stupid, goofy grin on my face.

I know this isn't traditional in any sense of the word, but it's still kind of fun.

I like Blake. We have fun together. He makes me feel special and adored. We have *amazing* sex. He's so much more underneath than I had initially thought. He's kind and funny and sweet and he accepts me exactly as I am.

And now he's my husband and if anyone thinks I'm not going to enjoy the hell out of that for as long as it lasts, they're nuts.

Before we stepped outside, he posted a photo of our hands with our wedding rings to his social media with the simple caption, "Did a thing today."

It's already blowing up.

I don't mean it's getting some attention.

I mean, it is *blowing up*.

As we hit the bottom of the steps, Blake turns and bands an

arm around my waist. "Come here." He pulls me in for a kiss and snaps a selfie. His long arm makes the shot pretty great. I grin at it as he shows me.

"Oh my gosh, did you just get married?" A woman who can't be more than twenty rushes up.

"We did," I tell her, giving her a bright smile.

"I can take a photo for you," she gushes.

"Amazing, thanks," Blake says, turning over his phone.

The woman steps back. "Dip her and kiss her," she instructs Blake.

"Yes, ma'am." He grins at me just before he dips me back and gives me a deep kiss.

"Oh yes!" she squeals.

She gives us instructions for a few more poses, then says to me, "That dress is *gorgeous*."

I beam at her. "Thank you."

"She makes dresses like this," Blake tells her.

The woman's mouth drops open. "No! Oh wow! You should put some of these up on your social media or something!"

She's right, I should.

"Here, do a few more," she says. She gets me to pose alone and snaps a few photos that show off the wedding dress perfectly.

"These look amazing." Blake peers over my shoulder. "God, you're gorgeous, sugar."

My heart swells. "Thanks."

"You two are so cute," the woman says with a hearts-in-her-eyes look.

But what's especially funny is that it's clear she has no idea who Blake is.

"Thank you for the photos," I tell her.

"Of course! I hope you're happy *forever*!" She waves to us as she moves off.

I keep my smile in place.

She's so sweet. But that last word hit me hard.

I mean, I *know* this is short term. Of course it is. That's been the plan all along. But I guess in the back of my mind maybe I've been thinking that even if we don't stay *married*, because that would be crazy, Blake and I could still see each other.

But forever? Yeah, that's not in the cards.

Even if I suddenly want it to be.

No, that's just insane.

Blake is moving far away.

I'm entrenched in Chicago.

But more importantly, he doesn't love me.

Even if I love him.

Oh, God, *I'm in love with Blake.*

My heart is suddenly racing and I suddenly grasp the obvious. I didn't offer to marry Blake because we're friends. I'm in love with him.

Houston, we have a *fucking problem*.

"Hey, you okay?" he asks, noticing that I'm still staring after her.

I look up at him and force a smile. "Yes. Of course. She was so nice."

"She was. I have some *amazing* photos to share on social media." He pulls me close and holds up his phone, scrolling through the shots so we can both see them. "We look good together."

I can't deny that. "We really do."

I look like I'm in love. It's written all over my face. I'm beaming. Glowing, even. It's so damn obvious. How does Blake not see that?!

Maybe because he doesn't want to see it.

"You ready to get out of here?" he asks, no idea I'm suddenly going through a massive existential crisis.

I'm definitely ready to get out of here. If I stay here any longer, or someone actually recognizes Blake, I'm going to panic a little bit.

I need time to regroup before tonight.

I give him a little smile. It's not really our wedding *night*, but he has a game tonight, so getting home to bed won't be until late. Me being at the game tonight as his *wife* was part of our plan. We're hoping to get a bunch of attention, make it as real as we can by using the fans and team, maybe even the media, and get even more social media posts circulating about our impromptu marriage. And someone—probably a broken-hearted Blake Wilder female fan—will definitely research the legitimacy of our marriage license. Heidi won't be able to argue with all of that proof.

Which now all feels very overwhelming. I need to pull myself together, and in order to do that, I need him to rip this wedding dress off of me. Hopefully, with his teeth.

"My place or yours?" I ask coyly, eager for the distraction.

Sex with Blake I know. It's neutral territory, so to speak.

Being in love with him is new and fresh and scary as hell.

"Oh, yours," he says. He takes my hand, but he's typing on his phone with his opposite thumb. "That way you can change before the game. Can you take an Uber tonight?"

"Sure." Taking a car service alone on my wedding night makes me feel like pouting, but it's *not really my wedding night.*

Maybe if I tell myself that enough times my traitorous heart will get the message.

God, how could I go and fall in love with Blake?

I'm also starting to think the reason I had such conflicted feelings about Simon and Aidan exchanging words of love is because I love them as well.

I'm in love with three men and they see me as just a friend. A sexy sidekick.

This was not how any of this was supposed to play out.

None of them did anything wrong. This is on me. I'm the one who went and fell in love.

Oblivious to my inner turmoil, Blake looks up and down the street, spots the car he called for before our little photo session, and waves. The town car pulls over and he opens the back door for me.

I slide in, and when he's closed the door, I expect him to turn to me, maybe lean over and kiss me. I'm even expecting some flirty words.

I need some flirty words.

Instead, he bends his head over his phone and presses some buttons, then he holds it up in front of his face.

I watch, confused, as the video call connects.

He grins. "Hey, Mom."

Mom? *Mom*?

Wait. *What*? We can't seriously be doing a video call with his parents right now.

"Blake! Hi honey! What are you doing?"

"I was hoping Dad was around. I have something to tell you guys."

"Oh sure. Jerry!" she calls. "Blake's on the phone! He wants to tell us some news!"

I'm dumbfounded.

Blake pushes another button. "Hang on. I'm connecting with Brooke and Gran too."

I just watch. I have no idea what to do. I actually lean closer to the door, trying to stay out of the shot.

As two other faces on two additional screens pop up, Blake looks over at me, notices how far away I'm sitting, grins, and loops an arm around my waist. He hauls me closer, sliding me over the leather seat.

"What's going on?" his mother asks. "Hi, Heidi. Hi, Brooke. I didn't know we'd all be talking today. Who's your friend?"

Damn it. She can see me.

I immediately shift out of view, a little panicked. I take a deep breath.

"I didn't either," Blake's sister says. "Is everything okay? You combed your hair and trimmed your beard. Is there a funeral somewhere I don't know about?"

"No funeral," he tells them happily. "Just waiting for dad. I want to introduce you all to my *friend*."

"Jerry!" his mom shouts again, louder this time. "Come on! Everyone's waiting!"

"I'm coming!" I hear a man's voice reply. "It's Blake?"

"Yes!" his wife answers.

"Ask him why the hell my texts are filling up with my friends asking why I didn't tell them my son got married!"

Blake's mom and sister both gasp.

I can see the phone and notice that his grandmother doesn't actually look surprised.

Blake chuckles. "You're not getting texts?" he asks. I assume that's directed to just...everyone.

They probably all have friends that follow the team. That would make sense.

"I haven't checked," his mother says.

"I just got out of the shower," his sister tells them. "I haven't looked either."

Suddenly, a man's face pops into the screen with Blake's mom. "What is going on?" he demands.

"Everyone, I'd like you to meet someone." Blake turns the phone so my face fills the screen. "Well, Gran's met her. Everyone, this is Elise. My wife. Elise, this is my mom, my dad, and my sister. You know Gran."

There is dead silence on the other end of the phone for about five seconds.

I swallow and smile. Then lift my hand in a little wave. "Hi."

Then they all start talking at once.

Except for Gran.

She waits until the, "What?", "How long have you *not* told me you have a girlfriend?", "Oh my God!", "But what about a wedding ceremony?", "You have to bring her home, no we'll come there, omg Jerry, we have to go to Chicago!" to die down.

I have no idea what to say or do, so I just sit, my hand squeezing Blake's huge, hard thigh, and try not to feel guilty as hell.

Finally, Gran says, "So, this is a surprise. I figured you'd do it this summer after your retirement. At the cabin. Like. We. Discussed."

Blake, smooth as top shelf whiskey, tightens his arm around me, smiles, and says, "It was all that talk about getting married at the cabin that got us talking." He looks down at me, and damn, that look of adoration is pretty convincing. "We talked about plans and who we'd invite and what kind of flowers Elise likes best and all of that, and our minds just started spinning, and I was laying there in bed that night thinking, 'why the hell are we waiting?'" He looks back at his family on the phone. "I'm in love. I want to be with her. She, thank God, feels the same way, so I said, 'let's do it now' and she laughed and said, 'you're on' and we went and got a license."

That's not at all how it went, but I find myself loving the story. It sounds like us. It's sweet and fun and part of me wishes it *was* our story.

I squeeze his thigh, and he leans over and kisses my temple.

I'm melting like chocolate in the sun under his touch.

When I look at the phone again, they're all looking at us with clearly convinced, happy expressions.

Even Gran.

"Well, this is…a surprise. But a *lovely* one," Shelby says. "Elise, we can't wait to get to know you better. But…welcome to the family."

I'm able to give her a genuine smile now. They are sweet. I'm looking forward to meeting them too.

But then it hits me—it would really be better if I didn't. I don't want to get attached. I don't want to really hit it off with them. When we call this off, I don't want to imagine their disappointed, maybe even angry, faces.

"Me, too," I say, weakly.

"Okay, we have to go," Blake says. "I have to get ready for the game. But it's going to be all over by then and I didn't want you in the dark."

"Thank you for that," his father says dryly. "So thoughtful.

Even if a text *before* the pictures went up would have been appreciated."

Blake laughs. "I'll send you photos that no one else has seen yet."

"You'd better!" his mom and sister say in unison.

"I love you guys," Blake tells them, then laughingly disconnects before they can say anything else.

He looks down at me. He seems happy. Content.

"So, that's my family."

"They seem great."

"They are," he agrees.

"A little warning would have been nice." I press a hand to my stomach. "Do you think they believed us?"

"Yes. And…" He clears his throat. "Thank you."

"For?"

"I guess…being you. Going along with this." He frowns. "I do hate lying to them."

I nod. "I don't even know them and I hate lying to them." I feel trepidation swoop through my belly. "It will be okay though. This is still the best way to handle this, right?"

He shrugs. "Too late now. We did it."

Yeah. We did it. For real. Whether we intend "til death do us part" or not, we are actually legally married.

Actually, I know he doesn't intend forever. That is just my wishful thinking.

I don't want this to feel like a mistake.

It's not Blake's fault it took us getting married for me to recognize that I truly love him. The last thing in the world I want to do is make him feel trapped in our relationship because I went and caught feelings.

I'm going to keep my mouth shut and enjoy whatever time I have left with Blake.

He squeezes my knee, but it doesn't feel sexual. It feels a little reassuring, mostly absent-minded. He's looking at his phone again.

My own phone is missing.

I was late getting ready for our appointment at the courthouse and I couldn't find it so I just left without it, trusting Blake would handle everything.

On the one hand, I'm glad I don't have it, because I'm not sure I could deal with dozens of notifications and news spreads on social media. But at the same time, my phone always gives me an excuse to mindlessly scroll and not have to just sit in a town car in my feelings while my legal, but fake husband, ignores me.

I adjust the bodice on my dress. My tits look great, but I didn't lift my skirt enough when I sat down and now the dress is dragging toward my stomach, exposing quite a bit of cleavage.

Blake makes a sound in the back of his throat.

A glance over shows he's noticed all the bouncing and adjusting. His eyes are narrowed, his hand scrubbing over his beard.

Oh, I know that look.

I give him a flirty smile. "See something you like?"

He nods, slowly. "My gorgeous wife, that's what I see."

Wife.

There is so much in that sentence, it makes my heart ache. I sigh and lean into him. "Do you think married sex is better than single sex?"

"We're about to find out."

Fortunately, when we get to Books and Buns, Luna is in the kitchen and Lydia is busy with a customer, so Blake just drags me past everyone and up the stairs. When he turns the knob and realizes I left my apartment unlocked, he gives me a stern look.

"It was an accident!" I say before he can lecture me. "I was in a hurry."

I don't mention I probably forget to lock my door once a week. It will give Blake a heart attack.

But I've managed to survive twenty-eight years without him. I'll survive without him again.

I hope.

Especially when he bends down and picks me up easily.

"What are you doing?" I laugh.

"Carrying you over the threshold. That's still a thing, right?"

"I have no idea."

Honestly, marriage has never been a goal of mine. I haven't been planning a wedding in my mind since grade school like some women. I've always seen myself as someone who probably should live alone, even if I'm in a serious relationship.

My three guys have challenged that viewpoint.

And I'm not going to say I don't gleefully enjoy having a hulking hockey player carry me into my apartment like it's no big deal.

He kicks the door shut with his foot behind us and that slam sends a jolt of heat straight through my thighs. I cling to him, arms around his neck.

"You're going to fuck me so hard, aren't you?"

I want that. Hell, I need that.

Blake clearly has something else in mind. He sets me down, slowly, so that all of my body slides down his, my chest pressed against his, his erection presses against my belly. When I'm on my tiptoes, he stares down at me, gaze sweeping over my features, as if he's memorizing them.

His hand sweeps into my hair and one by one removes the bobby pins that are holding my victory rolls in place. He lets them tumble to the floor, still not speaking.

It feels like time is standing still.

Our eyes are locked on each other and I feel very, very vulnerable.

Afraid he can see what I'm feeling, I try to distract him by kissing him.

I'm going for urgent. Hard, nipping presses of my lips on his, encouraging him to move faster as I wrap my thigh around his and grind myself against his hard cock.

But he slows me down. He cups my cheeks and presses a kiss

to the corners of my mouth and runs his thumbs across my jawline. He kisses my nose, my eyelids, my temples, my earlobes until I'm trembling with an ache I can't even describe.

I try again. I grab one of his hands and place it on my breast, inside the bodice of my wedding dress.

He obediently kneads my flesh before removing his hand and turning it over to brush his knuckles across my decollete in a soft, worshipful manner.

It feels too real.

Too devotional.

And I honestly feel like it might kill me.

"Take my dress off," I demand, presenting him with my back so that he can't see inside my heart, my very soul and see that I've been stupid enough to fall in love with him.

He sweeps my hair forward and does grip the zipper but at the same time trails kisses over my shoulder, and flicks his tongue across my earlobe. I'm a quivering mass of emotion and sexual need, my pussy aching, my heart breaking.

"The zipper is stuck," he murmurs, tugging it lightly. "It's caught in the fabric."

"Just rip it." I don't care.

"Elise, no. You must have spent a lot of time making this dress."

I never want to see this dress again. I'm going to either toss it in the trash after today or deconstruct it and dye the fabric black. I can't hang it in my closet and not feel a world of regret every time my eyes land on it.

"I don't care," I tell him. "Just get me out of this thing." I sound anxious and frustrated.

He manages to finesse the zipper down and he slips his hands inside, forcing the dress off of my shoulders. It drops to my hips and he shoves it down past my curves. When it thumps softly on the floor, I'm ready to walk straight to the bed, or even better, bend over the couch, but he holds me there, massaging my breasts from behind, teasing my nipples, palming my pussy.

I shudder as heat floods me.

Rocking my ass back against him, I finally have the satisfaction of hearing him moan a little under his breath. He does love my ass. He also has just realized that my panties have a slit in them, so his finger just sinks deep into me.

"You got the panties with the slit for me," he murmurs into my ear. "That's really sexy, Sugar."

"That's right. No shapewear."

"Thank you." He strokes over me so lightly I want to scream.

"You're welcome. See how wet I am for you?" I rock my ass back against him and my pussy forward onto his finger. "Fuck me, Blake."

But again, my *husband* has different ideas.

He scoops me up again and carries me to the bedroom, laying me down on the mattress so carefully and gently that for a minute, it really feels like this is our wedding day and we're married.

That he loves me.

Then as I watch him slowly strip out of his suit and tie, undoing the buttons on his suit while I prop myself up on my elbows, it occurs to me that this is it.

This is our goodbye.

I know Blake damn well by now.

After today, he's moving on. Literally and figuratively.

He will focus on securing the house for himself and finishing the rest of the Racketeers season, intent on winning the championship. There will be no space in his life for me, physically or emotionally.

So he's saying goodbye.

This is it. Our last time together.

He wants it to be more than just a quick wall bang, because he appreciates what I have done for him.

And because he does care about me.

For a second, I feel the words on my lips, threatening to burst forth.

I love you.

But I press them tightly together. If I tell him how I feel, right now, he might just panic and walk out and I'll never have this sweet, sensual memory he's clearly intent on making with me.

So I reach my hand out for him.

We'll do this his way.

Blake gives me a smile as he drops his pants. "See anything you like?" he asks, mimicking my earlier words.

I laugh softly. "Yes. My handsome husband."

It's meant to be tongue-in-cheek. To let him know I'm sticking to the plan.

But it has a different effect than I'm expecting.

"*Fuck*, Sugar." Then he's down on the bed, pressing into my thighs with a firm grip before sinking his tongue deep inside me.

"Oh, God! I wasn't expecting that!"

Then I can't breathe as he gets busy, nipping and sucking and licking me, taking full advantage of my newly purchased just-for-him panties. Falling back onto my bed, I decide to let go and just enjoy the attention.

He's giving soft moans of pleasure. "You taste so fucking good, Elise. God, I love—"

My heart almost stops.

But then he finishes his sentence.

"—your pussy."

That makes me annoyed with myself all over again.

Blake is not going to confess love to me with his tongue buried in my thighs.

Then he sucks on my clit and my mind blissfully empties. It's just him and me and a blinding hot orgasm that washes over me like a riptide.

Closing my eyes, I thrash and grip the sheets, shudders wracking my body.

Blake draws back and takes the corner of my panties and rips them, snapping first one side of the string, then the other. His strength and clear need for me has me eager for more. I shove the cups of my bra down and he immediately pulls my nipples into his mouth as he settles his weight over me.

"Hard or soft?" he murmurs, as his thick cock nudges against my very wet entrance.

I spread my legs wider and tell him emphatically, "Hard."

"That's my girl."

Then he thrusts inside me with a powerful burst that knocks the wind right out of my chest. I can barely recover before he's slamming into me over and over, his powerful biceps entrapping me between his arms, his muscular thighs giving him maximum speed.

I'm a mess of ecstasy and bouncing, trembling thighs, frantic thoughts and head-pounding pleasure.

Blake doesn't stop when my head hits the headboard and I don't care. The small amount of pain only seems fitting, only adds to the all-consuming intensity of what is happening between us.

He yanks my hip up higher and then he pauses, buried deep, and yells out, "Fuck, Elise, baby!"

I know the feeling.

I'm shattering apart, raking my nails down his back, yelling what may or may not be actual words, I'm not even sure. Maybe I'm not even breathing. I have no idea.

I'm certainly not thinking.

I'm just being destroyed and I fucking love it and him with all my heart.

Until my orgasm is over and he's crushing me and I realize there is no coming back from this.

I can't undo loving Blake and I don't want to.

My tongue is three sizes too big in my mouth and I try to swallow.

He gives me a grin and a head shake. "Whoa, that was hot." Then he slaps the side of my ass and climbs out of bed. He scoops up his clothes and disappears into my bathroom.

I lay there, a little shell-shocked, making no move to fix my bra or adjust my destroyed panties. When he returns, I'm still sprawled out, wondering how the hell I allowed myself to fall in love with a man who has no interest in doing the same.

Pick the man who aspires to be a hermit.

Great job, girl.

Blakes is already fully dressed. Even his tie is tied. He bends over and kisses my forehead. "Have a good night. See you after the game."

Then he swipes my panties and tucks them into his interior pocket.

"You're stealing my underwear again?" I ask, bewildered.

He grins and flips the cups of my bra back up over my breasts. "Yep. They're ruined anyway."

"That's weird," I say, because I don't know what else to say.

I actually think it's hot, but I need any kind of barrier between us I can create.

Blake just gives me a wave and leaves. When the front door closes behind him, I roll over and punch my pillow.

Hard.

"You're a fucking mess," I tell myself. "Pull it together."

I don't listen to myself.

Instead, I jump out of bed and go on a frantic search for my phone in my apartment so that I can scroll through the wedding photos Blake posted of us online.

Except I don't find my stupid phone.

CHAPTER 31
Aidan

"HEY BURKE," Wyatt calls as I walk into the common room. "I think your girlfriend just got married."

I frown at him. He thinks he's so hilarious. "What are you talking about?" I head for the fridge.

He's lounging on the couch across the room, but I can see he's scrolling on his phone.

"Do you know Blake Wilder?" he asks me.

I turned slowly. "Yeah. Why?"

"I'm a huge hockey fan. I follow the Racketeers. And they just shared a social media post from Wilder. I went over to his account and…yeah, he got married this afternoon."

I feel like a cold fist is suddenly squeezing my heart. What he's saying doesn't make sense. But I also have a terrible feeling that it might make a whole lot of sense and I am about to be very upset.

"Okay, so Wilder got married this afternoon. So what?" I open the soda in my hand and take a sip. I don't even taste it. I have no idea what flavor I pulled out.

"Well, I know I only met Elise briefly, but this woman in the white dress who he's dipping back and kissing the hell out of looks a lot like her."

I casually stroll toward him not wanting to let on that the icy fist in my chest is making way for a fiery anger.

What the fuck did these two do?

They wouldn't have *actually* gotten married, right? No way.

They've been fake engaged and we've all been in on it.

If they did a fake ceremony they should have told us. *Especially* if they were going to post it all over hell.

But they wouldn't have *really* done it, would they?

I hold my hand out and Wyatt places the phone in it. I look at the photo. Yeah, that is most definitely Blake Wilder dipping my girlfriend back and kissing her deeply. That would be bad enough, I suppose, but the dress she's wearing is absolutely a wedding dress. And if that wasn't enough, the caption under the photo says *skipped the chapel, but still got an I Do,* confirms it.

I scroll through the account.

There are a few other photos of them together, a couple of Elise by herself looking fucking insanely gorgeous, and then there's the first one. It's just of their two left hands, each with a ring, and the caption there says, *did a thing today.*

"When was the last time you and Elise talked?" Wyatt jokes. "If she's been telling you she's too busy to go out, I think you now know why."

I congratulate myself on the very mature way I hand his phone back rather than throwing it against the wall.

"Blake and I do know each other," I tell him. "She's been dating both of us."

There's not a great reason to fill in that information. It makes more sense to tell him something about Elise and I breaking up. But...we fucking didn't. I figured I'd bring her around the firehouse again, that she'd join me and my crew at our favorite dive bar, that she'd be my plus one to the firefighter's annual ball.

But now...

What the *fuck* is going on?

They can't intend to *stay* married, right? That they would *definitely* discuss with me and Simon.

But I'm not so sure. We don't really have any rules. We haven't discussed where this is going or how we all feel. Which is obviously a huge mistake.

"Well, I assume you're not going to keep seeing her now," another of our firefighter buddies jokes.

His words hit me a little harder than I would've expected.

I know this wedding is fake. Or at least the marriage is. They're doing it for Blake's cabin. But the fact that they actually had a ceremony, and the fact that they're kissing and posting photos on Blake's social media, somehow makes this feel far too real.

I feel a stab of jealousy, which is crazy. This man has been seeing Elise longer than I have. He's fucked her. Without me. With me. This has been an open relationship from the beginning. Her being with Blake is completely fine. What they do is between them.

Except maybe things that make her permanently only *his*.

I don't fucking like that at all.

Why didn't they tell us?

Wait, did they tell Simon? Maybe I'm the only one who doesn't know. I've been at work for fourteen hours. Maybe they just decided to do this, and I wasn't around.

My face must not have been as calm and collected as I think. Wyatt shoots the other guys a look and says, "Hey, leave Burke alone, you insensitive pricks." He turns to me. "You okay?"

No. Not even close. But I nod. I take my soda and head toward the bedroom area, thumbing through my phone. But nope. No missed calls or texts from Blake or Elise.

I go into my sleep room and shut the door. I set the soda down, slump onto the edge of the bed, suck in a deep breath, then punch in the first number.

But it rings and then goes to Elise's voicemail.

I sigh. She probably doesn't have her phone with her.

So, Blake Wilder has some explaining to do.

I hit his number and wait, anger and hurt churning through my veins.

"Hey," he answers after three rings.

Just hey. Like it's just any other day, and I caught him while he was hanging out or running errands.

"Hey," I say. "Anything interesting happen to you today? And is Elise aware that she doesn't have her phone with her?"

There's a long pause and then he says, "I don't know. I'm not with her right now."

That also pisses me off. "So you *married* her and then dropped her off at home? What the *fuck*?"

"She has all those dresses to work on!" He sounds annoyed.

Well, he can join the fucking club.

"And I have a game tonight."

"So you really did just drop her off?" I ask incredulously. "What the *hell*?"

"It's not…" He stops, then starts again. "It was for the cabin. My grandmother changed the rules. She was going to give it to us *at* our wedding and not before. So…we moved up the timeline and forced her hand." He pauses. "It was Elise's idea. For the record. I never would have asked her to do this."

I suck in a breath, then say, "So, it's real?"

"Yeah. It's real. I mean, it's legal." He stops again. "Fuck. I don't know what I mean. It's legal and all of that until we get it annulled."

I stand up and pace across the room. "Are you fucking kidding me? What the *hell*?"

"You knew we were going to do this," he says, some of that annoyance coming back.

"We knew you were *faking* being engaged."

"Yeah, well, Simon was in London and you were at work and we decided why not just do it this way?"

"Why not?" I ask. My voice rises. "Why not? I'll tell you why not! Because Elise is *my* girlfriend!" I exclaim. I realize how dumb that sounds at this point. "Because I'm in love with her! It's one thing for us to *consensually* all sleep with her, and for you to date her, and to *pretend* to be engaged. But you fucking *really* married her without a word to me? No. That is *not* okay. And Simon's in love with her too! Fuck! I mean, she deserves a *real* damned wedding, Wilder. Not a spur-of-the-moment trip downtown with no friends or family. What the fuck were you thinking?"

He's quiet for several long seconds. "You're in love with her? Both of you?"

"Yes!" I practically shout.

"Have you told *her* that?"

Okay, that trips me up. "Well, no. Not yet."

"Yeah, well, she overheard you tell Simon that you love *him*. And vice versa. She's pretty sure you two are just into each other for the long haul."

I drag a hand over my face. "Dammit."

"Yeah." He blows out a breath. "Fuck, man. If you both love her, then this wedding thing was kind of a dick move on my part."

I shake my head and almost laugh because…yeah. "You think?"

"I do. Except I can't read your mind, you know. At any rate, this is all becoming one big damned mess."

"But you're not planning on *staying* married, right?" I ask. "It's temporary, even if it's not fake."

"Well…about that," he says.

I scowl. And brace myself. "What about that?"

"I'm in love with her too," Blake says.

"Is she in love with you?"

"I have no idea because I didn't tell her that I *actually* want to love, honor, and cherish her as long as we both shall live before I married her."

CHAPTER 32
Simon

AS I LISTEN to an old codger, aka my father, drone on angrily about dividends, I stare at him and the rest of the board of Armstrong Enterprises in total irritation.

This could have been a fucking Zoom call.

I did not need to fly back to London to hear doomsday bullshit from old men.

I'm excellent in my position, in spite of my sometimes casual attitude. I can be a shark when I need to be, but I've always found I gain more traction using my charm than playing the heavy. My father is the opposite of me and he never trusts my abilities.

It's always frustrating, but even more so right now when I would much prefer to be back in Chicago in bed with my boyfriend and Elise.

And Wilder too, if he wants to be there.

I can never tell what exactly that man is thinking.

"Simon, you'll take the lead on that," my father says.

"Of course." My phone starts vibrating in my jacket pocket.

I pull it out and hide it under the table. We're in a private dining room at an exclusive club the Armstrongs have belonged to for generations. Dinner is laid out in front of each man or woman around the table, though no one is really eating. They're too busy getting worked up into a panicked frenzy over a dip in the market.

I glance at my phone. It's Aidan, calling me.

I frown. He's supposed to be at work. He doesn't usually call when he's at the firehouse. It's early afternoon in Chicago. I don't answer because my father's head will explode if I do, but I text Aidan surreptitiously.

> In a meeting. Everything okay?

> Not really. This happened.

An image suddenly pops up.

It's two hands, a woman's laying over top of a man's. That's Elise's hand, with the engagement ring Blake gave her. I'm used to seeing it now on her finger.

But that is also Blake's hand, next to hers, and he's wearing a wedding band.

The caption below from @OfficialBlakeWilder says, "Did a thing today…"

I stand up so fast my knees hit the underside of the table and everyone's silverware and glasses rattle.

"What the hell is wrong with you?" my father asks, astonished.

"I have an emergency. I need to make a phone call."

I'm striding out the door before he can even respond.

"My heavens," Dorothy Wilkinson, who has to be at least a thousand years old and has more money than God, says. "These young bucks today are just shockingly rude."

I don't even take the time to appreciate being called a young buck before I'm calling Aidan back.

"They got married?" I demand, when he gives a rough hello. "When the devil did they do that?"

"Apparently a few hours ago." Aidan says. "They didn't think it was a big deal, according to Wilder."

"You talked to him?" I am heading for the front door of the club before I'm even really aware that's what I'm doing. "How could he justify not telling us?"

"He said that we always knew they were engaged."

"*Fake* engaged. Was this a fake wedding?" I wave off the concierge, who jumps up to open the door for me. I shove it open, angrily.

I'm jealous.

Furious.

And hurt.

"No. It was real. They went to the courthouse and got married. Legally."

It's a gut punch.

Elise is married to Blake and Aidan and I didn't factor in it at all.

I thought we were a team, all four of us. I thought we were *all together*, on the same page.

"I'm fucking gobsmacked," I tell Aidan. "I can see Wilder not bothering to tell us, but why didn't Elise? Was she afraid we'd talk her out of it? Have you spoken to her?"

"No," he says tightly. "Wilder says she can't find her phone."

"Of course she can't find her phone." I step onto the sidewalk and pace back and forth. "Bloody hell! Let me ring you back. I need to arrange my flight to Chicago."

"You're coming back? You just got there. Don't you have important business?"

"Business can wait. I think the four of us need to sit down and talk about the horseshit that is two people in this relationship running off and getting married behind the other two's backs."

"Blake said Elise heard us the other night."

My mind goes blank. "Heard us what? Having sex?"

I don't see the relevance of that.

"Telling each other I love you."

I pause in my pacing. "Oh. Well, that wasn't really a shock to her, was it?" I ask, a little bewildered.

My relationship with Aidan has been progressing quickly.

Thinking about that moment when he confessed his feelings, even in the midst of this debacle, warms me from the inside out.

"I guess so. I don't know. Wilder was just speculating."

Then that means nothing.

I feel frustrated to be halfway around the world when I really just want to be face to face with Elise and ask her where her head was at. Where her heart is.

"Do you think she's in love with him?" I demand. "Is she heading north to rusticate in the woods with him?"

"I don't know, Simon. All I know is that I'm in love with her and I think you are, too."

He's right. I am in love with Elise.

What started out as just fun has deepened into friendship and much, much more.

"I do love her," I say gruffly. "And I love you."

"I love you, too."

I'll never tire of hearing those words from him.

Aidan is an amazing man. Being loved by him feels like I've accomplished something great.

"Maybe this is terrible timing, but I feel like it needs to be stated. I want to be with you, Aidan. Forever. I know the plan was for me to return to London, but plans can be changed. I want a real, permanent relationship with you."

"That's what I want too. I just wasn't sure if I could ask you to do that. You know I can't leave Chicago."

I blow out a breath, relieved. My voice softens. "I would never expect you to leave your career, your family. And you can ask me anything, just so you know. I'll jet across the world weekly to be with you if I have to."

Aidan laughs. "We'll figure it out. It's worth it."

"It is. You're worth it to me."

"And so is Elise. Now get your ass on a plane and come home to us."

Home.

I've never had much of one.

But if home is where the heart is, then my place is with Aidan, Elise, and Blake.

In freezing fucking Chicago.

I give an emphatic nod that he can't even see.

"I'll be there in ten hours. Then we'll go get our girl and talk some sense into her."

CHAPTER 33
Elise

I STARE at the dress hanging on the new rack Simon bought me.

It's mocking me.

I've been so productive lately. I've finished two dresses in less time than I expected. It's like the guys have been my muses and after they came over and found me drowning in fabric and plans, everything has been on track and better than ever.

Until now.

It's come to a screeching halt. And I know exactly who to blame.

My new husband.

My new *husband*.

The one I said *I do* to this morning. The one I realized I'm madly in love with this morning. The one who I just had blow-my-mind sex with. The one who just left me here afterward. Alone.

That was the fucking plan, calm down.

It was. It was the fucking plan.

The getting married thing was just one thing on both of our To Do lists today. I was also supposed to finish this dress. He was supposed to go through his pre-game routine. I was supposed to order...something. He was supposed to pick up toothpaste and socks.

It was going to be a normal day.

Except that I'm now somebody's wife.

And I have absolutely no idea what I was supposed to order. Probably something really important though.

And worst of all, I'm in love.

I suck in a breath.

I need the bakery.

I pivot on my heel and stomp toward my door. Not only do I need the routine of baking and frosting right now and plans that someone else put together that I just need to execute, I also need to surround myself with bright colors and sweet smells and baked goods that I can sneak samples of as I work.

I know Luna isn't here. She's catering a baby shower somewhere. But Lydia is holding down the fort and baking and frosting something like twelve dozen cupcakes for a going away party tomorrow.

That will be perfect. I'll be busy, feel productive, and won't think about the fact that I have a husband.

"Oh my *God*! You got *married*?!"

Okay, so I was wrong about one part of that.

I smile at Lydia, who pounces the second I step into the kitchen. 'Well...yes?" I maybe shouldn't make that sound like a question. I shake that off and try again. "Yes," I say enthusiastically. "It was really spontaneous. And romantic. And fun."

She laughs. "Obviously it was spontaneous. What are you doing here? Shouldn't you be with your new husband?"

The ironic thing is, I would be more enthusiastic about this, and selling this fake marriage harder if I *wasn't* in love with him. Which sounds so stupid. But if this was still just a part of the plan, and I had stuck to it, and was just doing this for Blake as a friend, I would readily be smiling and talking about the ceremony, and my dress, and how swept off my feet I was when he proposed going to the courthouse.

But my stupid-in-love heart just keeps reminding me that I would have rather had a real wedding with the man I'm in love with, with my friends, like Lydia, there watching us. And right now, three hours after that ceremony, I would rather be at a big party, with all of those friends, eating cupcakes just like the ones Lydia has spread out on the countertop.

Dammit. *Do not cry.*

I force a laugh. "It was so spontaneous, it didn't occur to us that we both still had to work today. He has a game tonight. So he's getting ready. I came home thinking I could get some work done on a dress. Turns out I'm too distracted." That's the truth at least. I smile at her. "Thought I could help you out."

"Sure! That would be fun." Lydia picks up her piping bag again and waves me to the spot across from her. "You have to tell me how he proposed. Actually start way back at the beginning when you first realized you wanted to date him."

I sigh. I can definitely tell the story, but it's going to be twisting a none-of-it-matters knife into my in-love-and-married-to-my-dream-man heart.

"And what about Aidan and Simon?" Lydia asks. "Where are they?"

Aidan and Simon have been around enough that our bakery family has met them. It doesn't phase Lydia that I'm dating three guys. Her boyfriend's dad is one of Luna's boyfriends. She is very familiar with poly relationships.

"Oh yeah, still… around. But both at work today." That has to be the strangest way I could've described that. And it suddenly dawns on me that Blake and I are going to have to tell Aidan and Simon that we got married.

It probably would be nice for them to hear it from us before they see it on social media.

Good thing they're both busy at work.

We begin frosting cupcakes, and I launch into my story about how I fell for Blake. I can mostly stick to the facts, including all of the things I love about him.

But I do give my mouth a squirt of icing after every three cupcakes. I need the strength that only pink buttercream can give me.

We've got three dozen cupcakes done, and I'm feeling a little sick from all the sugar I've eaten, when the bakery phone rings.

"I'll grab it," I say. I wipe my hands on the apron as I cross the room. "Books and Buns, how can I help you?"

"Yeah, uh, I'm calling for Elise Starling, please."

I frown. I never get phone calls here at the bakery. "Can I ask who's calling?"

"My name is Mark Gordon."

I don't know a Mark Gordon. "Can I tell her what it's regarding?"

"Yes. It's about her recent wedding to Blake Wilder."

I freeze. What? Shit, shit, shit. "Why are you asking about that?" I ask, working to keep my voice calm.

"I'm a reporter with an online entertainment and sports site. This is big news in the Racketeers world. We haven't been able to get a hold of Mr. Wilder. Thought I'd take a chance."

"Well if she just got married, why would she be here?" I ask. Such a great question really.

He chuckles. "Good point. Just trying everything I could think of. I assume you work there though, so you must know Elise pretty well."

My stomach dips. I should just hang up on him, but this is the business line. I have to be polite so he doesn't write something bad about Books and Buns. "I know Ms. Starling very well."

Lydia is watching me. She smiles at that.

"Well, I guess it's Mrs. Wilder, right?" The guy says with another chuckle.

Hey, I could keep my name. What a dick. But my stomach swoops again. And I regret that three-fourths of a cup of buttercream I have in it right now.

"Want to give me a quote?" he asks. "Tell me something about Elise that readers would like to know."

I think for a moment about telling him to fuck off, but then decide what the hell? "Elise is amazing. Everyone loves her. Blake's a lucky guy."

The guy gives another laugh, but says, "Okay, thanks. Can I get your name for the article?"

"How about you just do the thing where you say it's a source close to the couple?"

"Got it," he says. "Well, thanks." He disconnects.

I look at Lydia. "Well crap. A reporter knows that I work here and has already heard the news about our wedding."

She nods. "Most of Chicago has already heard the news about your wedding."

Right. That was the entire point. Blake's grandmother has to believe it's real. If it wasn't real, why would we let the entire city of Chicago, the entire Racketeers organization, think it was?

The bell on the front counter dings and Lydia sets down her piping bag. "My turn. Be right back."

I nod and bend over the tray of cupcakes again.

But a second later, I hear her say, "Hi, can I help you?"

"Are you Elise Starling?"

I straighten. Oh, *no*.

"No. I'm Lydia. Can I help you?"

"I'd like to talk to Elise," the woman says.

A customer? A design client? But I have a suspicion it's neither.

"Oh, well, she's not here right now," Lydia tells her.

I frown and move closer to the door.

"We saw Blake leaving his apartment alone. Wondering why his wife wasn't with him."

Yeah... *shit*.

"Sorry I can't help you," Lydia replies, her voice still upbeat and friendly. "Elise and Blake don't report to me."

"But she does work here?" the woman asks.

This has to be another reporter. I nudge the swinging door open just slightly and peek out. Then I freeze. There are like nine people in the bakery. At least that I can see. Four of them have cameras, five of them are holding out what look like recording devices. Definitely reporters.

Lydia shrugs. "Part time. She's a friend of the owner. But like I said, she doesn't report to me. If you need a story, you should probably ask the Racketeers or something."

I'm going to owe Lydia a free pinup dress for this. She's normally a pretty shy girl, but she's sticking to her denials and I'm grateful.

"No one's returning our calls."

Lydia crosses her arms. "Do I really look like I can be of any help?"

Shit. What am I gonna do now? If the reporters are here at the bakery, I need to slip back upstairs before anyone sees me. Then I need a plan for how to get out of here.

Just then the bell over the front door tinkles and I groan. *More* reporters?

"Wow! Are we having a sale no one told me about?"

I nearly sag in relief at the sound of Luna's voice. She's back. She will take care of this. Luna always knows what to do. Plus, she's pretty good with reporters. Dating Alexsei Ryan and Owen Phillips, one of the Racketeers coaches, has put her in the spotlight too.

"You all need to get out of here unless you're buying something." And that is the voice of Cameron Bach, Luna's third boyfriend. And grumpy multimillionaire tech genius, he doesn't take shit from anybody.

He'll get rid of the reporters. He might also be my best bet for sneaking out of here and getting to the arena without stumbling upon anyone I don't want to see.

Lydia comes through the swinging door. "This is crazy." She's smiling a smile that says she doesn't mind at all.

I blow out of a breath. "We didn't really think this through."

Luna comes through the door next, followed directly by Cameron.

"You are so lucky you filled me in on everything," she says. "Though a heads up on the actual *wedding* might've been nice before I saw it splashed over social media."

I pull Luna to the side and lower my voice. "It was really spontaneous. We honestly didn't think through anything other than letting his grandmother know that this whole thing was real enough that she'll give us the cabin."

"Well you better get upstairs. Get ready for the game, you can go with me and Cam. Then you won't have to worry about sneaking out of here on your own."

I pull her into a hug. "Thank you. You guys are the best friends."

She pulls back and gives me a wink. "And I assume you won't be coming home with us since you'll want to spend your *wedding night* at your new husband's house."

Yeah. That would make sense. But of course we didn't talk about that either.

We honestly hadn't made any plans past the courthouse.

And after the weird moments upstairs in my apartment where I felt that rocking connection, I really don't know what to expect from my new husband.

This was all supposed to be straightforward and easy.

But of course it got messy.

I make my way upstairs, planning to get ready for tonight. I do expect to have a lot of eyes and attention on me at the arena. I guess we did talk through that part. We knew that the news would break before the game tonight and Blake has filled in the PR department, so I expect that I'll be up on the Jumbotron a little bit. Now seeing how much social media coverage there has already been, I'm guessing the crowd will pay attention to me as well.

Again, I am thankful that I will be there with Luna and Cam. Dani and Nathan will also be there in the stands and between my two girls and their grumpy-rich-always-get-their-way boyfriend and husband, I'm not too worried about getting harassed.

The wall phone that Simon had installed for me two days ago starts ringing and I jump. I am still not used to that thing. I've only had three calls and it was the guys all calling to check to see if it worked. I press a hand to my chest, trying to catch my breath as I cross the room. I swear to God if this is a reporter, I'm ripping this phone back out of the wall.

"Hello?" I answer hesitantly.

"Elise Elizabeth Starling, this is your mother."

Oh, shit. My mother never uses my middle name unless I'm in huge trouble. And the fact that she's calling my landline reminds me I still have no idea where my phone is.

"Hi, Mom."

"You need to find your cell phone. It's pinging in your apartment, just an FYI."

My mother has me on Find My Phones because well, I lose my phone all the time. "I have looked for it. I don't know where it is."

Maybe it's in the refrigerator. I walk over, phone still pressed to my ear and open the door. No phone in the fridge.

"But first you need to explain to me why my friend Linda was the one to tell me that my daughter got married today."

Thankfully, the cord to the phone also reaches over to one of my stools. I slump down onto it. "I'm sorry. Mom, it's not real. Blake and I are doing it so that he can inherit his grandmother's cabin. She told him he had to be married for her to give it to him. That's it. I'm doing a favor for a friend. But it's gotten all blown up because he's a famous hockey player. And honestly..."

I trail off and my mom stays quiet for a moment, then she says, "And you didn't think it through."

Unlike when my father talks about me being scatterbrained or unorganized, my mother's words come out with affection. "I really didn't. And I should have. The thing is it doesn't mean anything to us so we didn't think about it meaning anything to anyone else."

"I see. Well, that is quite a favor."

"It is," I agree. "But I know what it feels like to have your family a little too involved in your life and the choices you are trying to make. So when he asked for my help, I agreed. Almost immediately. Plus, I really like him. He's a very good guy. And he really wants and deserves that cabin."

"You looked absolutely gorgeous in all the photos," my mother says. She pauses, then adds, "Those photos looked very real Elise. You looked extremely happy. Even in love, I would say. I know you're used to being on stage and playing a part. You're a very good actress."

There's something in her voice. Something that tells me she's not entirely convinced.

"Oh. Well, good. I want to sell it. For Blake's sake."

"Sure. For Blake's sake," she repeats. "And the marriage is not real, is that right? You just went to the courthouse together, all dressed up, to take photos so people would think that it was?"

"Well no. It is *legal*. But…" I have to swallow hard. "It's not *real*." My voice is definitely shaky now.

"Elise?" my mom asks in her I-know-you-so-just-cut-the-crap voice. "What's wrong?"

"I…I want it to be real." I feel tears stinging my eyes. And then I say the words out loud for the first time. "Mom, I'm in love with Blake Wilder."

CHAPTER 34
Elise

TRUE TO THEIR WORD, Luna and Cameron get me out of the bakery without anyone seeing me and then into the arena by parking in the players' lot and using a back door. The security people don't even blink, clearly used to seeing these two.

But my anonymity ends the second we step off the VIP elevator and onto the concourse. People start turning and pointing and talking.

And as I follow Luna and Cam down the steps toward our regular seats, suddenly the wedding march is blasting over the intercom.

I stop, the crowd erupts in cheers and whistles, and I look up at the Jumbotron to find myself front and center.

The only thing I can do is blush, smile, and wave.

I am Mrs. Blake Wilder. Legally. At least for now.

I look down on the ice and find Blake immediately. He has stopped his warm-ups and is watching me come down the steps.

I blow him a kiss, and he puts his hand over his heart as he gives me a huge grin.

The crowd goes wild.

Yeah, that's pretty sweet.

Well, so far, so good.

I'm only in my seat for about five minutes before Sammy, the Racketeers mascot, comes stomping down the steps and stops in the aisle at the end of our row.

"Jesus Christ," Cam mutters.

"Remind me why I haven't fired him," Nathan says.

"Oh, stop it," Dani tells him, grinning. "He's great. The crowd loves him."

There is definitely a love-hate relationship between Sammy and these guys. On one hand, he's the reason that Dani is with her men. Kind of. On the other, Cameron does not like the fact that Wade, the kid inside the malamute dressed in a gangster costume had a little crush on Luna. Cam was quite pleased, however, when Wade seemed to shift his affections to me.

I look over at Sammy. I wasn't told this was part of our show tonight. He tips his head to one side and plants his big furry paws on his hips. I glance up and see that, of course, we are on the Jumbotron.

Well, I can put on a show. I shrug as if to ask, "What?"

He holds up his left hand and points at his ring finger with his right. I hold mine up, wiggle it so the diamond sparkles.

The crowd cheers.

Sammy mimes a knife stabbing into his heart.

I laugh and shrug and mouth, "I'm sorry."

He holds out his hand to me then gestures up the stairs.

I point down on the ice toward Blake, put my hand over my heart and then shake my head at Sammy indicating that no, I won't run away with him.

Sammy sighs heavily, his shoulders slumping.

The crowd gives a collective, "Aw," in sympathy.

Then everyone starts laughing and cheering.

I look around, then realize that Sammy has turned to face the ice and has his hands up in surrender, shaking them and his head.

I look down to find Blake pointing his hockey stick up at Sammy and then dragging his opposite hand across his throat.

Obviously, there is a break in the game action.

I laugh and feel my heart skip.

How could I not fall in love with this guy? I'm not stupid at all. *Not* falling for him would have been far more ridiculous than losing my heart was.

Finally, Blake has to turn back to the game and Sammy wipes across his forehead as if massively relieved and I extend my hand as if to shake his hand.

But Sammy puts his hands up and starts backing up the stairs, as if to say no way, I'm staying far away from you.

The crowd loves it.

When I can finally take my seat again, Luna and Dani are delighted.

"I could never ham it up like that," Dani tells me.

"Yeah, I maybe could, but I would look ridiculous. You're a natural," Luna tells me.

I shrug. "It's pretty fun. I'm surprised Blake got into it."

"It would've been hilarious if Aidan and Simon had been here too," Luna says.

"Yeah, I've been dying to ask you—what were their reactions when you and Blake said you were going to actually get *married*?" Dani asks.

Dani and Luna are both in poly relationships, but Dani is the only one who actually has married her guys. So far anyway. And she did marry all three of them, but not at once. She had a commitment ceremony with Nathan and Michael first, and Crew later. And did create some angst amongst them, but they worked through it and are all wildly happy and fully committed now.

Of course, there's a huge difference between her foursome and mine. Hers intends to stay together.

I shake my head and lower my voice, "Nothing. I mean, we haven't told them. It's not real, remember?"

Dani and Luna both turn to look at me. "But it *is* real," Luna says. "I mean you really got married, right?"

"Yes." I don't know why everyone is so worked up about that. It's just a piece of paper. No one knows how I really feel about

Blake so they shouldn't be so invested in this. "But Aidan and Simon know that we were faking the engagement. And they'll know that the marriage is temporary. I don't expect them to have a reaction at all."

Dani and Luna exchange glances. I lift my brows. "What?"

"You don't expect them to have a reaction?" Dani repeats. "Really?"

"You guys, our situation isn't like yours."

"But there are feelings," Dani insists. "I mean, I've seen you together. I know you're having fun, but there are real feelings between you all."

Danielle always wants everyone to be in love. That's all that is. I tell my heart, which is now beating a little faster, to calm down. Dani has no idea how the guys feel.

I sit back in my seat and slump down. "Well, there are real feelings between Aidan and Simon."

Luna leans in closer. "What are you talking about?"

"I overheard them. They're in love with each other. Which is amazing. They're both the best. I'm so happy they're happy."

Luna narrows her eyes. "You don't look happy that they're happy."

I shake my head. "No. I seriously am. I love—"

Dani now leans in. "What was that?"

I press my lips together.

"Come on," Luna says. "Say it."

"I almost said I love them."

"See? Love." Dani seems almost giddy. "You're all falling in love."

I shake my head. "Well, that's the fucked up thing." I look from one to the other then I focus on the ice. On Blake. "*I'm* falling in love. I'm in love with all of them. But Aidan and Simon are in love with each other. Simon is going back to London eventually. I assume he and Aidan will work something out. And Blake and I have been faking all of this this whole time. I know they all love the sex. But nobody has said anything about love to me." And dammit, now I want to cry out of pure frustration.

I'm the one who is always up for a good time. And this has been a *very* good time. I know I can't do a long-term relationship with even *one* guy. There's no way I can juggle three.

But...I have been. Or rather, I've found three that don't need to be juggled. They roll with all of the messy parts of my life, with my quirks, and they make things easier, *better*. They also take care of each other so I don't have to worry about failing one of them. And they definitely take care of *me*. I've never felt this cared about in my entire life. Not only do they accept the ways I can make things more challenging, they find it endearing and strive to make it all easier. On me, not for themselves.

"Have *you* said anything about love to *them*?" Dani asks.

I shake my head. "No."

"Well you should. And you should've talked about this wedding thing with Aidan and Simon," Dani says. "Trust me, from experience I can tell you that communication is *the* most important thing."

"Seriously," Luna agrees. "Having a poly relationship has a lot of challenges. I mean, just the sheer amount of testosterone... And not in a good way all the time." She shoots a glance at Cameron. He pretends to be watching the game and not listening, but when she turns back to me, I see his eye roll.

"But you're in a relationship with three different guys. Individual relationships. But then they're also having relationships with each other. Obviously, in one case there's a romantic relationship. But there's also friendships with each of them and Blake. And then there's the whole group dynamic. It's honestly like you're having four relationships all at once. One with each of them and then the group. And communication and respecting all of that and everyone's place is the only way it works," Luna says.

My heart is pounding, my stomach is in knots, and I have officially decided that falling in love sucks.

I frown at both of my dearest girlfriends. "You know what? I don't need to hear any of this. I believe you, I think you're doing an amazing job in your relationships, but mine is not the same. This is a temporary thing the four of us are doing. And it's going to be over soon."

"But—" Dani starts.

But I see Nathan reach over and put a hand on her leg, squeezing gently. She presses her lips together.

On my other side, I hear Cam lean in and say, "You made your point, Pixie, give her a minute."

Thank you Nathan and Cameron.

I take a deep breath.

Thank God, just then Luna's boyfriend Alexsei shoots the puck down the ice to Crew, Dani's husband and everyone's attention is glued to the ice.

I know they mean well. I know they have experience and they know what they're talking about.

And these are the women I would want to talk to if I actually had a long-term, committed poly relationship.

But, fortunately I do not. Because it sounds like a big headache, to be honest.

I'll be single again soon. No more worries about the three men who have come in and turned my world upside down.

So, yeah, I'm really happy I avoided all of *that* long term.

Yep. Really, really happy.

CHAPTER 35
Blake

"WELL, THAT WAS A LONG DAY," I say as I shove open the door to my apartment and let Elise slip in before me.

I'm both keyed up and exhausted.

I hate the spotlight on a good day.

But today?

When I just wanted to be alone with Elise on our wedding day?

It was fucking torture.

There were reporters everywhere, mics in my face, lots of congratulations, and my phone hasn't seen that many notifications since I let the puck slide past me last season and I lost the Racketeers the championship.

But probably for the best, because if I was alone with Elise, I would have told her I'm in love with her and forced her to let me down gently.

Which would have really been torture.

"I had no idea people were so in love with love," she admits, dropping her overnight bag by the front door and bending over to yank off her boots.

She strips her winter coat off and just drops it on top of her shoes.

"I have a coat closet." I point to it.

She just shrugs. I leave the coat where she's tossed it.

She's stayed over here several times before but we were usually ripping each other's clothes off within three feet of my front door. Tonight, she looks like she needs a hug much more than she needs my dick.

She looks as exhausted as I feel.

Faking happiness is brutal. Or rather, faking that you're faking happiness is brutal, when you are, in fact, really happy, but it's all fake. Or something like that.

"Come here." I pull her into my arms and she sags against me. "Do you want to take a shower or a bath? Then we can watch a stupid comedy or a horror movie. Your pick."

"Oh, definitely horror," she murmurs against my chest.

"Works for me." The whole ride home I was worried about tonight.

This afternoon, after I stood there in the courthouse and realized I wanted to be married to her for real, and that I'm in love with her, I shouldn't have gone home with her. But I couldn't resist the urge to be inside her one more time, to touch her soft flesh, and kiss her gorgeous lips.

I think she sensed I was being weird. She kept trying to make it about quick sex, and I kept trying to make it romantic. Finally, I got myself so fucking wound up I ended up pounding her into the headboard with such ferocity she probably still has a headache.

Yeah. I was weird.

Hell, I even took her panties.

But I've never loved a woman the way I do Elise, and I'm kind of going out of my fucking mind.

Every moment in bed with her, every moment on the ice hamming it up for the crowd, then answering reporters' questions, I wanted it to be real.

I told Aidan I'm in love with her.

He and Simon are in love with her, too.

So now I don't know what happens.

But right now, Elise just needs time to decompress.

I do have to warn her though. "Aidan and Simon found out we got married. They were a little...caught off guard."

"Oh! Shit. I didn't mean for that to happen."

"Neither did I." I massage her lower back. Her muscles are tense. "You never found your phone?"

"No. Maybe it's in the garbage compactor. I've found it there before." She pulls back. "They didn't call the landline though. When did you hear from them?"

"Before the game I talked to Aidan. He said he spoke to Simon earlier and told him. I guess some of the other firefighters saw the social media posts."

She bites her lower lip. "We should have told them."

"Yep. But they'll understand. It wasn't meant to be a secret. Just..."

"Not a big deal," she finishes, her voice flat.

My stomach drops. "Exactly."

Frustration nearly overwhelms me.

This is nuts.

I don't want to live without this woman.

In the woods, or otherwise.

I'm going to let her take a bath, we'll watch a movie, get a good night's sleep, then I need to shoot my shot. I've spent most of my life blocking shots on the ice and in my personal life.

Not anymore.

I'm going to tell her how I feel and see if it lands in the net.

But right now, she needs some space.

"Bath or shower?"

"A bath sounds amazing."

I take her into my bathroom and I dig out some bath salts I use when my muscles are tired. Elise ties her hair up in a bun on her head as I turn the water on. I go and get her overnight bag and when I return, she's already in the water, piling bubbles up over her naked body so I can't see the good parts.

I'm going to assume that's a hint that she doesn't want me to touch her.

Pulling a towel out of the linen closet, I set it on the counter. "Here you go. Do you want a glass of wine?"

"That sounds amazing." She gives a sigh and leans back, closing her eyes.

In my bedroom I change into lounge pants and a T-shirt, then go and open a glass of the sauvignon blanc I know she likes. When I come back, I turn off the overhead lights and just leave the sconces on so the harsh glare isn't in her eyes. I set the wine on the little table I have next to the free-standing tub.

She opens her eyes and smiles at me. "Thank you. This tub is incredible. It's massive."

"I have a big body and I do love a good soak."

"Think how amazing you're going to feel in a year after you're done playing." She lifts the glass and sips the wine.

"Yeah. I'm looking forward to it. I'll miss hockey though."

I'll miss her.

I almost blurt out my feelings again, but she closes her eyes, so I just retreat and leave her be.

I debate reaching out to Aidan and asking him for advice, but I don't know where the three of us guys stand with each other right now.

Or where they stand with Elise.

All of that kind of seems like a conversation that needs to happen in person. The four of us.

Scrolling through all the messages I have on my phone, I see a text from Justin Fucking Travers. Annoyed, I open it, wondering what the prick has to say.

> Congratulations on your marriage, man. I'm genuinely happy for you. No more shit talk, let's keep it to hockey.

I don't know if it's genuine or not, and I still want to slam him into the boards, but it's something. I just text him "thanks" and leave it at that. If I think about him touching my wife, my head will explode.

Another twenty minutes pass while I scroll. I don't hear anything from the bathroom. Worried Elise might have fallen asleep in the tub, I go and check on her. She's asleep, but not in the tub. It's still filled with deflating bubbles and lukewarm water.

Elise is curled up in the middle of my bed, sound asleep under the covers.

I pause, debating joining her, but she looks too comfortable to bother. My bulk will drop the mattress the second I sit on the bed and I don't want to crowd her. I've crowded her enough today with my wants and desires.

So I grab my pillow and a spare blanket and head to the couch.

Not exactly the wedding night of my dreams and yet, I still feel very fucking grateful.

Fake or not, I'm married to the woman I love.

CHAPTER 36
Aidan

IT'S two a.m. and I don't give a fuck.

I've picked Simon up from the airport and we've had the drive to Blake's apartment to discuss what comes next.

But what comes next is simple—we tell Mr. and Mrs. Blake Wilder that we're in love with Mrs. Wilder, that we really like Mr. Wilder, and we'd like to live happily ever after with them.

See? Simple.

But they happen to be two of the most stubborn, emotionally closed off people we know so we're bracing for a fight.

Still, we know we'll win. Because they want this too. I know they do.

We just kind of screwed up by not telling them how we feel before now.

Is it fast? Maybe.

But how long should it take to fall in love with amazing people, anyway? As soon as you realize they're amazing and you have a pretty good sense that you will think they're amazing for the rest of your life, what else is there?

Miraculously, I find a parking spot on Blake's block and we stride through the lobby of his building minutes later.

His doorman recognizes us from previous visits. "Evening, gentlemen." He doesn't seem bothered by the hour.

"Evening, Victor," Simon says.

He remembered the doorman's name. I really love this guy.

We ride up to Blake's penthouse in silence. The doors swish open and we step off and into the dimly lit hallway. It's so weird to me that penthouses don't have doors. But I guess the elevator acts like a door. Not just anyone can come up here.

We start down the hallway to the living area, but Simon puts a hand on my arm, stopping me after only three steps.

"Wha–"

Then I hear it.

Snoring.

I frown. Why can I hear Blake snoring from here? We've been to his apartment. The bedroom is clear across the penthouse.

Simon sighs heavily. I look over at him.

"He's on the couch," Simon says.

"He's…" That sinks in. "He's *what*?"

Simon nods. "That has to be it."

The living room is five more paces in front of us. I stalk toward the sofa and the sleeping giant who is sprawled over the cushions on his stomach.

His hair is wild, covering his face, he's in lounge pants, and one leg is bent at what is a decidedly uncomfortable angle, while the other hangs off, his foot touching the floor.

The idiot.

"Blake," I say, nudging his foot. "Wake up."

He snorts, then rolls. But doesn't open his eyes.

"Blake!" I say louder. "Hey! Wake up!" I kick at his calf and start to lean in, but he suddenly jerks upright, his entire body tense. I step back in case he starts swinging.

He looks around. "What? Hey, what?" He scrapes his hair back from his face. "Who's there?"

Simon leans over and clicks on the lamp that sits on the end table.

Blake blinks in the sudden brightness. Then he focuses on us. He scowls. "What the hell, guys?"

"What the fuck are you doing?" Simon asks him.

Blake scrubs a hand over his face. "I was sleeping. Kind of."

"Elise better be in your bedroom," Simon tells him. "So help me God, if you dropped her off at her apartment on your wedding night–"

"She's in the bedroom," Blake breaks in, sounding very grumpy.

Oh, he's grumpy? The guy who married my girlfriend earlier today without telling me is grumpy?

"Why are you on the couch?" Simon demands. "What did you say or do to make her kick you out of bed?"

"She didn't kick me out. It's been a long day." He sits up and leans to rest his elbows on his thighs, his big hands hanging between his knees. He stares at the floor. "She took a bath and then she fell asleep. I didn't want to bother her."

"Bother her?" I repeat. "Why would sleeping in your bed with you bother her?"

He shakes his head. "This is all messed up." Then a thought seems to occur to him and he looks up at us, frowning. "What are you guys doing here? It's the middle of the night." He focuses on Simon. "I thought you were in London."

"I was in London," Simon says. "Until I found out from my boyfriend that my girlfriend got married. Decided I should come back and find out what the fuck is going on."

Blake looks at me. "You didn't explain it?"

"I did. And we decided that all of this bullshit about you two faking the engagement and this marriage being temporary and whatever else the two of you are telling yourselves, needs to end. Tonight."

Blake looks at us for a long moment. Then he takes a deep breath and blows it out. "Thank God you're here."

Simon lets out a long breath as well. I give a choked laugh. "Thank God?"

"Man, I'm so fucking in love with her," Blake says running a hand through his hair. "I don't know what to do. I got her wrapped up in this thing as a fake relationship. Then she agreed to marry me, but all because of the damn cabin. I don't know how to tell her I love her. How do I make that believable?"

I roll my neck and sigh. "You just tell her, man. You just tell her and you have to trust that she knows you well enough to know you're being honest." I look at Simon. "We haven't told her either. But we're going to storm in here at two a.m., and confess our feelings. It could easily look like we're just reacting out of jealousy because of the wedding, but the truth is, we're crazy about her. Neither of us can imagine our life without her. It hasn't been very long, but it just feels right. The four of us feels right."

Blake is watching me. He nods. "I guess that's another thing I wasn't sure about. Honestly, if I gave her the choice between me or you two, I'm sure she'd pick you. You guys have your shit figured out. You know what you want. You can give her whatever she wants. Hell until this morning, I really believed that what I wanted was to move to Minnesota by myself and live in a cabin in the woods."

Simon looks surprised. "That's not what you want anymore?"

Blake gives a soft laugh. "I mean, I still love that cabin. I'd like to spend time there. But I happened to fall madly in love with a woman who is not exactly, secluded-cabin-in-the-woods material. And I love everything about her.

Also, she has two other boyfriends. One of them is a firefighter and kind of has to live in the city. Chicago needs him to live in the city. The other one is a billionaire or something though I honestly don't really know what he does. Maybe he could do it from the cabin."

Simon and I both chuckle.

"But," Blake goes on. "It seems that he probably needs to be close to an airport. Or have really reliable Wi-Fi at the very least. So the full-time cabin thing is probably not going to happen."

"You would give that up for us?" I ask him.

He nods. "I have pretty quickly realized that being alone is not nearly as appealing as being alone with the three of you. I'm not saying that I want to go to a bunch of parties, and fundraising events, and galas, but, turns out there's two other people who can fill in for that stuff. This foursome thing is actually pretty great. So yes, I would stay in Chicago for this. For you."

Simon claps his hands together. "Excellent. This is going a lot better than I expected."

"Yeah, now we just have to make the pitch to our girl. She's the one who's going to take some convincing."

"Do you think so?"

We all swing around at the sound of Elise's voice.

CHAPTER 37
Simon

ELISE IS STANDING at the end of the hallway that leads to the bedrooms. She's wearing one of Blake's T-shirts. It hits just above her knees. Her hair is mussed, she has a pillow crease on her cheek, and her eyes look puffy, as if she hasn't gotten much sleep.

My heart aches in my chest.

She and Aidan are the loves of my life and I'm not letting her go. Even if she doesn't know it yet.

"Hey, Elise," Blake says, starting for her.

She holds up a hand. "You really came back from London early because you found out about the wedding?" she asks me.

"No," I tell her. "I came back from London early because I realize that I haven't told you that I'm in love with you. And I couldn't go another day without saying it. And I had to say it in person."

I take a step closer to her. Her eyes are locked on me and she's pressing her lips together.

"I'm in love with you, Elise. Madly."

"I thought you were in love with Aidan."

I nod. "I'm madly in love with Aidan too. I want you both. And I want you to stay married to Blake. But I want you and Blake to keep seeing me and Aidan." I take a step toward her.

"I'm moving to Chicago. I'll still have to go to London at times. And other places. But this is where I want to live. Where I want to make my life. With all of you."

I take a final step, stopping about a foot in front of her. "I'm very spoiled. I've lived a very privileged life. Please don't make me start learning the word 'no' now."

She's blinking her big brown eyes, but I see the corner of her mouth twitch.

Aidan steps up beside me and takes my hand. "Me too, Elise. I'm in love with you too. I've fallen for you both so fast, but it's completely real. Yes, I was jealous when I found out that you really married Blake. But only because I want to be a part of your forever too. We screwed up not telling you how we felt as soon as we realized it. I guess we didn't really have a great moment? We were waiting for a good time. But we shouldn't have. We should have just blurted it out."

She's pressing her lips together, staring at both of us. Her gaze goes to Blake.

"I'm in love with you, too," he says, his deep voice even gruffer than usual. "Asking you to marry me was the smartest thing I've ever done. I did it in a really stupid way, but the idea of having you forever, is the best idea I've ever had. I love you, Elise. And I am so sorry I didn't say that before now. In my defense, I just realized it as we were standing in front of the judge. So I didn't really have time before that. But...I was an idiot to not realize it before that."

She closes her eyes and takes a deep breath.

Aidan jumps in. "And before you say anything about how this can't work or how we can't deal with messes or disorganization or lost phones or whatever...no. It *will* work. It's already working."

"What messes?" Blake asks.

She opens her eyes and focuses on him.

"You mean your organizational style?" he asks. "None of us care about that."

I smile. I love Elise's "chaos" and I love how Aidan and Blake have embraced it as well. As I've gotten to know Aidan, it doesn't surprise me. He is loving and accepting and just a good man. I had my doubts about the big, burly hockey player, but he's all in. The way he cares for Elise and just rolls with all of the beautiful things that make her the unique, gorgeous woman who stole our hearts, makes me appreciate him and makes me look forward to a future with him in our lives.

"We will give you an entire room wherever we live and you can do whatever you want with it," Blake tells her, stepping forward until he's within touching distance. "Or you can have four rooms. Or hell, I kind of hope you'll set up some racks and stuff in every room with your dresses and accessories. You and your passion have brought color and creativity and sexiness and fun into my life in a way I would have never imagined and I want it around me all the time. I love being at your apartment. It makes me smile and feel surrounded by joy. This place—" He glances around his apartment. "Is empty and sterile and I hate it here now that I've spent time with you."

She gives him a shaky smile. "Wow."

He returns the smile, looking almost relieved.

Aidan continues where Blake left off. "And, as for your schedule, where sometimes you forget you need to do something until the last minute, that just means there's never a dull day. I never know what to expect and honey, I'm perfect for that. As a firefighter, I live with that kind of routine constantly. I'm so good."

I jump in. "And the phone thing is nothing. To me that just means you need one of us with you most of the time so people can call us if they need you." I shrug. "Needing one of us by your side all the time is an easy fix, because there's nowhere else we'd rather be."

Blake nods. "Yeah, sorry to break it to you, but if that's the best you've got to try to scare us off, you're stuck with us. Forever. Because that's nothing stacked up against love."

"He's right, love," I tell her. "You're going to have to do a lot more than just leave things lying around to scare us off."

Aidan gives her a grin. "Yeah, you've really screwed up trying to push us away. We are all completely head over heels and we're not going anywhere."

She swallows, then takes a breath and says simply, "I know."

We all just stand there, like dumbasses.

She watches us, her smile slowly growing. "I know that you are all okay with my messes, and my disorganization, and my phone issues. You've all been here, becoming a part of my life seamlessly. You've made me feel special and loveable and have never made me feel like a problem. I know this can work."

She stops and takes another breath. "But there is one big thing I screwed up."

"It's okay. Whatever it is," Blake says immediately.

"There's nothing too big," Aidan adds.

God, these two are gone for her.

Just like I am.

"What is it, love?" I ask.

She gives us all a dazzling smile. "I haven't told you all how much I love each of you either."

Blake steps forward, nearly on her toes. "Well, of course you do. We're *very* loveable."

That makes her laugh. "You already knew?"

He lifts a hand, cupping her face. "No," he confesses. "Not at all. In fact, I spent the whole day completely convinced you were just doing me a favor marrying me. But I'm so fucking happy to hear it."

She looks at me. "Did you know?"

I shake my head. "Hoped, love. Hoped."

She looks at Aidan. "How about you?"

"Did I think I might deserve to have an amazing, feisty, sexy, passionate, creative, special woman fall in *love* with me?" Aidan asks. "Girl, I was thrilled as fuck when you just let me *kiss* you."

She smiles, then a little pink touches her cheeks. "I think I *begged* you to kiss me."

He makes a little growling sound. "Yes, I believe you're right."

She takes a deep breath and looks at each of us again. "Well, I do love you. All of you. So much." She shakes her head. "I can't believe how much. I want this. I want all of you, all of us, together." She pauses and wet her lips. "Can we do that?"

"Yes," I say immediately.

"Absolutely," Aidan answers.

"Fuck yes," Blake says.

Her smile grows bigger and brighter. "Okay. Great. Awesome."

"Blake?" I say.

"Yeah?"

"I think maybe you should carry your wife into bed."

Now *he* growls. He immediately bends and scoops Elise into his arms. But he glances back.

"You guys are coming, right?"

I smile. That's how this needs to work and it looks like we're all on board.

"Right behind you," I tell him.

"Nowhere else I want to be," Aidan says.

Once in the bedroom, Blake settles Elise in the middle of the bed and climbs in on her right side.

Aidan and I strip down to our underwear, dropping on our clothes on the floor without concern for where anything lands.

I take Elise's right side and Aidan slides in next to me, moving in close and leaning over me.

He presses a kiss to Elise's mouth. "I love you, El."

"I love you too," she says softly, touching his cheek before he pulls back.

I lean in to kiss her next. "I love you, my love."

"I love you so much," she tells me, giving me a sweet smile.

Then her husband rolls her toward him. He cups her face and

kisses her deeply. He lifts his head and stares down at her. "Love you, Mrs. Wilder."

Her smile is bright. "I love you, Mr. Wilder."

Then he settles in, tucking her close, her back to his front, splaying his hand over her belly. My hand rests on her hip, and Aidan's hand is on my chest.

We're all quiet for a long moment.

Finally, Elise asks, "That's it?"

We all laugh.

"What do you mean?" I ask.

"We're not going to have celebratory we're-all-in-love-and-together sex?" she asks.

Aidan is hit by a huge yawn.

Blake shakes his head. "It's been a big day and it's the middle of the night. We're just going to sleep now."

"Oh." She sounds disappointed.

I lean in and kiss her cheek. "No worries, love. We have the rest of our lives to ravish you. You'll be trying to come up with ways to keep us off of you."

She grins up at me. "I can't imagine that. Danielle and Luna are two of the happiest people I've ever met."

We all laugh.

"You just keep that in mind," Blake tells her.

"How do you feel about being awakened by the smell of pancakes and bacon while your new husband eats your pussy?" Aidan asks. His voice is sleepy and mumbled, a sharp contrast to his words.

Elise giggles. "I think that sounds perfect."

"Great. See you in the morning. Goodnight, El," he says.

"Goodnight, love," I tell her softly.

"Goodnight, wife," Blake says.

She let out a happy sigh. "Goodnight."

I put my hand over Aidan's on my chest and close my eyes.

I have never been happier in my entire life.

I'm *home*.

CHAPTER 38
Blake

"OH, MY GOD!" Elise says emphatically, nearly jerking my arm out of the socket.

I wish it was mid-orgasm from pure ecstasy, but for once, it's because she's terrified.

We're flying in a single-engine plane chartered by Simon over the frozen lake to the landing strip on the south end of the island, en route to a cozy and intimate Valentine's Day weekend and my lake house—yes, mine.

Or rather, ours.

My *wife* and I both have our names on the title thanks to my grandmother—who, by the way, claimed she knew our engagement was fake the entire time when I finally confessed. In my mind, Aidan and Simon have a stake in it too, so I plan to add both of their names to the title, just in case.

This is the first time any of them are seeing the cabin and I'm excited as hell.

Elise is excited about the house and the time away from work for the four of us.

Not so excited about the flying part.

"Don't worry, in the summer, we just take the boat over," I

assure her, wrapping my arm around her shoulder and pulling her in tightly against my chest.

"Are we almost there?" Aidan asks.

To my surprise, he doesn't look entirely thrilled with this flight, either. He's gripping the armrests with white knuckles.

Simon, on the other hand, is used to a lifetime of private jets and aviation hobbies. He's sitting back, totally relaxed, sipping a bourbon.

"There's the landing strip right there," I point out, gesturing out the window.

"Thank you, Jesus," Elise breathes.

We flew from O'Hare to Duluth, then hopped on this charter plane to head out to the island the house is on. I've arranged for everything we need for the weekend to be dropped off at the house ahead of time, and a surprise for Elise is packed in my duffle bag. Well, one of her surprises.

I kiss Elise's temple and squeeze her reassuringly. "We'll be on the ground in five minutes."

"Not soon enough," Aidan mutters.

Simon puts his hand on Aidan's knee and squeezes. "I'm sorry this is making you nervous, yet at the same time I'm delighting in finding one way I'm actually tougher than you."

Aidan shoots his boyfriend a look of disbelief. "Seriously? I just have a sensitive stomach."

"I've watched you eat a twelve ounce steak and drink a six-pack of beer. You do not have a sensitive stomach." Simon gives him a smile. "But I find you very endearing right now."

"You're just lucky I love you," Aidan grumbles.

"You're going to love me even more later on tonight."

Aidan's eyes darken, but he doesn't respond. He just glances back out the window to check our flight status.

I assume Simon's comment was a sexual innuendo but Elise giggles and covers her mouth immediately to stop herself. Simon shoots her a sharp look.

Huh.

Why do I feel like those two are cooking something up for Aidan?

Maybe I'm not the only one planning a surprise this weekend.

It's been fun getting to know these guys better and figuring out how the four of us all work together, and separately. I never in a million years would have imagined I'd be willing to share my wife with two other men, but it's working damn well. When I'm on the road, I know Elise has one or both of them looking out for her, and I don't have to worry when she inevitably loses her phone for an entire day.

She gets all the love she needs and I get the camaraderie of best friends that I know I would have missed after retirement. As much as I wanted to live alone, it never really occurred to me that I've spent my entire life in the sport of hockey, surrounded by teammates. It would have left a void in my life.

Now I don't have to miss anything.

I've got everything I want, right here.

Plus, I have every intention of winning the championship this season and retiring in style.

"We're lucky the weather cooperated," I say.

The trees are covered in snow, but the skies are crisp and clear right now. No snow predicted for the entire weekend.

"I'm prepared to rusticate either way," Simon says, lifting up his foot and pointing to his brand-new expensive snow boots.

He looks like he's going skiing in Vail.

That makes me snort. "What, for the twenty foot walk from the truck to the house?"

"Precisely."

"Landing," Aidan says with relief as we descend over the trees.

A minute later, we're on the ground and Elise releases her death grip on my arm.

There are only ten houses on this island and the airstrip is owned by distant relatives of my grandmother's, and they always give anyone arriving a ride to their house. We pile into two different trucks and after another five minutes, we're pulling up to the cabin.

From the back, which faces the woods, it's not that impressive architecturally. The lakeside is the front of the house.

"Oh, this is so cute," Elise says. "Look at how peaceful."

"So peaceful," Simon says skeptically. Then he jumps. "What the fuck was that? I think I saw a bear."

He is pointing off to the right.

I turn and then burst out laughing as I see a familiar animal running back into the woods. "That is the neighbor's dog, Henley. She likes to come over and say hi."

Aidan is laughing too. "Tough guy, huh, babe?" He reaches for Simon's hand. "Here, let me protect you."

"Fuck you," Simon grumbles.

"Promise?"

They exchange heated looks.

"Hey, hey, let's at least get inside," Elise says. "Before we all freeze to death. Blake, there is heat, right?"

"Oh, dear God, there had better be," Simon exclaims in horror. "We're practically in the tundra."

I roll my eyes. "There is heat." I turn the key in the door and shove it open. "Enter and tell me what you think."

I hang back and let them crowd past me. There is a moment of stunned silence and then I hear lots of "wows" and "holy shit" and "now this is a cabin."

It makes me grin as I toe off my boots in the mudroom by the back door.

The cabin isn't really so much of a cabin as, well, a palatial lakefront estate with floor to ceiling glass, a massive modern kitchen with an island for seating ten and a twenty-five foot tall stone fireplace. It's still rustic, but rustic in the sense that my Gran is fond of buffalo check print on upholstery. Not rustic as in we-have-to-rough-it.

Elise has kicked off her boots and is hopping up and down in the living room. "Blake, this is amazing! I love this house and this view, it's *gorgeous*. I feel like I'm in a painting."

"I thought your grandparents were farmers," Aidan says, peeling off his winter coat and shaking his head in awe at the farmhouse table that seats thirty-two.

"There's a lot of money in dairy." I shrug. "Heidi Wilder likes nice shit."

"No wonder you wanted to fake an engagement for this property," Simon says, nodding in approval. "I would marry my Aunt Judith to secure this place, and trust me, Aunt Judith is a bulldog."

That makes me laugh. "My fake engagement was no hardship, as you know."

Speaking of…

I head over to Elise and I take her hand. "Come right here, Sugar. I want to show you something." I pause to light the fire that was already built and ready to burn, flicking open the flue.

"What?" she asks. "Is there a hot tub? You said there was a hot tub."

"There's a hot tub." I tug her into my chest and give her a soft kiss. "Look out the window. Can you see that deck next to the dock? It has the most brilliant sunsets there in the summer. The trees on the shore are thick with leaves and the water is still and serene. It feels like all of nature is putting on a show."

I reach into my pocket and fish out the box that's been burning a hole there. Dropping to one knee, I flick it open to reveal a wedding band that matches her engagement ring.

Her eyes widen and her free hand goes to her mouth.

"Elise, I love you with all my heart and soul. You've brought joy into my life with your laugh and your colorful spirit. I know we're already married, and I love being able to call you my wife, but I want to marry you all over again, with the people we love…" I glance over at Aidan and Simon. "With *especially* those two as witnesses, and to celebrate with us. So will you do me the honor of saying "I do" all over again?"

She nods rapidly. "I would love to marry you all over again in front of our friends and family. Yes, a thousand times yes."

When I stand up and kiss her, she reaches out and cups my cheeks. "Always yes," she whispers. "My answer with you is always yes."

I suddenly don't trust myself to speak. I just kiss her fiercely and click the ring box shut again.

"Wait, don't I get that?" Elise is trying to take it from me.

"No, not until the ceremony."

"Make a note of that," Simon tells Aidan. "Our girl likes shiny things."

"I feel like that's obvious. Don't worry, babe, I don't need shiny things."

"Oh. Right, of course. The ceremony." Elise looks disappointed.

I laugh. "I have something else for you though. Would you like that now?"

"Yes, please." She gives me a sweet smile. Then she holds out her hands with a sassy wink and closes her eyes.

Retrieving my duffel bag, I dig inside and pull out a vibrator that has a clit stimulator on top. I place it in her hands. "Open."

She does and her jaw drops. But then she immediately gets a look that goes straight to my dick. "I like," she says, running her hands over it. "Who wants to use it on me first?"

"Blake's gift, love," Simon says. "He gets first go at you with it."

"Agreed," Aidan says.

Then they both shake my hand and give her a kiss on the lips.

"Congrats, you two. We can't wait to be there for the wedding," Aidan says.

"I should be able to clear my calendar since you told us this time," Simon says with a grin.

Elise laughs, still holding the vibrator.

"Do you want champagne and the hot tub first or your new

toy?" I ask her. "Or how about your new toy and a glass of champagne in the hot tub?"

"That one," she says immediately. "Option two. Let me go put on my swimsuit."

"You don't need a swimsuit."

"Even better," Simon remarks.

I nod. "No one can see you out there but the birds. Let me show everyone the bedroom."

We've fallen into a pattern already back in Chicago, where we make a point to spend at least one night a week, all four of us together, either at my place or Simon's hotel suite, and we share a bed. The other nights when Aidan is at work and I'm playing hockey, Simon stays with Elise at her place. If there are any nights remaining, Elise and I are at my place, and Simon and Aidan are together.

It works for right now, but we've already talked about how to be together more moving forward, because Elise and Aidan do want time together as well, and I want to build on my friendships with both of the guys.

This house has five bedrooms, but one has a king size bed and the plan is to all share it this weekend.

After we haul our bags upstairs, I tell them, "Strip down to your underwear, then there are robes and towels in the bathroom downstairs."

Elise and Aidan are peeking in the primary bathroom and their heads are together. Elise is giggling again. It doesn't seem like their usual flirting, but something else. It has me curious and intrigued.

"What's with those two?" I ask Simon, who has already shed all of his clothes except for his black silk boxers.

"I have no idea. Maybe they're plotting to get me drunk and take advantage of me."

That makes me snort.

"Last one in has to stand back and watch during sex," Elise says suddenly, dashing past me in her bra and panties.

We end up all jogging down the stairs, jostling each other and laughing like a bunch of college kids. Elise is first out the door, shrieking as her bare feet hit the snow. She's jumping up and down and howling with cold and laughter as she realizes the lid to the hot tub is still on.

I strip off my boxer briefs at the door and pop open the lid and jump in. I reach out my hand for her and help her up the stairs. She is still in her bra and panties, but sinks immediately below the bubbling hot water with a sigh. I unhook her bra as Aidan just about cannonballs into the hot tub, still in his underwear.

Simon isn't even trying to win. He's still in the doorway, eyeing us with a superior smirk. He is somehow already wearing one of the thick robes and has one singular towel in his hand.

"I like to watch anyway," he says, stacking his towel on the edge of the hot tub.

"You didn't get towels for the rest of us?" Aidan complains, sinking to his knees in the water.

"I will if you ask very, very nicely."

"We forgot the champagne," Elise says.

"And the vibrator," I add.

"*Simon*," Elise says, sounding very sexy and pleading. "Will you go get them for us?"

He gives a long-suffering sigh. "Of course, love."

When he turns, she reaches out and smacks Aidan. "Now!" she hisses. "It will be just like the day you met. In the cold."

Aidan grins. "Good idea, because this ring box is cutting into my balls."

"And here I thought you were just happy to see me." Elise smiles at him, then shoos him toward the steps as Simon disappears into the house.

I finally understand what's going on. "You're proposing?" I ask in a low voice.

Aidan nods happily. "I know it's soon, but I don't want to wait."

I'm thrilled for him and for Simon. They're seriously amazing together, the perfect fit of opposites attract, and yet both genuinely good men. "Go get him," I say with a grin.

He leaps out of the water right as Simon reappears.

Then suddenly they are both on one knee in the dusting of snow on the deck.

Elise gasps. "Oh my God!"

My jaw drops.

They stare at each other in astonishment, each holding out a ring.

Then Simon grins. "You go first."

"I…" Aidan looks totally thrown off his game. But then he manages to choke out, "Will you marry me?"

"Yes. Will you marry me?"

"Absolutely."

"Good. Now let's finish this in the water because it's freezing out here."

Once they're both in the hot tub, kissing and slipping rings on each other, I pull Elise onto my lap so we can all enjoy the moment.

"I am so in love with you," Simon tells Aidan. "I thought you might think I was being impulsive, but I can't imagine a life without you." He turns to us. "Without you, love, and without you, Wilder."

He kisses Aidan again, passionately.

"I can't imagine a life without you either," Aidan says gruffly, pulling Simon up hard against his chest. "I can't wait until I can call you my husband." He reaches his hand out to Elise. "Come here, El, give us a kiss. If that's okay with your husband."

"Go for it."

I give her a little push toward her boyfriends and settle back, arms on the edges of the hot tub, to watch them take turns kissing her and each other. When it starts getting steamier and my dick starts to harden in response like it always does when I watch my wife being loved and cherished, I realize something.

"Damn it, Simon, you still didn't bring the champagne or the vibrator."

"We have all night," he says, kissing the back of Elise's neck.

"We have all weekend," Aidan adds, squeezing Elise's breasts.

"We have forever," Elise corrects, stretching her hand out to me.

Yes. We do.

Epilogue
ELISE

"I CAN'T TELL if that grin means you're a little drunk, you just got laid, or you're just really happy for your husband," Luna says, coming to stand next to me where I am observing Blake's retirement party from the edge of the room.

I've been in the midst of the party all night, and just wanted to take a minute to breathe and take it all in.

I grin at my friend and lift my half-empty lemon drop martini in a little toast. "How about all three?"

I got laid a few hours ago before we left for the party, but with my three men taking care of me, my post-orgasmic glows *last*.

She laughs. "That's my girl." She takes a sip of her martini and gives a, "Mmm."

They really are delicious. Blake chose the lemon drop martinis as the signature drink tonight. He'd given his grandmother a wink when he handed her the first one and the smile they had exchanged had made my heart squeeze.

"Well I know that you weren't in the storage room since Alexsei and I were just in there," Luna says.

Now that she mentions it, her lipstick could use a little touch up.

I shrug. "A lady doesn't kiss and tell."

Luna snorts. "Thank God we don't know any ladies."

I giggle. Turns out, we'd been on our way to that very storage room before the party really kicked off, but Blake and I had been waylaid by his mom, dad, and sister arriving and we hadn't had another chance to slip away yet. We, of course, have our choice of big beds only a few minutes away from the upscale bistro in downtown Chicago where we reserved the party room tonight, but sneaking around and playing as if we don't is always fun.

I find my men. They are all together across the room, drinks in hand, laughing with Owen Phillips, Michael Hughes, Crew McNeill, and Jack Hayes.

I love seeing how easily Aiden and Simon have been incorporated into Blake's group of friends. Blake has a small inner circle, but it's full of great people.

Though, looking around the room right now, you wouldn't know his circle was small. The room is packed with people wanting to celebrate his retirement with him.

I think the entire Racketeers team is here, including Wade, the mascot, and Nathan, the team owner. There is also, of course, a ton of family and friends.

Blake's whole family, including aunts, uncles, and cousins are here.

And my mother is even here somewhere.

Blake said that of course his mother-in-law should be invited, so I did, never expecting her to accept. But she immediately agreed and she's been here since the beginning. She and Blake's mom get along great. They're sitting together at a table along the far wall.

"So on a scale from zero to ten, how happy is he to be retired?" Luna asks. "And how long do you think it will be before he misses it?"

"I think he's about a nine right now," I say, honestly. "If the night they won the championship was a fifteen, he's a nine about retiring." We both laugh. The night the Racketeers brought that trophy home was amazing. I've never been that excited or proud of someone else in my life. "He's really happy," I continue. "I don't know if it's totally sunk in yet, though. But his doctor says that this last shot he gave him for his hip might actually do some good now that he can rest. And he has plenty to look forward to at home."

Luna laughs. "I know he does, babe. And I'm so happy for you."

I sip from my glass, hit by one of those moments that occurs every once in a while, where I can't believe how everything has turned out and how absolutely ecstatic I actually am. My life is full.

My business is going gangbusters. I am actually to the point where I think I'm going to have to hire someone to help me.

Simon has moved to Chicago and we're looking at places where we can all live together.

We've come up with a sort of routine. At least as much routine as having a billionaire who has to fly around the world occasionally and a firefighter who works twenty-four hours at a time can have.

But it's all just so fucking good.

"I do think he'll miss it though," I tell Luna. "Probably around the time the season is supposed to start. Coach has told him that he is welcome anytime he wants to come to practice and help kick the guys asses. And Crew has been talking to him about the kids hockey program he works with. I think that would be awesome for Blake. He'd love to work with kids."

Speaking of kids and Crew, his wife and daughter join us just then.

"Hey," a slightly harried Danielle greets us.

"Gimme," Luna says, handing her empty martini glass to me and reaching for her niece.

Dani surrenders the baby with a grateful sigh. I pass her the rest of my martini.

She doesn't even blink at the fact that I've drunk half of it. She lifts it for a sip and then sighs happily.

"This is an amazing party, Elise. But I am here to officially tell you that you still have to come to games. Even if Blake isn't playing, I want you sitting with us."

A year ago, I would've laughed. I did not show up at hockey games because of hockey. I showed up because of friends and the rowdy atmosphere. Then I kept showing up because of the hot hockey players. But now I actually appreciate the game.

"I think that can be arranged." Aidan has gotten into hockey as well, and Simon just likes to be wherever we are. I'm guessing it will be weird for Blake to sit in the stands after all these years, but he needs to try it.

"Oh, yay!" Dani says enthusiastically. She really is the sweetest person.

Again, I'm hit by a wave of happiness and gratefulness. I have two amazing friends. I'm so lucky.

I also have two amazing boyfriends and an amazing husband, and just then, Simon catches my gaze and tips his head in a 'come here' gesture.

"I think I'm being summoned," I say.

Luna and Dani both have men in the group as well so they cross the room with me.

But just as I step under Simon's outstretched arm and get a wink from Blake and a grin from Aidan, a loud wailing splits the air. The sirens draw close and a moment later, red flashing lights illuminate the front window.

I frown and immediately look at Aidan. He's also scowling.

"Oh my God," Dani says. "Are those fire trucks?"

Aidan is already striding toward the door. "Stay here," he orders. "I'll check things out." Blake moves to me and Simon, tucking me between them.

That's sweet, though I'm not sure they're going to be able to block *fire*.

There's a fire exit directly out of this room so I'm not overly concerned about anyone being trapped or harmed. We're in a restaurant, so I suppose the idea of a kitchen fire isn't too farfetched. But I'll feel better when Aidan tells us we're okay.

It's less than five minutes later when Aidan comes back into the room with a hard to read expression. I start to ask what happened, but the answer is right behind him.

Luke and Wyatt, the two firefighters I met when I visited Aidan at the firehouse, step through the door.

Blake meets them. "What's going on?" Blake asks.

"Capacity problem," Wyatt tells him.

Blake looks around. "We have too many people in here?"

Wyatt shakes his head. "No, you should have two more."

Blake frowns. "I...don't understand."

Aidan rolls his eyes. "He thinks he's being funny."

"For the record, this was his idea," Luke says. "And I didn't know he was going to use the siren or lights."

Wyatt laughs. He claps Blake on the shoulder. "We're just messing with you. Aidan told us about your party, and after all the gushing I've done and telling you I'm your biggest fan about forty times, we're kind of pissed we didn't get invited."

"He's pissed," Luke clarifies. "This was all his idea."

Blake stares at them then he looks at Aidan. "Are they serious right now?"

"*Him*," Luke says again. "His idea. I'd offer to fire him, but he's one of my best. And, you know, saving lives and being brave and shit makes up for him being a dumbass sometimes."

Blake looks at Aidan. Aidan nods. "It's true."

"Which part? The he's kidding part or the he's a dumbass but should be forgiven part?"

Aidan shrugs. "Both."

Suddenly there's a giggle from the back of the crowd. Blake, Luke, and Wyatt all turn.

It came from Brooke, Blake's younger sister.

Wyatt's face breaks into a huge grin. "See?" he says to Blake. "Funny."

"There is no *way*, Wilder is your favorite player though," Crew calls, and the tension is broken as everyone laughs.

We've gotten to know the guys that Aidan works with pretty well. Fire crews tend to be like little families, and there was no way that Aidan could be as close as he is to me, Simon, and Blake without introducing us to his crew. The guys have had some guys' nights at the Racketeers' favorite bar, and Blake thought it would be cool to go to one of their training exercises one Saturday.

Needless to say, being a hockey goalie is not quite the same as being a firefighter and carrying huge heavy hoses up and down ladders almost did him in.

His hip gave out way before anything else, but he confessed to me later that he truly wondered if his lungs were going to explode.

"I guess maybe I thought you guys had more important things to do," Blake tells them. "You know, like saving lives and keeping us all safe. But clearly you're able to just fuck around. So come on in."

Luke shakes his head. "Nah. He's just messing with you. But we did want to stop by and say congratulations."

"Thanks man," Blake says, extending his hand and shaking both of theirs. "But seriously stay. If you're not working."

"We're off shift," Wyatt says quickly. "We wouldn't do this if we were actually still on the clock."

"If you're gonna stay, you should maybe move the big red truck with the flashing lights," Aidan says dryly.

I am shaking my head as Simon pulls me over to the side. "How the hell did we end up in love with a hockey player and a firefighter *and* all of their crazy people?" he asks me.

I grin up at him. "Just very, very lucky I guess."

He leans down and kisses me. "Exactly right."

The party keeps going long past our reserved time and when I notice the clock, I start to worry until Simon assures me that he's taking care of it with the restaurant management.

It really is nice to be sleeping with a billionaire sometimes.

Okay, oftentimes. Especially this particular billionaire.

"Uh, oh," Simon says an hour later from where I've finally dropped into a chair and kicked off my heels.

I look up. "What? I don't like uh, oh."

"How old is Blake's sister?"

I look around and spot her across the room. I immediately see what Simon's uh oh is about. "Brooke's twenty-five."

"Okay. That's good. She looks younger."

Brooke does look younger. I think it's the very sweet, innocent air about her. She also doesn't wear much make-up and her hair and clothes are simple and understated. In other words, *very* different from me. But I love her and we get along great.

But she looks small and a little overwhelmed at the moment with Aidan's two best firefighter friends standing on either side of her. She's laughing though, even as her eyes are wide.

"How old do you think Luke is?" I ask. "He's at least your age."

Simon nods. "I'd say probably forty."

Simon is thirty-seven and I'm twenty-seven, and Blake has never said a word about our age difference.

I have a feeling that his sister being twenty-five and the guy who is looking at her right now with heated appreciation being forty might catch his attention though.

"I think he might have a problem with Wyatt as well," Simon says. "He is probably your age, but he is clearly a player."

Oh, for *sure*. Wyatt exudes confidence and I'm-a-good-time.

They're also both extremely good-looking and fuck, they're firefighters. I don't know any straight female who could *totally* resist that.

"Yeah, Brooke is quiet. And from what I've gathered, she doesn't date. Like at all," I tell Simon.

"Should we intervene?" Simon asks.

I don't love that idea. Brooke's a big girl. And she doesn't look *uncomfortable*. More…wonderstruck.

"They're both good looking and very charming and they're

good guys. I think she knows that all she has to do is say the word and they'll leave her alone."

"I actually meant should we intervene with Blake. Maybe try to distract him so he doesn't have a heart attack before he gets to enjoy his retirement?" Simon asks.

I grin. "Now that's not a bad idea."

"Any suggestions about how to do that?" Simon asks with a little smirk.

I spot my husband across the room. He looks so good in the dress pants, and button-down shirt, one hand tucked in his pocket, a bottle of beer in the other. He is laughing, relaxed, surrounded by people he loves, clearly happy.

God, happy and relaxed looks good on him.

"Well, I have it on good authority that the storage room is the right size for two people, including a hockey-player-sized person, and is fairly private," I say.

"Well, *I* can say, with authority, that the coat room is also very private and is a little more...intimate," Simon says, lifting his glass for a nonchalant sip.

"Oh, you can say *with authority*?" I ask, nudging him. "And experience perhaps?"

He grins. "Yes."

"And I didn't get invited to the coat room party?"

"You were busy. And it was rather...spontaneous."

I laugh. "Got it. So the coat room, huh?"

"Yes. I think Blake would enjoy it. It's about the size of, oh I don't know, an elevator car?" He smiles. "But there's not much light in there."

I laugh. "You don't say. Well, I think I can work with that." I get up from my chair and lean over to kiss Simon on the cheek.

"I'll send Aidan in to rescue you if you're not back in ten minutes," he says, giving my ass a little squeeze.

I laugh. "Don't you dare."

I take my phone from my purse and text my husband.

> We need to talk.

I watch him check his phone, grin, and then lift his head to search for me.

I tip my head toward the hallway.

He immediately excuses himself from the group he's chatting with and heads in my direction.

That, in and of itself, makes my heart flip. He will always be looking around any room for me. He will always want to be with me more than anyone else. He will always come to me with a simple tip of my head.

God. That is more of a gift than I ever expected to be given from any person. And I've been given it times three.

I hold out my hand as he draws close and he links his fingers with me. "Hey, Sugar."

"Hey. I need a few minutes with you."

"Only a few?"

"Yeah." I give him a sly little smile. "For now."

"I'm all yours." He leans in and kisses me. "Thank you for this celebration."

I smile. "I didn't do much. I just made the reservation and talked to the catering department."

"Not talking about just the party," he tells me. "I'm talking about the *celebration*. I'm celebrating the start of the next chapter of my life and all the good things coming up have to do with you."

My eyes widen and I feel tears sting. "Oh my God."

He chuckles. "Oh no. Don't get all mushy on me. I wanna know all about whatever dirty thoughts you had in mind when you beckoned me over here."

"How did you know they were dirty?"

He leans in. "Because I know you."

Well, what's the point of arguing? "I just had an idea about you and me and a tight space…"

His voice drops. "I do like *tight* spaces."

My body heats and I turn and start tugging him down the hallway. Yeah, I'm right back into my dirty thoughts.

And ten minutes later, Blake is officially distracted from the fact that his sister has two firefighters flirting with her at his retirement party.

In fact, he can't even spell 'retirement' when I'm done with him.

Truthfully, I can't either, because Blake never lets things be just about him.

So it's a good thing we don't really need to, because we are really just at the beginning of so, so many amazing things.

Want more of Elise and her trio of hot guys? To read a free bonus scene go to bit.ly/4cHJgpA

And coming in November... Light My Fire! Blake's sister Brooke gets snowed in with two firefighters, and their millionaire friend!

Find Emma on Social

Emma Foxx is the super fun and sexy pen name for two long-time, bestselling romance authors who decided why have just one hero when you can have three at the same time? (they're not sure what took them so long to figure this out)! Emma writes contemporary romances that will make you laugh (yes, maybe out loud in public) and want more…books (sure, that's what we mean 😉). Find Emma on Instagram, Tik Tok, and Goodreads.

Also by Emma Foxx

Chicago Racketeers

Puck One Night Stands

Four Pucking Christmases

Seriously Pucked

Permanently Pucked

Icing It

(Standalone in the Racketeers World)

Coming in November… Light My Fire!

Milton Keynes UK
Ingram Content Group UK Ltd.
UKHW030821200924
448513UK00005B/289